He remembered her now.

The Garlands had used to visit the Park every summer until Sir Alexander had married that frightful second wife of his. Ianthe had been too young to impinge upon his consciousness until that last summer, just before he had joined the army. She had dogged his heels, determined to join in his pursuits, and he had let her tag along on his fishing trips and rabbit-snaring expeditions. He had even taught her to ride something more lively than her fat little pony.

Actually, she had been a plucky brat, game as a pebble. Astonishing to find her grown into such a dreary pattern-card of virtue, too modest even to look him in the eye!

Maybe she had heard of his reputation, he thought cynically.

Gail Mallin has a passion for travel. She studied at the University of Wales, where she gained an Honours degree and met her husband, then an officer in the Merchant Navy. They spent the next three years sailing the world before settling in Cheshire. Writing soon became another means of exploring, opening up new worlds. A career move took Gail and her husband south, and they now live with their young family in St Albans.

Recent titles by the same author:

AN INFAMOUS PROPOSAL

Gail Mallin

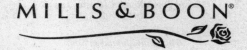

MILLS & BOON®

First published in Great Britain 2001
Harlequin Mills & Boon Limited,
Eton House, 18-24 Paradise Road, Richmond, Surrey TW9 1SR

© Gail Mallin 2001

ISBN 0 263 82762 3

Set in Times Roman 10¼ on 11 pt.
04-0102-90928

Printed and bound in Spain
by Litografia Rosés S.A., Barcelona

Chapter One

1819

'Lord Kildare? Is he not the son of your father's cousin?'

Ianthe Garland reluctantly raised her gaze from the piece of embroidery on which she was working in response to her stepmother's sharp question. 'I believe so, ma'am.'

Her quiet reply brought a satisfied smile to Mrs Turner's plump face.

'I thought I knew the name!' she declared triumphantly. 'And you say that he has made a large fortune during his travels, my love?' she continued, directing her glance towards the third occupant of Northwood's newly refurbished drawing-room.

Mr Augustus Turner nodded his sleek blond head. 'So I am informed.' He smiled. 'According to Irving, Kildare's wealth will set 'em all chattering when he arrives back in England at the end of this month.'

Ianthe, who had been delighted that morning to hear her detested guardian announce his intention of spending the whole day with his crony, felt a prickle of apprehension shiver down her spine.

She knew *that* smile! What was the devious creature up to now?

'How very clever of you to visit Mr Irving, Augustus!' Maria Turner exclaimed, conveniently forgetting her annoyance at his thoughtlessly staying on to dine in George Street without remembering to send word of his change of plan.

Augustus preened. 'Irving always has the latest gossip and I thought to garner something to amuse you, my dear.'

'So kind and thoughtful you are, my love! Have I not always said so, Ianthe?'

Ianthe nodded dutifully, curbing the temptation to point out that, miffed by his absence, Maria had been spoiling for an argument when Augustus had joined them in the drawing-room on his return from his crony's house in St Albans, the town which lay nearest to Northwood.

Her clear blue gaze sought out the giltwood clock which adorned the marble mantelpiece. Almost ten. Any minute now Hannah would bring in the tea-tray and she would be able to escape.

It was not by choice that Ianthe sat listening to Augustus gossip while Maria gazed at him adoringly, her fit of the sullens banished by his heavy-handed compliments. She would have much preferred to dine with her grandmother, but, on finding herself alone, Maria had demanded her company. Good manners obliged Ianthe to abandon her usual practice of dining at the Dower House, but it had been an uncomfortable meal, punctuated by Maria's sighs and complaints.

With grim amusement Ianthe reflected that it was her stepmother's dislike of solitude which had prompted the unexpected invitation. In fact, Maria's need for constant attention had provoked her hasty remarriage the instant her year of official mourning for Ianthe's father, Sir Alexander Garland, was up.

But how she wished her stepmother had not chosen Augustus Turner! Grandmama, in one of her lucid moments, had described him as a *penniless adventurer* and Ianthe was sure that the Dowager was right. For all his smart clothes and charming turn of address, there was something sly and cal-

culating about Augustus and he had made Ianthe's skin creep
from their very first meeting.

Maria, of course, saw no further than his florid good looks
and had ignored her advice not to rush into marriage, screaming that Ianthe was jealous.

'Just because you lost your own beau, there is no need to
try and deny me mine,' she had declared dramatically and,
biting her lip, Ianthe had fallen silent.

After the wedding, a lavish affair to which half the county
received invitation, the newly married couple set off on an
sumptuous bridal-trip to the Continent. Ianthe, whose nerves
had been stretched to breaking-point by all the fuss, delighted
in the peace which settled over Northwood.

On their return, however, her serenity was soon disturbed
by Augustus's wild extravagance. He set in motion a series
of improvements to the estate and refurbishments to the old
house that were as unnecessary as they were expensive.
Powerless to prevent him, Ianthe begged her stepmother to
intervene.

'Lud, Ianthe, you do worry needlessly! Augustus knows
what he is doing. He doesn't need advice from a chit of a
girl!'

Realising that Maria was too besotted to listen to any
doubts about Augustus's judgement or ability to run the estate, Ianthe eventually took the bold step of consulting her
late father's lawyer.

'I am afraid I cannot help you, Miss Garland,' Mr
Robertson had told her coldly, his expression leaving her in
no doubt that he disapproved of her unladylike forwardness.
'Your father's will clearly stated that although you are to in-
herit Northwood, his widow should have full control until you
attain your majority.'

During his brief final illness Sir Alexander had carefully
explained to Ianthe why he was leaving her in Maria's care.
'I know she is a feather-brain, puss, and it is likely to be the
other way around with you looking after her, but we lack male

relatives to whom I could entrust the task of guardianship and I do not want to burden you with a stranger.'

'Papa never envisaged her marrying again so soon,' Ianthe exclaimed bitterly. 'And certainly not to such a spendthrift nincompoop!'

Mr Robertson's frown deepened. 'It is not seemly for you to speak of a gentleman much older than yourself in such a fashion,' he reminded her stiffly.

Ianthe knew it, but instinct warned her that matters were too serious to worry about breaching polite convention. 'Are you sure that nothing that can be done to put a stop to his extravagance?' she persisted.

Mr Robertson sighed. Naturally, he knew about the new improvements at Northwood and his cautious mind found them alarming, but there was no evidence to suggest that Turner was lining his own pocket.

'You must be aware, Miss Garland, that it is perfectly proper for Mr Turner to manage his wife's business affairs,' he said firmly, his heavy features stern.

'I know a woman's property becomes her husband's on the day they marry, but Northwood does not really belong to the Turners,' Ianthe retorted stubbornly.

'In the sense that your father wished you to have it I agree, but, legally, they may do whatever they wish with the property. They could even sell it.'

Ianthe blanched. 'But, surely, I have the right to be consulted about changes that will affect my inheritance?'

He shook his balding head. 'I'm afraid not.'

Taking pity upon her stricken expression, he continued in a kinder voice, 'However, as your trustee, Mrs Turner does have a duty to guard your best interests.'

'I doubt their ideas on that score would chime with mine!'

Mr Robertson admitted that it might prove very difficult and costly to challenge any decision made by her guardians. 'However, I think you will find that they will not risk any truly drastic step, Miss Garland,' he concluded and with that cold comfort Ianthe had to be satisfied.

A knock at the door interrupted her unhappy reflections and she strove to dismiss her worries as Hannah brought in the tea-tray.

'You may go.' Impatiently, Maria dismissed the maid and, busying herself with the tea things, implored her husband to tell them whether Lord Kildare intended to remain in England.

'Irving's correspondent didn't mention it in his letter. He just said Kildare had left India and was coming home,' Augustus admitted. He shrugged his expensively clad shoulders. 'Don't ask me whence the fellow got his information. All I can tell you is that Irving swears he is reliable.'

Maria's round face creased in unaccustomed thought. 'But you think it's safe to assume that Lord Kildare will stay in England for while?'

'Aye.' Augustus accepted the cup of tea his wife handed him. 'He's bound to want to see his family.'

Maria agreed, a note of excitement entering her high-pitched voice, but as she turned to speak to her stepdaughter her hopeful smile faded. She repressed a sigh. What a pity the girl had grown so plain! Always dressed in those dismal blacks and no more colour in her thin cheeks than a bowl of whey! Still...

'You ought to write to Cousin Amelia, Ianthe,' she announced. 'It must be what...eleven years since you were at Kildare Park?'

'Twelve years. Just before you and Papa met, ma'am,' Ianthe confirmed in a subdued tone.

She had been eight years old, the apple of her widowed father's eye, and blissfully unaware that her safe, cosy world was about to change forever.

'Then it is high time you paid Lady Kildare a visit,' Maria continued briskly.

Ianthe's surprise showed upon her irregular features. Her father and Amelia Kildare had been first cousins, but since his death two years ago there had been very little contact between their respective families.

Cousin Amelia disapproved of the flighty young woman Sir

Alexander had chosen to be his second wife and Maria knew it!

'You will enjoy spending a month or two in Hampshire,' Maria insisted, her bland expression denying any hint of her oft-proclaimed dislike of her late husband's relatives.

'I should not like to leave Grandmama for so long,' Ianthe demurred, the warning prickle between her shoulder blades growing stronger. 'And, in any case, it would be unfair of me to impose on Cousin Amelia just when she must be expecting—'

'Nonsense! I am sure she will be delighted to see you,' Maria interrupted, her finely plucked brows drawing together in irritation as she waved aside these objections. 'Besides, there is no time to waste.'

'No, indeed.' Mr Turner's pale eyes met his wife's in a look of complete understanding. 'Such an eligible young man is bound to attract the notice of every matchmaking mama for miles around.'

He swivelled round in his chair and fixed his attention upon Ianthe. 'You will have the advantage of living in the same house. If you have any sense at all in that over-educated head of yours, you will find some way to secure Kildare's interest before anyone else can snap him up.'

Ianthe's lips tightened. It didn't surprise her in the least that Augustus should make such vulgar remarks, but it angered her that he imagined she would meekly fall in with his scheming.

'I have no desire to renew my acquaintance with his lordship,' she said fiercely. 'From all I have heard, he is much changed from the boy I remember from my childhood.'

'Tut-tut! You shouldn't listen to gossip, my dear. Most unladylike.' Mockery flashed in Mr Turner's ice-blue gaze.

He lifted the delicate porcelain teacup he held to his lips and took a sip. 'Kildare may have a wild reputation, but it is his money, not his morals, that you should think on.'

Gathering together her embroidery silks, Ianthe rose abruptly to her feet. 'I beg you will excuse me, ma'am,' she said through clenched lips. 'I fear I must retire to bed. I am feeling quite nauseated all of a sudden.'

Mrs Turner let out a hiss of annoyance. About to order her provoking stepdaughter to sit down, she changed her mind on receiving a nod from her husband. 'Oh, very well! You may go, but do not think you have heard the last of this, miss! You cannot keep on refusing to consider suitors!'

Ignoring this barb, Ianthe dipped a frigid curtsy and quietly left the room.

'Do you know, I think she persists in mourning that stupid boy just to vex me!' Maria exclaimed the instant the door closed behind Ianthe.

She sighed. 'What are we to do, Augustus? In less than four months she will come of age and it will be much more difficult to fob off her meddlesome enquiries. Marrying her off to Kildare would be the perfect solution to all our problems, but I fear she will refuse to go to into Hampshire.'

Well aware of the pressing need to recoup their fortunes, Mr Turner bit his thumb for a thoughtful moment. 'Don't worry, my dear,' he replied, his expression suddenly brightening. 'I shall speak to her in the morning. I think I may have hit upon the very way to…er…persuade dear Ianthe to encourage Lord Kildare's suit.'

'Thank you, my dear. I shall be very comfortable now.' Octavia Garland adjusted the woollen shawl Ianthe handed to her and smiled at her granddaughter.

They were sitting in the morning-room of the Dower House, a handsome stone-fronted dwelling which stood in the grounds of Northwood. Sunlight was pouring in through the sash windows, but when the Dowager mentioned she felt a little cold Ianthe had rushed off to fetch her a thick shawl.

'Are you sure you don't want me to ask Betty to make up the fire?' she said anxiously.

'Dearest, it's the middle of May!' The Dowager chuckled. 'It would be a shocking waste of coals.'

'I don't want you catching a chill.' Ianthe could not forget how ill her grandmother had been over the winter.

'My cough has gone completely.' Lady Garland's lined face took on a stubborn look. 'When one gets to my age it is quite natural to feel the cold, you know.'

'But, Grandmama—'

'Don't fuss, dearest. You know I hate it and, besides, I am perfectly all right.'

There was a slight catch in the old lady's voice and Ianthe made haste to apologise.

The problem, of course, was that they both knew her grandmother was not in the best of health. Two years ago she had contracted pneumonia. The doctors had advised the family to expect the worst, but to everyone's surprise the old lady had survived. By bitter coincidence, it was Sir Alexander, a healthy man barely into his forties, who had succumbed to the disease.

Her illness had left Lady Garland frail and to her great distress she was occasionally apt to forget things and grow confused. The doctors had muttered of the effects of high fever on the brain and told Ianthe that with time she would, hopefully, improve. This prediction had proved correct. Her grandmother's bad days were now thankfully rare, but she had changed. Once a lively and energetic woman who loved to entertain, she now preferred to live very quietly.

'You really mustn't worry about me, dearest.' Lady Garland patted Ianthe's arm in a gesture of reassurance.

Ianthe nodded obediently, but her expression remained slightly anxious as she resumed her seat opposite the cream-silk upholstered sofa on which her grandmother resided.

'Indeed, it is time you started to consider your own position,' her grandmother continued firmly. 'I have my lovely home...' she waved one hand to encompass the morning-room with its pretty striped wallpaper and comfortable furniture '...and enough friends in the vicinity to enjoy company whenever I wish. Whereas you, my pet, live like a hermit.'

Ianthe stared at her in astonishment. 'Whatever do you mean?'

'You never attend any parties, my dearest. Indeed, it is weeks since you had any kind of outing, unless you count riding one of the horses. I know you love your books, but you are in danger of dwindling into a veritable blue-stocking.'

Ianthe opened her mouth to deny the charge and then promptly shut it again as she met her grandmother's level gaze.

'I understand your reasons for shunning society.' Sympathy infused Lady Garland's thin voice. 'It was a dreadful shock to lose your dear papa so suddenly and nursing me has taken its toll, but you are young, dearest, and a girl your age should be out enjoying herself.' She smiled at Ianthe encouragingly. 'It is my belief that you need a change of scene.'

Ianthe shook her dark auburn head. 'You are mistaken, Grandmama. I like keeping you company.'

Lady Garland knew she spoke the truth. They shared more than the distinctive family colouring and above average height and the child had a kind, loving nature, but it wasn't right that she should bear such a heavy burden. 'I know you do, dearest, but you are in danger of letting seclusion become a habit. A holiday would do you good. All last winter you were cooped up in my sick-room. Summer is almost upon us and yet you still haven't recovered the roses in your cheeks.'

Ianthe bit her lip. She was aware that her looks had suffered in the last few months. Always slender, her recent lack of appetite had led to a loss of weight that did not suit her. Even her thick mahogany-coloured hair had grown dull and lifeless.

'You know I hold no brief for Maria,' her grandmother continued in the same firm tone. 'She is a very silly woman. However, I am sure she would not begrudge you the chance to spend some time away from Northwood. You could visit your Aunt Harriet in Devon, perhaps?'

It was on the tip of Ianthe's tongue to announce that the Turners had their own plans for her, but she decided against it. There was no point in mentioning Kildare Park since she had no intention of going there.. The idea of dangling after Luke Kildare was as absurd as it was undignified!

'I should not care to abandon you for so long, Grandmama,' she replied instead with an earnestness that made the Dowager frown.

'I should miss you, of course, but it is quite nonsensical to let mistaken notions concerning my welfare dictate your mode of existence!' Seeing Ianthe's look of incomprehension, Lady Garland shook her lace-becapped head in exasperation. 'You have your own life to lead, Ianthe. Indeed, I look forward to the day when a husband will take first place with you.'

'I have no particular desire for marriage, Grandmama.' Ianthe stiffened in her comfortable Sheraton armchair.

The Dowager swallowed a sigh. 'Don't you think it is time you stopped wearing the willow for that young man, my pet?' she said softly. 'After all, it is four years next month since he died.'

Ianthe's pale cheeks lost their remaining vestige of colour. 'I am not likely to forget the anniversary of the Battle of Waterloo,' she whispered.

'I'm sorry.' Seeing the distress flare into the great sapphire eyes that were her granddaughter's best feature, Lady Garland felt guilty, but she was determined to stick to her guns. 'I know you were in love with Lieutenant Fenton, but when all is said and done, he was the first eligible boy you had ever met.'

A little smile softened her expression. 'And very handsome he was too in his regimentals! I don't blame you in the least for falling for him! However, if he had lived, perhaps you might have discovered that your feelings were not as strong as you imagined?'

'On the contrary, my affections were deeply engaged,' Ianthe corrected stiffly, hardly able to believe that her beloved grandmother was echoing Maria's frequently voiced recriminations. 'Don't you remember? Just before Philip left for Belgium, Papa had agreed that we could become betrothed on my seventeenth birthday.'

'He could hardly say anything else since your mama was only that age when he married her!' Lady Garland retorted tartly.

She had thought it a mistake for her son to give his permission, but Alexander had always been something of a sentimental dreamer. His own marriage at an early age had been a happy one for the short time it lasted and he had not been able to resist Ianthe's pleading, although the young pair had not known each other long.

Was it merely that she had grown cynical in her old age to wonder if Alexander might have acted differently and advised caution had his Sarah survived Ianthe's birth? As it was, her death in childbirth barely two years after their wedding had inclined Alexander to put his late wife on a pedestal. He had never looked at another woman until he met Maria, who, unfortunately, bore a strong physical resemblance to Sarah. Bowled over, he had rushed into marriage within weeks of their first meeting.

No wonder, then, that he had not felt able to resist his daughter's persuasion!

'Very well, I shall say no more on that head since I have no wish to upset you, dearest.' Lady Garland decided a tactical retreat was in order. When, please God, the child did meet a real flesh-and-blood man she could love, she would realise that it was time to let go her memories of a ghost!

'But do promise me that you will think about my other suggestion. I am convinced a change of scene would help restore you to your old lively self.'

'I promise, Grandmama,' Ianthe agreed, hiding her consternation as she picked up the book, a leather-bound copy of the *The White Doe of Rylstone*, which she had been reading aloud for their mutual enjoyment before Lady Garland had spoken of feeling chilly.

Mr Wordsworth's poetry exercised its usual calming effect, but she was still feeling a little shaken when she parted from her grandmother an hour later. It was fortunate, she decided, that it was a fifteen-minute walk through the Home Wood to reach the main house. A stroll would give her time to compose herself before she had to face Maria again, knowing her stepmother wouldn't let the subject of visiting Kildare Park rest.

Ianthe had just emerged from the trees when a voice hailed her and she spun round to see Augustus Turner standing there. Since it was unusual for him to take exercise in the grounds she had a horrible feeling that he must have been lying in wait for her.

'Good morning,' she replied to his greeting with a politeness she was far from feeling.

'I will walk you home,' he announced, falling into step beside her. 'I wish to have a chat with you in private.'

'Really? You surprise me, sir,' Ianthe replied lightly, masking her dismay as the strange feeling of apprehension which had troubled her last night returned in force. 'I didn't realise you had any fondness for my conversation.'

Augustus chuckled. 'Now don't cut up at me, my girl,' he advised in a genial tone that worried Ianthe far more than his customary churlishness. 'What I have to say is important, so sheathe your claws and listen.' He waited for an instant and then, satisfied that she understood, continued, 'As you can probably guess, I want to talk about your visit to Kildare Park.'

'What visit?' Ianthe retorted sweetly.

'Don't interrupt,' he snarled, his jovial mask slipping. 'There is no point in arguing. You are going, like it or not. What's more, you are also going to worm a marriage proposal out of Kildare.'

Ianthe came to an abrupt halt. 'Are you mad? What on earth makes you think you can order me about in this high-handed fashion?'

'Mad, eh?' Augustus also halted and a sneering expression descended upon his florid face as he returned her angry gaze. 'Well, leaving aside my position as your titular guardian, how about the fact that I will sell the Dower House out from under the old lady if you refuse to do as I say?'

Ianthe felt the blood drain from her cheeks. 'You wouldn't dare,' she whispered.

He laughed and she knew he would. Worse, she doubted if she could prevent him. As Mr Robertson had warned, there was very little she could do to stop the Turners making changes to the estate.

'Let me put it to you frankly, dear Ianthe. I find myself a trifle over-stretched at present and the Dower House would fetch a tidy sum. However, I'm a generous fellow and I would be happy to accept the alternative of pocketing a handsome marriage settlement.'

'This is blackmail, sir!'

He shrugged. 'I would prefer to call it a sensible bargain. Agree to catch Kildare and your grandmama gets to live out the rest of her days in peace.' He paused significantly. 'A peace which we both know to be necessary for her continuing good health.'

Disgust rose in Ianthe's throat. Still, there was no use in expressing her repugnance to Augustus. He was much too greedy to let morals get in his way!

Striving to contain her outrage, she forced herself to think calmly and immediately saw the flaw in his infamous proposal. 'What makes you think that Lord Kildare will offer marriage to me even if I am the first eligible female he encounters? By my reckoning he must be twenty-eight and he has successfully avoided matrimony thus far.'

Augustus emitted a short bark of laughter. 'I certainly don't expect him to tumble into love with you at first sight, if that's what you mean!' His pale eyes roved over her slender form with insulting disparagement. 'You used to be quite an attractive wench. Too tall, of course, and a damn sight too self-opinionated for a female, but that's by the by.'

Ianthe glared at him. 'Since we are agreed that my appearance will never ensnare his lordship, I fail to see the point of my journeying to Kildare Park.'

'You know, for such a well-educated girl you are exceptionally naïve!' Augustus shook his head sorrowfully at her.

Ignoring his mockery, Ianthe demanded clarification.

'It's simple. All you have to do is engineer some means of being alone with him and then trap him into a declaration.'

Ianthe gasped. 'What do you mean?'

'Good God, girl, you ain't that much of a baby! You *know* what I'm talking about! If the pair of you are found in sufficiently compromising circumstances, he will have no choice but to offer marriage.'

Ianthe drew her breath in sharply. 'I cannot agree to such a monstrous scheme!'

'Not even to save your grandmother from having to leave the home she loves?'

'Grandmama would agree with me that your price is too high,' Ianthe spat back at him and whirled to leave.

'Hoity-toity little madam, ain't you!' Augustus grabbed her arm and dragged her round to face him. 'But you needn't play the outraged innocent with me. It won't wash.'

He let her go, but Ianthe made no move to escape. She felt sick as the meaning of his taunt sank in.

'Aye, I found your old diary.' He smirked at her. 'So I know this show of maidenly modesty is somewhat redundant.'

'You had no right to read my private journal.' Deeply shocked at his prying, Ianthe made the protest automatically.

A few days ago, sadness at the upcoming anniversary of Waterloo had driven her to get out her old journal. She had curled up in her favourite chair in the library and indulged herself in a bout of nostalgia before Maria had unexpectedly interrupted her. The diary had been in exactly the same place when she returned to retrieve it later.

It had never occurred to her that anyone would stoop so low as to pry into her private belongings. Remembering certain revealing entries, her cheeks flushed with hot embarrassment and, in spite of the light breeze playing over the greensward of the park, she felt scarcely able to breathe.

'It's your own fault for being careless and leaving it out for anyone to discover,' Augustus retorted. 'But don't worry,

I will keep your shameful secret providing you agree to my plan.'

The cruel glee in his pale eyes was almost more than Ianthe could bear. For an instant she longed to turn and run and then, gathering her courage, she met his gaze with all the determination she could muster. 'I would rather leave Northwood than submit to your coercion,' she said as firmly as her trembling voice would allow. 'If necessary, I shall take Grandmama with me and find a job to support us both until I come of age.' A faint smile touched her wide mouth at his stunned expression. 'I believe I am well qualified enough to obtain a position as a teacher.'

Fury made Augustus's cheeks bulge until they resembled two enormous red apples. 'And how do you think you would manage on the pittance they pay governesses?'

Ianthe felt she would rather starve than give him the satisfaction of bringing her to heel, but she couldn't allow any hardship to befall her grandmother.

The anger faded from Mr Turner's expression and his voice returned to its previous unctuous tone as he saw her resolution falter. 'My dear Ianthe, don't let's brangle. You must realise that your idea is simply unfeasible. No one would employ you as a governess once I exposed your folly to the world.'

Ianthe was unable to prevent herself from flinching. She was about to demand what purpose such heartless action would serve when she saw the answer in his face. He would blacken her reputation out of sheer spite if she refused to obey him!

'I should be reluctant to embarrass you,' he purred, enjoying her discomfiture. 'However, needs must as they say and I'm sure you would rather marry a rich man like Kildare than find yourself homeless.'

Her dark brows rose in enquiry and he shrugged.

'If I don't manage to raise sufficient money by the end of June, Northwood itself may have to go under the hammer.'

Ianthe stared at him in horror. 'But my father left a substantial fortune!' she gasped. 'How have you managed to squander…it's only been a year since you married Maria!'

His florid face took on a sulky pout. 'Don't lecture me, girl! The whys and wherefores are none of your concern, but I'll tell you straight that my creditors won't wait much longer. Unless Kildare agrees to settle the outstanding loans, we are in danger of losing everything.'

'Do you really expect Lord Kildare to bail you out if I trick him into marriage?' Ianthe asked scornfully.

'I hear he is a proud man. He won't want the world to gossip about his in-laws, not for the sake of a few thousand pounds which he can easily spare.'

'So you think it acceptable to fleece him just because he is rich!' Ianthe took a deep breath and fought off the revulsion, which was turning her giddy. 'Have you no shame?'

Augustus merely laughed. 'Most marriages are arranged for profit one way or another. So I suggest you put away your indignation, my dear, and concentrate on thinking how you are going to trap his lordship into a declaration.'

'I won't…I can't…it's dishonourable!' Ianthe's choked voice trailed away.

'Don't be a fool! Honour is for those who can afford it.'

Ianthe shuddered.

'Well, what's it to be?'

'You must give me time to *think*!'

'You can have twenty-four hours to consider my offer,' Augustus conceded. 'But if I don't have the right answer by then, I shall instruct 'em to put the Dower House up for immediate sale.'

Ianthe stared at him. In spite of the mildness of the day, an icy chill of dismay feathered down her spine as she realised he had left her no choice.

Hate the idea of compromising Lord Kildare though she might, she already knew what her answer must be.

Daylight came filtering in through the peach silk curtains, casting a soft glow over the bed where Luke Kildare lay.

He woke, coming instantly alert. The bedroom was unfamiliar and, for a moment, his body remained tense until his brain caught up with the instinct for self-preservation which had served him so well during the last six years.

Awareness of his true surroundings flooded over him. He was back in England, the luxuriant forests and damp heat of Ceylon a long sea-journey behind him.

He relaxed against the lace-trimmed pillows and the slight movement caused the woman lying at his side to murmur indistinctly in her sleep.

A smile softened the hard planes of Luke's face. He had not expected his first night in London to be so pleasurable...or so free from painful memories!

Virtue brings its own reward, he thought to himself cynically, his expression settling into its habitual harsh lines as he firmly relegated all thoughts of the past to the oblivion where they belonged. If he had not ordered his post-chaise to stop yesterday afternoon on sighting a carriage leaning drunkenly against a hedge and offered to take up the stranded traveller, it was likely he would have found himself brooding alone in a room at Grillon's Hotel in Albemarle Street instead of sharing the grateful lady's bed!

His gaze wandered over Lottie's delectable form, admiring the soft swell of bosom peeping out above the lavender-scented sheets. A year or two older than himself, she was young to be a widow, although, as she had soon informed him during their journey to London, her grief had been assuaged by a splendid inheritance.

Idly, Luke wondered if her elderly husband had died of exhaustion. It seemed quite probable if her energetic performance of last night was anything to go by!

He pushed the sheet aside and ran a hand lightly over the full curve of her hip. She stirred and opened her eyes.

'Good morning, Mrs Murrell.'

Charlotte blinked at him and then a smile brightened her sleepy face. 'Good morning, my lord. My, but you do look

wide awake and so early too! I swear it cannot be much past
dawn.'

'Force of habit, I'm afraid,' Luke replied and bent to silence
her with a kiss.

It had been very late when they had finally gone to sleep,
but he had no intention of trying to explain that he had spent
too long at the courts of Sultans and Maharajahs to indulge
in sloth. A man who did not keep his wits about him in India
was soon a dead man.

Charlotte wriggled pleasurably in his embrace, offering him
her body with a hoarse little murmur of anticipation.

Her delight in his touch was flattering, but as his fingers
tangled in her blonde ringlets Luke checked for an instant.
The bright colour of Lottie's curls might owe something to
her hairdresser's skill, but it was a sharp contrast to all the
dark-haired maidens who had floated through his life for the
past six years and it triggered a sudden memory of
Georgiana's ethereal fairness to sear his soul.

The unwelcome recollection brought anger in its wake.
What a stupid young fool he had been!

Deliberately, Luke allowed the wave of emotion to fuel his
passion for the woman in his arms until, in possessing her,
he was able to lose all conscious thought in pleasure.

'You are a wonderful lover, my lord,' Lottie cooed with a
little sigh of contentment when it was over.

She smiled up at him, idly stroking his chest with one hand,
and a familiar sensation of depression gripped Luke.

It always happened. Once the act of union was ended loneliness washed over him. Utterly ridiculous of course. What
the devil did he expect? To share his *mind* with a woman?

Unaware of his mental withdrawal, for she was not a perceptive woman, Lottie gave him a sunny smile. 'Do you intend to stay in London long?' she asked.

He shook his ebony-dark head. 'My family will be expecting me.'

'What a pity! We could have so much fun together.' Her

amber-coloured eyes twinkled at him naughtily and a reluctant laugh escaped Luke.

'A most tempting prospect,' he agreed with only a trace of irony.

Emboldened by this reply, Lottie persisted. 'Oh, please do stay for a few days, Luke. I am to go down to Brighton next week, but I shall be sadly bored until then. London is growing very thin of company.'

Luke nodded his understanding. During the summer months it was customary for the *ton* to visit fashionable seaside resorts or return to their country estates.

'I promise to keep you very well entertained,' Lottie breathed, her hand trailing south down over the hard flat plane of his stomach.

'I am sure you could, my sweet.' He laid a hand over hers, halting her explorations, and considered her suggestion.

He had intended to go straight into Hampshire after seeing his man of business. However, although he had written to his family the minute his ship had docked, he had not told them when to expect him, an oversight that owed more to his aversion to visiting Kildare Park than any reluctance to see his mother and younger brother again.

It was unfortunate, but his affection for his childhood home had been tainted by the events which took place just before he left for India. Those twin disasters had wrecked his hopes and he was in no particular hurry to revisit the scene of so much misery.

'It will do no harm to stay in town for a while,' he said, coming to a swift decision. 'After six years, a few more days cannot make much difference.'

In another week no doubt he would be bored and glad to say goodbye, but for now Charlotte Murrell amused him.

Lottie let out a little squeal of delight. 'Wonderful!' she cried. Visions of showing him off to all her friends chased through her head. 'I'm sure you must be longing to enjoy some civilised conversation and comfortable surroundings.'

Luke's black eyebrows rose, but he said nothing. He was

quite sure Lottie would not understand any attempt on his part to explain that there had been rich, cultured cities in India when people in England had been living in mud huts!

'Speaking of the social round, do you by any chance know if the Earl and Countess of Lomond are still in town?'

Lottie glanced up at him quickly. There was a rather strained note in his attractive voice. For an instant her curiosity bubbled up, but a more pressing need to avoid admitting that she did not move in such elevated circles preoccupied her.

'I believe they have already removed to Scotland for the summer,' she finally answered, remembering this piece of gossip with relief. 'Why? Are they friends of yours?'

He gave an odd little laugh, a queer mixture of relief and disappointment mingling in his breast. 'I suppose one might say so.'

Scenting an interesting mystery, Lottie wished, for perhaps the millionth time, that her Alfred had been better born. The son of a successful cloth-merchant, his wealth had provided her with ample luxury and allowed them to circulate on the fringes of society, but they had never had entrée to its first circles.

Luke came to a decision. Why not satisfy Charlotte's obvious curiosity? He had told himself that he was ready to face the whispers and inquisitive looks. Here was an opportunity to prove it.

'You see, I was once engaged to Lady Georgiana.'

'Oh!' Lottie's eyes widened. 'Was that before you went to India?'

He nodded. 'I was twenty-one and on leave from my regiment in Spain when we met.'

It had been at a ball given by his parents to celebrate his home-coming and he was the hero of the hour. Everyone had wanted him to tell them about Salamanca, Lord Wellington's most recent victory, but Luke didn't want to talk about the battle or the army's subsequent triumphal entry into Madrid. He had eyes only for the lovely Miss Hamilton.

She was the most enchanting creature he had ever beheld. From the top of her flaxen-gold head to her tiny feet in their pale pink satin slippers he'd thought her utterly perfect.

He had danced attendance upon her for the rest of his leave. When his parents had realised he was serious in his wooing, his father had summoned him to his study and gently pointed out that Georgiana had neither birth nor fortune to recommend her, being merely the daughter of an impecunious, if respectable, country squire.

'And I am merely a second son, sir, with my own way to make,' Luke had swiftly countered. 'I cannot offer Miss Hamilton a title or great inheritance but, with your permission, I wish to offer her my name.'

Unable to sway Luke from his purpose, his father, who was as indulgent a parent as his loud jolly manner would suggest, withdrew his objections to the match.

On the day before he was about to take ship to return to Spain, Luke proposed. He had hardly dared believe his angel would accept. For all her lack of dowry, Georgiana had the knack of attracting suitors like bees around a honey-pot and his rivals had given him several anxious moments.

To his immense joy, Georgiana had smiled in consent and he had sailed back to Spain, her shy kiss branded on his heart.

For almost a year he had bombarded her with letters, long rambling accounts of his daily doings and the progress of the war. Her replies were infrequent and short, but he did not let this worry him. She had blushingly confessed that she was no hand with a pen as they had said their farewells on his last morning in England.

What did matter was that all the arrangements for their wedding were at last in place; it had been agreed that they would be married as soon as he could obtain another spell of leave. Unfortunately, Lord Wellington strongly disapproved of his officers taking home leave and Luke knew his request would be refused, particularly now that there were only two pockets of French opposition, at San Sebastian and Pamplona, left to overcome in Spain.

In spite of his deep desire to return to Georgiana, Luke didn't want to miss the chance to invade France. For the last five years he and the rest of Lord Wellington's army had fought their way through the Peninsula and Luke shared the prevailing mood of optimism that the end was in sight. Napoleon's power was finally crumbling. His failure in Russia and Old Nosey's magnificent victory at Vitoria had strengthened resistance to his tyrannical rule.

Only the Pyrenees now stood between their advancing army and France. All he had to do was be patient and he would soon be going home to his lovely Georgiana.

'I have heard Lady Lomond is very beautiful,' Lottie remarked, her inquisitive tones jerking Luke from his reverie.

He nodded, his expression hardening.

'So what happened? Did the two of you decide you would not suit?'

Luke steeled himself to answer. 'Miss Hamilton broke off the betrothal when I was invalided home after the storming of San Sebastian and she saw this.'

He touched a finger to his right cheek.

'She rejected you because of your scar?' Lottie exclaimed.

The note of incredulity in her voice brought a wry smile to Luke's face. 'It was far worse in those days. Truly hideous, in fact.'

Lottie sniffed. Against the deep tan of his face, the scar was a jagged slash of silver, slanting from just beneath his eye down across his cheek almost to the firm line of his jaw. For sure, it spoiled his good looks, but it hardly seemed grounds for throwing away a man's love!

And he had loved her, Lottie thought. You could see the pain in those cool grey eyes of his for all that he was trying to hide it.

'Well, I think she was a fool to let you go,' she told him roundly.

'There were…other…factors involved.'

Sensing he would not elaborate, Lottie decided not to press him further. Instead she grinned at him cheekily and, curling her fingers into the dark hair that hazed his broad chest, said, 'How unfortunate for Lady Georgiana that society decrees young ladies must remain ignorant of love-making until they are wed. If she had only known what she was missing, she would have had more sense than to give you up!'

'You pay a pretty compliment, Mrs Murrell.' Luke hid a wince at her lack of tact, sensing that she meant only to cheer him up.

'Handsome is as handsome does,' Lottie chuckled.

She sat up and tossed her long hair over her shoulders. The movement set her full breasts jiggling and Luke eyed her thoughtfully.

He was grateful to Lottie for giving him a reason to postpone his visit to Kildare Park. He thought he had learnt to control his emotions, but, buried beneath the hard layer of cynicism and detachment he had cultivated, the bitter hurt of Georgiana's betrayal still existed. It was a weakness which angered him and he was determined never to make the mistake of falling in love again. Women were pretty playthings to be admired and cossetted…and paid off with generous gifts when they no longer amused!

'Are you hungry? Would you like some breakfast?' Lottie asked, wondering why he was suddenly looking so grim.

Luke shook off his demons. 'I would rather have you,' he said in a wicked drawl that set Lottie's pulse racing.

'Then breakfast can wait, my lord,' she replied with a breathless giggle as she slid back down into his waiting arms.

Chapter Two

The sound of carriage wheels crunching over the gravel of the driveway acted as a signal, impelling the butler across the marble-flagged hallway. He flung wide the heavy front door to reveal a tall, black-haired man dressed in a many-caped Benjamin strolling towards the house.

'My lord! You are here at last!' A smile of welcome wreathed Mr Tench's lined face. 'I trust you had a pleasant journey?'

'Capital, thank you, Tench.' An answering smile lit Luke's tanned features. 'You are looking well. Your arthritis not troubling you, I hope?'

'Not at the moment, my lord.' Mr Tench beamed with pleasure at this enquiry and made so bold as to ask after his lordship's own health as he ushered him inside.

'Never better.' Luke slipped off his driving-coat and handed it to the butler, who signalled a waiting footman to come forward.

'Did my mother receive my letter advising her I meant to arrive today?' Luke asked, removing his hat and gloves. Like his coat, they were passed into the care of the footman, a young fellow Luke did not recognise.

'Indeed, my lord. She is waiting for you in the Yellow Salon.' Tench dismissed the footman with a flick of his wrist. 'Shall I inform her of your arrival?'

Luke shook his head. 'I'll go straight up. I'm sure she'll excuse me from changing out of my dirt in the circumstances.'

Tench nodded approval. 'I shall send in refreshments presently.'

Luke strode up the stairs and entered the Yellow Salon. It was an informal apartment, often used by the family during the day because it faced south and received the best of the light. Even on a cloudy day like today the primrose-silk panelled walls seemed to hold a glow of sunshine.

Lady Kildare was seated upon a handsome Hepplewhite sofa upholstered in gold brocade which stood in the centre of the room. A book lay open upon her lap, but she was not reading. To Luke's surprise, she was talking to a darkish-haired young woman.

Luke, who had expected to find his mother alone, felt faintly irritated. He closed the door behind him smartly. 'Good afternoon, Mama.'

'Luke! At last!' His mother hastily shut her book and cast it to one side. 'We have been expecting you this past week and more!'

'I had business to conduct in town,' Luke replied easily as he crossed the room.

'Then I suppose I must forgive you.' Lady Kildare stood up and held out her arms to him. 'Oh, it is lovely to see you again. We have missed you dreadfully.'

A *frisson* of guilt flickered through Luke. 'I missed you and Harry too,' he said gruffly as he gathered her into his arms and kissed her soundly on both cheeks.

Lady Kildare blinked away the tears that threatened and said in a mock-reproving tone, 'Your absence might not have seemed so prolonged had you written a trifle more frequently.'

'They do not have post offices in the jungles of India, Mama,' Luke replied mildly.

She chuckled. 'I suppose I ought be grateful you bothered to write at all to your old mother.'

Luke held her out at arm's length and surveyed her fashionable morning-gown of striped gauze. 'Old? You are looking younger than ever, Mama. And devilish elegant too, I may add.'

She reached up and touched him gently on his undamaged cheek. 'I see you haven't lost your knack for flattery, dear boy.'

She allowed her gaze to roam over his face. There were new lines etched there, although his scar, thank God, had faded. It still spoilt his handsome looks, but it didn't startle in the way it had when he had left England.

Instinct warned her that he had changed in other ways too. His eyes, once so merry, now held a cool cynicism and she felt a pang of regret for the innocent young man who had disappeared for ever.

Swallowing hard, she summoned up a bright smile and slipped from his embrace. 'Dear me, I am neglecting my manners! Ianthe, my love, do forgive me and let me introduce my son to you.'

Luke had completely forgotten about the nondescript female sitting quietly on the sofa. As far as he could tell she had been staring into her lap the whole time they had been talking.

'There is no need apologise, ma'am,' she now said in low voice, still keeping her gaze downcast. 'Besides, Lord Kildare and I have met, although it was many years ago.'

Her voice was as colourless as her pale dress. Idly, Luke wondered why she had chosen such a fussy gown; it did nothing to flatter her pallid complexion or thin figure.

He couldn't place her at all.

'You were only a child then, Ianthe, not a young lady.' A speculative gleam entered Lady Kildare's dark eyes as she gazed at her guest. 'Come, do shake hands with my graceless boy or he will think you are cross with him for ignoring you.'

Ianthe obediently rose and extended her hand. 'How do you do?'

Luke noticed her gaze fixed itself upon his top waistcoat button. 'How do you do...?' He cast an urgent glance at his mother.

'Miss Garland,' Lady Kildare supplied helpfully. She laughed. 'Shame on you, Luke! You don't remember Ianthe, do you? My late cousin Alexander's daughter?'

'Of course. You must forgive me, Miss Garland,' Luke said smoothly, releasing her icy cold fingers. 'It has been a long time.'

'Twelve years,' confirmed Lady Kildare. 'However, Ianthe is staying with me until the end of the month, so the two of you will have plenty of time to get reacquainted.'

Luke smiled politely. 'How delightful,' he murmured, striving to keep the boredom out of his voice.

He remembered her now. The Garlands used to visit the Park every summer until Sir Alexander had married that frightful second wife of his. Ianthe had been too young to impinge upon his consciousness until that last summer just before he had joined the army. She had dogged his heels, determined to join in his pursuits and he had let her tag along on his fishing trips and rabbit-snaring expeditions. He had even taught her to ride something more lively than her fat little pony.

Actually, she had been a plucky brat, game as a pebble. Astonishing to find her grown into such a dreary pattern-card of virtue, too modest even to look him in the eye!

Maybe she had heard of his reputation, he thought cynically.

'Do sit down, Luke. I am dying to hear all about your adventures.' His mother waved him to the matching sofa, which stood opposite the one on which she now seated herself.

Luke nodded, but remained standing, politely waiting for his mother's guest to resume her seat.

'If you will excuse me, ma'am, I am sure you would like some time alone with your son.'

'How very thoughtful of you, Ianthe, but there is no need to hurry away, is there, Luke?'

'Not at all, Miss Garland.'

She darted a quick glance at him. 'You are too kind, my

lord,' she muttered, hastily dropping her eyes before their gaze could meet.

Perhaps it was his scar that repelled her? Luke gave a mental shrug. It was a reaction he had encountered many times before and it no longer troubled him the way it once had.

There was a tiny silence. Luke supposed he ought to reassure her of his desire for her company, but the truth of the matter was that he wanted to talk to his mother in private. They had many things to discuss, not least of which was George's death.

His elder brother had broken his neck on the hunting field barely a year after Luke had departed for India. News of the accident had taken several months to reach him. It had been a dreadful shock, although their tastes and interests had always been too different for them to be close friends. He would have returned home to offer what belated comfort he could, but in her letter his mother had pointed out that, given the distance involved, there was little to be gained by such action. She had Harry's support and all their friends had been kind.

Luke had accepted her decision that it was better not to disrupt his new career and he knew that time had softened the blow for both of them. However, George's loss was sharp in his thoughts today and he was in no mood for exchanging trivial drawing-room chatter with a stranger.

Out of the corner of her eye Lady Kildare noticed Ianthe edging towards the door and came to her rescue. 'Well, if you are sure, my dear, we shall see you at dinner,' she said agreeably.

The relief in the girl's voice was almost palpable, Luke thought, as she bade them a hasty farewell and fled the room.

'Am I to take it that Miss Garland is shy?' Luke enquired drily, disposing his long limbs upon the sofa.

Lady Kildare chuckled. 'She *is* somewhat quiet!'

'You must find her a difficult guest.'

Lady Kildare shook her silver-streaked dark head in vigorous denial, setting the lace on her pretty widow's cap a-tremble. 'Not in the least. Ianthe shares my interest in art so we have had plenty to talk about these past two weeks. I dare say you will find her equally agreeable once she gets over her shyness.'

Luke nodded carelessly. 'And how is your painting coming along, Mama?' he remarked, his brief flicker of interest in the dull Miss Garland evaporating.

His mother's gaze brightened and she launched into an description of her most recently completed work.

Luke listened to her enthusiastic outpourings and hid a smile. It was comforting to know that some things had not changed in his absence!

'Damn!'

Ianthe threw her silver-backed hairbrush on to the dressing-table and stared at her shaking hands. She would have to ring for Jenny to dress her hair since she couldn't stop herself trembling!

It was Lord Kildare's arrival which had set her nerves twanging like fiddle strings, of course. During the last fortnight she had allowed herself to forget her real purpose in coming to the Park. She had drifted along, enjoying Cousin Amelia's pleasant company just as if this had been a normal holiday.

Coming face to face with Luke had shocked her back into grim reality.

Ianthe sighed. She had been hoping against hope that he might have grown pompous or vain or even foolish. That way she might have felt a little less guilty at the thought of deceiving him, but the man who strode into the Yellow Salon this afternoon was no self-centred nonentity.

A shudder racked her slim frame as she recalled the cynicism in his cool grey eyes and the hard line of his well-cut mouth. Unless she completely missed her guess, he would not take kindly to any attempt to trick him into marriage!

And yet...what choice had she? Augustus had given her a scant month to accomplish this aim. Thanks to Lord Kildare's tardiness, she had only two weeks left until that deadline was reached.

Ianthe felt half-paralysed by indecision. No matter how she told herself that her Northwood and her grandmother were in danger, she knew what she proposed to do was indefensible.

But perhaps it wouldn't be so bad a bargain for his lordship? Few marriages between people of rank could be described as love-matches and, in spite of Augustus's meddling, she still had a handsome dowry to offer. What's more, she would do her utmost to please him. She would even try to disguise her distaste for the act of physical union, although how one coped without love to cloak its more distressing aspects she didn't know!

Glancing up, Ianthe saw her reflection in the mirror and let out an involuntary gasp.

'Hah! Just look at you! What makes you think he will find you attractive enough to allow you to engineer a situation alone with him?'

Ianthe let out a snort of self-mocking laughter. She scarcely recognised the pale, haunted-eyed ghost who stared back at her as herself!

She shook her head, biting back her bitter amusement before it turned into hysteria. Who would ever believe that she had been described as the prettiest girl in Hertfordshire only two years ago!

Abruptly, she rose to her feet and went to tug at the bell-pull to summon her maid.

Unable to sit still, she crossed over to the window and stared out into the garden, but her anxious gaze discerned little of its well-tended beauty as her tormented thoughts whirled round on their repetitive course.

A knock at the door roused her. 'Come in.'

Jenny, the raven-haired lady's maid who had been with her since Maria had dismissed her old nurse five years ago, came bustling in.

'Do you want my assistance in dressing this evening, my lady?' she asked hopefully.

Ianthe nodded wearily and the maid's face lit up in a satisfied smile.

Maybe the arrival of the handsome son of the house was just what Miss Ianthe needed to jolt her back into caring about her appearance. Only five years younger than herself, Miss Ianthe had always treated her kindly and she was very fond of her. It would be wonderful to see her restored to her former high spirits.

Jenny gestured for Ianthe to seat herself. Taking up the hairbrush, she brushed the heavy mahogany mass vigorously. There was a small bottle of jasmine oil in Ianthe's dressing-case and she sprinkled a couple of drops on to a large silk square, which she then used to polish Ianthe's hair for several minutes.

Ianthe found her ministrations soothing. Of late she had paid little attention to her hair, just pulling it back into a plain knot. It was a neat, practical style, but now she thought about it, it wasn't particularly flattering.

'Such pretty hair you have, Miss Ianthe, if only you would dress it right,' Jenny murmured, wielding a comb skilfully to coax a few curls to frame Ianthe's face.

Ianthe shrugged. What did it matter anyway? Her looks had gone and the new gowns Maria had insisted upon did not suit her. If she had not been so preoccupied and Maria had not been so vehement that she must discard her customary mourning, she might have sought an excuse to leave them behind at Northwood.

'There, that's better if I may say so, Miss Ianthe,' Jenny announced, laying down the comb.

Ianthe regarded her maid's handiwork in the mirror and a sudden flicker of pleasure pierced her gloom. 'Thank you, Jenny,' she said, surprised at how the new, softer style made her cheeks look less hollow.

Delighted to see her mistress smiling for what seemed like the first time in weeks, Jenny proudly handed Ianthe the yellow fan that matched her silk evening gown.

When she arrived downstairs Ianthe was relieved to find

the drawing-room was empty, but she had barely settled herself in a chair when she heard footsteps in the hall.

A moment later Lord Kildare strolled into the room and a
sense of panic swept over Ianthe. She wasn't ready to be alone
with him yet!

'Good evening, Miss Garland.'

Gulping hard, she struggled to contain her agitation. 'Good
evening, sir,' she murmured.

He had very properly left the double doors of the drawing-
room open. The long years he had spent in India had obviously not caused him to forget the convention which decreed
that young persons of the opposite sex should not spend time
together in potentially sinful privacy!

Luke thought he had rarely heard a less lively greeting. Her
voice had all the animation of an octogenarian on her sick-
bed!

However, he had been properly brought up and to allow
the conversation to wither into silence would be discourteous.

'It is a very mild evening, is it not?' he remarked, moving
towards the fireplace and casually leaning his elbow against
the mantelpiece. 'I had expected to find myself shivering after
Ceylon, but I dare say I shall not have to wear more than
three shirts and two waistcoats after all.'

Ianthe shot him a startled glance and then realised he was
joking. She forced a smile. 'June is often a warm month,' she
murmured absently, wishing he would sit down.

He had been a tall youth, she remembered. Now he was
well over six feet in height and he made her feel uncomfortable, towering over her like a giant out of a fairy story!

Her bland reply offered him little scope. Luke tried again.
'I hope you are looking forward to your dinner as much as I
am, Miss Garland,' he said with a heartiness that rang false
in his own ears. 'I know travelling is supposed to dull the
appetite, but I find myself sharp-set tonight.'

Ianthe cast about for something intelligent to say. She had
no appetite at all, but she could hardly tell him why!

The silence stretched out and Luke gritted his teeth. 'I trust you left your stepmother in good health?'

Ianthe nodded.

'I understand from one of my mother's letters that she re-married. To a Mr Turner?'

Ianthe confirmed it with another nod of her head.

Idly, Luke noticed that she had changed her hairstyle. She now looked less like a governess, but the acid-yellow gown she wore with its lavish trimming of silk floss was deeply unflattering.

'May I enquire if Mr Turner is related to the Hampshire branch of the family? Their country seat is quite close to here, as you may know.'

'I don't think…that is, I'm not really sure…' Ianthe mumbled, her eyes still glued to their study of the flowers woven into the drawing-room's Aubusson carpet.

'What a pity.'

Ianthe heard the note of boredom in his deep voice and could not blame him. A schoolgirl freshly launched into society could offer more interesting conversation than she had managed tonight!

He probably thinks me dimwitted, she thought with an illogical flash of resentment.

'Is it that you prefer silence or have I inadvertently done something to offend you, Miss Garland?' Luke asked with a dry irony.

Ianthe's mind went completely blank. Unable to think of a single sensible thing to say in reply to this question, she could only gaze up at him in consternation.

Even as he regretted his lack of patience, Luke registered how lovely her eyes were. It was the first time he'd had the opportunity to study her properly and he owned to a slight sense of surprise.

Cousin Alexander, he recalled, had been a very handsome fellow. His daughter shared the same oval shape of face and high cheekbones, but lacked his regular, classical features. With that wide mouth, rather *retrousse* little nose and determined chin, her thin face had character rather than beauty. However, her eyes were truly remarkable.

Framed by arching black brows and preposterously long eyelashes, they were a deep violet-blue, just like the prize sapphires he had discovered in Ceylon!

To Ianthe's immense relief, Lady Kildare chose this moment to walk into the room.

'I see I am the last!' She greeted them with an apologetic smile and took a seat near to Ianthe's. 'Still, my tardiness must have given the pair of you a chance to enjoy a little talk.'

Luke lifted his brows at his mother. She was no fool and must have noticed the tense silence as soon as she entered the drawing-room.

Lady Kildare cheerfully ignored his pained expression and began to chatter about her youngest son's forthcoming visit. 'Harry means to ask the Bishop if he will permit Miss Conway to accompany him so that she may meet you, Luke. You will like her, I'm sure. She is a pleasant girl and will make Harry a very suitable wife.'

During her stay at the Park Ianthe had learnt that Henry Kildare, now a clergyman, was employed in the Bishop of Dorchester's household. He was also paying court to the Bishop's elder daughter.

Apparently, Lord Kildare was *au fait* with this situation for he asked if the Bishop had actually given his permission for the couple to wed. 'In your last letter, Mama, I thought you said that he considered his daughter too young to enter into marriage?'

'Lud, Sophy is almost nineteen!' Lady Kildare exclaimed. 'Quite old enough, I should say.' She turned to Ianthe. 'What do you think, my dear?'

'It is difficult for me to judge, ma'am. I do not have the pleasure of knowing Miss Conway,' Ianthe said in colourless tone that disguised her fervent wish that the topic of marriage could be abandoned!

'But in general terms, Miss Garland? Surely you must have some opinion?'

There was a mocking note in his lordship's attractive voice and Ianthe could feel a blush rising in her cheeks. 'Generally speaking, I am not sure I approve of marriage at any age, my lord,' she retorted, stung out of her passivity.

'Really?' Abandoning his position by the fireplace, Luke strolled to take a seat close to hers. 'I thought it was every young lady's ambition to marry well.'

There was a hint of condescension in his baritone voice and this annoyed Ianthe so much that she forgot her previous apprehension. 'Women lose their rights when they marry,' she said hotly. 'I have no wish to become some man's shadow. Providing one has sufficient money, it must be preferable to remain an independent spinster.'

Luke's expression revealed his surprise and Ianthe experienced an instant of triumph. How dare he categorise her as a meek little mouse on such short acquaintance!

'I suspect you have been reading Mary Wollstonecraft's *Vindication of the Rights of Woman*,' Lady Kildare chimed in, her eyes twinkling.

Ianthe nodded, her eyes defiant.

'A most interesting work,' Luke said smoothly, recovering from his surprise.

'You have read it, sir?' It was Ianthe's turn to look amazed.

Her tone made it obvious that she considered him a brainless lump of brawn! 'A soldier's life contains many periods of inaction, Miss Garland,' he said, hiding his amusement. 'Reading was one of my favourite methods of occupying those idle hours.'

'Of course.' Aware that she had let temper lead her into rudeness, Ianthe forced herself to acknowledge his reply with a contrite inclination of her head.

Lady Kildare tactfully began to ask her son if he still liked strawberry tart. 'Cook baked one today specially in your honour,' she told him.

Luke laughed and said he would enjoy eating it. 'In India I used to dream of her wonderful pies and cakes!'

The conversation turned to the strange foods he had encountered on his travels and, as Lady Kildare exclaimed in horror at the thought of eating curried shark and buffalo-milk curd, Ianthe was free to pursue her own thoughts.

Good manners had forced him to solicit her conversation, but it was obvious Luke Kildare had decided she was a gauche blue-stocking with nothing to recommend her to his interest. Ianthe wondered why she found this realisation so upsetting.

She risked a direct glance at him. He was laughing at something his mother had just said and the cynical expression she suspected was habitual with him was temporarily absent. He looked suddenly much younger and a lot more like the boy she remembered.

Ianthe stared at him and, with a *frisson* of surprise, realised that she had been so nervous she hadn't really looked at him properly until now. All she had registered was his harsh expression and the jagged scar on his face.

It had been a shock, seeing him so changed. Cousin Amelia had written to Papa, of course, about his injuries, but hearing about it wasn't the same as seeing for herself. This afternoon, even amid the anguish of her guilty conscience, she had experienced a deep pang of sympathy for him.

He hadn't thought she was avoiding meeting his gaze because of his scar, had he? This notion made Ianthe feel uneasy. She had no desire to hurt his feelings and knew that, in normal circumstances, she would have tried to act as if there was nothing amiss.

Oddly enough, the way he was sitting now, with his undamaged profile presented to her, it was easy to see that he had matured into a very handsome man. His height and broad shoulders were striking and his features might have been modelled by a sculptor with classical inclinations. Even his unfashionably bronzed skin suited his dark colouring.

He reminded her, for some reason she couldn't quite fathom, of a big jungle cat!

He turned his head and their gaze met.

A little shiver ran though Ianthe. Lean, lithe and wickedly alert! No wonder he put her in mind of a dangerous predator!

At breakfast the next morning Ianthe found herself alone. Lady Kildare often had a tray in her room and, since it was after ten, she assumed that his lordship must have already eaten.

She had passed a wretched night, kept restlessly awake by her predicament, and risen later than her usual wont. However, since she had partaken of very little at dinner last night, she thought she might be able to do justice to a plate of buttered eggs. The Hampshire air seemed to agree with her and her appetite had improved since her arrival at the Park.

Adding a slice of the ham, which was sizzling under one of the silver chafing-dishes set out on the sideboard and giving off a most tantalising aroma, to her plate, Ianthe sat down at the table. She had just picked up her knife and fork when the door to the breakfast-parlour opened and Lord Kildare walked in.

'Good morning.'

Ianthe turned her squeak of dismay into a cough. 'Good morning,' she replied, hoping she didn't sound as nervous as she felt.

Luke sat down opposite her. 'Is that coffee still hot?' he asked, indicating the silver pot which stood in front of Ianthe.

Ianthe nodded. 'Tench brought it in just a moment ago.'

No sooner had she finished speaking than the butler appeared at his master's elbow with a cup and saucer. He poured the coffee and asked, 'Is there anything else I can get you, my lord?'

'No thank you, Tench.'

The butler nodded and melted away.

Luke sipped his coffee, which Ianthe noticed he took unsweetened and black.

'It is a lovely day. Do you have any plans made to enjoy it, Miss Garland?'

Chewing manfully at the bite of ham in her mouth, Ianthe swallowed and said hastily, 'Your mama requires my services.'

Did she think he had been about to ask for her company? Luke considered giving her a set-down and then realised he was being unfair. She was his mother's guest; if Mama hadn't yet asked him to entertain her, it was only because she knew he would be busy today with his bailiff.

There was a slight silence and, mindful of her disastrous showing last night, Ianthe sought to fill it. 'Aren't you going to eat anything, sir? I can recommend the ham.'

'I breakfasted earlier, Miss Garland.' Luke set down his empty coffee cup. 'Before I rode out to have a look at the estate.'

There was a faint amusement in his tone that made Ianthe bridle. He obviously thought her a slug-a-bed!

'Pray excuse me. I have many tasks to attend to today.' Luke rose to his feet, his mind already moving onto other matters.

After his long absence he felt it was his duty to acquaint himself with every aspect of running the estate. Wheat prices had fallen drastically since he was last in England. The price of iron, cloth and many other commodities had dropped too now that they were no longer fuelled by war. Already he had heard stories about the unrest and agitation for reform which was sweeping the country.

He had seen incredible poverty in India and knew how it could destroy a man's soul. He meant to do his utmost to ensure that there was enough work for the labourers here at Kildare Park to keep food on their tables.

'No doubt we will meet at dinner, Miss Garland,' he added dutifully and bade her good day.

Ianthe's guilty conscience made her acutely sensitive and she heard the lack of interest underlying his politeness. An irrational spurt of resentment filled her and there was still a hint of angry colour in her cheeks when she joined Lady Kildare in her studio a few moments later.

'You are very prompt, my dear,' Amelia greeted her, privately thinking how well the child was looking this morning. 'I have only just arrived myself.' She whisked the protective cover from the portrait which stood upon her easel. 'Your costume is hanging up over there if you would like to get changed.'

Ianthe took the costume and went behind the folding wooden screen that her cousin had installed. Slipping out of her morning-gown, she recalled her initial unease when Amelia had announced that she wanted to portray her as the Goddess Diana. Now, however, the flimsy white draperies which constituted her divine outfit felt perfectly normal.

'Shall I take my place?' Ianthe asked, gesturing towards the dais in the centre of the room.

'Please.' Amelia nodded, her mind elsewhere as she studied her efforts of yesterday.

Ianthe picked up her bow and adopted the required pose, leaning negligently against a broken marble column, which Lady Kildare had commandeered from the classical sculpture adorning the rose garden.

'Move a little further to the left...perfect!' Amelia glanced up from mixing her oil-paints and bestowed a smile of approval upon her young helper.

Amelia had asked her to sit for her a few days after Ianthe's arrival at the Park and Ianthe had been happy to oblige. The notion that she might be of use to her cousin eased her uncomfortable feeling that she was here under false pretences.

'You know, you have the fortunate knack of being able to keep still,' Amelia remarked some time later. 'None of my children could ever manage to do so, I assure you.'

Ianthe smiled. Holding a pose was harder work than it looked!

'Luke was the worst,' Amelia continued, her hands busy as she spoke. 'But then he has always been a restless soul!' She lifted her eyes from her palette and flicked a glance at Ianthe. 'What do you think of him? Do you find him much changed?'

'I…er…I cannot remember his lordship very well,' Ianthe murmured. 'However, he seems a most agreeable gentleman.'

If Amelia felt this reply lacked conviction, she made no sign of it. 'It is early days yet, but I am hopeful that he will be able to settle in England,' she said, loading her brush with more paint.

A tiny sigh escaped her. 'I knew he would never do so after his return from the Peninsula.'

'It must have been a very worrying time for you,' Ianthe ventured.

'Indeed! And not just because of his injuries! We were all dreadfully worried he might do something silly because of that stupid girl—' Lady Kildare bit off what she was about to say.

'Luke was a very romantic kind of young man,' she continued lightly after a moment. 'Unfortunately, he had little understanding of women and was forever fancying himself smitten by one unsuitable charmer or other! Typical behaviour of any dashing young man, you might say, but we used to fear that he would offer for some brainless beauty who would bore him senseless within a week!'

She shrugged, her expression somewhat rueful. 'I don't think he knew himself what he really wanted in a wife.'

Ianthe swallowed nervously. 'Lord Kildare doesn't give the impression of being a romantic,' she said quietly.

Amelia's expression lightened. 'No, indeed. I doubt if he would write poetry in honour of his beloved nowadays,' she chuckled. 'In fact, I suspect my son probably considers love an emotion felt only by the foolish.'

'Then I think his lordship is in danger of becoming a hopeless cynic!' Ianthe announced tartly.

Amelia flashed an amused glance at her companion. 'Perhaps, but many women find a cavalier attitude irresistible, you know. They imagine that they and they alone can pierce the armour surrounding such a man's cold heart and capture his love.'

Before she could stop herself Ianthe snorted inelegantly.

Her cousin laughed. 'I dare say you are right, my dear!' she said, waving aside Ianthe's hasty apology. 'It is nonsense to believe that one can change any man's nature. Luke, for example, thrives on challenge. He may have gone off to India to forget his broken heart, but he stayed there because he enjoys exploring new cultures and conquering the unknown.'

She added a touch of shadow to her depiction of Ianthe's draperies and stood back to evaluate the effect. 'It will take a very special kind of woman to succeed in taming him,' she added thoughtfully.

Ianthe gulped. Was she mad to think of trying to become his wife when even his mother seemed to think that Luke Kildare would make an awkward husband?

The next morning Ianthe awoke soon after dawn. In the hope of recapturing sleep, she lay quietly for a while, but her mind was too active to allow her to achieve her object. Last night at dinner her behaviour had been so gauche and stilted she was sure she must have given Lord Kildare a disgust of her. He did not betray any sign of it, of course, but she could positively *feel* the waves of boredom emanating from his tall, handsome person whenever he felt obliged to speak to her.

Abandoning her futile struggle, Ianthe threw back her covers and got up. Crossing to the window, she inspected the day and a smile suddenly touched her wide mouth. It was a beautiful morning and a brisk gallop before breakfast seemed an excellent way of banishing her megrim.

There was enough water left in the jug on her washing-stand to splash her face and hands and she dressed herself without bothering to ring for Jenny. Her riding habit, expertly tailored in dark blue broadcloth, was no longer new and it was loose on her these days, but it was comfortable and she felt far more at ease wearing it than any of the ornate dresses selected for her by Maria.

She gave her hair a quick brush and plaited it into a thick coil at the nape of her neck, securing it impatiently with several hair-pins. A few rebellious strands wriggled free, but

Ianthe didn't care. There would be no one except the servants to see her at this early hour.

Outside, she took deep lungfuls of the crisp air, her spirits rising. By the time she reached the stable block, the look of strain had disappeared from her eyes.

'Good morning, John,' Ianthe greeted one of the grooms who was sweeping the yard. 'Would you saddle Moonlight for me?'

The young man put down his broom. ''Course, Miss Garland.'

While she was waiting, Ianthe decided to go and inspect the litter of kittens which one of the kitchen cats had produced a few weeks ago. They were very sweet and she walked inside the building, humming cheerfully to herself.

Ianthe came to an abrupt halt as she realised that someone else was there. 'Lord Kildare! What are you doing here?'

His tall commanding figure turned in her direction. 'I'm waiting for my horse to be saddled, Miss Garland.'

'You are going riding?'

He inclined his dark head, his expression carefully polite.

Ianthe blushed. What a stupid remark to have made! Why else would he be here dressed in those immaculate riding clothes?

All thought of playing with the kittens fled her mind and with a feeble smile she backed out of the stable, horribly aware that he was watching her.

It's your guilty conscience that makes you so awkward around him, she told herself in despair, wishing that John would hurry up with her horse.

'It is quite unusual to find anyone else here at this hour. I am the only one in my family who is an early riser.'

The sound of his deep voice made her whirl round and she discovered Lord Kildare standing behind her. He had moved so quietly she had not heard him.

'Are you a lark by nature, Miss Garland?'

Ianthe nodded. 'I enjoy riding before breakfast when I can,' she murmured, determined not to make any more inane remarks if she could help it.

'So do I, especially on such a fine morning.' Luke made the discovery that the severe lines of her riding-habit suited her. Why the devil did she go about like an overdressed maypole when her tall slender body could look so elegant? he wondered, a spark of interest flickering in his breast.

It suddenly occurred to Ianthe that he was bound to offer her his escort. The thought made her feel so nervous that she almost missed what he was saying next.

'I acquired the custom of early rising when I was in the army. It was always something of a shock to discover that fashionable life required an exact reversal of my usual habits whenever I was on leave.'

'You spent part of your free time in London, I suppose, sir?'

'I stayed there on many occasions,' Luke confirmed. 'And you, Miss Garland, do you enjoy the Season?'

'Enjoy isn't the word I would have used.'

There was a rueful note in her pleasantly modulated voice and surprise lifted Luke's dark brows.

Seeing it, Ianthe wondered what explanation she might offer since she had no intention of telling him the truth. 'My stepmama brought me out when I was seventeen, but I did not take to fashionable life,' she prevaricated.

There was a touch of defiance in her manner and Luke felt his curiosity stir.

'London doesn't suit everyone,' he agreed smoothly. 'No doubt you found it too noisy and crowded.'

Ianthe agreed and, as John and one of the other grooms appeared leading out the two horses, was glad to be spared the necessity of further conversation.

In truth, she had unpleasant memories of her début into society. Maria had insisted on them taking a house for the Season the year after Waterloo, but it was too soon for Ianthe, who had not shaken off her grief. She had found the constant parties and balls wearisome and pleaded with her papa to allow her to go home. Maria had thrown a tantrum on learning of her request and her father had reluctantly refused.

Not that it had done any good, of course. Determined to stay true to Philip's memory, Ianthe paid no heed to the attentions of the young men who flocked around her and they had returned to Northwood without securing the betrothal to some eligible suitor that Maria had hoped to bring about.

Ianthe could feel Lord Kildare's eyes watching her closely as she mounted the lively grey mare. His attention remained fixed upon her as they set off at a sedate trot.

'Do you know the track towards Buttermilk Hill?' he asked.

'I have ridden that way once or twice,' Ianthe replied.

He nodded and began to chat amiably about nothing in particular as they turned in that direction.

He is gauging my skills, Ianthe thought to herself with a flare of indignation that swiftly faded when she realised that he probably did not want to humiliate her by setting a pace she could not match.

They skirted a copse of oak trees at a slow canter and, evidently deciding that she could keep up with him, Luke increased his horse's speed. Ianthe urged Moonlight forward and felt her own breathing quicken with excitement as they headed towards open country.

The wind blew into her face in an invigorating rush and it seemed to clear the cobwebs from her mind. Grandmama was right, she thought in astonishment. I *did* need to get away from Northwood! I *did* need a change of scene and new influences to stop me endlessly brooding about the past!

Out of the corner of her eye she caught a glimpse of Luke's surprised expression and she touched her whip to Moonlight's withers, a tiny crow of laughter escaping her as the mare shot forward in an intoxicating burst of speed. How annoyed Augustus would be if he knew she was actually enjoying herself!

The sound of the chestnut's hooves thundering behind her encouraged her crazy desire to race Luke to their destination and prove she wasn't the dull mouse he assumed. Moonlight responded to her skilful coaxing and they flew over a low stone wall with barely an interruption to their reckless speed. They jumped a narrow stream and sped on towards the hill, Ianthe barely aware that she had lost her hat although several loose tendrils of hair were blowing wildly about her face.

The realisation that Moonlight was beginning to shudder with effort finally cured her madness and she instructed the mare to slacken her pace until they came to a final halt at the crest of the grass-covered rise. A few seconds later Lord Kildare pulled up his mount beside her.

Ianthe saw that he held her riding hat. 'Where did you find it?' she gasped, suddenly conscious of her disordered hair and the perspiration beading her temples.

He held it out to her. 'It landed in a bush. I managed to pick it up with my whip as I rode past.'

'Thank you.' Ianthe took the hat and impulsively continued in the same breathless tone, 'Allow me to congratulate you, sir, on your horsemanship. I thought we were going much too fast to attempt such a rescue.'

Luke grinned. 'I assure you, my skills are paltry compared to those of the Mahratta tribesmen I knew in India. However, I am glad to have been of service.'

He was disturbingly aware of the rapid fall and rise of her breasts as she sought to catch her breath. She wasn't as flat-chested as he had thought! In fact, with that bright glow of animation in her eyes and that fresh colour in her cheeks, she looked positively pretty!

He smiled at her. 'You ride extremely well yourself, Miss Garland.'

His praise pleased Ianthe more than she cared to admit. To hide her confusion she said hastily, 'I had a very good teacher.' He looked at her blankly and she gave a little chuckle. 'You don't remember, do you?'

'Ah, but I do!' Luke's smile suddenly deepened. 'You are referring, are you not, to my persuading your papa into permitting me to put you up on my gelding instead of that fat little pony you used to ride?'

'You were very patient with me.' Ianthe laughed reminiscently.

'I was terrified you might start crying if I shouted at you!' Luke confessed solemnly, but there was a joking twinkle in his grey gaze.

How different he looked when he smiled properly with real warmth in his eyes! He had lost that usual trace of mockery in his baritone voice too. She had half-expected him to reproach her for galloping so madly, but either he was being tactful or he didn't care about her lack of decorum.

'I think you had better dismount and attend to your hair. Otherwise, you will have difficulty in seeing where you are going on the way home,' Luke said, observing her ineffectual attempts to tidy herself while holding her reins in one hand.

He sprang down from his saddle. 'Let me help you.'

He held out his arms to her and Ianthe put her hands on his shoulders.

She could feel the ripple of solid muscle beneath her fingers as he lifted her easily from Moonlight's back. Unexpectedly, her pulse quickened.

'Thank you,' she whispered in a voice that had become unaccountably hoarse.

He was still holding her by the waist. She lifted her gaze, intending to make a light-hearted announcement that he need not fear she would fall now she was safe on the ground.

Their eyes met and she heard the quick rasp of his indrawn breath.

'You have very blue eyes,' Lord Kildare said flatly. 'They are the exact colour of the finest sapphires.'

A thrill of triumph shot through Ianthe, although she could not have said why. She had heard the same remark dozens of time before. What's more, he hadn't even sounded as if he meant it as a compliment.

But, somehow, his cool statement made her heart leap and her nerves tingle!

Chapter Three

'You may release me now, my lord. I am in no danger of falling.'

Ianthe's breathing became a little easier as Lord Kildare promptly obeyed her request and stepped back. 'I must tidy my hair,' she murmured, still feeling inexplicably unsettled.

'Of course.' He moved off and began to admire the view.

Telling herself that her wild ride must have taken more out of her than she'd realised, Ianthe turned away and quickly braided her unruly locks into a fresh plait. Coiling it at the nape of her neck she donned her hat.

I won't stare at him, she thought, smoothing her skirts, but, somehow, the next moment her eyes turned in his direction and she discovered that he was no longer looking at the view.

'Are you ready?' Luke walked towards her.

He was smiling and Ianthe's face involuntarily lit up in an answering smile as she nodded assent.

'Then we ought to get back or they will imagine there has been some kind of accident.'

Ianthe nodded. They had been gone for longer than she had first thought. Would their absence give rise to gossip? If so, it might aid any future scheme of hers to have people think Lord Kildare was showing an undue interest in her.

She swallowed hard, pushing the thought away with distaste as she walked towards her mount.

'Permit me to assist you, Miss Garland.'

With an ease that betrayed he was used to far greater physical exertions, Lord Kildare threw her up into her saddle before mounting his own chestnut.

They rode in silence for a few moments before Ianthe decided she did not wish to take the risk of him thinking her tedious company. Not that she wanted his good opinion, of course. It was merely irksome to be thought a bore.

'Will you tell me a little about your travels in India, my lord? I am sure you must have seen many exotic sights.'

'Are you interested in foreign places, Miss Garland?' There was a note of slight surprise in Luke's voice. In his experience, his fellow countrymen were not much concerned with anything that went on beyond their own shores.

Ianthe nodded enthusiastically. 'I have not been further afield than France,' she admitted. 'However, I hope to travel more when I attain my majority.'

In the right company, she added silently. A trip to Paris had been conceived by her father shortly before his death in the hope of raising her spirits. Unfortunately, at the last minute Maria had changed her mind about remaining at home and insisted on accompanying them. The Channel crossing had been rough and Maria's bout of seasickness had induced a prejudice in her against the trip that nothing could shake off. She found fault with everything and her constant complaints had ruined the holiday.

'What would you like to know?'

Luke's velvet-toned voice recalled her to the present and Ianthe smiled shyly at him. 'Anything you can tell me! Tell me about the weather, what the people wear, what the scenery is like, what they eat. I know almost nothing about the country so anything you care to describe will be of interest to me.'

'Well, the first thing to realise is that India is vast. I think you could spend a whole lifetime exploring and never see all of it. It is also a land of amazing contrasts. There are wide flat plains and spectacular mountains, beaches of sugar-white sand and dark green jungles. You can find palaces and forts, abandoned ancient ruins and busy teeming cities bursting with people…or tiny villages where nothing seems to stir except for a wandering cow.'

He smiled faintly. 'India assaults the senses. It is difficult to explain, but somehow everything is more extreme there. Colours that dazzle the eye, constant noise in the streets, incredible wealth, utter squalor, weird customs…' He shrugged. 'Most Europeans hate it and cannot wait to leave. For others like myself, it gets into the blood like an intoxicating drug.'

Ianthe blinked. She had thought him much too cool and self-contained to make such a confession.

She has an expressive face when she forgets that maidenly modesty of hers, Luke thought. Still, she wasn't the only one who found his love for India perplexing. Many of his fellow Englishmen had thought him mad!

Not wishing to inadvertently offend, Ianthe searched for something neutral to say. 'I have heard that it is a hot country,' she ventured at last.

Luke grinned. 'I was never in the far north, but believe me, everywhere I went it felt as hot as Hades! It was often very humid and the rain…! My godfather had warned me, but I thought the climate couldn't be worse than Spain.' He shrugged. 'I was wrong! That kind of heat and torrential rain is impossible to imagine until you experience it for yourself.'

'Your godfather was an East India Company man, I believe?'

Luke answered her with a curt nod of his dark head. 'I went out there at his suggestion.'

There was a note of reserve in his voice and Ianthe reluctantly curbed her curiosity. Cousin Amelia had already let slip that his broken engagement had much to do with his decision to leave England. It was plainly a sensitive subject and she had no wish to rouse Luke's anger.

Not when they were getting on so well!

'And what of the natives, sir?' she asked. 'How were you able to communicate with them? Do any of them speak English?'

'A few do.' The brooding expression vanished from Lord Kildare's face. 'There have been Europeans in India for over three hundred years now and Portuguese and French is also spoken. However, I tried to learn a smattering of the language of whatever area in which I found myself.'

'Do you mean that there are several languages?' Ianthe exclaimed.

He nodded. 'They have several different religions too.'

'How very confusing!'

Luke laughed. 'You'd be surprised how quickly one can learn when one's safety depends on understanding local customs, Miss Garland.'

Cousin Amelia had mentioned that her son had a knack for languages, having learnt to speak both Spanish and Portuguese during his time in the Peninsula. He had obviously made good use of this talent in India too.

They had reached the oak copse and Ianthe had to give her attention to Moonlight, who took sudden exception to the flickering shadows cast by the wind-stirred trees. When this difficulty was overcome, she turned again to her companion and asked him to continue with his fascinating discourse.

'I have no wish to bore you, Miss Garland.'

'How can you think I am bored?' Ianthe demanded indignantly.

Luke directed a searching glance at her and decided that she was genuinely interested and not indulging in some girlish attempt to flatter his vanity.

Now what maggot had put that idea into his head? He'd lay odds she didn't even like him, let alone want to set up a flirtation with him!

'Very well,' he said crisply. 'Now let me see…ah, yes, you asked how the Indians dressed, I believe? Well, the men often wear loose trousers or something called a *dhoti*, which is a length of white cloth pulled up between the legs. The effect is rather like a pair of baggy breeches, not very elegant but much cooler than European clothes.'

Many white men, sweating in their tight woollen coats and

suffocating neckcloths, suffered from itchy rashes and debilitating illnesses or even died of heatstroke. Following Nicodemus's advice, Luke had decided to adapt to the climate.

'I had a tailor make me up several loose shirts and wide trousers, all in thin white cotton,' he told Ianthe. He grinned. 'Not the kind of attire that would be allowed to cross the sacred threshold of Almack's, but very comfortable.'

'Do the Indian ladies also favour white for their gowns?'

He shook his head vigorously. 'Good Lord, no! They are as bright as peacocks in their saris.' Seeing her look of incomprehension he attempted to describe this piece of female clothing. 'The Devil only knows how they get them to stay up without any fastenings,' he concluded with a chuckle.

'They sound quite lovely!' Ianthe exclaimed.

Luke had brought home several bolts of fine silk and delicate muslins and for an instant it crossed his mind to offer her one of them before he checked himself sternly.

Just because he had enjoyed their conversation there was no reason to let himself forget his resolve to keep women of his own class at a distance. She might get completely the wrong idea about his motives! Besides, such an expensive gift would be deemed inappropriate. A well-bred young lady might only accept trivial offerings such as a posy of flowers.

To cover his inner perturbation, Luke began to speak of random incidents and sights that had stuck in his memory. Ianthe listened enthralled to his description of a herd of elephants washing themselves in a river, of a white marble temple seen by moonlight and a flower-bedecked festival with a procession of strange, colourful gods paraded amid the clash of cymbals and the blare of horns.

'Do you know,' Ianthe said impulsively when he had finished speaking, 'at a party once in London I met an officer of the 33rd Foot, who was in India with Lord Wellington. When I asked him for his opinions, all he could say was that Calcutta stank, good beef was not to be had and India was much too dirty a place for a lady!'

A frown tugged Lord Kildare's black eyebrows together and for an instant she feared she had unintentionally destroyed their current mood of harmony. Then, to her relief, he laughed.

'It's true that Calcutta stinks,' he said frankly. 'But then London is little sweeter. The smells are different, that's all. Buffalo-dung smoke instead of coal fires, spice and dust instead of rain and damp.' He shrugged. 'Not that your story surprises me. Most of the Englishmen I knew out there were more interested in hard-drinking sprees and gambling after dinner than in learning anything of the country.'

'And the ladies? Did they hold the same narrow view?'

'There are far fewer white women out there than men. However, the ones I met were even more vehement in their complaints.' Luke reined in his chestnut who, smelling his stable, was showing a tendency to bolt. 'Why do you ask?'

'A woman's mind does not necessarily work in the same way as a man's,' Ianthe replied with a teasing note in her voice, hoping to make his attractive smile appear.

To her astonished dismay, a grim expression descended upon his face.

'Very true, Miss Garland,' he said. 'Unfortunately, it takes some men a long time to realise that simple fact.'

The bitter note in his voice alarmed Ianthe, but she couldn't resist the temptation to retort, 'I think one might safely say that it also takes women time to learn to understand men.'

'I disagree. Your sex was born with the power to beguile and deceive, Miss Garland. It is a lucky man who can withstand the wiles of a pretty woman.'

'I see that you do not hold a high opinion of us, sir!'

He gave her a cynical smile. 'On the contrary, I know how to appreciate a woman's charms. However, I do not expect her to share my notions of honour and loyalty.'

Ianthe sucked in her breath. Of all the arrogant…!

It was fortunate that they turned the final bend towards the stables as he spoke or Ianthe was sure she would have lost her temper. Instead, she cantered into the yard, where she quickly made use of the mounting-block.

One of the grooms ran up to take the mare and Ianthe thanked him with a smile, which vanished as Lord Kildare brought his chestnut to a halt next to her.

'Thank you for your escort, my lord.' Good manners prevented Ianthe from leaving without a word as she would have preferred to do, but her tone was curt.

'My pleasure, Miss Garland.' Luke raised his whip in acknowledgement, a mocking expression on his face once more and Ianthe whirled away.

By the time she reached the house Ianthe had convinced herself that while he might not deserve to be trapped into an unwanted marriage, Luke Kildare most certainly deserved to be taught a little humility!

Lady Kildare laid down her paint brush. 'Shall we call a halt for today, Ianthe? You look tired, my dear.'

Ianthe felt exhausted, but she did not wish to inconvenience her relative. 'I am quite all right, Cousin Amelia,' she said stoutly.

Amelia smiled and tactfully did not enquire why her young companion had spent the morning trying to stifle her yawns.

They worked for another quarter of an hour and then Amelia insisted it was time they finished. 'I have reached a good place to stop and, besides, it is growing too warm for comfort in here,' she announced.

Ianthe concurred. The late Lord Kildare had built the painting studio as a present for his wife when they were first married. It was situated in a small pavilion in the grounds close to the house. Tall windows stretched almost from floor to the ceiling on all sides, giving the maximum amount of light, and the estate carpenter had constructed a clever set of shelves and cabinets to hold Lady Kildare's paints and other equipment.

On a hot summer's day like today sunlight flooded the pavilion's single room, washing the paint-splattered floorboards to the colour of honey. Even in her scanty costume, Ianthe felt the heat.

'I think I shall take a nap after our nuncheon,' Lady Kildare remarked, leading the way back into the main house. 'I find this hot weather enervating.'

Usually, it had been her custom to take Ianthe for a drive or to pay calls. On the rare occasions they had stayed at home, they had occupied themselves in the gardens if it was fine or with their embroidery if the weather was inclement.

'We had several new volumes of music delivered recently, which you will find in the music room if you wish to amuse yourself in that way,' Lady Kildare announced after they had finished their simple meal of cold meats and fruit. 'And you know, I'm sure, that you may help yourself to whatever book you fancy from the library.'

When she had retired to her rooms, Ianthe pondered these suggestions. Neither appealed and she decided to emulate her cousin's example. She didn't expect to be able to sleep, but an hour's rest upon her bed would help restore her energy.

To her surprise, the afternoon was far advanced when she woke. Scrambling from the bed, she rang for her maid.

'I was just about to come and see if you wanted my help in dressing for dinner, miss,' Jenny informed her, arriving with commendable promptitude.

It was already past five and Lady Kildare, who would not have dreamt of sitting down to her dinner before seven when in town, kept earlier hours in the country.

'Thank you, Jenny. I fell asleep and now I see I must make haste if I am to make myself presentable.'

'The rest has done you good, if I may say so, miss. You got a nice colour in your cheeks.'

Ianthe laughed and shook her head. 'The sun was strong today and I was out riding for a long time, that's all.'

'You ought to wear a veil, miss!' Jenny exclaimed in a scandalised tone. 'You don't want to go spoiling your complexion with nasty freckles!'

'I shall use some Denmark Lotion tonight, I promise,' Ianthe soothed.

Jenny sniffed. What her young mistress lacked was a proper sense of vanity. Still, she was so pretty her harum-scarum ways didn't make no difference or at least they hadn't until a couple of years ago. It was such a shame her father had gone and died just when she'd at last been recovering from Lieutenant Fenton's loss. Since the old master's death Miss Ianthe had been so wrapped up in gloom she'd lost all her sparkle, but Jenny had detected a revival in her spirits since they'd got here.

This impression was strengthened when Ianthe sighed in response to her question about what gown she wished to wear this evening.

'Oh I don't know, Jenny! They are all equally hideous!'

Jenny surveyed the gowns hanging up in the wardrobe and silently agreed. Whatever had Mrs Turner been thinking of? Everything she had chosen had been selected with her own plump blonde charms and fussy tastes in mind. Not a thought had been given to what might suit her much taller stepdaughter.

'What about this one?' she asked, lifting out a white silk dress. 'Now you have some colour in your cheeks, it will look quite nice.'

Her bracing tone did not deceive Ianthe. The dress was decorated with numerous flounces and ruffles that merely emphasised her thinness. 'It will do, I suppose.'

'I could take off some of these frills,' Jenny offered.

'There isn't time,' Ianthe said regretfully.

'Then I hope as how you will allow me to do some alterations soon, miss.' Enthusiasm shone in Jenny's brown eyes. 'If I stripped the decoration off some of 'em, you could see the pretty fabrics underneath and they'd look better.'

Ianthe considered her maid's suggestion. 'Do you think it will make much difference?'

Jenny ignored the doubt in her tone. 'You'll not recognise yourself,' she said cheerfully.

'Very well. Please do whatever you can, Jenny.' Ianthe decided that there was no harm in giving her permission for the experiment. After all, the gowns could hardly look any worse!

When she was dressed Jenny arranged her hair in the same flattering style she had devised the previous evening and Ianthe hurried downstairs.

Lord Kildare broke off his conversation with his mother as she entered the drawing-room.

'I hope I am not late,' she murmured.

'Not at all, my dear,' Lady Kildare greeted her kindly. 'Do come and sit down.'

Luke remained silent. Ianthe had told herself that she was not going to pay him any special attention, but it was difficult not to notice how well his formal evening clothes became his tall, athletic figure. His superbly cut black coat stretched without a crease across his broad shoulders and a single ruby gleamed in the intricate folds of his snowy neckcloth.

Their gaze met and locked for an instant before Ianthe looked away, her pulse thumping.

'Did you enjoy your afternoon, Ianthe?' Lady Kildare asked. 'I hope you found something interesting to do.'

'I did, thank you,' Ianthe replied evasively. She had no desire to admit to taking a nap. Luke Kildare thought she was boring enough as it was!

Luckily, Tench, the butler, arrived at that moment to announce dinner.

'Allow me to escort you, ladies.' Lord Kildare offered one arm to his mother and the other to Ianthe.

Ianthe accepted with a cool smile. She was determined to put Augustus's ultimatum out of her mind and behave in a rational manner this evening.

They took their places in the elegant dining-room where the first course was already laid out in readiness upon the long mahogany table. 'I ordered Cook to prepare a few light dishes for this evening,' Lady Kildare announced. She smiled at her son. 'I know *you* won't mind the heat, Luke, but I thought our appetites might be dulled by it.'

Luke took a spoonful of turtle soup and hid a grin. His mother's notions of a simple family meal were enough to feed a regiment!

Glancing across at Ianthe, who was seated opposite, he detected the same gleam of amusement in her blue eyes.

'Next week we must contrive something better,' Lady Kildare continued blithely as the soup was removed. 'I did not want to inflict guests upon you when you were first arrived, Luke, but we must entertain while Harry and Sophy are here.' She gave a little shudder. 'I should not wish the Bishop to think us lacking in the proper attentions to his daughter!'

'I'm sure everything will pass off well, Mama,' Luke said soothingly. 'Even a high stickler like Dorchester couldn't find fault with the way you conduct this household.'

During her stay at the Park, Ianthe had become aware of her cousin's deep dislike of scandal and gossip. Although not at all stiff or formal in her own manner, she was very insistent on observing the proprieties. 'You are a wonderful hostess, ma'am,' she chimed in impulsively, anxious to reassure Amelia. 'And I will think Miss Conway very top-lofty if she does not enjoy her stay at the Park as much as I have.'

Luke shot her a considering look. For the last two evenings she had sat in almost total silence, only returning monosyllabic answers to remarks made directly to her. He'd begun to think that her shyness bordered on stupidity. It wasn't until their ride this morning that he realised his mistake.

Perhaps their conversation about India had broken the ice? Luke hoped so. It would be a pity if she retreated back into her shell now that she had demonstrated that she wasn't the little ninny he had imagined her to be.

Lady Kildare waved away the dish of sole with wine and mushrooms offered to her by one of the footmen. 'Thank you, my dear,' she said to Ianthe. 'It is kind of you to say so, but all the same I must own to some slight anxiety. Harry is extremely fond of Miss Conway and I should hate anything to go wrong while they are here in case it prejudices the Bishop against the match.'

The table was cleared and the second course brought in. Lord Kildare carved the pair of roasted ducks. Ianthe admired his deft skill, but settled instead for a small helping of macaroni.

'I thought we might visit the Fairhursts tomorrow,' Lady Kildare informed Ianthe. 'We ought to repay their call and they have a very pretty garden, which you might like to see.'

The Fairhursts lived a few miles away on the other side of Alton. They had visited the Park last week and Ianthe had found Lady Fairhurst a pleasant woman, although she had not taken to her daughter.

'Of course, ma'am. When do you wish to set out?'

'Around eleven, I believe.' Lady Kildare spooned green peas on to her plate. 'Should you care to accompany us, Luke?'

'No thank you, Mama.' Luke managed to restrain a shudder. 'I intend to visit Tom Fisher over at Lime Tree Farm tomorrow.'

Times were hard now that the wartime boom had faded and Amelia knew that he wanted to speak to all their tenants as soon as he could to see what he could do to help. However, she suspected that in this case duty marched alongside desire. 'You were never one for paying morning calls upon our neighbours,' she murmured softly.

Luke did not bother to deny it.

When the ladies retired to the drawing-room, Lady Kildare confessed to a slight headache. 'Should you mind if I excused myself, my dear?' she asked Ianthe.

Panic fluttered along Ianthe's nerves. Although she felt she had acquitted herself tolerably well over dinner, she wasn't sure if she was up to maintaining a conversation with Lord Kildare on her own.

Politeness demanded, however, that she smile and bid her hostess goodnight with every appearance of calm!

Amelia went out into the hallway and Ianthe heard her

exchange a few words with her son, who had not lingered over his solitary port. A moment later he strolled into the room.

'Well, Miss Garland, it seems we must manage without my mother's company this evening,' he said, taking a seat close to hers.

Quelling the urge to flee, Ianthe forced herself to acknowledge his remark with a little nod of her head.

Should she ring for Jenny to fetch her embroidery or the book which she was currently reading? She could avoid conversation by immersing herself in either pursuit, but that would be the coward's way out.

Luke noticed how her hands twisted restlessly in her lap. 'You are uncomfortable, Miss Garland. Would you prefer it if I left you in solitary peace?'

His perceptive comment brought her head up with a jerk. 'Actually, I was just wondering what on earth we could talk about,' she said frankly, surprising herself.

'Am I such an ogre?' Amusement danced in Luke's grey eyes.

Ianthe began to protest and then realised he was baiting her and stumbled to a confused halt.

'Forgive me,' Luke said gruffly. Damn it, but he hadn't meant to make that apprehensive look return to her face! 'It was unfair of me to tease you, but I am interested to know why you find it awkward to talk to me now when you appeared to have no difficulty this morning.'

'It was different somehow when we were riding,' Ianthe murmured.

It was true. She had forgotten Augustus's infamous proposal in the excitement of their gallop and then Luke's tales of India had caught her imagination, preventing her guilty conscience from making its tongue-binding presence felt. She gave a little shrug. 'I suppose I am more at ease on horseback than in the drawing-room, sir.' Which was also true, if not exactly the whole truth!

Luke concluded that she had been too busy controlling

Moonlight to think about her shyness. 'Then we need another diversion tonight.'

'You mean something like a game of cards?' Ianthe asked cautiously.

'Yes, but I am not a great hand at cards.' Luke shrugged in apology.

'Neither am I!' Ianthe's wide mouth curved into a smile.

Luke caught his breath. She wasn't beautiful, but when she smiled like that a man might be forgiven for thinking her so!

There was a tiny silence. Ianthe wondered what he was thinking. He was looking at her most strangely!

Still, the usual mockery was absent from his deep voice and she sensed that he genuinely did not wish her to feel uncomfortable in his presence.

Ianthe's pulse quickened. Was it possible that he was beginning to like her?

'Your mama mentioned that there were plenty of song sheets in the music-room,' she said impetuously. 'We could attempt a little music, if you are agreeable?'

He considered her suggestion. 'I should enjoy that, but are you sure you want my company, Miss Garland?' he asked bluntly. 'It occurs to me that you were offended by certain of my remarks this morning. I am afraid that I cannot apologise for I believe what I said to be true.' He lifted his dark brows at her in challenge, his expression hard. 'Nor can I promise to guard my tongue in future, so I shall quite understand if you would prefer to forgo my company and retire.'

'Are you always so forthright, sir?' Ianthe gasped.

'I have little time for polite prevarication, Miss Garland.'

Ianthe gathered her courage. 'Then to match your frankness, sir, I have no wish to retire,' she said firmly. 'What's more, I did think your remarks arrogant, but, on balance, I enjoyed our conversation.' She shrugged lightly. 'If you are willing to take the risk that we might quarrel, then so am I.'

Luke's face relaxed. He had expected her to cry off and yet he found he was pleased she had not. A twinkle appeared in his eyes. 'I'm sure you play beautifully, but I must warn you that my friends have compared my singing to a crow's caw-ing,' he informed her solemnly.

An answering smile lit her irregular features. 'Then perhaps you had better confine yourself to turning my music for me.'

He grinned. 'I should be delighted to do so, Miss Garland.'

They both rose to their feet. He held out his arm to her and she placed her hand upon it. Beneath her fingers she could feel firm hard muscle, just as she had this morning after their wild gallop to Buttermilk Hill.

Her mouth turned suddenly dry and she could feel her heart thumping. Not since Philip had she been so aware of a man's presence! Several would-be beaux had attempted to court her since then, but none of them had had this effect on her!

Luke stood very still. She was so close he could see the pulse fluttering at the base of her white throat. It was hard to tear his gaze away. Her skin was like satin, encouraging a desire to touch...

Mastering a ridiculous urge to pull her into his embrace, he said casually, 'By the by, I should welcome your company if you should happen to fancy another early morning ride before church tomorrow.'

His expression was as cool as his voice, but instinct told Ianthe that her answer mattered to him.

'If I should wake up in time, I might join you, my lord,' she replied in the same casual manner, forcing herself to ig-nore the quiver of excitement that shook her knees.

Luke nodded and began to chat lightly about his favourite music as he escorted her from the room.

But they both knew that she would be at the stables in the morning and that he would be there waiting.

Ianthe's early rides with Lord Kildare quickly became the high spot of her day. The weather continued kind and over the following week they were able to explore the estate for an hour or two each morning before returning to enjoy a hearty breakfast.

'Riding out with my son seems to agree with you, my dear,'

Amelia announced with a smile as Ianthe came hurrying into
the painting-studio on the Thursday morning.

She waved away Ianthe's apologies for being late. 'I like
to see you with that healthy colour in your cheeks.' She
paused and added delicately, 'I hope you will not be offended
by my saying so, but you are looking much more robust than
when you first arrived here three weeks ago. You were so
pale and thin I was quite worried about you, but now I believe
you have put on a little weight and you look all the better for
it.'

Ianthe thanked her for the compliment and went to change
into her draperies before assuming her pose as Diana.

In the silence which followed as Lady Kildare concentrated
on the portrait she had time to think about what her cousin
had said. In spite of the anxiety which gnawed at her whenever she thought of Augustus's ultimatum, she was enjoying
her stay at the Park far more than she had dreamt possible.

Not that she could truly forget the threats Augustus had
made, but, away from the sad memories and frustrations of
Northwood, her spirits and health had improved.

Perhaps my recovery has given me new strength, she
mused. Her situation was still desperate, but the black despair
which had engulfed her had vanished and she no longer
flinched whenever Luke came near.

In fact, Ianthe silently admitted to herself, she looked forward to their rides. Now that he knew she was able to keep
up, Lord Kildare gave her no quarter and they had enjoyed
some exhilarating gallops. The sheer pleasure of the exercise
had overcome her anxiety and guilt, allowing her to drop her
guard and behave in a much more natural manner with him.

A tiny smile touched her mouth. The first time she had
abandoned her insipidity and made a witty retort to one of his
provocative sallies, Luke had stared at her in shocked surprise.
Then he had given a shout of laughter.

'This will never do, Miss Garland. Don't you know that a
young lady must never betray her intelligence?' he'd said, a

teasing gleam in his grey eyes. 'Not unless she wishes to be thought a blue-stocking.'

'I have no objection to that description, sir,' Ianthe had replied demurely.

'What? Will you confess to knowing Latin and reading Shakespeare?'

Laughing, Ianthe admitted it. 'Now you will say that my papa educated me too well.'

'Sadly true, I fear.' Luke sighed with theatrical solemnity. 'However, I do not despair. Your handicap could be banished by a few weeks in London.' He slanted a grin at her. 'A touch of Town polish and you'll look suitably bewildered if anyone asks you for any opinion more taxing than what colour bonnet will best go with your newest gown.'

Ianthe gave a choke of laughter. 'You are too absurd, my lord.'

'Shouldn't you like another try at conquering society?' Luke asked, dropping his bantering tone. 'I rather fancy you'd be a success; the combination of brains and beauty is quite rare, you know.'

Startled by the unexpected compliment implied in this speech, Ianthe coloured. Staring at a point between Moonlight's ears, she sought to repay him with an honest reply. 'I dare say I might like London better now,' she murmured at last. 'Not that I have any desire to conquer society, as you put it, but I think I should enjoy the entertainments on offer now that I am older.'

She lifted her gaze to his. 'And you, my lord? May I ask you a question about your future?'

He inclined his dark head.

'Will you stay quietly at home or will you be off on your travels once more?'

'Ah, now you have caught me out, Miss Garland. I must own that I find cosy domesticity boring after a while, but so far I am content to remain at the Park.' He had shrugged his broad shoulders. 'Truth to tell, I am not yet sure of my plans.'

There had been nothing in his deep voice to betray unease,

but Ianthe had sensed he did not wish to discuss the matter further and she had not pursued it.

Thinking over that conversation, Ianthe now wished she tried harder to find out his intentions. Perhaps if she told Augustus that Lord Kildare meant to leave for some far-flung foreign shore he would acknowledge the impossibility of such a marriage and release her?

But what would happen to her grandmother and Northwood then? Augustus had declared that his creditors would not wait!

Her grip on the hunting bow she held in one hand faltered and it trembled violently in her grasp.

'Let us stop for a few moments,' Lady Kildare announced, laying down her palette. 'I expect you could do with a rest and we both deserve a glass of orgeat after our efforts.'

Amelia's suggestion reached Ianthe through the sudden haze of panic which had turned her dizzy. She stepped down from the dais and accepted the glass of cordial her cousin poured for her.

'Thank you,' she murmured, taking a sip. The almond-and-orange-flavoured liquid was cooling to her dry mouth, but Ianthe scarcely tasted it in her anxiety.

'Come and sit down, my dear, and have some of Cook's excellent cherry cake.' Lady Kildare uncovered the cake which waited on a small side-board and cut two generous slices. She loaded two plates and carried them over to the sofa which stood against the back wall.

The servants brought new supplies of refreshments to the pavilion every morning, but it was unusual for Amelia to interrupt her work in this leisurely manner. Sitting down next to her cousin, Ianthe wondered if her face had betrayed her distressed thoughts just now.

If so, her relative was much too tactful to add to her anxiety by demanding to know why she had suddenly turned pale and begun to shiver. Instead, she spoke calmly of her youngest son's arrival, which was expected on the morrow, and insisted that Ianthe eat her cake.

This sensible treatment soothed Ianthe's nerves; by the time she had finished the cake she had recovered her composure.

'Shall I resume my pose, ma'am?' she asked, brushing crumbs from her fingers.

'If you are sure that you wish to continue.' Lady Kildare regarded her carefully.

Ianthe rose to her feet. 'I am quite certain, ma'am.'

She crossed the room, her step firm, and took her place by the broken column. Amelia hesitated for an instant and then, apparently reassured, returned to her easel and took up her brush.

'Are you ready, my dear?'

Ianthe nodded. 'As I will ever be.'

It was time she faced reality. She had been living in a dream, allowing herself to forget the invidious nature of her position at Kildare Park. But she could not halt time's relentless march. She had barely a week left until the deadline Augustus had set was reached.

She could not go on ignoring her plight. The stark choice facing her would not disappear if she pretended it did not exist! She had to make her mind up. Was she to risk destroying her grandmother's happiness and possibly losing Northwood itself or should she throw away her own honour and compromise a man she had grown to like?

And how, if she could bring herself to do it, was she to accomplish this fearful task?

'I thought we might attempt a longer ride today, Miss Garland,' Lord Kildare suggested the next morning as they trotted out of the stable-yard. 'The Wey valley is lovely at this time of year and you might like to view the ruins of the old Cistercian abbey there.'

'I should indeed, sir.'

They took the track which would lead them to the eastern boundary of his lordship's park. Beyond this lay the estate's gently rolling farmland. Fields of wheat swayed in the warm breeze and in the distance sheep and cattle grazed upon lush green grass.

Ianthe gave a sigh of pleasure. 'It's very beautiful,' she murmured.

Luke nodded. 'On a morning like this I wonder why I stayed away so long.'

He had dreaded returning to the Park, fearing that his last unhappy memories of the place would sour all pleasure in his homecoming. But after the first day back he'd found that the good memories outweighed the bad.

He glanced across at his companion. In part, at least, Miss Ianthe Garland had something to do with his change of heart. She was such an odd mixture of shyness and sharp intelligence that she intrigued him and his interest in trying to fathom her out had kept him from brooding. One minute she was blushing and unable to meet his eyes, the next she was arguing with him over some point of history or politics most females wouldn't pretend to understand!

An oddly attractive wench!

'Your brother and Miss Conway will have a pleasant day for their journey if this weather holds,' Ianthe remarked, interrupting his thoughts. 'What time are they expected to arrive?'

'Around two, I believe. My mother tells me that they meant to break their journey at Romsey last night. Apparently, the White Horse Inn is owned by a relative of the Bishop's late wife and he gave his approval for them to rack up there.'

'It must be a very respectable hostelry,' Ianthe replied gravely.

Luke noted the laughter dancing in her lovely eyes. His heart gave an unexpected lurch, but he ignored the tug of attraction and said lightly, 'But of course, my dear Miss Garland. The Bishop is such a great stickler for convention that he makes my mother seem positively decadent!'

Ianthe grinned. She was tempted to ask him if he knew why his mother was so careful of propriety when her nature was somewhat unconventional, but at that moment a rabbit shot out almost beneath Moonlight's hooves and set the startled mare to rearing.

The next few minutes were lively and Ianthe was quite breathless by the time she regained control of the horse.

'Well done, Miss Garland! I thought she must unseat you!'

The admiration in Lord Kildare's tone set Ianthe's pulse racing afresh, but she managed to sound nonchalant as she said, 'So did I!'

They continued their ride and Moonlight behaved impeccably. Satisfied that the mare had recovered from her fright, Ianthe allowed herself to relax and enjoy the lovely scenery.

'You were right. This is a very pretty valley,' she said to her companion, pointing with her whip to the profusion of wild flowers growing beside the river Wey.

Luke smiled. 'This was one of my favourite places when I was growing up. Each season has its own special charm, but I like it best in the autumn when the beech trees turn to fire in the sunlight.' He stared at her thoughtfully. 'Just like your hair.'

His unexpected comment startled Ianthe far more than Moonlight's rearing had done.

'Why, sir, I suspect you are bamming me,' she succeeded in retorting airily.

'I was making a statement of fact, Miss Garland. When we first met I thought your hair was brown, but it is not.' Luke kept his voice cool, unwilling to admit even to himself how a desire to touch those glowing tresses had begun to torment him. Glints of copper, gold and amber shone in the lustrous mahogany depths, brought to life by sun or candlelight.

'Red hair runs in my family,' Ianthe murmured.

She told herself it was silly to feel unsettled by his remarks. There was nothing in his manner to suggest he had meant to pay her a compliment.

The ruins of Waverley Abbey, the earliest Cistercian house in England, came into sight.

'Did you know that Walter Scott is said to have taken the

name of his first novel from here?' Luke said, bringing his chestnut to a halt.

Ianthe confessed that she had not heard this piece of information before, although she admired Scott's work. 'Actually, I think I prefer *The Antiquary* to *Waverley*, but these ruins are magnificent,' she said as they dismounted.

Luke tied the reins of their horses to the branch of a nearby tree and they walked into the abandoned abbey's grounds. Time and the hand of man had attacked the stonework, but enough remained intact for Ianthe to admire its delicate carving and the perfect proportions of the nave.

'Take care where you step,' Luke warned as she wandered towards the cloisters. 'Some of these stones are loose.'

Ianthe assured him she would be careful.

They continued to explore for a while and then Luke announced it was time they were getting back. 'Mama will scold if I keep you out too long,' he said with a rueful grin.

His words reminded Ianthe that they had set out not long after seven and could not expect to return before ten, which was pushing the bounds of propriety to the limit.

'I thought we might stop briefly for something to drink on the way home,' Luke continued. 'There is an inn I know on the Farnham road where the landlord serves an excellent ale.'

She wrinkled her nose at this offer and he laughed. 'I'm sure he can find something more to your taste if ale is too strong for you.'

'It is at this hour,' Ianthe said firmly. 'However, I would certainly appreciate a cool drink.'

The sun was now high in the sky and the gentle warmth of the early morning had developed into a thirst-inducing heat.

'I'm glad you suggested coming here,' Ianthe said, taking one last look at the soaring arches graceful in the sunshine.

'The pleasure has been all mine.' There was an odd note in Lord Kildare's voice and he turned abruptly away.

What had she said wrong now? Ianthe gave a mental shrug. She was feeling too relaxed and at peace with the world to take offence at his sudden moodiness!

His long stride was carrying him rapidly away in the direction of the horses and Ianthe, knowing that they could not afford to waste time, abandoned the temptation to deliberately dawdle just to annoy him.

'Wait, my lord!' She darted forward to catch him up, but, in her haste, forgot that the chancel steps, on which she stood, were broken. Her foot slipped on the crumbling stone and she lost her balance.

Unable to stop herself, she pitched forwards with a cry of alarm and Luke whirled round just in time to see her go tumbling down the steps.

Chapter Four

'Miss Garland, can you hear me?' Lord Kildare knelt beside Ianthe and took one of her hands in his. 'Can you tell me where you are hurt?'

Ianthe's eyelids fluttered open, but the breath had been knocked out of her lungs by her fall and she felt dazed.

She was dimly aware of Lord Kildare muttering a smothered curse and then very gently he lifted her head, cradling it in the crook of his arm. He smoothed a stray lock of hair from her brow and then unfastened the top two buttons of her riding-jacket.

His fingers were warm and strong against her skin as he sought the pulse which beat at the base of her throat. Ianthe closed her eyes, an inexplicable languor stealing over her. She knew she ought to sit up, propriety demanded it, but it felt much too pleasant where she was.

'Ianthe, for God's sake, can you tell me where it's hurting?' Lord Kildare's voice shook with urgency, penetrating her shocked haze. 'I can't risk moving you until I know what is wrong.'

Ianthe forced her eyes open and found herself staring directly up into his worried face. Still too breathless to speak, she reached out instinctively and brushed the tips of her fingers against his damaged cheek.

Immediately he became very still, his expression switching to a blank mask.

Acutely embarrassed, Ianthe allowed her hand to fall back to her side. How strange! It must be the after-effect of shock that had made her want to touch him.

Lord Kildare carefully disengaged his arm from beneath her head. 'It would be helpful if you could indicate where you are hurt,' he said coolly.

'I am only winded.'

'That is good news.'

Ianthe struggled to sit up.

'Allow me to assist you.' The formality of his lordship's tone was matched by the impersonal courtesy with which he efficiently eased her into a sitting position.

'Thank you.' Ianthe avoided his gaze. Common sense was returning with every breath.

'Are you certain you have no other injuries?'

Ianthe wriggled her ankles and ran her hands swiftly over her limbs. 'I shall be bruised, but there's nothing serious.' She attempted a smile. 'It will teach me to mind my footing more carefully in future!'

Lord Kildare stood up and held out his hand to her. 'Permit me, Miss Garland.'

Ianthe was about to protest that she did not need his help to stand when she saw that he looked strained, his mouth a hard tight line. Did he blame himself for her inattention?

She put her hand in his. 'My fall was an accident,' she said softly. 'My own fault entirely.'

He nodded, his expression indecipherable, and pulled her to her feet.

Ianthe removed her hand from his, but when she took a step forward she found that she had overestimated her recovery.

At once his arm went around her waist, supporting her.

'Thank you.' Ianthe's breathlessness returned. 'I shall be all right in a moment.'

'Are you sure?' He looked down at her with what she could have sworn was genuine concern in his eyes.

'Perfectly. It was merely a touch of dizziness.'

Ianthe hoped God would forgive her the lie. Her heart was hammering in a way she had never known before and her senses swam every time she looked at him.

'Take my arm.' Lord Kildare led her towards the horses, his pace slow. 'If you are fit to ride, I suggest we return home immediately. You ought to rest.'

Ianthe assured him that she was quite capable of managing Moonlight. 'If you will assist me into the saddle, sir, you shall see that I am fully recovered.'

On the way back to Kildare Park Ianthe noticed his gaze resting on her in an assessing fashion several times, but he did not plague her with enquiries on how she felt.

At the stables he helped her dismount and insisted on escorting her up to the house. When they arrived he rang for her maid, staying with her until Jenny came into the hallway. His manner continued to display the same formality as he bade her goodbye and Ianthe concluded dismally that he was relieved to be rid of her.

A hot bath and the application of a soothing cream made with marigold and lavender helped restore her physically, but her mood was pensive as she watched Jenny tidy up the bedroom.

'You put your feet up on that day-bed and have a nice read, Miss Ianthe, and I'll bring you up a tray of refreshments in a little while,' Jenny promised.

'Lady Kildare will expect me to join her for our usual nuncheon.' Ianthe sat down on the elegant couch, which stood at the foot of her bed, but she did not open the leatherbound volume which Jenny had handed to her.

'His lordship said he would tell his mama that you'd had a fall,' Jenny countered firmly. 'I reckon he won't be pleased if you ignore his advice to rest.'

Ianthe shrugged irritably. 'I doubt it. My welfare is no concern of his, after all.'

Jenny had her own thoughts on this subject. Proper shook-up the man had looked! 'It's not my place to say, miss,' she murmured, wisely deciding not to argue. 'But I do know that you need to recuperate if you want to be fresh for meeting Lady Kildare's visitors this afternoon.'

Ianthe sighed. She had no desire to lie here, her thoughts in a turmoil of wondering and worrying. On the other hand, she did want to make a good impression on Mr Kildare and Miss Conway. 'Oh, very well, but I shall get up the minute I've finished eating.'

Jenny grinned. 'I'll have that blue sprigged muslin finished and ready for you to wear by then.'

Ianthe produced a smile of thanks, but when her maid had gone her face creased into lines of unhappy anxiety.

Augustus had claimed that it would be simple for her to compromise Lord Kildare. With painful clarity Ianthe now saw that her stepfather had been correct. It was very easy to picture herself in some lonely spot with his lordship…just like today!

The sensation of his arms around her returned with vivid force. His head had been close to hers, his beautiful mouth only inches from her own lips. It would have been so easy to pull him towards her…

Ianthe gasped aloud, horrified by the trend of her thoughts. What was the matter with her! Anyone would think she *wanted* Luke Kildare to kiss her!

No, of course she didn't yearn for his embrace. What an absurd idea! Passion was something only men, or women of dubious virtue, experienced.

For an instant Ianthe wondered if what she had been taught could be wrong.

She bit her lip. She was being foolish beyond permission! Surely, after what had happened on the night before Philip had left, she need not look for further proof of the truth in-herent in society's dictate that a lady tolerated her husband's desires solely out of duty?

Obviously, it was the shock of her unexpected fall that had

made her feel so safe in Lord Kildare's arms. He had represented the security she had unwittingly craved at that particular moment. Her ridiculous longing for him to kiss her was merely the result of her dazed confusion.

Logic satisfied, Ianthe opened her copy of *Persuasion* with a determined flourish, but somehow Miss Austen's story failed to exert its usual charm and she was still staring at the same page when Jenny came back an hour later.

Within five minutes of meeting Harry Kildare Ianthe was convinced that he was a most amiable gentleman. He had the placid manner of someone entirely happy with his situation in life and his smile was serene as he declared that indeed he did remember Miss Garland.

'Delighted to renew our acquaintance,' he said, bowing over her hand with a stately grace.

Ianthe heard the slight but distinct sound of his corset creaking and hastily smothered a grin.

Lord Kildare was not so circumspect and began to roast his brother over the weight he'd put on since their last meeting.

It was undeniably true that Mr Kildare was stout. Not as tall as his brother, his figure displayed a plumpness that even his excellently cut clothes couldn't disguise.

Ianthe's initial impression was strengthened by his good-natured acceptance of Lord Kildare's teasing.

'I dare say I wouldn't keep m'tailor so busy if I'd managed to retain my figure the way you have,' he'd retorted with a lazy grin.

Miss Conway, who appeared to be scandalised by Luke's quips, said gravely that in her opinion Mr Kildare was quite as active as any clergyman was required to be.

A hint of boredom appeared in his lordship's eyes.

Seeing it, Ianthe experienced a flicker of relief, which she instantly regretted. It was very mean-spirited of her to be pleased that Lord Kildare did not seem to admire Miss Conway!

She'd been sure he would. Sophy possessed a pretty face

and a neat figure displayed to advantage in a smart travelling costume of golden-brown cambric. Its colour exactly matched her beautifully cut and dressed hair.

Perhaps Luke disliked her formal manner? Ianthe wondered if she was shy, but as the day wore on she realised that Sophy was, in fact, very aware of her own worth. She expected to be heeded when she spoke in her quiet way.

By the time dinner was over Ianthe had also realised that Sophy had little sense of humour. Whenever Luke made one of his wicked cracks, her mouth had tightened in disapproval.

The two brothers lingered over their port. After a while a slight frown appeared between Sophy's brown eyes and she asked Lady Kildare to excuse her.

'You must be tired after all your travelling, my dear,' her hostess nodded, tactfully choosing to ignore Sophy's displeasure at Harry's dilatoriness. 'Sleep well.'

'So what you do think of my youngest son?' Amelia asked Ianthe after the housekeeper had been summoned to escort Sophy to her bedchamber.

Ianthe's warm response brought a proud smile to Lady Kildare's lips.

'Although they share the same colouring, he isn't very much like his brother,' Ianthe continued without thinking and then blushed in embarrassment as she realised how her remark must sound.

'Poor Harry!' To her relief, Amelia merely chuckled. 'He used to be such a slim youth!'

Thoughtfully, she adjusted the set of the handsome Norwich shawl she wore draped over her arms. 'My sons are dissimilar in character too. In temperament, as well as appearance, Harry favours his father.'

Ianthe remembered the late Lord Kildare. A big jolly man with a loud laugh, he rarely lost his temper and always had a kind smile for children.

'Luke favours my side of the family, a sadly belligerent set of persons, I'm afraid.' There was a rueful twinkle in her ladyship's dark eyes.

Ianthe's expression revealed her scepticism and Lady Kildare laughed and told her that she had learnt to govern her temper long ago. 'I do wish Luke could do so. He has a tendency in a rage to hit out without thinking. I know that afterwards he often regrets the harsh things he has said.' She shrugged. 'George was the same. It was Harry who ended up acting as peacemaker whenever they quarrelled. He is quite the diplomat, you know, which no doubt makes him extremely useful to the Bishop.'

'Mr Kildare appears very fond of Miss Conway.'

Hearing the note of surprise in her young relative's voice Amelia smiled. 'I must confess that I did not much care for Sophy the first time I met her. I thought her rather dull and strait-laced, but she has many worthy qualities. Beneath her formal exterior she has a kind heart and, although she sometimes seems to suspect Harry of too much frivolity, I believe her to be as devoted to Harry as he is to her.'

A little sigh escaped her. 'I worry far more about Luke's future than I do about Harry's. Sophy will suit Harry very well, but I live in dread of Luke obstinately refusing to take a wife.'

Ianthe's mouth fell open. 'But, Cousin Amelia, you said the other day that he would have trouble finding the right woman!'

Amelia nodded. 'I know, but I am convinced he will never experience true peace and contentment if he remains a bachelor.' A sad smile touched her mouth for an instant. 'He was a very warm-hearted boy. So merry and full of fun. It is quite lowering to see him grown hard and cynical!'

Ianthe nervously smoothed her cream satin skirts. Like the blue-sprigged muslin which she had worn earlier, it was one of the dresses Jenny had altered to appear more flattering. Ianthe had been secretly gratified to notice Lord Kildare's look of surprise when she had walked into the drawing-room tonight, but her mind was not on that small triumph now. 'Do you think that it would be beneficial for Lord Kildare to marry even if he was not in love?'

'I wish I had the power to arrange a suitable match for him!' Lady Kildare exclaimed in response to this timid question. 'Luke loves children and he ought to have a dozen of his own. Providing I could be sure that he liked and respected the lady, I think a marriage of convenience would be infinitely preferable to him dwindling into an embittered and lonely old age!'

Hope flickered inside Ianthe's heart. Perhaps she would not be acting *too* wickedly if she compromised Lord Kildare? He needed a wife in order to have a legitimate heir. She would bear his children willingly and make no demands upon him. In fact, she would be so dutiful a wife he would never have cause to regret the unsavoury start to their union.

With luck, he might even come to forgive her!

Over the next three days Ianthe's mood swung between feverish optimism and dark despair. It was almost impossible to put thoughts of the future out of her mind and only when she was riding with Lord Kildare was she truly able to relax.

Miss Conway was not a keen horsewoman and, although Harry joined them one morning, Ianthe rarely had any occasion to exchange more than a few conventional words with Sophy. However, as she began to grow used to Sophy's reserved manner, she realised Lady Kildare was right. Sophy took a serious view of life, but she wasn't a prig.

She enjoyed sharing their entertainments and, during an archery contest organised by Lady Kildare on the Tuesday afternoon after her arrival, her sense of fun and willingness to help made Ianthe feel quite ashamed of her first uncharitable thoughts.

'Thank you,' she said as Sophy patiently showed her how to cock her arrow for what seemed the hundredth time. 'You are very kind.'

'Not at all, Miss Garland. Unlike you, I have practised for many years.' She smiled, revealing her slightly uneven teeth. 'My papa is very fond of archery, but even he will admit that it is difficult for a novice.'

Ianthe grinned. 'I'm glad this is just a family occasion,' she confessed. 'I should be embarrassed to be so clumsy in front of guests!'

Knowing that Sophy was keen on archery, Lady Kildare had decided to have butts set up on the south lawn. Her own family had often used to take part in this form of entertainment. Only Ianthe had never tried to draw a bow, but she had declared herself happy to take part if the others would excuse her lack of skill.

After a spell of rain, the weather had favoured their plans with an afternoon of windless sunshine. Ianthe had felt rather self-conscious at first, but everyone was so encouraging that she soon began to enjoy herself.

'Well done, Miss Garland.' Lord Kildare gave her a broad grin as her arrow encountered the target for the first time.

Ianthe laughed and walked over to join him where he awaited his turn to fire his next arrow. Together they watched Sophy, who stepped forward and hit the bull's-eye with deceptive ease.

Everyone clapped and Sophy thanked them, her blushing smile making her look much more vivacious than usual.

'Perhaps I have done Miss Conway an injustice,' Lord Kildare said softly, watching the happy expression on his brother's face as he gave Sophy's hand an affectionate little squeeze.

Wondering if he had also revised his opinion, Ianthe looked at him expectantly.

'You know very well I thought her a dead bore.'

'You are very frank, sir!'

'A failing of mine which you have remarked upon before, Miss Garland, but I see no need to need to be coy with you.' He shrugged. 'We are friends, are we not?'

Ianthe stared at him, a sudden lump in her throat preventing speech.

'Luke! Come on, man! It's your turn.'

Summoned by Harry's shout, he made her a brief bow and walked off.

Ianthe could feel her knees trembling. Swallowing hard, she watched him step up to the mark. In response to the needs of the activity and the hot afternoon, the gentlemen had removed their tight coats. She could see the powerful muscles in Luke's shoulders rippling beneath his white shirt as he drew back the bow and let fly his arrow.

It found the bull's-eye, landing next to Sophy's and causing a shout of congratulation and amusement to go up.

Waylaid by his mother, who offered him a glass of lemonade, Luke glanced back at Ianthe.

Why the devil was she looking so pale?

'I think I must encourage Ianthe to sit down in the shade for a while,' Lady Kildare said, following the direction of his glance. 'Hot sunshine can be so tiresome for redheads.'

'She is wearing a broad-brimmed hat, Mama,' Luke replied, unwilling to accept this obvious explanation.

Her look of discomfort had been brief, but he was sure he had not imagined it. Perhaps he had been wrong to assume she wished to be friends with him? And yet they had been getting on so well it had become something of a habit to speak his mind freely to her.

Now that his assumption had been challenged, Luke discovered that he had enjoyed Ianthe's company more than he realised. These last two weeks he had slipped into the way of treating her almost as if she had been one of his male cronies, discussing all manner of things with her.

He had never known it was possible to have such a friendly relationship with a woman. As a youth he had tended to put women on a pedestal, treating them with a somewhat nervous awe. Later, after Georgiana had opened his eyes, all he had wanted from them was to satisfy his desire. Laughter and companionship had not figured largely in either kind of situation.

Ignoring his acerbic comment, Lady Kildare hurried over to Ianthe and pressed her to sit down for a moment and sip some cool lemonade. Still feeling shaken by his lordship's totally unexpected announcement, which had aroused desperate feelings of guilt, Ianthe obeyed.

By the time Harry and Lady Kildare had shown off their prowess, she was feeling more composed and declared that she was able to take her turn when her hostess asked if she wished to carry on.

To her dismay, however, she found that her concentration was not up to the task and her arrow once more veered off at a wild tangent and completely missed the butt.

'Oh, bad luck, Miss Garland!' called out Harry. 'Do take another turn, I think the wind caught that one.'

Since there was scarcely a breath of air, Ianthe began to protest, but her voice faltered. It was incredibly foolish of her, but she felt almost close to tears!

'Harry's right.' Lord Kildare strode towards her and Ianthe fell silent.

He stood behind her. She could feel his warm breath on the back of her neck as he gently put his arms around her and said, 'Allow me to show you the proper stance once again, Miss Garland.'

With his help she drew back the bow.

'You're trembling,' he whispered in her ear.

'I know,' Ianthe replied helplessly.

'Relax,' he murmured, his deep voice soft and gentle. 'Look straight ahead and let me guide you.'

Ianthe could feel waves of sensation rippling along her nerves from each point where their skin made contact. She could barely hear his calm instructions for the loud thudding of her heart.

'Now.'

Acting more from instinct than any conscious decision, Ianthe obeyed the change of pressure in his touch and released her arrow. It winged forward and landed creditably near the centre of the target.

Cries of congratulation rent the still air, but it was only when Lord Kildare released her and stood back that Ianthe roused from her dreamlike state.

'Thank you, my lord,' she murmured.

'We make a good team,' he replied lightly.

There was an echo of his earlier question in his eyes as they rested upon her flushed face and Ianthe felt a tiny shiver feather down her spine.

Until this moment she hadn't known how much she desired his friendship!

'Miss Garland? Is something wrong?' A new urgency filled Luke's voice. She looked as if she was about to faint!

Ianthe's tongue seemed glued to the roof of her mouth. Frantically, she shook her head.

He wanted to be her friend and she was proposing to betray him!

'Ianthe—'

Unable to meet his eyes, Ianthe murmured, 'I...I am a little too warm, that's all.'

Disappointed by her reply, which was undoubtedly a prevarication, Luke's expression assumed its usual harsh lines.

'Then I suggest you go indoors,' he said shortly.

'I think I will.' Ianthe struggled to stay calm.

Lady Kildare, who was approaching, caught the end of their exchange. 'There! What did I tell you, Luke? Is this bright sun giving you a headache, my dear?' Motherly concern infused Amelia's tone and, without waiting for an answer, she continued, 'Do go and sit in the drawing-room. It is cool in there and I shall tell Tench to bring in another tray of lemonade.'

'I do not wish to spoil—'

'It is quite all right, my love. We shall all join you in a moment, won't we, Luke?'

'Of course. Otherwise none of us will be fresh for our dinner party this evening,' Luke drawled.

His sarcastic tone made Lady Kildare shoot him a startled look. Now what had occurred to put him out of curl?

Her dark eyes turned to gaze uncertainly at Ianthe.

'I must inform Mr Kildare and Miss Conway of my withdrawal,' Ianthe said hastily and walked away with a rapidity that put Luke strongly in mind of a panic-stricken retreat.

'What do you think of this, Miss Ianthe?' Jenny entered Ianthe's bedchamber and held up a dress, a broad smile on her round face. 'Just the thing for tonight's party, I reckon!'

'Where ever did you get it, Jenny?' Ianthe reached out to take the celestial blue evening gown from her maid. She held it up against herself. 'It's beautiful!'

The softly shimmering silk flattered her pale complexion and brought out the vivid colour of her eyes.

'It's one of the gowns Mrs Turner chose for you,' Jenny chuckled. 'Mind you, I'm not surprised you didn't recognise it. I took off all that lace and those pink roses which decorated the bodice. Then I reshaped the neckline a bit and shortened the sleeves.'

'It looks completely different,' Ianthe agreed happily. 'Thank you, Jenny. Such a miracle must have taken a lot of hard work and I appreciate it.'

Jenny flushed bright pink with pride. 'It was no trouble, miss,' she said gruffly, delighted by her mistress's reaction.

Ianthe, who had already bathed, sat down at her dressing-table to allow Jenny to arrange her hair.

'Shall I try that new style I was telling you about?' Jenny asked, picking up Ianthe's hairbrush. 'Lady Kildare's maid says it's all the crack.'

'Why not?' Ianthe was feeling reckless.

Lady Kildare had invited several neighbours, including the Fairhursts, to this evening's dinner party. Ostensibly, it was to celebrate her son's return, but, knowing Luke had no love for what he described as *starchy affairs*, Amelia had persuaded him into agreeing by pointing out that she was obliged to offer Sophy at least one formal entertainment.

It would be a glittering social occasion and Ianthe had no intention of letting her inner despair dictate her behaviour. She would act the part of a young lady without a care in the world if it killed her! Pride demanded no less, to say nothing of her obligations as a guest.

The only way to achieve her object, she decided, was to avoid Lord Kildare as far as possible. Not that he seemed inclined for her conversation. They hadn't exchanged a single word since their awkward parting by the archery butts. What's more, his grey eyes were stormy whenever they rested upon her and his beautifully shaped mouth kept thinning to a hard line.

'The pearls or your grandmama's earrings and necklace, miss?' Jenny asked, interrupting Ianthe's thoughts.

'The gold set, I think.'

Jenny blinked in surprise. She had suggested the jewellery loaned by the Dowager in honour of this visit because it would enhance the beauty of Ianthe's new gown, but she hadn't expected her mistress to agree. She had always said that the lavish leaf-and-flower design was too elaborate for her taste.

'My grandfather bought this in Paris.' Ianthe's fingertips brushed against one of the intricately wrought gold flowers which made up the necklace. 'A jeweller there named Jean Pouget created a fashion for the style.'

She put on the matching drop earrings and surveyed the effect. They looked very well against the curls which Jenny had cunningly arranged to tumble down her neck from a high, upswept knot. A few more curls strayed artistically across her forehead.

A touch of pearl powder and pink lip salve was followed by a discreet dab of her favourite rose-scented perfume. Then it was the work of a moment for Jenny to slip the refurbished gown over her head.

The maid fastened the row of tiny silk-covered buttons with practised ease and gave the skirt a final twitch into place. She stood back to admire her handiwork. 'You look lovely, Miss Ianthe. I haven't seen you look so well since—' She bit off what she had been about to say, an expression of dismay spreading over her face.

'It's all right, Jenny.' Ianthe achieved a reassuring smile. 'My papa wouldn't have wanted me to grieve for ever.'

'Aye,' Jenny nodded. 'It's time you started to enjoy yourself again.'

This sage advice stayed with Ianthe as she descended the handsome main staircase and made her way to the drawing-room. Mr Kildare broke off his conversation with his brother at her entrance and exclaimed, 'Miss Garland! No need to ask if you are fully recovered. Indeed, you look more beautiful each evening!'

Ianthe smiled at his jovial flattery, but her attention was caught by the unguarded look on Lord Kildare's face. For a single heartbeat she could have sworn admiration gleamed in his eyes, but as he became aware of her scrutiny his features returned to their customary expression of cynicism.

Before she'd had time to decide whether she was imagining things, Lady Kildare and Miss Conway walked into the room. They were followed swiftly by the first guests, the local vicar and his wife. Ianthe had already met this pleasant couple and was delighted to talk to them.

Over the next quarter of an hour Tench was kept busy announcing new arrivals and the drawing-room was soon full of chatter and laughter as her ladyship's guests greeted one another. The Fairhursts were the last to arrive. Sir James was a tall shy man whose lack of social conversation was so well known that it occasioned no comment. However, as he was reckoned to be a generous landlord and an excellent sportsman, this deficiency was forgiven him.

His wife was also popular. Quite the opposite in appearance to her husband, she was tiny and plump with an infectious smile and sunny nature. Ianthe could quite see why she was one of Cousin Amelia's closest friends.

Miss Lucy Fairhurst more than made up for her father's silence. Favouring her mother in height and colouring, she reminded Ianthe of a beautifully dressed doll with her rosy cheeks and mass of golden curls threaded with pink ribbons piled high atop her head.

Her china-blue eyes darted around the crowded room and fixed with unerring precision upon the most eligible bachelor present. 'Lord Kildare,' she said huskily as her hostess introduced him to her, 'I am thrilled to meet you at last. I have heard so much about you.'

'None of it good, I'll be bound,' Luke replied lightly.

Lucy giggled and fluttered her long eyelashes. 'On the contrary, sir. Everyone tells me you are a hero and I am longing to hear all about your battles.'

Ianthe, who was standing quite close to them, talking to another guest, thought she saw a flicker of irritation cross his lordship's features, but then he smiled down at Lucy so charmingly she decided she must have been mistaken.

'It will be delightful to have such an appreciative audience,' he drawled. 'My family have heard my stories so often that they are bored by them.'

'I could *never* be bored listening to you, Lord Kildare.' Lucy's somewhat pouting lips parted on a sigh of admiration. 'You kept us all safe from that dreadful monster.'

'You mean Napoleon, I presume, Miss Fairhurst?' Luke's voice was carefully bland.

Lucy gave a pretty little shudder. 'Indeed I do, my lord. You must be *so* brave! It quite terrifies me to even say his name.'

Lord Kildare's gaze encountered Ianthe's and, seeing an answering gleam of amusement at such absurdity in her eyes, he grinned. Then his smile abruptly faded and he returned his attention to his young companion, who continued to gasp and flutter her fan as he obliged her with several stories about his time in the Peninsula.

Excusing herself to the elderly widower with whom she had been chatting, Ianthe moved away. For some reason she didn't care to examine, it annoyed her to watch that silly girl flirt so shamelessly with Lord Kildare.

'I perceive you also do not care to see one of our sex making such an exhibition of herself,' Sophy said gravely as she joined Ianthe.

Furious that she had accidentally betrayed her feelings, Ianthe forced a carefree smile. 'Perhaps it is uncharitable of us to be so critical, Miss Conway. She is only seventeen and barely out.'

Sophy nodded. 'I dare say she will learn discretion in time.' She winced as a particularly loud burst of laughter from Lucy reached them. 'It would be a pity if she gained the reputation of being fast. Her mama has just been telling me that she is most accomplished.'

Ianthe had also heard Lady Fairhurst go on at length about Lucy's talents. According to her doting mother, the young lady sang like an angel, played several instruments better than her teachers and could paint almost as well as Lady Kildare.

'Indeed, it would be unfortunate if anything were to spoil her chances. She is a very pretty girl,' Ianthe replied, striving for the charity she had advocated.

The announcement of dinner brought their conversation to an end. Ianthe found herself seated between the Reverend Mr Burton and young Mr Harper, the hopeful scion of a local squire, who had been invited along with his parents. Unfortunately, the table arrangements afforded her an unimpeded view of Miss Fairhurst's continuing flirtation with Lord Kildare and she was hard put to it to maintain her laudable intentions.

Spooning white soup without tasting any of it, she listened with grim determination to Mr Harper telling her all about a recent cricket match in which he had played. The soup was removed and she turned politely to her other table companion who engaged her in a discussion of her favourite hymns.

Good manners compelled her to appear interested in what the vicar was saying, but she could feel a strange turmoil of emotion erupting inside her whenever she glanced up and saw how Lord Kildare's dark head was bent close to Lucy's. It was an effort to swallow even a few morsels of asparagus dressed the Italian way, a dish she had selected from the vast choice the first course offered her.

Suddenly, it dawned on her what was wrong with her. She was almost literally choking on jealousy!

Ianthe put down her fork abruptly, her hand unsteady. She was jealous of a girl barely out of the schoolroom! And all because Lucy was the recipient of Luke Kildare's smiles!

She drew in a deep breath, afraid to look up from her plate in case anyone saw her agitation. She tried to tell herself that she was mistaken, but the emotion seething within her was too strong to be denied.

She wanted Luke to show interest in *her*, not some silly little ninny with more beauty than sense! She wanted him to tell *her* that she looked beautiful!

Confused and ashamed by the intensity of her feelings, Ianthe redoubled her efforts to be an entertaining dinner companion and throughout the rest of the long meal she carefully avoided looking in his lordship's direction.

And thereby failed to see how often Lord Kildare looked across the table towards her!

Ianthe slept badly that night and awoke later than usual. Glancing at the pretty little French porcelain mantel clock which adorned her bedroom, she realised that there was no point in hurrying. Lord Kildare, if he had decided to ride, must have already set off.

No doubt he would think the weather had dissuaded her from joining him. She could hear rain lashing at the windows and, when Jenny arrived with her morning chocolate and drew back the curtains, Ianthe saw that the sky was filled with thunderclouds.

'I think I should like to breakfast in my room, Jenny, if you would be so good as to bring me up a tray. It is such a dismal morning that it hardly seems worth the effort of getting out of bed.'

Jenny gave her a sharp look at this uncharacteristic pronouncement. 'Are you tired, miss?' she asked.

Last night there had been a full moon, which had permitted their visitors, some of whom lived at a distance, to stay on

and it had been well after midnight before the last one left.
'A little,' Ianthe admitted with a rueful grimace.

'You'll probably feel better when you've eaten,' Jenny announced and bustled off, leaving Ianthe to her reflections.

Today was her last day of grace. Augustus was to arrive
tomorrow to escort her home and he would be furious that
she hadn't found an opportunity to snare Lord Kildare.

Ianthe chewed her lower lip. All her heart-searching had
brought her no nearer to an answer. Every time she reached
a decision, her conscience demanded she think again and she
had become mired in vacillation.

Not that it was going to be easy to entrap his lordship in
any event! Ianthe had turned over several schemes in her mind
and come to the conclusion that an *accident* whilst out riding
was the only solution if she decided to go ahead. She had
studied a map of the estate in the library, looking for somewhere where she could stage a convincing tumble, which was
also remote enough for help not to arrive too quickly. There
was a risk, of course, of hurting herself more seriously than
she intended, but there was little she could do about that.

At least such a scheme had the merit of looking accidental.
Moonlight was prone to skittishness and there was a faint
possibility that Lord Kildare would not realise she had deliberately staged the event. It was a rather forlorn hope, but
Ianthe couldn't think of any other way to achieve being alone
with him for long enough for their absence to be remarked
upon and her reputation put in jeopardy.

Unfortunately, due to the arrival of his brother, Lord
Kildare had spent less time in her company than previously.
Last night when she couldn't sleep, Ianthe had realised that
she was going to have to persuade Lord Kildare into undertaking another long expedition. However, unless the weather
improved, it would be impossible to make such a suggestion
today.

Would Augustus be willing to give her more time? He had
been very insistent that his creditors would foreclose at the
end of the month unless he could buy them off. Ianthe had

no idea how long it would take for him to squeeze money from the prospective bridegroom, but Augustus had assured her that once the announcement of her engagement appeared in the *Gazette* Northwood would be safe.

Ianthe shuddered as she remembered her final conversation with Mr Turner before departing for Hampshire. 'We'll hold the wedding as soon as possible, of course,' he'd told her. 'Don't want any hint of gossip, but you needn't fret. They'll give me an extension until Kildare hands over the readies.'

He had then fixed her with a warning look. 'Just make sure you've done your part by the time I get there or, by God, you'll regret it!'

Ianthe's stomach churned with anxiety and when Jenny returned with her breakfast tray she found her appetite was unequal to more than a single bite of a buttered roll.

'You'll need long sleeves today, I think, miss,' Jenny announced, taking a blossom-pink morning gown out of the wardrobe. 'It's colder than yesterday, but I was talking to one of the gardeners and he reckons that this rain won't last.'

Ianthe put aside her tray. 'I hope not. I should hate it if the weather prevented me from enjoying one last ride around the estate.'

'You'll be sad to say goodbye to the place,' Jenny nodded. 'And his lordship too, o'course,' she added innocently.

A sudden rush of colour stained Ianthe's cheeks. 'I'm going to be late for my final sitting with her ladyship if I don't hurry,' she said abruptly. 'Please go and fetch my hot water, Jenny.'

Hiding a grin, her maid hurried off.

She was so quick that Ianthe was in time to greet Lady Kildare in the hallway as that lady prepared to leave for her studio.

'There you are, my dear! If you are ready to leave, shall we make a dash for it?'

Ianthe nodded and Lady Kildare smiled. 'I told them to light the brazier in there an hour ago so you needn't fear that you will freeze in your short tunic.'

Since the studio was quite close to the house they did not get very wet and were soon ready to begin on what Lady Kildare described as her final tinkering.

'Do you think you will be able to complete everything to your satisfaction today, Cousin Amelia?' Ianthe asked, taking up her customary pose.

Lady Kildare nodded vigorously.

'Everyone has been asking to see it,' Ianthe said.

'My family know I make it a rule not to let anyone view my daubings until they are finished.' There was a teasing note in Amelia's voice. She knew very well that Ianthe, who had also been forbidden to look at the portrait, was curious.

'Perhaps I shall invite everyone for a viewing tomorrow,' she mused. 'We could make a little celebration of it.'

Ianthe coughed. 'How…how delightful.'

'Do you think we should wait until your stepfather arrives?' Amelia was too absorbed in placing one last highlight to the marble column to notice her young relative's nervous hesitancy.

'Mr Turner is not much interested in art.'

This time Amelia could not fail to hear the edge in Ianthe's voice. The note of dislike was unmistakable!

She put down her brush. 'My dear, I haven't liked to ask before in case you thought me interfering, but I cannot help but wonder if everything is well with you at Northwood?'

Ianthe hesitated. She was sorely tempted to disclose the truth. It would be such a relief to pour her troubles into a friendly ear, but she swiftly rejected the idea. Cousin Amelia was a kind woman and would want to help, but there was little she could do.

'Perfectly, thank you, ma'am. It is no secret that I do not get on particularly well with Mr Turner,' she said, her tone deliberately casual. 'We have no interests in common, you see, but we contrive to rub along.'

'I am glad to hear it. However, if you should ever feel the need to talk over a problem, I should be very happy to give you my advice.' Lady Kildare smiled at her warmly. 'I have always been very fond of you, my dear, and I was so pleased when Maria wrote to me. It has been delightful having you here. I only wish you could stay longer.'

'Thank you, but I believe my grandmother will be missing me,' Ianthe murmured, a lump in her throat.

'It would be selfish of me to keep you,' Amelia agreed, picking up her brush. 'However, the house is going to feel very quiet. Mr Turner gave me to understand that he would only stay one night before escorting you home to St Albans and Harry and Miss Conway must also leave on Friday.'

'You will still have Lord Kildare to keep you company.'

Amelia's brush paused in mid-air. 'Didn't Luke tell you? He is off to visit his godfather later today.'

'Today?' Ianthe echoed, her heart suddenly racing.

'I must admit his sudden decision surprised me too. I knew, of course, that he would want to visit Mr Stratton. In spite of the gap in their respective ages, they are good friends, but I fail to understand the need for such haste. However, Luke insists he wishes to be off this afternoon.'

'What a pity,' Ianthe said unsteadily. 'He will miss the viewing of my portrait.'

Chapter Five

Ianthe and her hostess had just returned to the house when a knock at the door sent Tench hurrying across the hallway.

'I wonder who could have been brave enough to venture out in such inclement weather?' Lady Kildare asked, pausing as she reached the threshold of the Yellow Salon.

Ianthe, who had excellent hearing, suddenly paled as she recognised the voice of the visitor Tench had admitted.

An instant later a footman, dispatched by Tench to appraise his mistress of the identity of the caller, confirmed her fears.

'Show him up at once, John, and then tell Cook we will be six for nuncheon.' A slightly irritated note had entered Lady Kildare's voice, but her smile was serene as she turned to greet the gentleman who was now making his way towards them.

'Mr Turner. How do you do. We had not expected you until tomorrow.'

'Lady Kildare.' Augustus Turner bowed with showy grace over Amelia's hand. 'I hope you will not mind. I had business in this direction and it seemed more sensible to bring my plans forward by a day than retrace my steps.'

'Of course.' Lady Kildare nodded graciously. 'You are welcome at any time, sir.'

Augustus, who was under no illusions that she approved of him, hid a satisfied smile. He had known that good breeding and his connection with her family, slight though it was, would override her ladyship's personal feelings.

Although Amelia—on her way to London some ten months ago—had paid a courtesy call to congratulate Maria on her new marriage, it was plain that she did so only out of duty. Augustus, who was shrewd concerning such matters, sensed that she had not taken to him. Her warmth had been reserved for her late cousin's daughter and she had spent most of her brief visit talking to the chit.

'Ianthe.' He turned to greet his stepdaughter with a jovial smile. 'You are looking very well, my dear. I knew this holiday would bring the roses back to your pretty cheeks.'

Ianthe would have dearly loved to slap his smirking face! 'How do you do, sir,' she said instead through gritted teeth.

Lady Kildare led the way into the salon and behind her back Augustus hissed, 'Well?'

Ianthe ignored his whisper and marched off after Amelia.

He gave her a furious look, but had no choice but to follow her.

'I trust you left Mrs Turner well?' Lady Kildare asked politely when they had all settled themselves comfortably.

Augustus confirmed it, and, since he could not speak privately to Ianthe, decided to launch an attempt to charm his hostess.

He was in the middle of paying her a flattering compliment when Lord Kildare walked in.

'Mama, would you mind if I took that book of Indian sketches I gave you to show Nicodemus—' He broke off, becoming aware of the stranger sitting with his mother. 'I beg your pardon. I did not realise you had a visitor.'

'Luke, this is Mr Turner. Ianthe's stepfather.'

Augustus had risen to his feet and now he came forward, holding out his hand. 'Good day, my lord. I am very pleased to meet you at last.'

Luke eyed the older man. Around ten years or so older than himself, he would guess. His extravagantly cut coat and the very high points to his shirt smacked of dandyism, as did the

carefully curled blond hair and the multitude of fobs and seals
which hung about his bright waistcoat, but he was a tall, well-
set up sort of fellow with the kind of smooth good looks
which often appealed to the ladies.

'How do you do.' Luke shook the outstretched hand.

Turner gave him an ingratiating smile. 'I was just saying
to your mother how delighted she must be to have you home.'
He paused and then continued with an even wider smile, 'May
I ask if you mean to make your stay in England a long one
this time, my lord?'

Luke raised his black brows. 'I haven't yet decided, sir,'
he answered frostily.

Ianthe winced. She knew why Augustus was keen to know
Lord Kildare's future plans, but even someone so thick-
skinned couldn't fail to realise that his lordship found the
question impertinent.

'Of course. Of course,' Augustus simpered. 'You young
fellows are always on the go. I dare say you have a hundred
invitations to hand and can scarcely tell me what you mean
to do tomorrow.'

Luke, who was beginning to think that Miss Garland deserved sympathy, returned nothing more than a faint look of
contempt to this fawning sally.

'As a matter of fact, Mr Turner, my son means to venture
north to visit his godfather directly after we have finished our
nuncheon,' Lady Kildare said, feeling obliged to come to her
unwanted guest's rescue.

Augustus's sleek head spun round back to her son. 'You
are leaving the Park *today*?'

Luke wondered why the fellow looked so shocked. 'I am,
sir,' he said shortly, his clipped tone indicating that he found
the topic under discussion a dead bore.

Augustus's Adam's apple bobbed up and down and then
he managed a feeble smile. 'Mr Stratton lives in
Cockermouth, does he not? A most delightful part of the
world, although a little remote, I fancy.'

Obeying the pleading look directed at him by his mother,

Luke resisted the blighting snub which rose to his lips and merely asked if they would excuse him. 'I have several things to attend to before I may sit down to eat with you.'

Lady Kildare nodded and told him that she had no objection to him taking his sketch-book to show Nicodemus. 'Do not let him keep it, mind,' she added playfully. 'I do not intend to surrender such a thoughtful gift!'

A smile lightened his lordship's severe expression. His talent was far inferior to his mother's, but he had known she would appreciate his efforts to sketch the Indian countryside for her.

'I wouldn't dare, Mama,' he replied, giving her such a warm grin that it lit a flame of envy in Ianthe's heart.

Luke heard her tiny sigh and his grey gaze flicked in her direction.

For a heartbeat their eyes locked and then Ianthe quickly lowered her gaze to her lap.

Luke saw how her fingers were twisting a fold of her gown with restless repetition. So, she was not as calm as she would have him think!

They had barely spoken a word since yesterday when she had refused to acknowledge his offer of friendship. For reasons he didn't care to dwell on, her apparent rejection had made him furious.

Luke knew he was in grave danger of letting the intriguing Miss Garland slip beneath his hard-won armour. His ridiculous flirting last night with the empty-headed Fairhurst girl was proof of his idiocy. If he had not wanted to annoy Ianthe, he would never have singled out that chit!

He had undoubtedly succeeded, but it was, he had discovered, a somewhat Pyrrhic victory. Which was why it behoved him to quit the Park at once before he fell victim to further folly.

He had intended to visit Nicodemus next week in any event. They had much to discuss but, looking at Ianthe's pale unhappy face, he felt an involuntary pang of regret for having brought his journey forward.

He moved towards the door. 'I shall join you in half an hour.'

'Oh, before you go, Luke, I have just remembered something!' Lady Kildare detained him. 'Pray tell your valet he will find all your clean shirts still in the laundry. Mrs Blenkinsop decided to take advantage of the good weather yesterday to order a huge wash of all the linen the maids could lay their hands on, but I believe they should be ironed and ready for you by now.'

'Thank you, Mama. I will certainly tell Whinlock. Otherwise, he will be hunting through all my cupboards.'

Ianthe's eyes followed him as he quit the room. Her heart felt as heavy as a lump of lead and she knew her dejection had nothing to do with the inevitable interview which her stepfather would shortly demand.

She could sense anger bubbling behind Augustus's polite smiles but, in spite of the danger to her reputation, Ianthe found nothing seemed to matter now that Luke was leaving and it was unlikely she would see him again!

Lady Kildare's cook had risen to the occasion and provided a splendid nuncheon. In addition to the usual cold meats and fruit she normally provided for the ladies, there was a chicken pie, a savoury omelette, a dish of buttered prawns and several assorted kinds of vegetables.

Cheese, cakes and gooseberry tart were also on offer, but it could not be said that any of the party other than Mr Kildare seemed to have much of an appetite. It was Sophy's usual custom to eat sparingly and the others seemed intent on following her example.

'Will you stay and drink tea with us, my love?' Lady Kildare enquired of her elder son when he laid down his knife and fork.

'I think not, Mama.' Lord Kildare rose to his feet. 'Whinlock should have finished packing by now and we can travel several stages before we have to rack up for the night if we leave immediately.'

'Very well.' Lady Kildare managed to produce a creditably cheerful smile. 'At least the weather has cleared up for your journey.'

Luke nodded. The sun had come out as they sat down to the table and it was already warm again. 'I'll come and say my goodbyes to you in—' he began, but broke off abruptly as one of the footmen entered the dining-room and spoke softly to him.

A frown descended upon his brow. 'Pray excuse me,' he said curtly.

He strode out of the room and Ianthe met Lady Kildare's puzzled look with an equally baffled glance.

'I dare say there is some slight problem with one of his horses,' Lady Kildare murmured.

'Don't fret, Mama. I'm sure Luke will tell us everything shortly,' Harry said. 'In the meantime, shall we retire to the drawing-room?'

They all rose to follow this sensible suggestion and Ianthe happened to glance across at Augustus. There was a smug expression in his pale eyes.

In the flurry of leaving the room, Ianthe managed to waylay her stepfather. 'What have you done?' she whispered, laying an urgent hand on his arm.

'Found a way to salvage the mull you've plainly made of things, you stupid jade!' Augustus shook her off. 'Hold your whist, we cannot talk here. I'll come to your room later.'

Ianthe glared at his retreating back. However, since there was nothing else she could do, she followed him into the drawing-room, where her curiosity was soon satisfied in part at least.

'I won't be leaving today after all, Mama,' Lord Kildare announced, entering the room. 'Someone has decided to play a foolish trick and thrown every one of my shirts out into the mud. I have ordered them to be washed again, but they won't be ready in time for me to set off at a reasonable hour.'

Lady Kildare exclaimed in horror at this piece of news.

'I'm sure I don't know why any of the servants would do such a thing!'

'Nor I.' Lord Kildare shrugged. 'However, it doesn't signify. I can just as easily set off in the morning,' he added, his frown easing.

He was unwilling to admit it aloud, but he couldn't help but feel secretly pleased. He had discovered that he didn't want to part on bad terms with Ianthe and the delay would give him time to talk to her before he left.

Ianthe did not dare look in Augustus's direction. However, she could feel the wave of triumph emanating from his well-dressed figure. He had slipped out earlier, declaring that he must tidy himself before they sat down for their nuncheon and, no doubt, had ordered his man, a sly individual whom Ianthe had never liked, to perform the deed.

The ploy had worked. Lord Kildare would spend another night under his ancestral roof and Ianthe was willing to bet all Lombard Street to a China orange that her odious stepfather was about to demand that she make good her failure to carry out his hateful scheme before it was too late!

'Out!'

Jenny looked at her mistress with wide-eyed indignation.

'Please do as Mr Turner says, Jenny.'

'As *you* wish, ma'am.' Ianthe's maid whisked from the bedchamber with a look of venomous dislike at Augustus.

He ignored her and strolled across the room to seat himself in the raspberry silk elbow-chair placed by the window.

Ianthe, who was standing by her dressing-table, closed her lips against a gasp of outrage at his lack of manners. He could not have made his contempt for her plainer, lounging there at his ease, surveying her through his glass!

'Very pretty!' Augustus approved. 'I wasn't jesting, you know, when I said your looks had improved.'

Ianthe had just completed her toilette for the evening. She was wearing another of the gowns that Jenny had altered, an open robe of soft peach mull worn over a white satin slip.

The narrow bodice had a revealing neckline now that Jenny had stripped off its excessive trimming and Ianthe had been a little worried her bare shoulders looked too thin.

Evidently, her concern had been misplaced if Augustus's leers were anything to go by!

'Spare me your compliments!' she snapped, picking up a gold-spangled net scarf from the bed and draping it to veil her bosom. 'I know why you are here.'

'Do you? I am glad to hear it, miss, for I don't see any other sign that you've been using the brains God gave you.'

Ianthe met his ugly frown with an outward show of composure, but her knees were shaking behind their fragile protection. 'I have had a good deal of time in which to think,' she said calmly. 'And I have decided that I cannot agree to your infamous proposal.'

'What?' Augustus straightened up abruptly. 'What are you talking about? We agreed—'

'Your memory is at fault, sir. I said I would consider it.' Ianthe collected her fan from the dressing-table with apparent tranquillity. 'A man of your stamp may have difficulty in understanding the concepts behind my reasoning, but, believe me, I cannot deceive Lord Kildare.'

'Don't preach to me of honour, you mealy-mouthed little fool!' Augustus's face turned bright red with rage.

Ianthe shrugged gracefully. 'You may insult me if you wish, but you won't change my mind.'

She'd spent the afternoon in confronting the spectre which had haunted her waking hours ever since arriving at the Park. In spite of the problems which lay ahead, she could not bring herself to betray the friendship Luke Kildare had offered her, and in realising that simple fact, she had known there was no point in torturing herself any more.

It was a question of honour, she told herself stoutly. Her personal feelings for the man had nothing to do with it. She would have felt the same even if she hadn't liked him.

'Oh, I think I can!' Mr Turner gave her a spiteful smile.

'Only consider, my dear, how all your acquaintance will view your little peccadillo!'

Ianthe paled. 'Knowing you, sir, I don't doubt that you will vent your spite by revealing a secret that does not belong to you. However, have *you* considered the result of such a course? You will not come well out of it, I assure you.'

Augustus bit his lip and for an instant Ianthe hoped she had reached him, but then he shook his blond head. 'Nay! I'm done for anyway if I can't raise that money, so what does it matter?'

'And what about Maria? You have always disliked me, but have you considered how the scandal would affect her?'

A short bark of laughter escaped Augustus. 'Don't waste your sympathy on Maria. She'll be too busy complaining about *her* troubles to spare a thought for either of us!'

This savage comment was so apt it silenced Ianthe.

'Look, I know we don't see eye to eye,' Augustus said, employing a more conciliatory tone than she had ever heard him use to her before. 'But would marriage to Kildare be so bad? He's a handsome fellow in spite of that damned scar and he's rich. You'll enjoy all the comforts that rank and money can buy.'

Ianthe shook her carefully dressed head. 'The price is too high. I prefer to keep my self-respect.'

On her return home she would do what she should have done in the first place. She would approach Mr Robertson and beg him to help her. He had told her that her guardians had to act in her best interests. The Dower House might have to be sacrificed, but surely the lawyer would be able to think of some way of stopping Augustus from signing away the rest of the estate?

'In less than three months' time I shall come into my inheritance,' she said firmly. 'I know you will try to make it difficult for me, but I believe that I can manage to survive until I can throw you out of my house.'

'So, the little kitten has claws,' Augustus sneered. 'But it all rather depends on whether Northwood is still yours come September, doesn't it, my dear?'

Ianthe paled. 'It's a risk I'll have to take.'

Augustus's plump mouth tightened. 'You are a fool.'

Ianthe shrugged. 'Better a fool than a liar and a cheat.'

She saw her remark hit home and experienced a brief flicker of satisfaction as his florid face paled.

'You will regret this, mark my words.' He rose abruptly to his feet.

'Perhaps.' Ianthe was honest enough to admit her doubts. If she could not stop Augustus, she might lose everything: her good name, her home and all hope of finding respectable employment to support herself if insufficient money remained after the legal wrangling was over! She could only pray that she would have enough courage to face whatever problems the future would throw at her. 'However, since I cannot do what you ask, I have no other choice.'

'How brave of you!' Augustus made her a mocking bow.

He strolled to the door. With his hand on the knob, he paused. 'Oh, by the way, I almost forgot. Your grandmother charged me with conveying her good wishes to you.'

Ianthe stiffened warily at his suddenly dulcet tone.

'Such a pity she was feeling too unwell to write to you. I'm sure you would have liked to have a letter from her.'

Ianthe stared at him, her pulse tumultuous. 'My grandmother is ill?'

'Oh, don't worry, my dear. It's nothing too serious. I just happened to mention the idea of moving house to her and she took it badly.'

'You devil!'

Augustus chuckled.

'I don't believe you. You are just trying to scare me!'

'Am I?' Augustus gave her an evil grin. 'Just think about it, my dear. Are your high-minded principles worth risking your grandmother's health?'

'I can take care of her!'

'Perhaps.' Augustus threw the word back at her in a mocking echo.

Ianthe took a deep breath. She was shaking so much that the gold bracelet she wore was jangling. 'Even if I cannot obtain a position as a governess,' she gasped. 'I can sell my jewellery and take both of us away from your malicious influence.'

'I suppose you could run away.' Augustus nodded thoughtfully, stroking his chin. 'And your jewellery would probably yield enough for you to live on until September, but, even supposing that I did not use the law to pursue you as a runaway minor, can you really imagine dragging that fragile old woman into such a sordid adventure?' He wagged a finger at her playfully. 'You are living in a dream world, Ianthe. Wake up and face reality. You can neither save her beloved home nor save her from the shock of learning that her adored granddaughter is nothing more than a trollop!'

He laughed at her appalled expression. 'Oh, yes, Ianthe, I will most certainly drag you down with me if you do not follow my sensible suggestion and compromise Kildare before he leaves tomorrow!' He opened the door and turned back to smile at her with poisonous sweetness. 'So think on what I have said while you still have time!'

Dinner that evening seemed to stretch out endlessly to Ianthe. She could barely eat a thing—her previous good appetite had fled in the face of Augustus's renewed threats—and she took no part at all in the conversation.

When the ladies retired to the drawing-room Sophy came to sit down next to her. 'Is there something bothering you, Ianthe?' she asked kindly. 'You are so quiet tonight I scarcely recognise you.'

Ianthe forced herself to look cheerful. 'It is nothing. I...I am not looking forward to leaving tomorrow.'

'Neither am I.' Sophy's solemn face broke into an unexpected smile. 'I have greatly enjoyed my visit here and, although I am longing to see my papa, I shall be sad to say goodbye to you all.' She gave a little shrug. 'I shall even miss Lord Kildare.'

She met Ianthe's startled look with a faint shrug. 'I know we have little in common, but I believe him to be a good man. What's more, he has Harry's interests at heart.'

A shy blush coloured her cheeks. 'He has promised to try and use his influence to persuade Papa to let our marriage go ahead.'

'Oh, Sophy, I am pleased for you!' Ianthe's anxious gloom lifted for an instant.

'I am persuaded Lord Kildare's bark is worse than his bite.' Sophy slanted a sideways glance at her companion. 'Do you not feel the same?'

Ianthe swallowed hard. 'No doubt you are referring to the coolness between myself and his lordship,' she muttered gruffly.

Sophy nodded. 'I do not mean to pry, but I had noticed that the two of you no longer seem to be on speaking terms.' She hesitated. 'Forgive me if I offend, but should you not try to mend the quarrel before you leave? It is always upsetting, I think, to part on bad terms with any acquaintance and you and Lord Kildare seem to have become rather more than that.'

'What do you mean?' said Ianthe, her voice rising so shrilly that Lady Kildare looked up in surprise from the sketch-book she was examining.

'Noth…nothing.' Sophy fidgeted with the fringe of her silk shawl in uncharacteristic confusion. 'I merely meant that the pair of you seemed to get on so well together and that it was a pity to let a quarrel spoil your friendship.'

Ianthe bit her lip. 'I'm sorry, Sophy. I know you mean well, but I really cannot discuss it.'

Sophy nodded. 'Then I shall say no more.'

In spite of her smile, Ianthe saw the look of rejection in her brown eyes.

An unladylike desire to curse assailed her. She had just undone all her previous efforts to thaw Sophy's reserve!

She thinks I don't trust her. If only she knew! Ianthe real-

ised that she was clasping her hands together so tightly that
her knuckles shone white.

But when she unclasped them, she could see how they
trembled as if she had a fever.

'Will you excuse me, Cousin Amelia?' She stood up
abruptly. 'If you do not object, I will not stay for the tea-tray,
but will retire early. I believe Mr Turner wishes to make an
early start and there are a few things I need to do.'

'Of course, my dear.' Lady Kildare looked regretful. 'However, I hope Mr Turner does not mean to leave before we
have shown off our portrait?'

Ianthe had forgotten all about the planned viewing. 'I'm
sure he will wish to see it, ma'am,' she murmured.

Naturally, Augustus had made no mention of leaving early.
She had invented the excuse because she did not think she
could bear to linger here at the Park in the circumstances. But
her cowardice was no excuse for disappointing Amelia.

'Good. Then I shall expect to receive everyone at the studio
after breakfast.'

With an obedient nod, Ianthe quickly said her goodnights
and made her escape.

Once in her room she rang for Jenny and asked her to take
down her hair. Mustering her patience, she allowed the maid
to complete the thorough brushing she considered necessary
to maintain its recently restored shine, but she felt too on edge
to let Jenny disrobe her.

'I shall undress myself. I'm not ready for sleep just yet.'

'Very well, miss.' Aware of her mistress's tension, Jenny
did not argue and merely asked if she should begin Ianthe's
packing.

'There will be plenty of time tomorrow. I do not expect we
shall leave before mid-morning at the earliest.'

Jenny nodded and Ianthe dismissed her with a word of
thanks.

The minute she had gone Ianthe jumped up from her dressing-stool and began to pace the room with restless haste. She
was too agitated to keep still, let alone think of going to bed!

An hour later she sank exhausted into the elbow-chair by the window. It was no good. She could not outpace her thoughts!

Ianthe thrust her fist against her mouth to prevent a wail of despair from escaping her clenched lips. Dear God, what was she to do? She had been so convinced this afternoon that she could remain strong and face her uncertain future without flinching, but since Augustus had renewed his poisonous threats she had felt sick with fear.

Had she the right to sacrifice her grandmother's happiness on the altar of honour? *She* might think her principles were worth the loss of her reputation, but how would Grandmama feel when the scandal broke?

Ianthe's instincts told her that the Dowager would not condemn her for following her heart. Her grandmother would understand that she had loved Philip, just as she would understand and agree with Ianthe that it was monstrous to entrap Lord Kildare. But Ianthe knew *she* would never forgive herself if her grandmother's health suffered as a result of her refusal to surrender to Augustus's hateful blackmail.

Ianthe desperately wished that she might ask for Grandmama's advice. She had considered telling her the truth before she left Northwood, but had decided it was too great a burden to lay upon her grandmother's fragile shoulders. To leave her worrying for weeks on end while she was away in Hampshire would have been cruel!

Now it was too late. She had to make the decision by herself and make it quickly! Tomorrow morning would be her last chance to ride out alone with Lord Kildare, her last chance to engineer a situation which would compromise him.

Her head spinning with tension and indecision, Ianthe poured herself a glass of water from the carafe kept upon the night-stand by her bed. The room was over-warm in spite of the window she had opened earlier, in defiance of Jenny's belief that night air was injurious to the health, and she was thirsty.

Pouring herself a second glass, she moved to the window.

Moonlight played over the dark garden. Sipping her water slowly, Ianthe realised how quiet the house seemed.

She glanced at the pretty clock on the mantel-shelf and was surprised to see it was well gone eleven. All the half-heard sounds of people going off to bed, which she had unwittingly registered during her endless pacing, had ceased.

It wasn't surprising if everyone had retired, she supposed. Apart from Lady Kildare, they were all to set off on journeys in the morning and no one would wish to stay up late.

The water had helped, but Ianthe still felt over-warm. She thought of how much cooler it would be out of doors and suddenly the idea of remaining imprisoned in this hot bed-chamber was unbearable. Maybe out in the garden her head would feel clearer! Without giving herself time to dwell on the fact that young ladies were not supposed to wander around out of doors in the middle of the night, she slipped light-footed from the room.

Luke Kildare threw down the butt of his cigarillo and stamped it out with unnecessary force. The impatient gesture did little to relieve the tension coiled within his lean frame.

With a muttered oath he rose to his feet and strode off down the moon-washed path. He had hoped that a few minutes spent in the peace of the garden would soothe his mood, but he had the distinct feeling that sleep would continue to elude him.

Restful nights had been in short supply of late. Luke's mouth twisted in a wry grimace. Insomnia had never troubled him in India! On the other hand, he had never given his future a second's thought until he had come home.

It was distinctly unsettling to think of settling down!

The dark outline of his mother's painting-studio loomed ahead. Luke paused, breathing in the sweet scent of the honeysuckle that grew by its door. He had not yet told his mother that he intended to leave early, before the viewing she had spoken of.

He hoped she would not be disappointed and would understand that he preferred to examine the portrait in a more

leisurely manner on his return. Standing around listen͏
that mincing fool, Turner, fawning over her work would g͏
him the bellyache! A slight shudder of distaste ran through
him. Poor Ianthe! Fate had saddled her with an unattractive
pair of guardians!

Still, that was no concern of his. Miss Ianthe Garland would
disappear out of his life tomorrow and his foolish fantasies
would, hopefully, disappear with her.

Luke tried to dismiss the mocking little voice in his head
which told him he was sadly mistaken if he thought he could
so easily escape the disturbing sentiments that young lady
aroused in him.

He gave a hollow laugh, which sounded much too loud in
the stillness. Fool! Who was he trying to gammon? He didn't
even want to fight the temptation that was pulling him towards
the studio like iron to a magnet.

As he had expected, the door was unlocked and opened at
his touch. Moonlight filled the room, guiding his footsteps
towards the shelf where he knew his mother kept a tinder-box
for those occasions when artistic inspiration would not wait
for morning. A bronze-and-ormolu candelabrum sat next to
the tinder-box. It was fashioned in the shape of a tall column
topped by the figure of a cupid. In each outstretched hand the
infant god held a new wax candle.

Luke lit both candles and carried the heavy candelabrum
over to the easel, which had been set in the middle of the dais
ready for the morning. He knew that this was where his
mother must have posed her sitter, but the background props
had been cleared away, leaving the easel in solitary splendour.

An affectionate grin curved his well-cut mouth. His mama
had a taste for the dramatic!

Ianthe's portrait rested upon the easel and, as the candlelight fell upon it, Luke's grin vanished and he sucked in a
deep breath. By God, but his mother had no need to go to
such lengths to impress her audience!

The portrait was magnificent! Easily the best work she had
ever painted, it conveyed a wonderful feeling of a moment

caught suspended in time when, against a backdrop of a tender blue sky, flecked with high floating clouds, the graceful young goddess of the hunt stood paused, resting for a brief instant before resuming the chase.

Sunlight played over Diana's hair, which gleamed with glowing tones of copper and gold. Her long slender limbs were exposed by a short white tunic and her bare skin had the delicate sheen of fine pearls.

Luke was unable to drag his eyes away from the inviting smile which curved her soft red lips. In spite of the chaste nature of the pose, there was a subtle air of eroticism about the painting. This was no cold stern goddess. His mother had chosen to remind the observer that Diana was not only worshipped as the Maiden, but also as the Nymph, an orgiastic deity who took a male consort.

A slight sound broke the silence and his well-honed instinct for survival immediately roused Luke from his enchantment. He spun round, staring into the darkness beyond the candles' reach. 'Who's there?'

Ianthe moved out of the shadow of the doorway. 'I...I saw a light and came to investigate,' she murmured shyly. 'I'm sorry if I startled you.'

He stepped down from the dais and walked slowly towards her. 'What were you doing in the garden at this hour?' he asked, ignoring her apology.

'I...I needed some fresh air. I couldn't sleep.'

'Neither could I.'

They stared at each other in silence for a moment and then Lord Kildare said softly, 'What a fortunate coincidence, Miss Garland. I had hoped for an opportunity to speak to you in private before I left.'

There was an edge of mockery in his deep voice, but Ianthe was too disconcerted at finding him here instead of Lady Kildare to notice it.

One of the doors in the service area of the house had been left unlocked, allowing her to slip out. A variety of fresh herby scents had greeted her and she realised she was in the kitchen garden. It had been easy to find her way along the moonlit path into the main pleasure-grounds and, with no particular goal in mind, she had wandered aimlessly for several minutes, savouring the coolness of the night.

Then she had spotted the light shining in the studio and it had drawn her like a moth. She hadn't meant to do more than take a quick peek to satisfy her curiosity, but as soon as she had seen Luke she had found herself unable to tear herself away.

Ianthe could feel herself growing rigid with tension. He had come to a halt less than a yard away, so close she could have touched him if she stretched out her hand. 'I think we ought to leave any discussions until the morning,' she said stiffly.

'It is already morning.'

Ianthe was only too well aware of the lateness of the hour and she couldn't help wondering if Fate was enjoying playing such a perverse trick on her. Their presence here, unchaperoned in this warm, honeysuckle-scented darkness, was far more scandalous than any scheme she could have devised!

She crushed an hysterical impulse to laugh. She was even dressed as if for an assignation! Her loosened hair flowed down her back and her low-necked gown displayed her charms.

She had been too warm to think of wearing her gold-spangled scarf, but she wasn't feeling hot any longer. In fact, the impropriety of their situation was sending icy shivers racing up and down her spine! It didn't matter a tinker's curse that they had not planned to meet. In the eyes of society, they were already damned.

This realisation made her gasp. The opportunity she had sought was here, all she had to do was grasp it!

'Miss Garland?'

Unable to speak, Ianthe shook her head.

She couldn't do it! She couldn't go through with Augustus's scheme. She liked Luke much too well to want to compromise him. No matter the difficulties ahead, she would have to find some other way to solve her problems!

A tremendous feeling of relief that her decision was finally, irrevocably, made swept over her, releasing her tongue. 'I must return to the house,' she said quickly.

'Without even a glimpse of your portrait?'

'Your mama wishes us to view it tomorrow.' Too late Ianthe remembered it was after midnight. She half-expected him to remind her, but he merely smiled.

'What iron resolution you possess!'

There was a warm teasing note in his baritone voice that made Ianthe think of their friendly sparring during the long rides they had taken together.

'I would never make any such claim,' she answered lightly, unconsciously relaxing. 'But your mother did say that she made it a rule not to show her work to anyone until it was finished and I feel I ought to respect her wishes.'

'But the portrait *is* finished,' Lord Kildare pointed out provocatively.

Ianthe hesitated. Curiosity was one of her besetting sins! *'Get thee behind me, Satan,'* she muttered and then blushed to realise she had inadvertently said the words aloud.

Luke laughed. 'A man might take offence at such a comparison, Miss Garland!'

Ianthe grinned back at him. She had missed their banter and so, it seemed, had Lord Kildare. All the same, she couldn't help wondering at his insouciance. Why was he lingering here talking to her? Didn't he realise what the consequences of being discovered would be?

'Is my suggestion really so devilish?'

A spirit of rebellion stirred in Ianthe. She knew she ought to walk away, but the temptation was too strong. Luke didn't seem to think that there was anything to worry about and, surely, another moment or two's delay couldn't matter?

'Not at all, my lord,' she answered him. 'In fact, you have convinced me that there can be no harm in taking a *quick* look.'

They walked towards the dais and stepped up to view the

portrait. 'Allow me.' Luke obligingly lifted the candelabrum higher.

Ianthe's eyes widened as she studied her image. 'Do I really look like that?' she asked, impulsively turning towards her companion.

He nodded. 'I think it reveals your strength of character. Don't you like it?'

'It is very striking,' Ianthe said doubtfully. 'But it isn't at all what I was expecting.'

'Artists are notorious for portraying sitters according to their own interpretation.' Amusement laced Lord Kildare's voice.

Ianthe hadn't realised that her costume would reveal quite so much flesh, but it wasn't the depiction of her bare limbs that disturbed her. The girl in the portrait wore a mysterious expression. It hinted at something hidden, something passionate beneath her smiling façade.

No innocent goddess this! The Maiden of the Silver Bow had secrets.

Ianthe shivered. She had the uneasy feeling that Cousin Amelia had seen into her soul!

'Are you cold?' Luke immediately put down the candelabrum. 'Here. Take my coat.'

'No, thank you,' Ianthe protested hastily as he began to strip it off.

Luke gave her a mocking grin. 'Do you think I'm such a frippery fellow that I demand my tailor make my coats so tight they cannot be removed without assistance?'

'Of course not!' Ianthe retorted with a touch of amused exasperation. 'I merely meant that your chivalry is quite unnecessary. I am quite warm enough and, besides, I must go back to my room now.'

'And there was I, trying to make up our quarrel.' Luke casually dropped his discarded coat onto the floor by the candelabrum.

'Careful! You'll give poor Whinlock a heart attack if you

singe that masterpiece of Weston's making!' Ianthe couldn't help laughing.

'Never mind my valet.' Luke's expression became serious. 'Are we going to part with things still in a stupid muddle between us, Ianthe?'

She stepped back, her face paling.

'I'm sorry. Should I still call you Miss Garland?' he asked quickly, taking a step towards her.

Ianthe shook her head. 'I am not such a poor creature, I hope, as to be offended by the use of my given name.'

'Then why—'

'I am honoured that you appear to value my friendship,' Ianthe interrupted, her voice shaking. 'But this is not the time for us to discuss it.' She took another step backwards. 'If you wish, we can ride together before breakfast. I promise I'll listen to you then, but now I must go.'

In her eagerness to get away Ianthe had failed to notice how close she was to the edge of the dais. She turned hastily, thinking there was still time to step down from the platform, and found empty space beneath her dainty sandal.

'Watch out!' Luke leapt forward and caught her before she fell.

His arms locked around her waist and he lifted her bodily away from the edge until they were both standing well clear. Too shocked by her near escape to pull away from him, Ianthe could only look up into his dark face.

'My God! Must you make a habit of scaring me?' Luke demanded unsteadily.

They stared at each other and Ianthe forgot to breathe. In some dim corner of her brain she knew she ought to defuse the tension spiralling between them with some light-hearted quip about her clumsiness, but it was totally beyond her capability. Instead of thanking him politely for his assistance and removing herself from his embrace, she could only tremble with anticipation as his arms tightened around her and his head bent to hers.

Ianthe closed her eyes. Slowly, gently his lips caressed hers and she felt a responsive explosion deep inside her. Her hands, trapped between their two bodies, clutched at the lapels of his waistcoat.

Nothing in Ianthe's life had prepared her for the intensity of her reaction to Luke's touch and she shuddered with bewildered pleasure as he drew her more tightly against him. Ripples of excitement were flowing through her veins and her head was spinning.

Mindlessly obeying the expert pressure of his mouth, she let her lips part. She had no idea why he wanted her to open her mouth to him, but a sharp arrow of sensation ripped into her as she felt their breath mingle.

This sensation swiftly became a new wave of pleasure as his tongue curled intimately around hers. The darkness surrounding them seemed to shimmer, mirroring her tingling delight.

Philip had never kissed her like this! His kisses had been sweet and somewhat clumsy. They had never aroused such a depth of longing in her body. Ianthe could feel the elegant buttons of Luke's waistcoat pressing into her breasts and she was suddenly assailed by a fierce desire for him to touch them.

The thought shocked her back to sanity. Jerking her head away, she gasped, 'No! This is wrong! You must not kiss me, my lord.'

'Oh, but I must,' Luke said firmly.

His mouth captured hers once more and, unable to resist, Ianthe surrendered to the flame consuming her. Her eager response caused him to deepen the kiss, and as he crushed her to him a strange liquid heat unfurled in the pit of Ianthe's stomach and her hands crept up to tangle themselves in his thick black hair.

'No doubt you have an excellent explanation for this behaviour, Luke. Pray enlighten us, I beg of you!'

Lady Kildare's clipped voice broke the silence with all the

force of a cannon-shot. Wrenched back to reality by the brutal impact, Ianthe looked over Luke's shoulder and saw her hostess standing in the doorway, a lantern in one hand and an expression of outraged disbelief on her stern face.

Chapter Six

With a little gasp of horrified dismay, Ianthe pulled free of Lord Kildare's hold.

Luke turned round to face his mother. 'Good evening, Mama.'

In a fever of embarrassment, Ianthe wondered how his voice could be so coolly unconcerned. She was shaking all over and desperately wishing that the earth would open up and swallow her!

'Well, we are waiting!' Lady Kildare moved forward and Ianthe saw that another figure stood in the shadows.

'Indeed, my lord, I am extremely anxious to hear what you have to say.'

With a feeling of sick horror, Ianthe recognised Augustus's unctuous tones. Her throat was so dry that she could barely speak, but anger gave her the strength to mutter gruffly, 'Go away! I don't want you interfering.'

Mr Turner stepped into the light. 'My child, you are over-wrought and no wonder,' he said with a reproachful sigh. 'Pray remain quiet, dear, and let me handle this.'

'There is nothing to handle,' Lord Kildare announced impassively. 'Miss Garland stumbled and would have fallen from the dais if I hadn't managed to catch her.'

Augustus tittered. 'You were doing a little more than *catching* her, my lord!'

Ianthe shot a quick look at Luke's profile. His mouth had tightened to a hard line. 'Do you doubt my word, sir?'

Augustus visibly thought better of his mode of attack. 'I do not dispute that you acted to prevent an accident,' he said with some haste. 'What concerns me is what happened afterwards, indeed, what was happening even as we entered this building.'

'He is right, Luke. You cannot expect to fob us off with such a feeble explanation,' Amelia said testily.

'Please don't blame Lord Kildare. We did not plan to meet. It was by coincidence that we both came in here and decided to look at the portrait.'

'At *this* hour of the night?' Augustus interjected.

Ianthe shot him a look of acute dislike. 'I...I couldn't sleep and came into the garden for some air.' She turned back to her hostess. 'I noticed a light in here and discovered his lordship studying the portrait. Perhaps it was ill-judged of me to stay, but I was just about to leave when you arrived.'

Lady Kildare's brows rose in disbelief and Ianthe could not blame her. Her explanation was true, but it failed to clarify why she had been locked in Luke's passionate embrace!

'May I ask what made you follow us into the garden, Mama?' Luke asked with a hint of irony.

'Mr Turner remembered an urgent message he ought to have given to Ianthe. Hoping that she might not be asleep, he tapped upon her door and found it ajar and made the discovery that she was absent from her room. Naturally, he was concerned and he came to speak to me.'

'What was this important message?' Something in Turner's manner disturbed Luke. He was altogether too gleeful for a man who had just discovered his ward in a compromising situation!

'A private matter, sir,' Augustus replied huffily.

Ianthe let out an involuntary snort of derision. She would lay odds that there was no message. Augustus had come to her room to badger her again!

Luke threw a puzzled glance at her. His instincts told him there were undercurrents here he knew nothing of.

Mr Turner drew himself up to his full height. 'What is important, Lord Kildare,' he stated with a pomposity that made Ianthe long to hit him, 'is that several of your servants witnessed my ward leaving the house.'

'Yes, and even more of them knew you were already out in the garden, Luke,' his mother continued.

'Your point, Mama?' enquired Lord Kildare softly.

'Do not fence with me, Luke!' Amelia's expression was grim. 'You know very well how the under-stairs chain of gossip works. By breakfast time every servant at Kildare Park will know that you and Ianthe were together unchaperoned in this building. By dinner time the story will have spread to all the surrounding villages. In a few days it will come to the ears of people like the Bishop of Dorchester!' She shuddered. 'Even worse, it will have gained extra embellishments with every retelling. I dare say that before the week is out they will be claiming that you had removed more than just your coat!'

Ianthe had the unpleasant feeling that the dais was rocking beneath her feet. 'I am truly sorry, Cousin Amelia,' she whispered. 'I never meant to cause any trouble.'

'It is too late for regrets,' Lady Kildare said with unwonted sharpness. 'Apologies will not mend *this* situation.'

She turned a basilisk gaze upon her son. 'I am sure, Luke, that I do not have to remind you of your duty.'

Lord Kildare inclined his head with an ironic smile. 'I know what society expects of me, Mama, but in this instance I fail to see the need to comply with the usual dictates. What happened here tonight is of no concern to any one other than Miss Garland and myself.'

Ianthe sucked in her breath as she realised what was being discussed. 'I agree,' she said quickly, her voice shaking. 'It was only a kiss, Cousin Amelia. I know it was wrong of us, but there is no need for talk of marriage.'

She could feel Augustus's pale eyes boring into her.

'Be silent, Ianthe! You do not know what you are talking
about!' Augustus switched his angry gaze to Luke. 'I am surprised at you, sir! You cannot wriggle out of your obligations
as a gentleman so easily. When word of this gets out—'

'Why should it?' Luke demanded ruthlessly. 'No one else
apart from my mother and yourself knows for certain whether
or not Miss Garland and I met here tonight.'

'The servants—' Augustus began to bluster.

'Are all loyal and will not gossip if my mother requests
them to stay silent,' Luke pointed out with cool logic.

'It will not be as easy as you think to silence wagging
tongues,' Augustus snapped. 'And it is not your reputation
which will suffer when a careless word leaks the secret.'

The lantern in Lady Kildare's hand betrayed her sudden
trembling. 'He is right, Luke,' she said in a strained tone.
'Remember the vicious gossip which began after your father
died. You know what people were saying then and there was
not a word of truth in those rumours!'

A look of concern crossed his lordship's face. 'Do not distress yourself, Mama.' He stepped down from the dais and
moved swiftly towards her. 'There is no need to worry—'

'Do not try to comfort me with false promises, Luke!'
Amelia interrupted. 'You cannot guarantee that there will be
no gossip.' A shudder shook her slight frame. 'I do not think
I can bear to go through all that again!'

Tears suddenly glistened in her dark eyes and the lantern
in her hand was swinging so wildly that Ianthe feared she
might drop it.

She risked a glance at Luke. His expression was carefully
shuttered, but a muscle twitched at the corner of his well-cut
mouth.

What was going on? Ianthe wondered. Why did the mere
threat of scandal upset Amelia so badly? She had often been
puzzled why her cousin was so careful of the proprieties. Now
it appeared that her deep aversion to gossip had its roots in
what happened six years ago when her husband died.

Her father had declared that Ianthe was too young to attend

the funeral with him. All she knew was that Lord Kildare had suffered a fatal heart attack. But it was obvious from the sly look, swiftly veiled, on Augustus's face that he had heard something.

'Aye, think of what harm such tattle would do to your brother's prospects, my lord,' he chimed in, his tone oozing sympathy. He rescued the lantern from Amelia's trembling grasp and patted her hand in commiseration. 'The Bishop would never allow his daughter to marry Mr Kildare if your family name was tainted by scandal a second time.'

Sickened by his hypocrisy, Ianthe opened her mouth to tell him to be quiet, but was forestalled by Lord Kildare.

'Thank you for your advice, sir,' he said icily. 'However, I do not need you to remind me of my obligations.' He turned to his mother. 'Will you permit me a few moments alone with Miss Garland?'

Lady Kildare had recovered her composure. 'What you ask is very irregular but, given the circumstances, I suppose there could be no harm in allowing the two of you to talk in private. If Mr Turner has no objections?' She glanced enquiringly at Augustus, who hastily shook his head.

'Very well. You may have ten minutes and then I shall expect you to join us in the Yellow Salon.'

Augustus held out his arm. 'Allow me to escort you back to the house, ma'am.'

With a nod of thanks Amelia took his arm and they left the studio.

There was a tiny silence and then Luke said abruptly, 'I feel stifled in here. Let's go into the garden.'

He returned to the dais and held out his hand to her. She hesitated and then took it shyly. He released her the instant she stepped down and moved to pick up his coat.

'I must blow out these candles.'

Ianthe nodded. 'Your mother would never forgive us if we were responsible for her studio burning down,' she replied with a gallant, if shaky, attempt at humour.

She saw the startled look he gave her before the light went out.

'Come. We haven't much time.'

Ianthe decided he must have eyes like a cat. Her vision was still adjusting to the greater darkness and she was thankful for the moonlight to guide her footsteps. She wasn't surprised that he did not offer her his arm, but she noticed that he slowed his long stride when he realised she was having difficulty in keeping up.

It was cooler in the grounds. Luke headed towards the house, but paused as they reached the terrace which overlooked the Sunken Garden. 'Shall we sit down?' He indicated the stone bench which had been placed in the centre of the terrace.

Ianthe agreed in a subdued voice. Her heart was thumping wildly against her breastbone and it was difficult to appear calm when she longed to know what he was thinking.

They sat down on the bench. To her surprise Luke was silent, his enigmatic gaze fixed upon the moon-washed garden which lay below the terrace. Amelia had told her that a previous Lady Kildare had modelled it after the style of the Privy Garden at Hampton Court. It was famous for the hundreds of rare tulips which bloomed in the spring. These had now been succeeded by marguerites, pinks and Amelia's fashionable new dahlias to set off its neat grass lawns and formal hedges.

Ianthe breathed in the floral perfume wafting up to them on the warm night air and struggled for patience.

At last Luke turned to her. 'Forgive me,' he said coolly. 'I have been considering what was said just now in the studio.'

'Have you come to any conclusions, sir?' Ianthe asked, trying hard to disguise her anxiety. 'I'm afraid I have no idea how to rescue us from this predicament.'

'I have.' To her surprise he rose abruptly to his feet. 'Miss Garland,' he said formally, sweeping her a graceful bow, 'Will you do me the honour of becoming my wife?'

For one brief shining moment Ianthe's soul sang with blissful relief. Without stopping to think why his proposal should make her so happy, she silently rejoiced that he wanted to marry her even though she had not deliberately compromised him.

Then, as her giddy rush of elation subsided, what she saw in his face made her happiness instantly evaporate. He was angry!

'Pray do not keep me in suspense, ma'am.'

Ianthe flinched at the coldness of his tone. She had to hide her hands in her lap to conceal their trembling, but she lifted her chin and faced him resolutely.

'Thank you for your kind offer.' Miraculously, her voice was as indifferent as his own. 'It is generous of you to wish to redeem my reputation, but I see no reason for us to be tied together in a marriage neither of us wants.'

'You are *refusing* me?'

Ianthe bit her lip to stem a hysterical impulse to laugh. 'I believe your mother is mistaken and the level of gossip we may face will be quite small. However, even if she is right, I do not intend to let a few rumours worry me.'

'My mother is rarely mistaken about such matters,' Lord Kildare replied curtly. He sat down again. 'What's more, I know she feels a double responsibility to safeguard your reputation since you are both a guest under her roof and her cousin's daughter.'

'Perhaps, but I will not marry you just to placate her inordinate fear of scandal!'

Luke stiffened.

Ianthe took a deep breath. 'Please excuse my unruly tongue,' she said in a quieter tone. 'I appreciate your mother's good intentions, but I do not think that anyone can hold her responsible for my behaviour. For heaven's sake, I'm not a child! In September I will come of age and take control of my own life.'

'Until that moment, however, Mr and Mrs Turner are your guardians,' Luke reminded her drily. 'And Mr Turner seems set on our marrying.'

Ianthe shivered as if he had thrown a bucket of cold water over her. 'Let me deal with Augustus,' she gasped.

Luke raised his brows. More than ever, he sensed that there was an undercurrent at work which he did not understand. It was obvious that Ianthe disliked Turner intensely and he could not blame her. The man was the worst sort of toad-eater, but he was sure there was something more than mere dislike behind their mutual antipathy.

'I will not pretend that I have taken to Mr Turner,' he said with one of his cynical smiles. 'However, his wish to see you creditably established is quite natural.' He shrugged. 'Gossip about tonight would not reflect well on his guardianship.'

Ianthe dropped her gaze to stare at her sandalled feet. How she wished she could tell him that Augustus was blackmailing her! Yet if she dared to explain, she felt sure he would recoil from her in disgust and, bad as things were now, at least he didn't despise her!

'Nor would it reflect well upon me,' Luke added softly. 'I do not care much for the opinion of society, but I must admit it goes against the grain to desert a lady in distress.'

Ianthe's head jerked up. 'I am not in distress,' she retorted, but her voice wobbled precariously. 'I…I can manage perfectly well on my own. I don't need you to sacrifice yourself in an unwanted marriage.'

'And what if I told you that the idea of a match between us was not entirely distasteful to me?'

Ianthe's eyes widened. 'Are you saying you *want* to marry me?'

'As my mother has been at pains to point out since I came home, I need a wife.' Luke's voice was cool. 'I have been thinking of settling down and I will need someone to act as the mistress of my household and to provide me with an heir.'

'And you think I might fit the bill?' Ianthe asked unsteadily.

He inclined his dark head. 'You possess the right background and breeding. Also I believe you to be a woman of intelligence and good sense, which I think important. I could not abide to be married to a simpering ninny.'

Ianthe took a deep breath. For one absurd moment she had foolishly imagined he might speak of love. 'You are very practical, sir,' she said in a colourless tone.

A cynical smile appeared on his face and his excellent teeth gleamed in the darkness. 'You think my approach lacks finesse, Miss Garland? Alas, I hoped you were a sensible girl who might prefer the truth to a pretty speech.'

Ianthe winced.

Luke was silent for a few seconds and when he spoke again the note of mockery was absent from his voice. 'I'm sorry. That was unfair of me.'

'You are angry,' Ianthe blurted. 'And I cannot blame you. This is all my fault!'

In the moonlight she saw surprise etched upon his handsome features. 'How so? We both knew we were breaching the conventions. In fact, one might say that this predicament is mostly of my making. *I* encouraged you to stay and view your portrait and *I* initiated what followed.'

Ianthe wriggled upon the hard bench. Guilt had prompted her outburst. It still distressed her to think how very close she had come to abandoning her principles and deliberately trapping him.

'I don't regret kissing you,' Luke murmured softly, mistaking her reaction for embarrassment. 'It was worth any amount of parental scolding, I do assure you!'

Ianthe was glad of the darkness which hid the sudden heat which rose to colour her cheeks as she remembered how his arms had felt around her.

'However, you are correct in thinking that my mother's attempt to coerce me *did* make me angry,' Luke went on, his tone turning hard. 'I will not be forced into marriage to suit other people's notions.'

'Nor will I,' Ianthe retorted, indignation restoring her composure in a trice.

'Please let me finish.' A quick authoritative gesture of his hand silenced Ianthe. 'Unfortunately, my mother and your guardian do have a point. We are in the suds and it would be foolish to pretend otherwise.'

Ianthe bit her lip. He was more right than he knew. A spiteful desire for revenge would prompt Augustus to fan the flames of rumour to vicious heights and, although she tried to tell herself that gossip did not matter, it would only add to her own difficulties and her grandmother's inevitable distress.

'Ianthe, listen to me.' Luke laid a hand gently upon her shoulder. 'Our betrothal would silence wagging tongues, but nothing could make me offer for you if I did not think we could make a success of our union.'

Suddenly breathless, she stared at him. 'What do you mean?'

'We have many interests and tastes in common and I believe that is a solid foundation upon which to build a good marriage.' He paused and then continued quietly. 'You told me once that you did not wish to become some man's shadow, but would you really be happy remaining a spinster all your days?'

'Married women may enjoy higher status, but it doesn't automatically make them happier,' Ianthe murmured in confusion.

'Spinsters miss out on other things too. You may not need a husband to provide for you, but you don't possess the solace of a close family.'

Ianthe could not deny it. Sir Alexander had been an only child and her mother had but the one sister, Aunt Harriet, a childless widow who lived in Devon. She was a nice woman, but Ianthe rarely saw her.

'Loneliness need not be a problem when one has friends,' she said with all the firmness she could muster.

'But don't you want a family of your own? I overheard you saying how much you liked children the other day when you and Sophy were discussing her ambitions in that direction.'

Ianthe was reluctant to admit it, but his objections were sound. In spite of her inclination towards independence, she didn't really feel that a spinster's life would suit her.

'I promise you that I do not want a clinging wife. In as far as it is possible, I would allow you the freedom to go your own way.'

'Am I to assume, sir, that you do not look for love?'

His hand dropped from her shoulder. 'Love, Miss Garland, is a delusion. I have no faith in romantic promises of eternal bliss.' A harsh laugh escaped him. 'A marriage of convenience will suit me very well.'

Ianthe suspected that his sour attitude had been caused by the failure of his previous betrothal and her heart sank. How could the woman he married combat its grim influence when he was wary of letting anyone else get close to him?

Her expressive face betrayed her dismay. 'I see that you do not agree with me.'

'Think me a foolish romantic if you wish, but I do not believe I could endure a life where cold detachment was the order of the day!' Ianthe declared with conviction.

To her astonishment a faint smile curved his mouth. 'Who said anything about cold detachment? Think *me* a foolish coxcomb if you wish, but I do not believe we need worry about a lack of passion in our marriage.' He reached out a hand and gently tipped her face up to his. 'You must know that I have been attracted to you since that first morning ride we undertook together and I do not think you are indifferent to me.'

Innate honesty forbade Ianthe to contradict him. Even if she had wished to do so, her passionate response to his kiss would declare her a liar.

'I always thought it might be restful to marry a woman who knew the value of silence,' Luke said lightly.

It was the hint of laughter in his voice that pierced Ianthe's defences. In a sudden flash of understanding she knew that the liking and respect she felt for him had turned to something deeper.

I have fallen in love with him, she thought, with a sense of shock that robbed her of the power of speech.

'On this occasion, however, my dear Miss Garland, your refreshing tendency not to chatter puts us at a disadvantage.

Time, and my mama, will not wait. We must rejoin the others or have them descend upon us like the wrath of God to discover what we have decided.' He smiled down into her eyes. 'So tell me, is it possible you might reconsider your answer?'

Beneath his humour Ianthe sensed he was deadly serious and her heart began to turn somersaults.

He was offering her what she had just realised she wanted most in the world, but did she have the right to accept? He had listed the qualities that would make her a suitable bride, but there was one important attribute he had not mentioned.

The touch of his hand, warm upon her skin, wasn't helping her to think straight! Ianthe knew she ought to confess her secret, but she couldn't bear to watch his smile change to a look of revulsion. Her courage seemed to have been all used up in defying Augustus!

'I realise that marriage could not have been upon your mind any more than it was on mine,' Luke said with an unconscious irony that made Ianthe's pulse skip several beats. 'In other circumstances I would not press you for an answer, but we are out of time.' He released her. 'You must decide now whether or not you wish to marry me.'

Ianthe's heart was pounding so loudly she was convinced he must be able to hear it. Was it so very wrong of her to keep silent? Might it not be better for everyone to simply accept her unexpected good fortune, particularly when refusing him would bring disaster in its wake?

After all, there was no reason for him to find out that she had misled him. Augustus certainly wouldn't tell him! And she would do her utmost to ensure that he never regretted his choice.

'May I take it that your silence means consent?' Luke asked, hoping he sounded calm. It was strange. He had proposed marriage purely for practical reasons and yet his pulse was racing faster than when he had faced the French in battle!

'Yes, Lord Kildare,' Ianthe said clearly, crushing the protests of her conscience. 'I have made my decision. I will become your wife.'

* * *

It was unusual for Lady Kildare's family and guests to partake of breakfast at the same time, but the next morning found everyone gathered around the table in the breakfast-parlour.

'I have an announcement to make,' Amelia said happily. 'Which is why I requested you all to join me.'

'I suspected something was up when I received your note, Mama,' Harry chuckled. 'You have a surprise for us, I'll be bound.'

Lady Kildare smiled. 'I rather think I have.' She glanced across the table at Ianthe, who turned pale and dropped her gaze to her plate. In contrast, her son was drinking his coffee with every appearance of unconcern.

She curbed a sigh. Last night there had been a faint, but distinct, glow of happiness around the pair of them. Surely they hadn't begun to regret their sensible decision? Not that it mattered. She would see to it that the wedding went ahead.

Her spirits revived. They might not yet realise it, but she was convinced that this marriage would turn out splendidly. She had seen how they looked at one another when they thought no one was watching.

It was this obvious attraction which had prompted her to play matchmaker, absenting herself whenever possible to give them a chance to become better acquainted. Not that she had expected to find them in such an intimate embrace, of course. She had been genuinely shocked, but in an instant she had seen that this was her opportunity to give Luke a push in the right direction.

He'd been furious and she'd spent a very bad quarter of an hour, worrying that he might fail to honour his upbringing as a gentleman. Her deep relief when he and Ianthe had returned to the house as an engaged couple was not prompted solely by the removal of the threat of scandal.

Everything would work out for the best in the end!

'We are holding our breath in anticipation, dear lady,' Augustus reminded her in a somewhat impatient voice.

Amelia nodded. She would never like Turner, but on this issue their thoughts were one.

'I am delighted to inform you that Ianthe has accepted Luke's hand in marriage and the wedding will take place very shortly.'

A twinkle appeared in Amelia's eyes at the reaction to her announcement. One of the footmen had dropped a cup, fortunately empty, and Sophy had mis-swallowed a bite of bread and butter and was coughing. Harry, looking astonished, patted her automatically on the back.

Then he rose quickly to his feet to cross to where Ianthe sat. 'Please accept my warmest felicitations, Miss Garland. It is a pleasure to welcome you into the family. Luke is a lucky man.'

'Thank you. You are very kind.' Ianthe lifted her gaze to smile at him shyly.

Harry moved round the table to shake his brother's hand. 'Congratulations, Luke. I am very pleased for you. You have made an excellent choice.'

Luke thanked him and Harry returned to his seat.

Having recovered her breath, Sophy added her good wishes to them both. 'Have you decided where the ceremony will take place?' she asked Ianthe.

'I'm...I'm not sure. Perhaps at St Michael's, my parish church.' Ianthe flashed a look of uncertainty at Luke.

'I have no particular preference,' he said. 'You may choose the location and whatever else you wish.'

'Careful, Luke,' Harry laughed. 'It's plain that you know little about weddings. There's more involved than you might think.'

A sharp pang of memory assaulted Luke. He had been in Spain when all the arrangements had been put in place for his marriage to Georgiana.

'Harry is right,' Lady Kildare chimed in. 'There are many considerations to be decided. Once the formal announcement is made we must begin to draw up a guest list.'

There was a gleam of anticipation in her dark eyes and Luke frowned. It was time to put a stop to these transports! 'I hesitate to spoil your fun, Mama, but the one thing I am quite sure of is that I do not want half the fashionable world invited to my nuptials,' he said crisply.

He turned to Ianthe. 'Should you object to a quiet wedding?'

She shook her head. 'A simple ceremony with just family and close friends would suit me very well.'

Lady Kildare swallowed her disappointment. 'It shall be as you wish, of course.'

On reflection, it was better to have a small private wedding. A simple affair could be arranged more quickly, which was a distinct advantage. She knew Luke was much too honourable to withdraw now that the betrothal was made public, but she would feel happier once the knot was tied!

'Good. That's settled, then.' Luke turned his head to smile at his fiancée and saw that her gaze was glued to her plate again.

A feeling of surprise mixed with irritation swept over him. Why the devil was she so subdued? She had barely said a word throughout the meal and she was as pale as on the first day they had met.

It did not require great intelligence to realise that she was unhappy. Weren't brides supposed to glow with content? Far from glowing, she seemed almost reluctant!

For reasons not entirely clear to him, Luke felt affronted. He did not expect babbling delight. They were a rational couple who had taken a sensible decision based on logic, not emotion. Nor did he expect gratitude—the idea that his bride should feel beholden to him was repugnant. On the other hand, he knew his wealth and rank made him a good catch. Surely she ought to look a little pleased?

A sudden knot of uneasiness twisted in his stomach. Money was not everything, even for a pretty young woman. Perhaps she found his scar repellent. In which case, how in God's name would she react when she saw the results of his other injuries? He had been wounded twice in India to add to the battle scars he had acquired in Spain.

'Do you still intend to visit Nicodemus, Luke?' Lady Kildare asked, spreading honey upon a slice of bread.

Wrapped up in his uneasy thoughts, Lord Kildare failed to hear her and she had to repeat the question.

'I beg your pardon, Mama.' Luke threw off his unwelcome introspection. 'Unless Miss Garland has some objection, I believe I will stick to my original plan. In fact, I shall ask him to be my best man.'

He saw a flicker of disappointment flit over his brother's face. 'I can't choose you, Harry. You are going to marry us.'

Harry grinned. 'I was hoping you would ask!' He glanced at Ianthe, who, seeing that he was trying to frame a way of confirming that this *fait accompli* was acceptable to her, quickly reassured him.

'Although I think we must consult my stepmother before sanctioning your services, sir,' she added a little doubtfully. 'The Reverend Pickford, who is the incumbent of our parish church, is a personal friend of the family and she will not wish to offend him.'

'Leave Maria to me, my dear,' Augustus interjected smoothly. 'There is no need for either of you to fret. Pickford will not object once it is explained to him that Mr Kildare is the bridegroom's brother.'

Ianthe nodded, knowing it would do scant good to argue. Augustus would ride roughshod over any quibble which threatened to upset Lord Kildare's wishes!

The discussion turned to wedding clothes and the three gentlemen hastily excused themselves. While Augustus hurried upstairs to check that his valet had completed his packing to the high standards he demanded, the two brothers strolled out into the sunshine with the intention of ensuring that their respective horses were in fine fettle for travelling.

'Do you know you could have knocked me down with a feather when Mama made her announcement,' Harry declared. 'I could see you liked Miss Garland, but I had no idea you were thinking of marriage.'

'It came upon me suddenly.'

One glance at his brother's shuttered expression was enough to inform Mr Kildare that the subject of the forthcoming nuptials was taboo. A thoroughly vulgar curiosity raged in his breast. He strove to repress it with an inward sigh. Luke could be as close as an oyster when he chose!

The stables came in sight. 'Do you think the Bishop will make any difficulties about giving you leave again so soon?' Luke asked abruptly.

'I hope not,' Harry replied. 'I should hate to miss your wedding.' He hesitated and then said, 'I'm sure I can square things with this Pickford fellow, but if I were to put off my journey today it might adversely affect my chances of obtaining permission to conduct the ceremony.'

Luke glanced at him with a slightly puzzled frown. 'There's no need for you to stay, Harry.'

Mr Kildare coughed. 'Didn't know if you wanted some support, old boy. Love and the prospect of marriage can affect a fellow oddly sometimes, you know!'

Luke laughed. 'Thank you, but I think I can still manage to carry on in a rational manner.'

It struck Harry that there was little mirth in his brother's laughter. 'I must say that it seems odd that you intend to leave Miss Garland at this juncture,' he blurted, wondering at Luke's apparently blasé attitude.

Surely Luke felt something for the girl? If he didn't, Harry was blowed if he knew his reason for offering for her. 'I'm sure Nicodemus wouldn't object if you visited him another time.'

Luke's mouth tightened. 'I have business matters to discuss with him,' he said curtly. 'And if I do not leave now, it will be difficult to return in time for the wedding.'

'And Miss Garland doesn't mind?' Harry persisted delicately.

'Why should she?' Luke enquired with raised brows.

Harry blinked. His brother had returned from his travels changed in character. He was certainly a cool customer nowadays, but, even so, this complete insouciance was disconcerting.

'Besides, you forget that Ianthe is also leaving today. The first banns are to be called this Sunday and there are various arrangements that need to be made.'

'Aye, she will be busy. You wouldn't have much time to spend together,' Harry remarked with relief, glad of a reason to abandon his anxious suspicions.

They entered the stable-yard and Harry allowed himself to be drawn into a lively discussion about the merits of Luke's bays.

However, he couldn't help hoping that one day, not too far distant, his brother would unbend sufficiently to tell him what had really happened last night!

Lord Kildare returned to the house alone, leaving his brother still deep in discussion with the head groom. He was hoping to find Ianthe and speak to her. They hadn't exchanged more than a formal greeting this morning and he must leave soon. However, when he walked into the hallway he found Turner loitering and the man's eager smile told Luke that he had been waiting for him.

'May I beg the favour of a word in private, my lord?'

Luke's hackles rose at the man's ingratiating tone. He had no wish for Turner's company, but he supposed it behoved him to listen to what the fellow had to say given that they were shortly to be connected by marriage.

'I do not have much time,' he warned, leading the way into the library. As he had expected, this comfortable book-lined room was empty. 'Well, sir?' he asked.

Augustus looked a little put out at not being invited to sit down, but as his host had remained standing he realised Kildare had meant what he said about keeping the interview short. 'I had hoped to discuss the matter of Ianthe's dowry with you,' he announced jovially, trying to hide his anxiety.

Luke suspected Turner's real purpose was to ascertain what

settlement he planned to bestow upon his bride. It was a perfectly legitimate question and Luke would have thought better of him if he had come straight out with it.

'I am sure Sir Alexander provided satisfactorily for his daughter,' he drawled. 'Naturally, I will furnish your lawyer with the name of my bankers and details of my assets. If you will let me have his direction, I'll get my fellow to get in touch with him and they can sort out the details.'

Turner's florid face lost most of its colour. 'Of course, of course. But there is a slight problem, sir, relating to…ahem…money that I need to bring to your personal attention.'

'If you are worried that I may not be inclined to generosity because of what happened last night, you are far out.' Luke's expression was mocking.

'The thought had never entered my head,' Augustus protested mendaciously. He whipped out a large spotted handkerchief and mopped his damp brow. 'I am sure you will do all that is expected of you, my lord.'

'Thank you,' Luke said ironically.

'It is not of the settlements exactly that I wish to speak.' Augustus cleared his throat. 'Dear me, I hardly know how to begin. The matter is a delicate one, you perceive, sir.'

'In that case, I suggest we postpone our discussion until I return from Cumbria and we have more time at our disposal,' Luke replied crisply.

Augustus's pale eyes bulged. 'But…but, my lord—'.

'Mr Turner, I do not wish to cause you inconvenience.' His lordship's tone was bored. 'However, you must see that I cannot do justice to any *delicate* business in the few minutes which remain to us.'

The impatience in his deep voice convinced Augustus that it would do more harm than good to persist. He needed Kildare in a benevolent mood before he broached the subject of the debts he wanted paid!

He bowed with a showy flourish of assent. 'I understand,

sir,' he murmured, racking his brains. Would his creditors accept his word that Kildare would pay up if he could give them no details of the settlements?

'Then let me bid you farewell, Mr Turner,' Luke said and headed towards the door.

Inspiration struck Augustus. 'May we travel in convoy with you, my lord? I'm sure Ianthe would appreciate the chance to enjoy your company for a little longer.'

Luke checked in surprise. He had imagined that Turner would take a different route than himself, but when he said so Augustus hastily denied it. 'I prefer to go north, sir, and then swing west,' he announced breezily. 'We could travel together as far as Abingdon before our ways parted. Indeed, I think I shall dine there with Ianthe. The Crown keeps a good table. Perhaps you would care to join us?'

Luke hesitated for a fraction. He had intended to travel beyond Oxford before stopping to dine, but, as Turner said, this arrangement would give him some extra time to spend with Ianthe.

Luke was perturbed to realise how much he would relish such an opportunity.

'Very well,' he said slowly. 'If you and Miss Garland can be ready to leave within the next half an hour, I am happy to acquiesce to your plan.'

'We shall not keep you waiting, my lord,' Augustus promised.

Lord Kildare gave a curt nod and went out of the library, leaving Augustus to hurry off and appraise Ianthe of this change of plan.

'Tell your maid to make haste. I don't want Kildare thrown into a bad mood,' he concluded.

Ianthe did not need to ask why. She had been fretting herself to flinders wondering what Lord Kildare would say when he realised that her hand in marriage came accompanied by large debts!

Last night she had gone to bed too exhausted to allow her

thoughts to dwell upon the future, but from the minute she had woken up this morning she had been plagued by apprehension. She felt as if the sword of Damocles was suspended over her head and could only be grateful that Augustus was determined to get his confession over with today instead of waiting until Luke returned from Cumbria.

Pushing aside the lowering thought that she ought to emulate Augustus's example and make a clean breast of her past, she changed into her travelling outfit while Jenny completed her packing. With a few minutes to spare, she joined Augustus and Lord Kildare on the front steps of the house where everyone had gathered to wave them off.

'I shall say *au revoir* rather than goodbye, my dear, since we shall see each other again in just three weeks.' Lady Kildare gave Ianthe a fond kiss on the cheek.

'Aye, and I will write as soon as I have spoken to the Bishop,' Harry promised, shaking her hand.

Sophy nodded, her solemn face displaying an unusual excitement. 'If Papa allows me to be your bridesmaid, I will show your sketch to my mantua-maker and send you full reports on how my dress progresses.'

'I hope your father agrees.' Ianthe impulsively gave the younger girl a hug as she said goodbye. She had no female relatives of the right age to ask and, as her future sister-in-law, Sophy had seemed the obvious alternative choice. To her delight, Sophy's enthusiastic reaction seemed to hold out a promise that their tentative friendship would develop into a stronger bond one day.

They walked to the carriages. Ianthe had half-hoped that Luke would offer her a seat in the new curricle he had purchased in London, but to her disappointment no invitation was forthcoming.

Augustus was driving the showy phaeton he had acquired soon after his marriage to Maria. Accepting the assistance of one of the grooms, Ianthe joined him on the high seat of this vehicle.

'Do take the lead, my lord,' Augustus urged politely. 'You know the local roads.'

Luke raised his whip in acknowledgement and they set off, with Jenny and Augustus's valet bringing up the rear in the Turner gig.

The chorus of goodbyes had scarcely faded from their ears before Augustus started grumbling about the narrowness of the roads and the speed of Lord Kildare's driving. Ianthe hid a smile. Augustus had pretensions to be a dashing whip, but his skills, although tolerable, did not match his ambitions.

On the other hand, Lord Kildare, she observed, could drive to an inch. Luckily for Augustus, the country lanes were quiet and their progress was not impeded.

They stopped to rest the horses and enjoy a light meal in the village of Basing before driving on to Newbury. Sheep reared on the nearby downs had been responsible for the wealth of this town, which had once been a centre of the cloth trade. It was still a busy place, lying as it did on the Great West Road, and they had no difficulty in procuring horses for the next stage of the journey.

Since his lordship did not wish to linger, one of the inn servants brought out a tray of drinks to quench their thirst while fresh beasts were put to. The day was warm, if somewhat cloudy, and Ianthe was glad of the lemonade and the chance to stretch her legs for a few minutes while the ostlers were busy.

Lord Kildare had also decided to take a little exercise and Ianthe approached him shyly as he returned to his vehicle when the change-over was completed. Last night when they had parted after telling his mother their news, his mood had seemed reassuringly amicable. Now his expression was aloof, but she couldn't suppress her longing to speak to him.

'How far is it to Abingdon from here?' she asked at random, desperately hoping he wasn't having second thoughts about his proposal.

'Around nineteen miles, I believe,' he replied. He paused

and then added abruptly, 'Would you care to join me for the next stage?'

A beaming smile broke out on Ianthe's irregular features. 'I would be delighted to do so, sir!' she exclaimed, her nervousness dissipating.

Luke's stern expression relaxed. 'Then come,' he said, holding out his hand to assist her into the curricle.

Ianthe put her hand in his and felt a strange tingling warmth invade her palm. She glanced up at him quickly and saw the unguarded look in his eyes.

An unexpectedly tender look that sent an irrepressible happiness fizzing through her veins!

Chapter Seven

The Crown Inn in Abingdon turned out to be as comfortable as promised and Lord Kildare decided to dine there before driving on. His decision was based on good sense—obtaining a tolerable dinner on the road could be a chancy business. It had nothing at all to do with his enjoyment of his fair companion's company.

Or so he told himself.

Ianthe had also been sorry to see the abbey which graced the old town come into sight. She had greatly enjoyed their drive through the beautiful Vale of the White Horse. His lordship had lost his worrying air of remoteness and they had chatted together as easily as they used to do on their morning rides at Kildare Park.

On their arrival at the inn, the landlord's wife showed her up to a bedchamber where she was able to remove her bonnet and wash her hands and face. When Jenny had tidied her hair and brushed the dust from her emerald cambric travelling-costume, she decided she looked presentable.

Augustus had told her that, once the meal was over and he had spoken to Lord Kildare, they would take advantage of the long summer evening to travel on so there was no point in changing her gown. It would have been nice, though, Ianthe mused with a sudden burst of vanity, to wear something pretty to impress her fiancé.

Her fiancé. How odd it sounded! She had not yet grown accustomed to the idea, but it was undeniably pleasant.

On her way to the private parlour they had hired, she met Lord Kildare.

'I've just seen mine host, who assured me that our dinner was ready,' he informed her.

Ianthe smiled. 'Are you hungry? I remember you saying that travelling gave you an appetite.'

Luke nodded. He was hungry, but not, he realised, for food! Standing there with a shaft of evening sunshine from the window at the end of the corridor playing upon her glorious hair, she looked so lovely that his heart gave a queer little lurch.

'Shall we go and find Mr Turner?' Ianthe asked tentatively, wondering why he was looking at her so intently. 'He will be growing impatient.'

'No doubt. He hopes there will be time after we have eaten for the two of us to have a private conversation.' Luke's tone was deliberately droll and she obliged him with a smile, but he noted the shadow that flickered in her eyes.

'Miss Garland…Ianthe…' He hesitated. He wasn't accustomed to seeking to understand the women who had passed through his life. He hadn't cared what they were thinking or shared his own thoughts with them, but Ianthe was different.

'If something was troubling you, would you let me try to help?' he said abruptly.

For an instant Luke thought he saw a film of tears shimmer in her beautiful eyes and then she smiled at him and he decided that it must have been a trick of the light.

'When we are wed and our butler gets foxed or the cook ruins our dinner I shall have a fit of hysterics and remind you of your kind offer,' she said saucily.

'I think it unlikely you would need my help in such circumstances,' Luke replied. 'I'll wager that you are more than capable of handling any domestic crisis.'

She was not going to confide in him. Luke felt a momentary stab of disappointment, which he promptly dismissed as absurd. His imagination was at fault. There was no reason to assume that she was concealing anything from him.

'You have a flattering tongue, sir.' Ianthe hid her feelings behind a playful smile. She hated having to rebuff his attempt to befriend her, but she could not confide in him. It was too shaming to admit that Augustus hoped to use their betrothal as a lever to persuade him to hand over a large sum of money.

It was also too risky. Augustus would be furious with her if she warned Luke and the betrothal did not bring him the financial advantages he desired. Ianthe was prepared to brave his wrath, but she suspected he would take revenge by blackening her character to Luke and she had too much to hide to let that happen.

'We ought to hurry. Our dinner will be growing cold,' she said lightly, laying her hand upon his arm.

Luke nodded, staring at her wordlessly as his blood ran hot with a sudden need to embrace her. She was so invitingly close…

Ianthe blushed. She did not have much experience of the world, but there was no mistaking the desire which darkened his eyes to the colour of storm clouds. 'Luke,' she murmured, barely conscious of saying his name.

Silently, he reached out and brushed his thumb over the sensual curve of her bottom lip.

Ianthe quivered and involuntarily swayed towards him.

Luke stopped fighting the temptation to take her into his embrace.

For an instant Ianthe allowed herself to enjoy the feel of his strong arms holding her close before she tried to pull away. 'Luke, we should not…you must not…a servant might come…'

He ignored her reluctant protest and stared down into her brilliant eyes. In spite of her alarm, they were glittering with the same desire which tormented him. 'You called me by my given name,' he said softly.

'I know.' Shy laughter lit up the sapphire depths of her gaze. 'Do you mind?'

'I believe I shall insist upon it in future,' he replied hoarsely.

Her wide mouth curved in an answering smile and it proved to be Luke's undoing. 'You are much too lovely to resist,' he muttered and bent his head to hers, finding her lips in a long slow kiss.

At first Ianthe struggled to remain unresponsive. Young ladies did not allow themselves to be kissed in the corridors of inns. It was not proper! Her head spinning, she knew she ought to push him away, but her arms crept up of their own volition to wind themselves around his neck and when he deepened the kiss she was lost. Her lips parted beneath his and she pressed herself against him eagerly.

With a considerable effort of will, Luke raised his head and let her go. He stepped back, leaving a safe gap between their bodies. Desire still held him in its savage grip, but this was no place to satisfy the hunger which threatened to rage out of control whenever he touched her.

'Forgive me. My behaviour is inexcusable,' he said, drawing a deep breath. 'I promise you I will not repeat it again.'

'Never again?' Ianthe asked in a small voice, her gaze downcast.

'I give you my word.'

She lifted her head and he saw the mischief sparkling in her vivid eyes. 'What a pity,' she murmured huskily. 'I quite liked it, you know.'

Her mouth had curved into a little smile and Luke almost pulled her back into his embrace. Only a lingering vestige of common sense prevented him.

'We must not keep Turner waiting any longer,' he said gruffly, indicating that she should precede him down the narrow corridor.

Ianthe sighed regretfully and obeyed.

Watching the gentle sway of her hips as she walked ahead of him, Luke began to think that there was a great deal to be said in favour of a quick marriage by special licence!

* * *

'Shall we stretch our legs before we depart, my lord?' Mr Turner asked as a servant arrived to clear the table at the conclusion of their excellent meal. 'There is a small garden at the back of the inn, I believe.'

'I am at your disposal, sir.' There was a note of dry irony in Lord Kildare's tone.

He might as well get this interview over with, he thought, rising lithely to his feet. It was obvious that Turner wanted something from him.

'Wait here for us, my dear,' Augustus instructed Ianthe.

She nodded, hiding her anxiety, as she watched them leave.

Would Luke agree to Augustus's demands? Ianthe sat like a stone, oblivious of the clatter as the waiter gathered up the dirty plates and dishes and departed.

Reputedly, Lord Kildare was so rich that the money Augustus needed would be an insignificant sum to him, but she hated the whole sorry business. There was only one small consolation. Augustus had announced that he would not reveal her knowledge of the debts which threatened Northwood's future.

'It is better Kildare thinks you ignorant,' he'd declared earlier that afternoon as they had neared Newbury. 'We don't want him smelling a rat and guessing you tricked him into proposing.'

While she was glad that Luke would not think she approved of him redeeming Augustus's personal folly, anger had filled Ianthe at this remark. Unfortunately, at that moment they'd encountered heavy traffic on entering the town and Augustus had ignored her attempt to rebut his assumption, roughly telling her to be quiet while he concentrated on handling his horses.

It still rankled that Augustus had not been listening, but Ianthe was growing too anxious to think of anything other than what was happening in the inn garden. With no occupation to distract her, her curiosity was running riot!

What could be taking them so long? Unable to bear her

disordered thoughts for another minute, Ianthe jumped to her feet. She would go and see for herself.

A helpful chambermaid directed her to the garden, which lay behind the inn and was reached by a narrow path which ran down one side of the building. This path was somewhat overgrown and dark, but when Ianthe emerged into the light again she gave a little gasp of surprise. Although quite small, the garden was attractive and well kept.

Someone, she suspected the landlord's wife, had planted a pretty flower border and there were damask roses scenting the rather sultry air. However, at first glance, she could see no sign of either Augustus or Lord Kildare. Then she spotted the older man, who had just emerged from behind a large syringa bush. He was adjusting his breeches and Ianthe guessed he had been relieving himself on the bush. A moue of disgust at this lack of consideration wrinkled her features. He was an uncouth creature behind his pretence of fine manners!

'What are you doing here? I told you to stay indoors,' Augustus was frowning as he came towards her and Ianthe forgot about the unfortunate syringa.

'Where is Lord Kildare? Did…did your discussion not go well?' she asked apprehensively.

'Don't worry.' Augustus laughed at her sudden pallor. 'Kildare's only gone to settle the reckoning. We are to meet him in the yard in a few minutes. You can say goodbye to him then.'

Relief bubbled up in Ianthe. 'And the money? Will he help you?'

A broad smirk appeared on Mr Turner's well-fed features. 'He agreed to settle twenty thousand pounds on you *and* pay all the debts secured against Northwood.'

Ianthe gasped. She had not expected such magnificent generosity!

'Aye, we are in the clear!' Augustus's voice was filled with satisfaction. His lordship had set but one condition. Management of the estate was to be handed over immediately to Robertson, Ianthe's lawyer. Augustus knew this was to pre-

vent him dipping his fingers into the pot again before the
wench married and Northwood passed out of his control. He
would regret losing its revenues, but, all in all, Kildare had
been exceedingly generous.

'Aren't you glad now that you followed my advice?' he
said to Ianthe in a tone of smug self-congratulation.

Ianthe glared at him. 'If by that remark, you mean am I
glad I decided to visit Kildare Park, then I must concur.'

Augustus laughed. 'Doing it too brown, my dear! You've
got more to be grateful to me for than suggesting you visit
Cousin Amelia and you know it! Kildare would never have
proposed to you if I hadn't shown you how to trap him into
marriage.'

A flood of anger swept over Ianthe. 'How can you possibly—' She broke off as her sharp ears caught a slight rustling
sound and she whirled round to stare in the direction it was
coming from.

'What's wrong now?' Augustus asked impatiently.

A large tabby cat strolled into the garden. It halted on seeing them and then paced slowly over to a rustic bench which
was bathed in evening sunshine. Jumping up, it settled itself
and began washing its paws.

'Just a cat, my dear.' Augustus gave her a nasty smile. 'No
need to let your guilty conscience get the better of you.'

'I do not need to feel guilty,' Ianthe snapped.

'Quite right! I always say there's no point in lamenting after
the deed is done,' proclaimed Augustus jovially, but his pale
eyes gleamed with spiteful mockery.

'Will you listen to me!' Ianthe could feel her temper slipping. 'Why are you deliberately twisting what I—'

'No, you listen to me, my girl!' Augustus's face had lost
its veneer of amusement. 'I am sick of your airs and graces.
You think you are superior to me, but we're no different. You
can claim I pushed you into it if that makes you feel better,
but the plain fact remains that you went to Kildare Park with
the express intention of compromising Kildare so that he'd be
forced to marry you. Aye, and very cleverly you set about

snaring him too! You deserve to get your hands on his fortune. I couldn't have arranged that little scene in Amelia's
studio better myself.'

Lord Kildare did not wait to hear Miss Garland's reply. He
turned on his heel and stormed down the path, anger drumming in his ears so violently that he could not have heard
what she said even if he had wanted to listen.

A burning need to put a large distance between himself and
the scheming pair sent him in search of his curricle. 'Whinlock,' he shouted to his valet, who was gossiping to Turner's
man in one corner of the inn-yard. 'To me. We are leaving
now.'

The reckoning had been paid and the horses put to. About
to spring up into his vehicle, Luke paused. He ground his
teeth. God knows, she didn't deserve the courtesy, but he
supposed he ought to leave some sort of message!

Roundly cursing under his breath, Luke strode back into
the inn. He'd seen Ianthe's maid earlier in the coffee-room.
She was still there and he hailed her in an impatient voice.

She hurried over to him and bobbed a respectful curtsy.

'Please tell your mistress that I have decided to leave.'

Jenny blinked in surprise. 'Aren't you going to say goodbye
to her, sir?' she asked timidly, alarmed by his black frown.

'I cannot wait.' The coldness in his voice warned Jenny not
to protest. 'I shall write to her in due course.'

'Yes, sir.' Jenny bobbed another curtsy.

Luke returned to his curricle. Whinlock had taken his seat
and, better acquainted with his master's moods than Jenny,
took care to remain silent as Luke drove away from the inn
at a spanking pace.

It was perhaps unfortunate for Lord Kildare's present state
of mind that the road north was comparatively empty. With
nothing to distract him, his thoughts whirled in a furious
tangle of bitter anger and regret.

The last six years had obviously not taught him wisdom,
he reflected rancorously. Once again a beautiful woman had

beguiled him into making a fool of himself. And this time he could not even plead the excuse of youth!

Luke could scarcely believe that he had been on the brink of falling in love with that calculating hussy. He had sworn when Georgiana betrayed his affections that he would never allow another woman to get close to him. Well, he was certainly paying for his folly!

He had thought Ianthe Garland different to the rest of her sex. She had seemed so warm and sincere, but her only purpose in pretending affection was to deceive him.

Luke's long fingers clenched the reins. Most women were satisfied, he'd discovered, by a few gifts. Ianthe's greed went further. She had planned to get her hands on his entire fortune!

He had been in danger of becoming so besotted that she would have had no difficulty in persuading him to indulge her every whim. He would have willingly given her whatever she asked for: only look how he had dipped into his pocket to save Northwood! He had wanted to shield her from anxiety and distress. Hellfire, he'd even believed that she knew nothing about the debts which threatened her home until he had overheard her talking to Turner.

After paying their shot, he had realised that he had not given Turner Nicodemus's address. Deciding that it might be needed, he had requested pen and paper from the landlord and quickly written it down. Approaching the garden, he had heard raised voices. Under normal circumstances he would have immediately made his presence known, but he had froze to the spot when he grasped what was being said.

Luke overtook a waggon with barely an inch to spare and never heard his valet's gasp of alarm.

How clever Ianthe had been! Her tactics would have done credit to Wellington. First she had intrigued him by her silence and seeming indifference, then, once his interest was caught, she had drawn him deeper into her toils by asking him about his travels and displaying her intelligence. With each passing day she had tightened her net, offering him the kind of perfect friendship he had never expected to find with a woman.

Nor had she neglected to fan his physical desire. Her gowns had grown steadily more revealing, their fussiness slowly discarded to show off her slender curves. At the same time, she had maintained a wide-eyed innocence which was more enticing than direct invitation. Unlike some women, she knew the value of restraint! A teasing smile here, a languorous sigh there, and all the while keeping him at arms' length, even on that day at Waverley Abbey when they had been alone for hours.

Had she meant to force a proposal out of him then? Luke stared moodily at a point somewhere above his horses' ears. Perhaps she had been reluctant to make the attempt without witnesses to seal her triumph.

A flood of bitterness washed over him as he remembered how soft and yielding she had felt in his arms. He could have sworn her response was genuine. Her mouth had trembled beneath his as if she had never before experienced the thrill of arousal. What an actress she was! She could give the performers at Drury Lane a run for their money and no mistake!

Ianthe Garland had almost persuaded him that it was safe to love again, but he had discovered her true nature just in time. He had not yet decided on the method, but he was going to teach her that her intended victim was not so gullible as she imagined.

And his revenge was going to taste very sweet!

It began to rain heavily as Ianthe and Augustus arrived home. The downpour continued over the next few days and Ianthe found the dreary weather echoed her mood. Confined to the house by the constant rain, she tried to convince herself that the lack of activity was responsible for the hours seeming so endless and empty.

The absence of a letter from her fiancé had nothing to do with her gloom, she assured herself. In her heart, however, Ianthe knew she was lying. She couldn't understand why

Luke had gone off in such a hurry without even a word of farewell. A horrible suspicion that he might have regretted his generosity, perhaps even regretted proposing to her, kept insisting on rearing its ugly head.

She did her best to hide her uneasiness. The announcement of her engagement brought many callers to Northwood and she had too much pride to let anyone see her without a smile. Everyone imagined she must be happy and excited and she made sure she fulfilled their expectations.

She had toyed with the notion of confiding in her grandmother, but the Dowager's transparent joy had curbed her tongue.

'I cannot tell you how delighted I am by your news, my dearest,' her grandmother had exclaimed. 'You must tell me all about your young man. I have not seen him since he was in leading strings and I dare say he has changed more than a little!'

Ianthe had duly obliged, consoling herself with the knowledge that her betrothal had at least achieved its objectives. Her grandmother was safe and so was Northwood.

Or at least they would be, providing Luke Kildare kept his word!

Ianthe's gloom deepened as another week passed without any communication from Cumbria and she became convinced that he was having second thoughts about marrying her.

The third banns were called and the next day a letter arrived for her. A footman brought it into the morning-room, where she was sitting with Maria waiting for the carriage to be brought round so that they might visit the mantua-maker. Ripping it open eagerly, she saw that it was from Sophy.

'Does she say if her dress is finished?' Maria demanded on learning the identity of the writer.

'You may read it if you wish, ma'am.' Ianthe handed over the letter, concealing her disappointment behind a polite smile.

Maria scanned it and gave a nod of satisfaction. 'Your own dress ought to be ready today.' She returned the letter to

Ianthe. 'You did remember to tell your grandmother that you had the final fitting this morning?'

'I explained that I could not visit her as usual,' Ianthe replied in a quiet voice.

'Good. She will have to get used to your absence. You will be a married woman soon and cannot dance attendance upon her.'

Ianthe had already discussed this problem with her grandmother, who had firmly told her not to be a goose.

'I shall employ a companion,' she had announced. 'Mrs Pickford has a niece who sounds suitable.'

Ianthe had been a little startled to discover that the parson's wife had already written to this lady, a widow in her thirties.

'She is to come for an interview immediately after your wedding.' The Dowager had smiled at her granddaughter. 'I dare say we will rub along nicely if she is as agreeable as Caroline Pickford claims.'

'Are you sure this is what you want, Grandmama?' Ianthe asked doubtfully.

'I am.' The Dowager's tone was firm. She understood that Ianthe felt disturbed at the thought of someone else assuming her role and she longed to tell her that no one could ever take her place, but it was necessary to make a clean break. 'Employing Mrs Clarke will help me keep my independence. I do not wish to have to rely on Maria for anything.'

She patted Ianthe's hand. 'I shall miss you, dearest, but you must not worry about me. You will have other duties and concerns. Even if you return to live at Northwood at some future date our lives cannot go on in the same way.'

Ianthe had reluctantly agreed. Her marriage would change everything.

The ceremony was to take place this Friday. Harry and Sophy were to arrive the day before, the Bishop having given the visit his blessing. The Reverend Pickford had agreed to yield his role and acceptances from all the guests had been received.

Maria was in her element. She had escorted Ianthe on trips

to the mantua-maker, drawn up an elaborate menu for the
wedding-breakfast and organised how the ancient church was
to be decorated with flowers.

She hadn't said a word to Ianthe to indicate that she knew
what had actually happened at Kildare Park and Ianthe had
come to the conclusion that Augustus had not told her how
he and Lady Kildare had surprised herself and Luke in a compromising situation. Maria did not like to know unpleasant
details, although she was perfectly prepared to go along with
her husband's dubious activities!

Augustus himself was keeping out of Ianthe's way. She
suspected that, after their furious argument in the garden of
the Crown, he was wary of provoking her in case she thwarted
him by withdrawing from the betrothal. She had been so angered by his refusal to accept that she had not tricked Luke
that she had screamed at him like a fishwife, venting many
months' pent-up frustration and disgust in a scathing casti-
gation of his faults.

Her tirade had lasted a full five minutes and he had been
so taken aback that he had sought refuge in offended silence
all the way home. She knew she ought to be ashamed of
losing her temper in such a spectacular fashion, but she could
not bring herself to regret it.

'The carriage will be at the door by now,' Maria announced, getting to her feet. 'Let us be off or we shall be late
for our appointment with Madame Claudine.'

Ianthe followed her stepmother from the room. They were
not the only ones who were cutting it fine. In four days' time
she was supposed to be marrying Luke Kildare and she had
still not heard a word from him.

She smiled bitterly to herself. It was beginning to look as
if it was the bridegroom refusing to go ahead with the wedding that Augustus ought to be worrying about!

Lord Kildare and Mr Nicodemus Stratton arrived in London
on a rainy Wednesday evening. Mr Stratton had elected to
stay at the Clarendon and this exclusive establishment re-

ceived them with its customary lavish hospitality. After an elegant dinner, Mr Stratton announced his intention of seeking his bed after their long and tiring journey from Cumbria.

'I'm not as young as I was,' he'd murmured by way of apology.

Luke, who had been surprised at the deterioration in his godfather's stamina since their last meeting three years ago, had not attempted to persuade Nicodemus to change his mind, but had taken himself off to Watier's where he played faro and drank a great deal of brandy without displaying any sign of pleasure in either pursuit.

In the morning he breakfasted with Mr Stratton in his room and his godfather asked him if he had enjoyed his evening.

'I won several hundred pounds,' Luke shrugged carelessly. 'But I've a devilish head.'

'You don't look it.' Mr Stratton stifled an envious sigh. Fifteen years in India had left their mark upon his health, which even the clean air of his native Cumbria had not been able to eradicate.

Not that he regretted his service with John Company. He had amassed a very considerable fortune, a fortune which could indeed have been even larger had he been inclined to be rapacious. But he had liked India too much to be greedy.

When Luke had come to stay with him six years ago to recuperate in wounded body and spirit, he had planted the idea of going there in Luke's receptive mind.

'Now that the Company's monopoly has been abolished, I've a mind to do a little trading on my own account,' he'd announced. 'Would you care to join me?'

Luke had been concerned that he had no experience of anything other than soldiering, but Nicodemus had reassured him. 'You're an intelligent lad, Luke, and you learn fast. Even better, you are used to handling men. Oh, you'll make mistakes, but if you will accept my tutelage I think you shall do very well.'

The livid scar on Luke's face had stood out as he coloured in pleasure at his godfather's praise, but he had said slowly,

'I don't want to let you down, Nic. We owe you too much already.'

Mr Stratton had frowned theatrically at him. 'I do hope you are not going to harp on again about that trifling sum—'

'It was not a trifling sum, Nic,' Luke interrupted quietly. 'Your generosity has saved my family from financial ruin.'

Nicodemus had abandoned his attempt to defuse the subject with levity. 'Your father was my best friend, Luke. I consider it a privilege to have been in a position to help.'

'But that money must be a loan, not a gift,' Luke had insisted. 'I cannot allow you to pay for my father's disastrous gaming losses.'

Nicodemus had hesitated, wondering how to answer.

Edmond's weakness for cards had grown slowly over the years. A jolly man with no eye to the future, he had closed his mind to the way his gaming was bleeding the Kildare estates dry. When at last he had realised how serious the situation had become, his attempts at retrenchment were futile.

He had kept his losses a secret from his family, but the strain had killed him. On discovering the extent of his debts, Nicodemus had stepped in to prevent Kildare Park going under the hammer.

'Very well, I'll be frank with you, Luke. Paying off your father's debts has wiped out my reserves. That's one of the reasons why I am thinking of going out to India. I've contacts there and I believe I can restore my fortune, but it's not my only reason for wanting to go.' He smiled. 'I'm bored and I'd like one last adventure before I'm too old. You can help me achieve that dream.'

Nicodemus had seen from his sudden eager expression that his words had touched a chord in Luke. He sensed that Luke, even more than his desire to repay the loan, yearned to make a fresh start. His father's death and that treacherous little madam's heartless rejection, coming on top of the injuries he had received at San Sebastian, had left him dangerously low in spirits. It was Nicodemus's hope that a complete change of scene would bring Luke the peace of mind he craved.

Nicodemus's faith in his beloved India had been justified. That strange and magical land had restored his godson's shattered self-esteem and confidence. Unlike many of his contemporaries, Luke had learnt to appreciate native culture and enjoy it and India had repaid his efforts generously. Even before he had acquired that gem mine in Ceylon, his talent and industry had amassed enough money to pay back Nicodemus's loan twice over.

Sadly for himself, after three busy years Nicodemus had been forced to return home to England when he could not shake off a recurring fever which drained his strength. They had wound up their trading partnership and closed their books, but Luke had elected to stay in India. He had wandered with no other aim in mind than satisfying his curiosity and taste for adventure. His letters home had delighted Nicodemus, who had rejoiced that his godson had so fully recovered his zest for life.

Finding the sapphires had made Luke very rich indeed. No doubt their discovery had tipped the balance in favour of coming home. However, Nicodemus was convinced that something had happened recently to disturb Luke's hard-won equanimity. He was concealing it much better than he had been able to do six years ago, but Nicodemus suspected that it was once again a case of *cherchez la femme*!

Which led him to say with apparent innocence, 'Do you mean to visit Northwood this morning?'

Luke set down his coffee cup. 'I think not. There are several matters which require my attention in town.'

'May I ask you something, Luke?' Nicodemus received a swift nod of consent, but took a thoughtful moment to smooth the lapels of his silk banjan before speaking again. 'Are you sure you want to go ahead with this marriage?'

'Why do you ask?' Luke's voice was utterly toneless.

'You haven't seen Miss Garland in three weeks, but you don't seem in any hurry to visit her,' Nicodemus replied mildly.

'As I've already said, it is a marriage of convenience.'

'Even more sensible, then, to call it off if you've decided you ain't keen.'

'The announcement of our intention to wed has been posted. I cannot in honour withdraw.'

'True. However, if you've changed your mind, it might be better for you both if you asked Miss Garland to release you.'

'I doubt she would care to do so.' Nicodemus saw a flash of anger darken his godson's grey eyes. 'And in any event, I have no desire for the world to think me jilted a second time!'

Luke shrugged. 'I know you have my best interests at heart, Nic, but you are wasting your concern. I intend to go ahead with the wedding for the reasons I outlined to you previously.'

Nicodemus suppressed a snort of disbelief. Luke had told him that his mother wished for the match and that there had been a threat of scandal, but he knew Luke too well to think that any power on earth could compel him to marry for such commonplace reasons. There had to be some other incentive!

'Is she very pretty, this Miss Garland?' he asked craftily.

Luke laughed. 'You'll see for yourself tomorrow.'

He stood up. 'May I execute any commissions for you after I have called in on my tailor?'

Nicodemus, who intended to visit Hamlet the silversmith in Cranbourne Alley to choose a wedding gift, shook his grey head and Luke went off to finish dressing.

After he had gone Nicodemus poured himself another cup of coffee and sat drinking it, his expression thoughtful. More than anything else in the world, he wanted Luke to be happy. It had grieved him to see how cynicism had changed the lad. A good marriage might restore his natural optimism, but he suspected that this union was already under threat.

Unfortunately, it was also obvious that his godson was not going to either confide in him or listen to advice. All he could do was pray that his misgivings were unfounded!

On the eve of her wedding Ianthe returned from a visit to the Dower House to find that a small package had been delivered for her.

'The courier brought this for you too,' said Maria, handing a letter to Ianthe. 'I take it they are from Lord Kildare?'

Ianthe opened the letter and nodded as she caught sight of Luke's bold signature. Her knees were trembling so much that she had to sit down on the scrolled armed sofa that adorned the rear drawing-room to read the few lines he had written.

'Well, what does he say?' Maria demanded impatiently.

'He has sent me a gift,' Ianthe replied, unable to prevent a little quiver in her voice as she explained that Luke did not intend to visit them before the wedding.

Maria put up her finely plucked brows. 'How very provoking! After all my efforts to welcome him with a celebratory dinner tonight! Now I suppose I shall have to make do with a brief exchange of greetings before the ceremony!' She heaved a petulant sigh. 'Still, I suppose I must not grumble. Business must have kept him in town.'

Ianthe thought how very like Maria it was to consider the situation solely from her own point of view. A less self-interested stepmother might have wondered at his lordship's lack of enthusiasm for his bride's company, but Maria was too wrapped up in her own disappointment to consider Ianthe's position.

Maria eyed the package in Ianthe's lap curiously. 'Aren't you going to see what it is?'

Mechanically, Ianthe opened the small box.

'Lud, you are a lucky girl!' Envy filled Maria's tone as a magnificent betrothal ring was revealed.

Ianthe stared down at it, her heart thumping wildly. Set in heavy gold and flanked by two large diamonds, the enormous sapphire glittered in the light.

So lavish a gift…and yet sent without a single kind word!

'Aren't you going to try it on?'

'Later.' Ianthe snapped the box shut and rose abruptly to her feet. 'Pray excuse me. I must change for dinner.'

In her own room she stared at her wedding dress which was hanging up in readiness for morning. Everything was prepared for the ceremony. Sophy and Harry had arrived earlier together with Lady Kildare, who had travelled with them from Kildare Park. They were even now dressing for the elaborate dinner Maria had devised. All that was lacking was the bridegroom.

A wry grimace twisted Ianthe's mouth as she placed the ring-box upon her dressing-table. She supposed she ought to be grateful that Lord Kildare had bothered to inform her that he would be at the church at ten o'clock tomorrow as planned.

The cool formality of his letter danced in her brain. He had sounded so distant and withdrawn!

Tomorrow she was going to wed Luke Kildare and it felt as if she was marrying a complete stranger!

The morning of Miss Ianthe Garland's wedding to Lord Kildare dawned bright and clear. Freshened by the recent rain, the cottage gardens of St Michael's village glowed in the sunshine, competing with the pealing bells to welcome the bride as her carriage drove past on its way to the church.

Within its ancient stone walls sat the wedding guests, all happily commenting on this auspicious start to the marriage. The arrival of the bride on the arm of her guardian sent a collective sigh of admiration echoing around the pews.

Her gown of white lace over a white satin slip was deemed both fashionable and flattering to her tall slender figure. Modishly arranged ringlets peeped out from beneath an Angoulême bonnet of white threadnet trimmed with a white lace veil while pearls shone in her ears and around her neck.

Her bridal attendant was a brown-haired girl, demure in pink-sprigged muslin and plainly nervous as she approached the altar. Everyone noted the broad grin she received from Mr Kildare, who was conducting the ceremony, and smiled indulgently at her blushing response, which quickly changed back to serious concentration again as the bride handed her the posy of white and pink roses she carried.

It was the first time many of the guests had laid eyes on the bridegroom. His tall, broad-shouldered figure was clad in a superbly cut blue superfine coat, cream pantaloons, gleaming Hessians and an exquisitely tied cravat. A buttonhole of clove pinks completed the elegant picture, which so dazzled the guests that the extent of his fortune was not raised for at least a pair of minutes at the lavish reception which followed the ceremony.

Maria had spent many hours organising every detail of the wedding-breakfast and ensuring that Northwood looked its best for its future master's inspection and she was not at all pleased when her new in-law politely informed her that he and his new bride would depart within the hour.

'My apologies, Mrs Turner,' Lord Kildare said coolly. 'If we are to reach Hampshire before nightfall we must not linger.'

'Of course.' Maria forced a smile. Augustus had instructed her to comply with his lordship's wishes, whatever they might be, but she hadn't expected to find the man so stand-offish and abrupt! Not that he was rude exactly, but his grey eyes were as cold as ice.

And cursed with that dreadful scar too! Really, in spite of his vast fortune, she felt quite sorry for poor Ianthe!

Watching them from the other side of the drawing-room, Ianthe wondered what Luke was saying to put Maria into a flutter, but she didn't have time for further speculation as she was surrounded by well-wishers anxious to congratulate her.

'Lady Kildare.'

For an instant Ianthe failed to respond to her new name and then with an apologetic smile she turned to greet the man who had spoken.

'Mr Stratton.' She held out her hand and he bowed over it with a grace at odds with his frail appearance.

'Since my deplorable godson has neglected to introduce me, I hope you will excuse my approaching you in this manner.'

'I am very glad to make your acquaintance, sir. Luke has often spoken of you.'

Nicodemus wished he could return the compliment. She

wasn't what he had expected at all. Not a conventional beauty, but decidedly attractive and he liked her frank smile.

'A very interesting church, your St Michael's,' he said easily, choosing a safe opening gambit. 'Is it very old?'

'It was originally built in the tenth century, I believe, although there are many later modifications,' Ianthe replied shyly.

Nicodemus nodded. He had noted the splendid Jacobean pulpit, which prompted him to remark, 'I thought Harry conducted the service very well, didn't you?'

'Oh, indeed. He told me earlier this morning that he was nervous, but no one could have guessed it,' Ianthe commented, trying to study Luke's godfather without appearing too obvious.

She guessed that he was in his early fifties because he had been at Eton with the late Lord Kildare, but he looked much older. His skin had an unhealthy yellowish tinge to it and was very heavily lined, probably as a result of his years in India. Once upon a time he must have been a fine figure of a man, but now he was extremely thin and stooped so that his height was not immediately obvious.

However, his dark brown eyes retained their keenness and Ianthe felt sure that ill health had not affected his sharp wits. He was watching her like a hawk and she realised he was evaluating her suitability for her new position.

'I understand that you have invited Lady...my mother-in-law to be your guest at the Clarendon for a few days,' she murmured, her pulse fluttering nervously.

'I thought it wise to give you and Luke a little privacy and Amelia agreed with me.' He shrugged. 'I am a bachelor, so I cannot speak from experience, but it seems to me that embarking upon marriage is a tricky business. Both parties have to adjust to living together and that requires great patience and magnanimity. Or so I am told.'

Was he trying to warn her? Trying to advise her to be careful of Luke's present mood? She had barely exchanged a word with her new husband, but she had sensed a puzzling anger behind his mask of formal courtesy.

Ianthe put up her chin. 'I am perfectly prepared to be a tolerant wife, Mr Stratton. I just hope Luke will be equally forgiving of my shortcomings.'

He smiled at her as if her firm answer pleased him, but before they could continue their discussion Lord Kildare came up to them.

'We are required to cut the bride-cake,' he said to Ianthe in the same cool tone he'd used to take his vows.

Ianthe nodded and, after dipping a curtsy to Nicodemus, allowed her new husband to escort her to the flower-decorated table where they performed this little ceremony to the applause of their guests.

The final toasts were drunk and Ianthe excused herself to change into her new travelling-costume of bronze-coloured French cambric. Within a few minutes of her reappearance they were saying their farewells.

'Take good care of her, Luke, and I shall see you both in a week,' Amelia said, giving Ianthe an enthusiastic hug with no thought for crushing her own cherry-red figured muslin gown.

'Be happy, my dearest,' Ianthe's grandmother whispered, blinking away a sudden tear as Ianthe kissed her goodbye.

Ianthe smiled mistily at her and moved on to exchange embraces with Sophy and her new brother-in-law. Then she quickly kissed Maria's cheek, but Luke noted that she avoided Turner's attempt to return the same gesture and merely bade him farewell in a formally polite voice.

This deliberate snub stayed in his mind as he gave his horses the office to start and the curricle set off down the drive to a final chorus of good wishes.

Northwood was soon left behind as the curricle picked up speed. Lord Kildare's attention seemed to be focused upon his driving. Apart from a few polite enquiries as to her comfort, he made no attempt at conversation and Ianthe did not try to fill the silence.

In all honesty, she was feeling so confused and bewildered that she hardly knew what to say or think. The man who had returned to her from Cumbria was the cool cynical stranger she had first met at Kildare Park. It was as if all their long enjoyable conversations had never taken place!

She risked a glance at her new husband. His averted profile might have been carved in stone. A tiny sigh escaped her.

It was becoming clearer by the minute that his lordship did not share her hopeful view that today marked the start of sharing their minds, hearts and souls. In fact, his aloof attitude seemed to indicate the opposite, that he wanted no truck with tender sentiments at all.

Unless she wished to have her heart broken, she had better remember he wanted a marriage of convenience and banish any romantic daydreams of winning his love!

Chapter Eight

'Good evening, my lady.' Mrs Blenkinsop dropped a respectful curtsy. 'I trust you had a good journey. Your maid arrived safely a little while ago.'

Ianthe thanked the housekeeper, who had lined up all the staff at Kildare Park to greet their new mistress. Ianthe was tired and would have preferred to postpone this formality, but she summoned up a smile and said a few words to each of them.

Luke made a gesture of dismissal and the servants melted away leaving only the housekeeper behind. 'Cook has prepared a light supper, my lord, which is ready to be served at your convenience.'

'Excellent. We will sup in an hour, if that suits you, ma'am?'

Ianthe returned a nod of consent to his enquiry.

'Mrs Blenkinsop will show you to your rooms. I am sure you would like to rest for a while before we eat.'

'You are most thoughtful, sir.' Ianthe couldn't prevent a sharp edge entering her tone.

He raised his brows, but said nothing. Feeling tears spring to her eyes, Ianthe turned away quickly before she made a fool of herself.

It is just because you are exhausted that you find his icy courtesy so depressing, she told herself firmly, following the housekeeper to her new abode.

She had been given the spacious set of rooms which adjoined the apartments traditionally occupied by the owner of the house. Ianthe felt embarrassed at ousting her mother-in-law, but Amelia had insisted upon removing to another room.

'No doubt you will wish to redecorate, my love,' she'd told Ianthe cheerfully. 'But there isn't time before the wedding so I am afraid you will have to endure my tastes for now.'

Ianthe thought the bedroom charming with its Chinese silk wallpaper and beech furniture which had been carved and painted to simulate bamboo. A thick Axminster carpet in pale green covered the floor and curtains in a matching shade hung at the windows.

A cosy fire had been lit to ward off any hint of evening chill and for some strange reason Ianthe had to blink away fresh tears at the sight of it. She could have been so happy here, if only Luke's attitude was different. As it was, she felt an intruder, a wife who was unwanted.

Jenny, who had been unpacking, bobbed a curtsy at her entrance. 'Welcome home, your ladyship,' she said with a big grin.

'Shall I send up some tea, ma'am?' Mrs Blenkinsop asked.

'Please.' Ianthe untied the bronze silk ribbons of her chip-straw hat and removed it.

'If there is anything else you require, my lady, you only have to ask.'

Ianthe murmured her thanks and the housekeeper whisked out of the room, leaving her to sink into a comfortable chair placed to one side of the hearth. She ran a weary hand through her hair.

'You look tired, my lady,' Jenny said. 'I ordered some hot water to be made ready for you. A bath should help revive you.'

'You are an angel, Jenny,' Ianthe replied gratefully. 'I feel as if I have been bouncing over those roads for ever!'

'It's been a long day,' Jenny sympathised.

It had been necessary to get up early to be ready in time for the ceremony, which Jenny had unfortunately had to miss. As soon as she'd finished helping Ianthe into her wedding dress, she'd had to leave in order to arrive at Kildare Park ahead of her mistress so, while Ianthe sipped her tea and had a bath, she asked questions about how everything had gone.

By the time Ianthe went downstairs again she felt like a new woman. Soaking in warm rose-scented water had banished the weariness from her limbs and she had the satisfaction of knowing that she looked extremely elegant. Jenny had arranged her hair in a flattering style and her new aquamarine satin evening-gown suited her colouring to perfection.

Entering the drawing-room, she was determined not to let pointless doubts spoil her first evening in her new home. It was only natural that Luke should be feeling wary. He wasn't used to sharing his life and it was silly of her to expect him to act the part of a lover. She had to give him time to become accustomed to her presence. In the end his reserve must surely melt.

Lord Kildare rose to his feet at her entrance. He stared at her in silence for a moment and then said, 'You look lovely, my lady.'

Ianthe smiled at him, delighted by the compliment. 'Thank you.'

He did not smile back, but moved to ring the bell.

Tench appeared so promptly that Ianthe realised he had been waiting for the signal.

'You may serve supper now,' Lord Kildare told him and he offered Ianthe his arm to escort her to the dining-room.

Ianthe placed her fingers upon his sleeve. Beneath her touch she could feel firm muscle and bone, but she sensed his mental withdrawal. Dismay flickered through her, attacking her hopeful optimism. He was as remote as if he were on the moon!

Two places had been laid close to each other at the long table. 'I thought you might prefer things to be informal, my lord,' Tench murmured.

Luke nodded. 'A good idea. In fact, I think we shall serve ourselves.'

Tench nodded and, after fetching a decanter of wine from the sideboard and placing it on the table within his master's reach, he bowed and left the room taking both footmen with him.

'Would you care for some claret?

Ianthe nodded and he poured the clear red wine for her. She picked up her glass, but checked when he said, 'We ought offer up a toast to mark this special occasion, don't you think?'

Ianthe smiled at him uncertainly, unable to understand the mockery in his deep tones. 'You are right. It is our first meal together in our home,' she said shyly. 'Shall we toast our future happiness?'

'I was thinking more of saluting your cleverness, my lady.'

Ianthe coloured. 'Such praise is more than I deserve.'

He laughed and swallowed his wine in one long draught.

Ianthe set down her glass untouched.

'You do not drink, dear wife.'

'I find that I have no thirst.'

'Then perhaps I can tempt you with some food.' His lordship selected a dish of tiny lamb cutlets which gave off an enticing aroma of rosemary and placed several upon her plate for her. 'You will need to keep up your strength.'

Her great blue eyes flew to his in alarm and for a moment Luke almost relented. She looked so defenceless, so touchingly eager to please that his anger wavered, but it flared up again when she picked up her knife and fork and began to eat in a composed fashion.

How dare she sit there so calmly as if her conscience were clear!

New potatoes and baby carrots flanked the lamb and Cook had also sent up several side dishes to tempt their appetites. Tender chicken breasts poached in wine, asparagus, a dressed salad...everything looked delicious and Ianthe was sure that it must all be as good as it looked, if only she could taste anything.

'If the claret is not to your liking, what do you say to some champagne?'

'Why not? A wedding is an occasion for celebration, I believe,' Ianthe replied defiantly.

He smiled at her coolly. 'Indeed. And you have every reason to celebrate, do you not? You achieved your aim so easily.'

Ianthe stiffened. What did he mean by that remark? Surely he could not have guessed why Augustus had sent her here? Too afraid to ask, she took refuge in pretending interest in her meal.

Luke waited for an instant to see if she would answer him and then, his mouth compressing to a hard line, rang for his butler.

Tench speedily produced a bottle of champagne, which to judge by its chill, he must have had ready and waiting for them. He poured it out into two glasses and discreetly withdrew again.

'Drink up, my lady. We are celebrating.'

Ianthe promptly tossed back the contents of her glass. She had an immediate urge to sneeze as the bubbles exploded in her throat, but managed to hang on to her dignity. She set down her empty glass and stared at her husband across the table.

'You keep an excellent cellar, my lord,' she said pleasantly, trying to introduce a note of normality into the strained atmosphere.

Luke inclined his dark head. 'Thank you.' He refilled her glass.

'My father always said you could judge a man by the wines he served,' she murmured, an unconsciously wistful note in her voice.

'You still miss him, don't you?'

Startled by his abrupt question, Ianthe nodded. 'I kept wishing he could have given me away today.' She fingered the aquamarine and diamond necklace she wore, her thoughts regretful. 'I disliked having to accept Augustus's services.'

The mention of Turner brought the frown back to Luke's face and Ianthe sighed.

'Not regretting your bargain already, my dear? It is rather late for second thoughts.'

Ianthe picked up her glass, her eyes suddenly ablaze with temper. She was growing very tired of his persistent mockery. 'I think it is *you* who are having second thoughts, sir,' she said curtly, taking a large gulp of champagne.

It lit a glow in her stomach and gave her the courage to meet his angry gaze. 'However, I would point out that I didn't force you into this marriage. As you remarked at the time, we were both to blame for the circumstances that led to your proposal.'

Luke's attention appeared to be upon a bowl of hot-house nectarines and he took his time answering. 'Is that what you wish to claim? That our marriage was a mere accident?' he said at last, his voice harsh.

Guilt brought a flood of colour into Ianthe's face. 'What else?' She hastily put down her glass and hid her shaking hands in her lap where they could not be seen. 'And, since you ask, I do not regret marrying you.'

'I am glad to hear it.' Sarcasm fringed his lordship's deep tones. 'Although, I suppose, it is a little early to make such a declaration. Will you still hold to the same answer tomorrow, I wonder?'

There was a dangerous flame glittering in his eyes and Ianthe felt a little shiver run down her spine.

'I apprehend that you refer to my marital duties,' she answered in a completely toneless voice. 'However, I am perfectly prepared to fulfil my obligations.'

He laughed without mirth. 'Obligations? Hellfire, I hope you can do better than that, my lady! A little enthusiasm would not come amiss, you know. Considering what I have paid for the privilege.'

Ianthe felt her cheeks burn. She had no idea of what reply

to make. He seemed to want to hurt her and she could not understand why!

'If you have finished eating, perhaps you would care to retire to the drawing-room?' Luke cursed himself for a fool, but the sight of her stricken expression made him feel a brute.

'If you don't mind, I think I would prefer to go straight to bed. As I may have mentioned earlier, I am a little tired.'

'Not *too* tired, I hope.'

Ianthe lifted her chin. 'Naturally, I shall await your lordship's pleasure,' she said defiantly.

'I am sure you will.' Abruptly, Luke rose and, striding towards the sideboard, poured himself a large bumper of brandy from the decanter kept there. 'After all, I suspect you are about to reveal another of your talented accomplishments.'

Ianthe stared at him in bewilderment. 'I...I don't understand.'

'Don't you?' Lord Kildare's voice was as smooth as silk. 'Ah, well, we shall see. Now go to bed. I will join you when I have finished my brandy.'

He moved to open the door for her and, angry at being dismissed in such a manner, Ianthe stood up and walked stiffly across the room.

As she reached the door, however, she could see the bleak misery in his eyes and she made one final effort. 'Luke, please, don't let's quarrel.'

He ignored her outstretched hand. 'Until later, ma'am.'

Ianthe bit her lip and left the room in a furious rustling of satin skirts.

There was no sense in trying to prolong their discussion. She might as well leave him to his drinking!

'Goodnight, my lady.' Jenny gave her mistress an encouraging smile.

'Goodnight, Jenny, and thank you for all your help today.'

When her maid had gone Ianthe sat down in the chair near the fire and stared into the newly banked flames, her mind in a whirl. Too tense to relax, she stared across the room at the wide bed. Jenny had turned the covers down and it looked invitingly soft and comfortable.

Ianthe gulped and, unable to sit still, jumped up and began to pace about the room. Lord Kildare was in for a disappointment if he thought she would prove accomplished in the amatory arts!

Why on earth he had got such an idea in his head she couldn't fathom. Was it because she had stupidly responded to his embrace? A little snort of derision escaped her. According to rumour, he'd had dozens of mistresses. Did the coxcomb therefore think all women were mad for him?

Ianthe sighed. She was being unfair and she knew it. Luke could be high-handed and arrogant, but he didn't have a puffed-up opinion of himself. What's more, she *had* returned his kisses with passion. However, she hadn't a clue what would please a man. In spite of her brief interlude with Philip, she knew very little about the business!

Perhaps if her mother had lived she could have talked to her. As it was, when she was fifteen and her monthly cycle had begun, Maria had merely informed her that she was now capable of bearing children.

'You must keep yourself pure until you marry when, of course, you will submit to your husband's demands,' she'd said coyly without going into further details.

Ianthe had been too shy to ask questions, even of her grandmother. It hadn't really seemed important. Like the rest of her friends, she had been content to giggle in corners over a rare stolen kiss. Their youthful daydreams of romance had seemed far removed from what happened in the marriage bed.

Ianthe shuddered. Innocence was a virtue much prized!

Her restless pacing suddenly halted as she caught sight of herself in the long cheval mirror which stood near the washstand. What had made her buy such a revealing nightdress, she wondered? Normally she wore white lawn made sensibly high to the neck, but for her trousseau Madame Claudine had suggested this delicate cream silk. The material was beautiful and Ianthe had given way to the little Frenchwoman's persuasion.

The bodice had been exquisitely embroidered, but the neckline was cut shockingly low and the garment clung to her curves in a most vulgar manner. Ianthe eyed her reflection uneasily.

'Be honest,' she whispered to herself. 'You agreed to Claudine's suggestion because you wanted to wear something pretty tonight. And why? Because you still have hopes of capturing Luke's heart.'

She observed the hectic flush which rose instantly to her cheeks. 'You are a fool, Ianthe Gar—'

Ianthe Kildare. The name was now hers, but she could hardly believe that she was Luke's wife. She had actually married him, a man she scarcely knew.

Ianthe swallowed hard, remembering how she had felt when he had kissed her. It hadn't seemed to matter then that she didn't know him.

A knock sounded, loud in the silence. She spun round to see the door which connected her room to the master bedroom opening.

'You look surprised, dear wife. This is our wedding night. Surely you were expecting me?'

Lord Kildare stood on the threshold. He was wearing a dressing-gown of dark blue silk and he held a brandy glass in one hand. In the flickering candlelight, he seemed taller than ever as he advanced into the room, an enigmatic expression upon his dark scarred face.

Ianthe's pulse quickened. With a swift surge of dismay, she realised that it wasn't surprise but a queer mixture of fright and anticipation that was making her stomach churn.

'What? No reply?' A mocking smile curved Luke's well-cut mouth. 'Still, I don't suppose we have any need for conversation.'

He came to a halt just a few feet away and Ianthe felt her mouth turn dry. It seemed absurd that this stranger had the right to stroll into her bedchamber. Unable to speak, she stared at him in wide-eyed silence.

Luke stared back at her, his grey gaze travelling over her slender body. 'You are even more desirable than I imagined.'

His gruff words tightened the knot in Ianthe's stomach.

She watched him set down his glass on a side-table. He took a step towards her.

'I think it is time I...I explained something,' she gasped.

Luke raised his black brows. 'Now?' he said silkily, taking another step nearer.

Ianthe gulped. It was now or never! 'I want to apologise for the way our betrothal came about,' she said breathlessly.

'You told me a short time ago that it was my fault as much as yours,' Luke reminded her, his handsome face suddenly wary.

'I know.' Ianthe hung her head. Oh, how was she to explain? She so wanted to confess the truth, but she was scared that he would never feel the slightest particle of respect or affection for her if she did.

The silence hung heavy between them for an instant and then Luke took one last stride to close the gap which separated them.

'Just at this moment I'm not sure I care to listen to explanations,' he said hoarsely, reaching out to pull her into his arms.

Ianthe flung up her hands to hold him off. 'No, wait!'

'Is this your idea of being a dutiful wife?' Mockery infused Luke's tone, but his eyes were glittering with desire.

'I meant what I said over supper,' Ianthe whispered unsteadily, her breathing ragged. 'I will try to be a good wife to you.'

It was horrifying to discover just how much she wanted him to touch her, how much she yearned for him to find her desirable!

'But, please, I beg of you, listen to what I have to say first!'

Luke took a deep breath and reined in the desire which raged in him. 'Very well. What is it that is so urgent?' he demanded, folding his arms across his chest and surveying her through narrowed eyes.

'I have a confession to make.'

Luke became very still.

'I did not come to Kildare Park just to visit your mother. I came because I wanted to meet you.'

'Why?' Luke snapped the word with all the force of a whip-crack.

Ianthe screwed up her courage. 'Because you were an eligible *parti* and I hoped I might be able to capture your interest.'

Luke expelled his breath in a hiss. 'So you planned a trap for me to walk into,' he declared roughly, fixing her with a fierce gaze.

It required all Ianthe's resolve to meet it without flinching. 'That idea did cross my mind,' she admitted. 'But I found that I could not go through with it.'

'May I ask the reason behind your attack of conscience?' There was a wealth of irony in his tone and Ianthe shivered.

'Because…oh, because whatever you may think, not all women lack honour!' she exclaimed.

'Is that the only reason?'

Unwilling to confess her deep feelings for him, Ianthe hesitated and then nodded jerkily.

She was lying. 'I don't believe you,' Luke said flatly.

Ianthe gasped. 'Then at least believe that I had no idea you were in the garden that night! It was totally by accident that we met in Amelia's studio.'

She drew in a deep breath to try and calm herself. 'I swear I never wanted to compromise you.'

Luke looked down into her lovely eyes, which were misty with unshed tears. Could he trust her?

'Why are you telling me all this?' he demanded gruffly.

'It was on my conscience.' Ianthe gave a fierce shrug. 'And I don't want secrets between us.'

Her vehemence surprised a faint smile out of him and, encouraged, Ianthe laid a timid hand on his arm. 'Please, Luke, don't be angry with me. I know you didn't really want to give up your bachelor freedom, but we are wed now. Can't we try to live together without quarrelling?'

Cynicism warred with Lord Kildare's desire to believe in his wife's integrity.

Her unexpected confession had thrown him into confusion. What possible reason could she have for admitting to her deception except a genuine desire to be honest with him? Obviously, she had realised that he was angry and she must have decided he regretted being thrust into an unwanted marriage.

She seemed so sincere! Dare he believe that he had been mistaken? It was Turner who had said that she had planned to trap him. He had not actually overheard her reply.

Luke's anger began to dissolve. He knew Turner for a deceitful rogue, but until that evening at the Crown he had believed Ianthe to be that rare exception: an intelligent woman of principle. Even now, he noticed, she had taken responsibility for her behaviour and not tried to lay any blame upon Turner's shoulders.

He frowned. Turner had certainly had reason to push for the marriage. He'd been up to his ears in debt. Had he also been pressuring Ianthe in some way?

Ianthe saw his frown and felt sick. Her hand fell from his arm. Oh God, he didn't believe her! She had taken the risk of confessing and it had all been for nothing!

She turned so white that Luke instinctively grabbed her by the shoulders. Startled, Ianthe stared up at him, her breath catching in her throat.

'I...I thought you were about to faint,' Luke apologised, his voice a husky thread of sound.

'I did feel dizzy for a second,' Ianthe admitted softly.

He was still holding her. Ianthe could feel the warmth of his hands penetrating the thin silk of her nightgown.

'I don't want to fight with you, Luke,' she murmured. 'I want us to be friends.'

He stared down into her eyes and suddenly his severe expression softened. 'Do you know, I was thinking the same thing myself,' he said quietly.

Relief made Ianthe feel almost light-headed. 'Oh, Luke, I'm so glad!'

Her brilliant smile set alight the desire which had smouldered in him all evening. 'And I'm glad I married you, Ianthe,' he said huskily as his hands slid down to her waist and he drew her to him.

Their lips met in a passionate kiss and a wave of pleasure swept over Ianthe. The same liquid heat which she had felt when he had kissed her that night in Amelia's studio flowed through her veins. She clung to him for support, her very bones feeling as if they were melting.

A delicious languor stole over her as he expertly deepened the kiss. Obeying the pressure of his demanding mouth, she opened her lips. Their tongues entwined in an exciting duel of sensation that Ianthe wanted to go on forever.

Luke lifted his dark head and she had to stop herself from protesting.

He smiled down at her. 'Will you do something for me?'

She nodded shyly. Her whole body was tingling in a way she had never experienced before and, with a blush, she realised that she wanted him to do more than just kiss her. Strange, she had not felt this way when Philip had come to her room...

Ianthe suddenly stiffened. Oh God, she had not told him about Philip!

'Will you undo your braid for me?'

'My...my hair?' Ianthe found it hard to concentrate. Her mind was a chaotic jumble of thoughts. 'Jenny has just plaited it for the night.'

'I know,' Luke replied gently. 'But you have such beautiful hair and I would like to see it loose upon your shoulders.'

Mechanically, Ianthe undid the ribbon which tied the thick braid. Dare she tell him about Philip? She wanted no secrets to spoil their marriage, but would he understand?

Her fingers untwisted Jenny's tight weaving, freeing the

heavy mahogany mass. Even more important, she thought anxiously, would he be able to forgive her?

'That looks better.' Luke wondered at her sudden pallor.

'It needs brushing,' Ianthe murmured automatically.

'Then let me act as your maid.' Luke took her hand and led her over to the dressing-table. 'Sit down and I will brush it for you.'

She was nervous, which was hardly surprising, he supposed. Maybe if he could help her to relax, that look of agitation in her big blue eyes would vanish.

Ianthe watched him pick up her silver-backed brush. He began to draw it smoothly through her hair. With a slight stab of bitterness she realised he must have had considerable practice.

The rhythmic movement was soothing. Slowly, she fought down her sense of panic. She must tell him about Philip. Otherwise, guilt would eat away at her happiness. It wasn't in her nature to keep secrets. Only look at how miserable trying to conceal Augustus's plan had made her!

Luke was a reasonable man. Beneath his cynical manner, he had a kind heart. Her youthful indiscretion had been wrong, but surely he would be able to understand that she had been too love-struck to think of anything but the fact that Philip was leaving to go off to war?

No doubt Luke would be disappointed. She had broken the sacred rule of society and custom and she wouldn't blame him if he became angry. Gathering her courage, she looked into the mirror. 'Luke, there's something else I must confess,' she began nervously.

His gaze met hers. 'If it is about the debts Turner incurred, there is no need,' he said softly.

A wave of colour rushed into Ianthe's face. Oh God, this was so difficult! He had been more than generous already and she hated the thought of letting him down again!

Luke's brushing halted mid-stroke and his free hand tightened on her shoulder. 'Sweetheart, don't worry. I don't blame you for Turner's behaviour.'

Ianthe's mouth was dry with anxiety. She ran her tongue over her lips to moisten them and in the mirror she saw Luke's expression change as he watched her.

'Forget the past. I'm only interested in the here and now,' he said thickly, clasping her about the waist and drawing her effortlessly to her feet.

'Luke, I must tell you something first,' Ianthe's voice came out in a whisper.

'No.' He kicked the velvet padded dressing-stool which stood between them to one side. 'Not now. What ever it is, it can wait for the morning.' He pulled her against him and buried his face in her neck.

The touch of his lips against the soft skin of her nape made Ianthe sigh with delight, but her conscience prodded her into making one final effort. 'Luke, please. It's important.'

He lifted his head and she heard the rasp of his indrawn breath. 'Not as important as making love to you,' he said hoarsely, his hands sliding up her body to cup her breasts.

Ianthe gasped. In the mirror she watched him caress her nipples. Pleasure rippled through her.

Luke's gaze locked with hers. 'I've wanted you for too long. I won't wait any longer,' he declared fiercely and spun her round to face him.

Ianthe closed her eyes as his mouth descended to hers. The kiss was long and deep and the last faint protest of her conscience went unheard as she twined her arms around his neck and pressed herself eagerly against him.

She felt his rigid arousal. But, to her astonishment, she was not repulsed by it, but excited!

Before she could guess what he meant to do, he gave a tiny groan and swept her up into his arms. He carried her over to the bed and set her down gently. Still cradling her in his embrace, he took passionate possession of her lips once more.

Ianthe kissed him back with untutored enthusiasm and when they finally broke apart for want of air, Luke raised his brows at her. 'If this is your idea of duty, I am all in favour of it, my lady.'

There was a hint of laughter in his voice and Ianthe blushed. She didn't understand it, but his intimate touch had a completely different effect on her than Philip's. Instead of feeling embarrassed and repelled, she didn't want him to stop.

'I like it when you kiss me,' she whispered.

'Then let me kiss you again,' he replied wickedly.

Ianthe gave herself up to bliss and after a few moments felt his lips leave hers to blaze a trail of fire down the slim column of her throat. She trembled in his arms as he kissed the tops of her breasts, which were exposed in her low-cut nightgown.

He stopped as he reached the edge of her bodice. Sitting up, he slanted a smile at her. 'This is very pretty, but it is in my way,' he murmured. 'Come, let me take it off.'

Ianthe couldn't believe her ears! 'You want to remove my nightgown?' she gasped.

She had never expected him to make such a scandalous suggestion. Was this what married people did? She stared at him in wide-eyed shock.

Luke, habituated to more frank India customs, misunderstood her objection. 'Don't fret, I promise I will be careful not to tear it.' He pulled her gently upright. 'Just lift up your arms.'

'But…but you are wearing your nightclothes,' Ianthe protested.

He laughed. 'So I am. Do you think that unfair of me?'

Ianthe nodded shyly. To her surprise, he immediately stood up and untied the belt of his robe. With one quick movement he shrugged it off and let it fall to the carpet.

'Oh!' It had never occurred to Ianthe that he might not be wearing a nightshirt.

His body was beautifully made. Broad shoulders, deep chest, narrow waist and hips and long, long legs…muscle and bone had been sculpted into a perfection to rival the marble statue of Apollo which graced the rose garden. But, unlike Apollo, he was warm and alive!

Realising she was staring at his naked body, Ianthe hastily averted her gaze.

'Your turn, sweetheart.' He bent towards her and Ianthe, who wanted to please him, blushingly abandoned modesty and raised her arms.

Her nightgown joined his robe on the carpet.

Luke stared down at her and the laughter died out of his face. 'My imagination did not do you justice,' he said huskily and sank down on to the bed beside her.

His hands slid over her smooth skin, exploring her slender curves with an intense delight. 'You are so lovely, sweetheart,' he murmured.

Ianthe sighed with pleasure at his touch.

Luke caressed her breasts, trailing his fingers gently over her nipples. 'Do you like this?' he asked softly, rolling each one between finger and thumb until they grew hard and tight.

Ianthe answered him with an eager kiss.

Luke's hands strayed lower, moving over the fascinating curves of her hips, stroking the gentle swell of her stomach.

Ianthe stiffened as he touched the soft mahogany curls at its base and Luke lifted his mouth an inch away from hers.

'It's all right, there's no hurry,' he whispered, removing his hand.

Ianthe stared into his eyes. They were glittering like bright silver and his breathing was ragged, but when he smiled at her, her nervousness fell away. Silently, she took his hand and returned it to its former position.

Luke caught his breath. 'Are you sure you are ready, sweetheart?'

She nodded. 'You are my husband, Luke,' she whispered. 'I want to love you.'

'And I am aflame for you,' he replied hoarsely.

His mouth swooped down to her breast and covered her nipple. The hot moist rasp of his tongue, gentle at first and then harder, against her sensitive skin made Ianthe gasp. Delight flowered in her and she clutched at his broad shoulders with a little moan of satisfaction.

Encouraged by her response, Luke's fingers slipped between the cleft of her thighs and began to stroke her most sensitive flesh.

Ianthe clung to him, bewildered by what was happening to her own body. The feelings he was arousing in her were utterly new and so exciting she couldn't keep still. She wanted something to happen, but she didn't know what.

'Gently, my sweet! I won't be able to wait if you keep doing that,' Luke gasped with a hint of laughter in his voice as her hips writhed against him.

Ianthe wasn't entirely sure she understood what he meant, but instinct told her that he held the key to satisfying the need that burned within her.

'I can't help it,' she whispered against his lips, one hand caressing the firm muscular expanse of his chest. A soft haze of dark hair covered his tanned skin. She ruffled it experimentally and, growing bolder, stroked his flat copper nipples.

Luke seized her hand and pressed a kiss into her palm. 'You are utterly adorable,' he muttered.

Ianthe smiled at him confidently, revelling in her new-found power. She had never imagined how marvellous love-making could be! 'I want to know what pleases you,' she murmured.

'Then touch me the way I have touched you,' Luke said, releasing her hand.

Ianthe realised that she wanted to explore his body the way he had explored hers. With a smile she ran her fingers over his ribs. Just above his waist she felt a raised ridge of thickened tissue and paused, saying quickly, 'Luke, you were hurt! What happened?'

'A dispute with a *chasseur à cheval* at Fuentes de Onoro.'

Ianthe's exploring touch discovered two further scars. 'Indian souvenirs,' Luke said laconically. 'Do you find them repulsive?'

Ianthe shook her head. 'I don't like to think of you having been hurt, though.' She lifted her hand to his damaged cheek and touched it with butterfly lightness. 'You never speak of how you were injured at San Sebastian.'

'Sheer stupidity.' Luke forced himself not to flinch away. 'I didn't have enough sense to avoid a Frenchman determined to decapitate me.'

He frowned at the memory. The storming of San Sebastian had been unsurpassed in horror. After hours of murderous heat, an appalling thunderstorm had broken over their heads as the men marched into the trenches. The eerie darkness had only added to the mounting tension. When it had begun, the slaughter in the breaches was so ghastly that there were not enough officers left alive to control the victorious troops when they finally entered the town.

He'd been injured trying to protect a Spanish family who had got in the way of some French soldiers trying to escape. The pain had been indescribable, the worst he'd ever known. At first, he thought he had been blinded; there had been so much blood that he couldn't see. Later, he had been so weak from the wound-fever that followed, the surgeons reported that he would die. It had been weeks before he was strong enough to be sent home to England.

Worn to skin and bone, his cheek a weeping mass of horror…God, was it any wonder he'd frightened the ladies!

'I'm sorry. I shouldn't have asked,' Ianthe said softly.

Luke shrugged off his demons. 'One day, if you wish, I will tell you about it,' he promised. 'But I don't want to talk about the past now.'

Ianthe nodded. 'Tonight is just for us,' she whispered in agreement and, stretching up, she kissed his damaged cheek to show him that she didn't care about his scar.

Immensely touched by her gesture, Luke smiled and, turning his head, found her mouth with his.

The kiss, gentle at first, swiftly became passionate and the tide of excitement rushing in Ianthe's veins became a flood of wild abandonment. She felt she was dissolving, her body melting in a fierce hot pleasure.

Each caress tightened the spiral of tension within her. Every nerve in her body was alive and screaming for satisfaction.

Breathless and giddy, she gasped his name, her voice sounding strange in her own ears.

Luke could feel her liquid heat beneath his stroking fingers. 'Sweetheart,' he breathed and moved above her.

Her thighs parted eagerly to receive him, but anxious not to hurt her, Luke clung to self-control and was as gentle as possible. To his astonishment, there was no resistance to his entry and he slid home in one long thrust.

Shock held him motionless. He stared down at her. Her eyes were closed and she was breathing hard, an expression of pure pleasure on her face.

'Oh, don't stop! Please don't stop!' Ianthe gave a little moan, her nails digging into his broad shoulders.

'Damn you!' Luke muttered.

Deafened by ecstasy, Ianthe didn't hear him and arched her hips instinctively to urge him on.

With a groan, Luke thrust into her yielding softness. He couldn't stop, couldn't fight the desire raging in him. By God, she might be a deceitful bitch, but he wanted her more than he had wanted any other woman in his life!

Ianthe began to quiver in his arms as he moved rhythmically inside her. The knot in the pit of her stomach was growing tighter with every thrust and she could hardly bear the intensity of such pleasure.

She could feel her heart beating as if it must burst and heat enveloped her as a new urgency ripped through her body in scalding waves of ecstasy. Pleasure coursed through her, climbing and climbing...

'Oh, Luke!'

Delight exploded within her in a dazzling burst of sensation that left her dazed and speechless with wonder.

An instant later she felt Luke's body go rigid. She clung to him, holding him close as she felt him shudder in convulsive release.

They lay entwined for the space of another heartbeat and then abruptly Luke rolled free.

Ianthe opened her eyes, reluctantly floating back to earth. She felt so deliciously exhausted. 'Where do you get your energy from, my lord?' she asked in a tone of sleepy amusement as she watched Luke get up.

To her surprise he did not answer her, but bent to pick up his dressing-gown. Ianthe felt a prickle of alarm down her spine. She could not see his expression, but she sensed the tension in his body as he pulled on his robe. 'Luke? Is something wrong?'

Luke turned to face her and Ianthe gave a little gasp. In the candlelight, his classical features were a hard savage mask.

'Do you need to ask? Or do you imagine me to be a complete fool?'

Ianthe blinked. Surely she was asleep and dreaming? How could his deep voice be filled with contempt after the incredible sweetness they had just shared?

'I…I'm afraid I don't understand what you are talking about,' she said with a hesitant smile.

'You disappoint me, my dear. I thought you had more intelligence than to go on pretending once the game was up.'

He really did mean to insult her. Ianthe sat up hastily. 'Please, Luke! What is—?'

'Cover yourself, madam!'

Ianthe recoiled from the harshness in his snapped command. Snatching up the bedsheet, she draped it around herself with trembling hands. 'You are angry with me. Why?'

'Ianthe, spare us both this charade of wounded feelings, I beg of you!' Luke's well-cut mouth curled in disdain. 'It is a little late in the day to act the innocent.'

Every vestige of colour fled her face. She wasn't asleep. This nightmare was real!

'Exactly so, dear wife,' Luke said with a deadly softness as he watched her expression change. 'I knew that Turner was a cheat and a liar, but I hadn't realised that you were tarred with the same brush.'

'I tried to explain,' Ianthe exclaimed wildly. 'You wouldn't listen. You said that it could wait—'

'That was before I discovered the truth,' Luke cut in ruthlessly. He gave a harsh laugh. 'A man expects his bride to be a virgin, you see.'

Ianthe flinched, but remained damningly silent.

Luke clenched his teeth against a cry of anguish. Reason warned him that he was a fool, but he had longed to hear her protest that he was mistaken.

She looked so small and defenceless sitting in the middle of the wide bed, her hair tumbling about her shoulders. It blazed against the whiteness of her soft skin and her eyes were inky pools in the pallor of her face. He *wanted* to believe in her innocence.

'Am I wrong? Will you deny that you have lain with a man before tonight?' Luke strove to keep the eager hope out of his voice. A hymen could be broken by vigorous exercise and she was an excellent horsewoman.

Ianthe drew in a deep breath. 'No,' she said flatly. She stared down at her hands clasped in her lap. Her nails were digging into her palms, but she couldn't feel the pain. 'I gave myself to the man I hoped to marry the night before he left for Belgium.' She lifted her eyes to meet his fierce gaze. 'He didn't come back from Waterloo.'

'How very touching!'

The sarcasm in Luke's tone brought the colour back into her cheeks. 'I know it was wrong, but I was madly in love with Philip and—'

'Be silent!' Jealousy ripped through Luke. 'I don't want to know the sordid details.'

'You will condemn me without a hearing?' Ianthe gasped in dismay. 'How can you be so unfair?'

Luke gave a bitter laugh. 'You are in no position to prate to me of justice, my lady. You are a liar and a cheat, and you trapped me into this marriage for the sake of my money.'

'No! I swear I didn't—'

'Stop lying!' He stared at her in disgust. 'You planned a deliberate campaign down to the last shabby detail, even playing on my mother's fear of gossip, knowing how she dreaded loose talk after rumour painted my father's death from a heart attack as suicide.'

Ianthe swallowed the sob that rose in her throat. 'How can you imagine I would risk hurting Amelia? On my oath, I didn't know anything about his debts or those cruel rumours until I asked Maria about your father's death on my return home from my visit here.' Her voice quivered in distress. 'I know you are very angry with me, but, please, try to understand I didn't mean you to be hurt.'

'I understand that you are selfish and unprincipled.' Scorn blazed in his stormy eyes. 'Your stratagem may have brought you the marriage you craved, but you needn't think I will play the part of a besotted husband now that I know your true nature.'

Ianthe shrank against the pillows, her protests involuntarily silenced by the look of absolute fury on his face.

'Oh, don't worry! I don't believe in offering violence to women,' Luke snapped.

He had never hit a woman in his life, but, by God, he wanted to strangle her! She had taken his dream and smashed it and the pain was far worse than that of the sword slash which had destroyed his cheek.

'Luke, where are you going?' Ianthe demanded in a panic-stricken cry as he turned and strode towards the door which connected their rooms.

'Away from you, ma'am.' Luke wrenched open the door. He couldn't bear her expression of injured innocence a moment longer. It was salt in the wound that she continued to play-act in this ridiculous manner!

'Luke! Wait! Don't—'

The slam of the door answered her.

'Go.' Ianthe breathed the last word on a sigh that became a sob as she threw herself face down on the bed and wept as if her heart would break.

Chapter Nine

The experience of his wedding night convinced Luke Kildare that his wife was a dangerous woman. It would be all too easy to become a slave to the pleasures of making love to her delightful body. Logic therefore insisted that he avoid her bed.

It was not so easy, however, to avoid Ianthe during the day. He refused her repeated requests for a private interview and insisted that they took their meals in a state of utmost formality. By keeping a plethora of servants always about them it was possible to ensure that their conversation was confined to trivialities, but Luke was aware of her presence in a thousand subtle ways. No matter how he tried to ignore her, no matter how many long hours he spent in riding round the estate, he could not banish her from his thoughts.

Damn the woman! She was like a particularly irritating burr trapped under his skin!

After three days of torment, Luke decided to take action.

When the servants had removed the covers and set out their dessert of nuts, fruit and candied sweetmeats on the fine polished table at dinner that evening, he dismissed them. Ianthe, who was seated at the other end of the table, looked up in surprise at this change in routine.

'I've something to tell you,' Luke announced curtly. 'I'm going away.'

Ianthe's heart began to beat rapidly. 'To London?'

He shook his head. 'Brighton. London is dead at this season.'

His mother was also in London and he had no wish to face a barrage of questions.

Ianthe paled and Luke was furious with himself for the stab of sympathy which pricked him.

'I see,' she said quietly, toying with the hot-house peach upon her plate. 'When will you return?'

'I haven't decided yet.'

She was trying to mask her reaction to his brusque announcement, but her eyes betrayed her.

'Would you care to accompany me?' Luke couldn't believe what he had just said. Was he mad? Why the devil had he invited her along when the whole idea was to get away from her?

A dazzling smile transformed her face. 'I have never been to Brighton,' she said a little breathlessly. 'I should very much enjoy visiting it with you.'

Ridiculous pleasure flickered through Luke at her words. Suppressing it sternly, he shrugged. 'It makes very little difference to me one way or the other. Just don't expect me to spend all my time squiring you around.'

'I'm sure I shall manage to amuse myself,' she replied with a determined cheerfulness.

Luke conquered the impulse to retract his statement and assure her that he would be happy to show her the sights. 'I thought to set off tomorrow. Will that suit you?'

'So soon? Won't it be difficult to find accommodation at such short notice?'

He gave her a cynical smile. 'The place will be bursting at the seams, but I'm sure I can find us a suitable house.' He poured himself a glass of Carcavellos wine. It had been a favourite of his when he had been in Portugal and he'd ordered a case from his wine merchants on his return home. Its rich topaz colour reflected its sweet strong taste and he allowed himself to savour it upon his tongue for a deliberate

moment before slanting a cruel glance down the table.
'Money can buy anything.'

Ianthe bit her lip. He was mocking her again.

Luke saw the excitement die out of her face. An odd pang
of regret filled him. She'd looked so happy.

He cracked a walnut between his strong fingers. Fool! Did
he have to remind himself how basely she had treated him?
He'd come dangerously close to losing his head over her.
Even now when he knew her for a liar and a cheat, her lovely
smile still had the power to make his heart perform somersaults.

'Will you excuse me?' Ianthe pushed back her chair. 'If we
are to leave tomorrow, I must speak with the housekeeper and
give my maid instructions about packing.'

Luke nodded, aware of a perplexing annoyance at losing
her company.

He rose and courteously held open the door for her, fighting
the desire to ask her to stay.

His butler discreetly re-entered the room. 'Is there anything
further you require, my lord?'

'Aye, pass me the port, Tench,' Luke replied, sitting down
heavily.

The butler placed the decanter at his elbow. 'Will that be
all, sir?'

Luke nodded and, left alone with his port, stared moodily
into the ruby heart of his wineglass. A bitter sense of frustration filled him. He had no idea how to breach the barrier he
had erected to separate Ianthe from him. Even more confus-
ingly, he had no idea why he should wish to tear it down.

Apart from the fact that he still wanted her, of course. One
night had not slaked his appetite. A bitter smile passed over
his features. Experience had taught him that it was not necessary to like a woman to desire her. Lust did not depend
upon friendship or intimacy.

Luke took a swallow of port and then set down the glass.
There was no use in attempting to get drunk. He'd tried that
solution these last three nights and much good it had done

him! He'd ended up pacing his bedroom floor, fighting the compulsion to barge into her room and snatch her into his arms.

'Bloody fool!' he castigated himself in a savage undertone as he abruptly abandoned the dining-room.

It was a fine evening and he decided to take a turn about the garden. The exercise might help take his mind off his treacherous wife.

Half an hour later, having made a brisk circuit of the ornamental lake, Luke settled on his favourite bench in the rose garden. He pulled a flat silver case from his pocket and took out a cigarillo. He'd acquired the habit in Spain and, although he only smoked occasionally, he usually found it soothing.

He lit the cigarillo, using the tinder-box he had left on the bench earlier. His walk had been as useless as his other methods of forgetting Ianthe.

He watched smoke drift upwards on the gentle breeze. Why had he asked her to come with him to Brighton? It was sheer folly! Well, he'd just have to make the best of it. The place was noted for its amusements. With luck, he'd be too busy to find her presence disturbing.

Anyway, it was too late to withdraw the offer now. She'd have told the housekeeper that they were leaving and he was damned if he'd give the servants any more opportunity to gossip.

Luke frowned. He'd seen the reproachful looks cast his way. Ianthe was very popular with everyone at Kildare Park and his coldness towards her had not gone unmarked. Not that he cared a tinker's curse what they thought, but it irked him to be assigned the role of an unfeeling brute when *he* was the one who had been maligned.

He tapped ash off the end of his cigarillo. Unless he revealed the truth, his mother would also take Ianthe's part. She would want to know, for example, why he wasn't taking his bride to Italy on honeymoon. Luke had planned to surprise Ianthe with the trip once the weather had grown a little cooler.

She was well educated in the classics and he had thought she would enjoy seeing Rome.

A sour smile twisted his mouth. Brighton wasn't much of a substitute! On the other hand, it was more than the little wretch deserved. If he had any sense, he would lock her up in some deserted dungeon and leave her to rot!

That way at least he might be able to forget about her!

Luke threw down his half-finished cigarillo. Rising to his feet, he stamped it out with unnecessary force. Nothing seemed able to calm the angry irritability which festered in him!

Perhaps he would try reading. A book might help him to get to sleep. Otherwise, it was going to be a very restless night. Again.

Ianthe raised her hand to knock at the library door and then paused. She smoothed a wayward curl nervously. Perhaps she should have asked Jenny to redo her hair? Still, it was too late now. Gritting her teeth, she gently knocked on the wooden panel.

'Come in.'

Luke was standing at the large reading table which stood in the centre of the room. He was bent over it, studying a large volume and didn't immediately look up at her entrance.

'May I speak to you?'

His dark head jerked up at the sound of her quiet voice. 'What are you doing here?' he growled, straightening to his full height.

'Luke, we cannot carry on in this ridiculous fashion.' Exasperation gave Ianthe the courage to meet his fierce gaze. 'You have asked me to accompany you to Brighton. We *must* straighten things out between us before we leave!'

'You could always remain here.'

Ianthe's temper rose to meet the note of provocation in his deep voice. 'I could, but you would still have to face me when you got back. Unless you intend to keep on running away, of course.'

By God, she was accusing him of cowardice! Luke glared at her. 'What is there to discuss?'

'Our...our marriage,' Ianthe faltered, her boldness deserting her under the onslaught of his icy gaze.

'Our marriage is a business transaction, ma'am,' Luke retorted in clipped tones. 'Providing you behave yourself, I shall treat you generously. You shall want for nothing.'

Nothing, except any sign of affection, Ianthe thought with a sharp stab of pain.

'Now, if I have satisfied your concern, you may go.' Luke turned away, ready to return to Tacitus's *Annals*.

'*No!* You shall not dismiss me as if I were a housemaid.' To her own astonishment, Ianthe grabbed his arm.

Luke stared down at her white hand. It looked very small and delicate against the sleeve of his formal black evening coat. He couldn't quite bring himself to shake it off.

'Luke, please!' Misery rendered Ianthe's voice husky. 'Surely you cannot want to go on quarrelling?'

He lifted his gaze to meet hers and Ianthe immediately removed her hand. 'I beg your pardon,' she said in a trembling tone, trying not to let him see how his scorn had affected her. 'Only you must see that we need to talk.'

Luke leaned his hips against the edge of the table and crossed his arms. 'I see that I shall get no peace until you have satisfied your need to enact me a Cheltenham tragedy,' he drawled in a bored tone.

Ianthe prudently curbed her impulse to box his ears. 'I'm so glad you are willing to listen,' she said sweetly and crossed the room to where a settee in the Egyptian style with lotus arms and feet stood. She sat down and arranged her aquamarine skirts neatly before looking up at him with a determined expression.

A reluctant flicker of admiration stirred in Luke. By God, she was as tenacious as a bulldog puppy!

Ianthe waited for him to sit down. She hadn't been in this room since her return to Kildare Park. She had always liked its mellow oak panelling and old-fashioned furnishings, but now with a start of surprise she realised that a new portrait had been added to the collection which adorned the walls.

In the place of honour over the mantelpiece, expensively mounted in an ornate gilded frame, Amelia's study of her as Diana had been hung. She stared at it, a dozen conflicting emotions flickering over her expressive face.

Luke followed her gaze. 'My mother thought you would be pleased to find it displayed,' he said, his cool tone hiding the fact that he had been tempted several times to throw the damned thing on the fire.

'How...how kind.'

Ianthe belatedly realised that he intended to remain standing. 'I want to apologise,' she began in a low voice. 'I did not realise that you would be able to tell that I was not a virgin.'

She gulped, horribly conscious of his sardonic gaze. She had never been told the details of what to expect on her wedding night. Minor discomfort, nothing more, had accompanied Philip's fumblings, but the embarrassing act had been over almost before it had begun and it wasn't until she had managed to question Jenny yesterday, in what she hoped was a discreet fashion, that she learned it was usual for a girl to experience some pain and bleeding when deflowered.

'If I had known, I would have made more effort to enlighten you before...before it was too late. Please believe me, I never meant you to be disappointed.'

'What makes you think I was disappointed?' Luke demanded coolly. 'I knew exactly what kind of woman you were when I married you.'

She stared at him in confusion.

'I overheard Turner talking to you in the garden of the Crown Inn,' he informed her.

Ianthe swallowed hard. So it hadn't been that cat after all.

'I knew about your plan to trap me into marriage before you staged your little confession on our wedding night,' Luke continued in the same hard tone. 'A clever move that, my dear. You deflected my suspicions about you very neatly.' He paused and then added coldly, 'For a short time, at least.'

'I didn't even know you were suspicious!' Ianthe protested. 'Why should I?'

'Didn't it strike you as odd that I didn't write or attempt to see you before the wedding?'

Ianthe shifted uneasily upon the settee's green brocade upholstery. 'I thought you were having second thoughts about marrying me,' she admitted.

'Oh, I did!' Luke said silkily.

Ianthe stared at him. Why had he gone ahead and married her if he thought so little of her?

'As I told you before, it was time I took a wife and my mother approves of you,' Luke answered when she put this question to him. 'What's more, I had no fancy for the world to think me jilted.' His brow darkened for an instant and then he shrugged. 'However, all these considerations were nothing against the fact that I wished to enjoy your delectable body.'

Ianthe coloured hotly.

'I realise now that I could probably have got what I wanted without a wedding, but at the time marriage seemed the only way to achieve my object.'

Ianthe gasped. 'There is no need to be insulting!'

'And there is no need for you to go on pretending to be modest!'

Ianthe recoiled from the fury in his face. After a moment she found her voice again and said quietly, 'You have every right to be angry, but I beg of you to believe that I only gave myself to Philip on that one special occasion.'

'Why should I believe you when I know you for a liar? With your talent for deception, you could have slept with half the men in the county and no one the wiser.'

Pain seared Ianthe's heart. She had destroyed his trust in her!

Her blush had faded to a bleached bone pallor. Anguish had made him cruel and Luke silently wished he could retract his words.

'Never mind. Don't look so glum, my dear,' he said, using mockery to hide his true feelings. 'Just think of all the fun you can have spending my money.'

'If you knew me half as well as you seem to think you do, then you would realise that money is not high on my list of priorities!' Ianthe retorted with a flash of spirit.

'No?' Luke's expression was derisive.

'No! I would never marry a man simply because of his money.'

'Then why did you agree to marry me?' asked Luke with deceptive calm.

Ianthe's eyes widened in sudden dismay.

'Come, my sweet,' Luke insisted softly. 'I have given you my reasons. Pray return the compliment. If it wasn't my fortune that prompted you to accept me, what did?'

'I…I fell in love with you.'

The simple words echoed in the sudden silence and then Luke laughed.

'You disappoint me. I thought you much too intelligent to try such an old ruse!' His amused tone did not entirely hide his bitterness. 'Can't you think of a more original lie to try and convince me of your sincerity?'

Ianthe closed her eyes to try to shut out the pain invading every fibre of her being. She had known he would not believe her, but it still hurt.

'You asked for the truth,' she said, opening her eyes again and meeting his scornful gaze. 'I have given it to you. I wanted to marry you because I love you.'

'Stop it!' Luke commanded angrily. 'There is no need for this tedious pretence. I am not interested in love, real or otherwise. All I want from you is your presence as my hostess and your enticing body in my bed.'

Ianthe gasped, outrage overcoming her anguish. 'How dare—'

'When you have presented me with an heir and I have tired of you, you may go your own way.' Luke ignored her ruthlessly. 'Until then I demand fidelity and the appearance, in public at least, of a dutiful, complaisant wife.'

Ianthe shot to her feet. 'Go to hell!' She had no intention of allowing him to see the wounds he had inflicted.

'What's the matter? Aren't my terms generous enough for you?'

Infuriated beyond bearing, Ianthe hurled herself across the short distance which separated them and slapped his dark mocking face.

Luke grabbed her upraised hand. 'You little—' He bit off what he had been about to say as he stared down at her. She was breathing so hard that her breasts were threatening to pop out of her low-cut narrow bodice and desire leapt in him.

Ianthe realised her mistake as she saw his eyes cloud with passion. 'No!' she exclaimed as he dragged her into his arms.

She wrenched her head sideways to avoid his lips, but his strength was so much greater than hers that she could not prevent him from crushing her against his aroused body. A flicker of excitement flared in her, but, stubbornly ignoring it, she twisted violently in his hold.

'Let me go!' Too late, she understood that her frantic efforts to free herself were inflaming his desire...and her own!

'It's time you realised that I call the tune, my lady!' Luke said thickly.

His mouth claimed hers in a long hard kiss. Ianthe tried to concentrate on feeling outraged by his brutal tactics, but a slow insidious delight began to unfurl in the pit of her stomach.

Sensing her response, Luke gave a little growl of triumph. With an expertise that made Ianthe's knees buckle, his lips caressed hers, invoking a dizzying, terrifying pleasure.

'Luke, please don't do this,' she whispered as he eventually raised his dark head.

'Why not?' Luke's gaze rested insolently upon her bosom. 'Don't you like it?'

Ianthe blushed to the colour of a corn poppy. His touch gave her pleasure and he knew it!

'Deny it if you will, but your body tells me that you want me to make love to you.' Luke's fingertips brushed against her erect nipples.

Ianthe shivered. 'Not now. Not when you are still so angry with me,' she whispered.

A wave of tenderness unexpectedly swept over Luke. The scared look in her sapphire eyes made him long to tell her that she need not be afraid of anything ever again.

The knowledge that he wanted to keep her safe from all harm made him angrier than ever!

'What about your vow to obey?' he asked tauntingly. 'Do you mean to deny me my marital rights before we've even been wed a week?'

Ianthe bit her lip. 'It is my duty to admit you to my bed,' she agreed in a voice so low that he had to strain to hear her. 'But this feels *wrong*!'

She had not said it aloud, but Luke knew what she meant. He was treating her as if she was his whore and not his wife. For an instant, his conscience stung him, but he could not withstand the desire that raged in him.

'You must know that I would never hurt you,' he murmured persuasively, his arms tightening around her waist. He bent his head to kiss her. 'Have you forgotten how good it was between us?'

His lips brushed against hers. 'How could I?' Ianthe sighed.

Her mouth quivered under his. If she had not cared so deeply for him, she might have been able to hold on to her wrath and resist his expert caresses. But her heart undermined her mind's dictate. In his arms nothing seemed to matter, not pride, not anger, only love.

Luke's heart began to race as she kissed him back with the passion he had longed to know from her again.

His hands slid over her body, caressing her with a wild excitement. 'Shall we go upstairs?' he whispered in her ear.

An enchanting flush coloured Ianthe's cheeks. She nodded shyly.

He swept her up into his arms and carried her out of the room.

'Luke! The servants!' Ianthe gave a little scandalised cry.

He merely laughed and bore her up the main staircase to his room. He kicked open the door and carried her inside, setting her down gently by the enormous four-poster bed.

'Your maid?' he asked, busy pulling out the pins which secured her hair.

'I've already dismissed her for the night,' Ianthe murmured, running her fingertips down his spine.

Luke wondered if she knew what her touch was doing to him.

Her hair was loose now, tumbling down her back in a silky flood that glinted in the candlelight. He picked up one long strand and breathed in its perfume before pressing it to his lips.

'Let me help you.' He unfastened her gown and it slid into a puddle at her feet.

Ianthe stepped out of it. Clad only in her delicate lace-trimmed chemise, she watched him shrug off his coat. He tossed it carelessly onto an elbow chair placed near the bed. His pale lemon waistcoat followed.

Ianthe saw how his hands were shaking as he ripped off his elegant cravat and pulled his shirt over his head. These items joined the rest of his discarded clothes and she couldn't resist the temptation to trail her fingers over the tanned skin of his bare chest.

Luke caught her hand in a fierce grip. 'Tell me the truth,' he demanded urgently, pulling her close in one swift movement so that she fell against him. 'Do you do this out of duty or because you want to?'

His chest hair rasped softly against her breasts. 'I want you to make love to me.'

Luke expelled his breath on a sigh of satisfaction. For some reason he had *needed* to hear her say it aloud.

They helped each other off with their remaining garments.

'Maybe I'll dismiss Whinlock and give you his job,' Luke said somewhat breathlessly.

'But I don't know how to mix boot blacking,' Ianthe said with a tiny choke of laughter and Luke gave up trying to control his need to kiss her.

Still entwined in each other's arms, they fell onto the bed. Ianthe curled her hands around his neck, burying her fingers in the thick hair at his nape.

'You're shaking, sweetheart,' Luke said softly, gently stroking the curve of her hip.

'So are you,' Ianthe replied. She smiled up at him, all her fears banished by the sweetness of the moment. 'Do you, by any chance, know of a cure for our affliction, sir?'

He nodded solemnly. 'I do, my lady,' he answered and found her lips with his own.

The tender kiss swiftly turned to passion and a burning heat enveloped them both, melting the barriers between them. Each touch brought new ecstasy, binding them together and forging a bond that transcended suspicion and doubt.

Luke's last coherent thought before he was swept into a vortex of pure delight was that whatever else had been a lie, this intense passion they shared was unmistakably real.

Brighton, thanks to the Prince Regent's patronage, had been for some years the most fashionable resort in England. The Season was at its height and Ianthe had her first view of it at its gay, faintly raffish best.

The morning was bright and sunny, the sea a sparkling blue. A light breeze, tangy with salt, stirred the diaphanous pastel-hued muslins of the fashionable ladies promenading down the Steyne.

Ianthe felt a delightful sense of anticipation as she looked about her. It had been too late when they arrived last night to do other than take a little supper and retire to the best bed-chamber that the Castle Inn, the town's leading hotel, could provide. Waking refreshed, Ianthe had enjoyed a leisurely breakfast of hot rolls and coffee in bed while Luke had disappeared to confer with an agent about renting a house for their stay.

She had no idea how he managed it, but when he returned he informed her that they would be taking over the Earl of Dover's house in Royal Crescent.

'Would you like to go for a walk and see something of the town while it is made ready for us?' he asked.

Ianthe agreed eagerly. In his absence she had dressed in a pretty sprigged muslin gown and all she had to do now was select a broad-brimmed Villager hat in satin straw to complete her modish appearance.

While Luke's manner was still reserved, their journey from Kildare Park had proceeded amiably and Ianthe had high hopes that their stay here would result in a reconciliation.

Brighton was such a delightful spot, she thought to herself, surveying the bright gardens laid out in geometrical designs which bordered the glazed red-brick pavement of the Steyne. Surely amidst its lively pleasures, Luke would relax and realise that his suspicions of her were unfounded?

'What do you think of Prinny's Pavilion?' Luke enquired, enjoying the excitement playing across her expressive face.

The fantastic pile of domes and minarets gleaming in the morning sunlight met with Ianthe's approval. Others might cavil at the Regent's extravagance, but she found it delightful and said so with a vigour that made Luke smile.

'It reminds me of the drawings in your Indian sketchbook,' Ianthe continued. 'Do you think you will do any sketching while we are here?'

'I might,' Luke replied, secretly pleased by her remark. 'Especially if this fine weather keeps up.'

They progressed slowly towards the sea and Luke pointed out Donaldson's Circulating Library, one of the most popular gathering places in the town. In its elegantly appointed rooms, one might change a book, show off a new *toilette* or meet one's friends.

'They also hold card-assemblies and concerts most evenings,' Luke informed her.

Ianthe had already discovered that balls were held at the Assembly Rooms of the Castle Inn and its rival, the Old Ship. 'I hope I have brought enough evening gowns,' she murmured.

Luke raised one eyebrow and she fell silent, a sudden chill darkening the bright day. Was she presuming too much, too soon? He had warned her that he did not intend to squire her around.

'The shops here rival those in London. I'm sure you could purchase more gowns if you need them,' he said.

Ianthe gave him a brilliant smile, her spirits rising buoyantly at his unexpected words.

'It is also probable that we shall be invited to attend one of the informal receptions or concerts that Prinny is fond of giving when he is in residence at the Pavilion,' Luke continued.

Ianthe's eyes widened. She had met the Duke of York during her brief Season in London, but to be hobnobbing with royalty would certainly put her on her mettle!

Brighton was obviously a place where fashion ruled. The Marine Parade, with its bow-fronted houses decorated with Corinthian columns and entablatures, was thronged with well-dressed strollers. Ianthe noted several particularly attractive bonnets before her attention was caught by a row of odd box-like contrivances on wheels drawn up on the beach.

'Are those bathing-machines?' she asked Luke.

'Indeed they are.' Luke viewed her excited expression with an amused smile. 'Should you like to try being dipped in the sea by one of the bathing-women?'

Ianthe hesitated and he laughed. 'Aye, that water is deuced cold and I'm told that if you do not submit meekly to their ministrations, they hold you under quite ruthlessly.'

Ianthe indignantly protested that she wasn't a coward, but Luke had meanwhile remembered that the bathing-machines at Brighton, unlike those at the more staid resorts of Ramsgate and Scarborough, did not possess awnings. It was the custom of certain rakish young gentlemen visitors to provide themselves with telescopes to spy upon ladies about to enter the sea and he had no wish for his wife to be subjected to their curiosity.

Luckily, it was easy to change the topic of conversation when there was so much else to be seen!

They had just finished admiring a particularly smart yacht out at sea when a loud feminine voice hailed Luke.

'Lord Kildare! Well, I never! Fancy seeing you here!'

Ianthe turned round. The owner of this voice was a lady of around thirty, dressed in the height of fashion in blossom pink muslin. The style with its deeply flounced hem and elaborate neck-ruff was a little young for her, as was the green chip hat *à la* Pamela perched upon her bright blonde curls, but her figure was good and she was decidedly attractive.

She was also smiling at Luke in a very familiar manner as she excused herself to the party she was with and came over to speak to them. Ianthe's high spirits suddenly sank.

'Mrs Murrell.' Luke bowed over the hand Lottie was holding out to him. He had fond memories of the dashing widow, who was as good natured as she was wealthy, and he had no hesitation in presenting her to Ianthe.

'So you are married!' Lottie exclaimed. Hiding her disappointment, for she had hoped that they might renew their brief affair, she decided to make the best of the situation and lost no time in introducing her companions and making herself agreeable to Ianthe.

She succeeded so well that Ianthe's initial flicker of jealousy had faded by the time they all said their farewells with a promise to meet up again the following evening at the ball to be given at the Castle Inn.

'Mrs Murrell seems a pleasant woman,' Ianthe remarked as they strolled off in the opposite direction to the other party. 'Did you know her before you went to India?'

'No, we met more recently,' Luke said and went on adroitly, 'She's the widow of a rich cit. She don't exactly move in first circles in London, but Brighton ain't stuffy and I dare say that here she's accepted everywhere.'

What he did before he was married was no business of Ianthe's. On the other hand, he had come straight from Lottie's bed to Kildare Park. It was possible Ianthe might find this idea upsetting and now that they were getting on so much better, he didn't want another quarrel.

Luke was unsure of his feelings. His head and heart seemed at war. He wanted to believe Ianthe when she said that she had not deliberately deceived him, but the carapace of cynicism he had grown to protect himself was too thick to allow him to trust her.

His anger had faded, but he wasn't ready to give in to the feelings of affection which frequently assailed him when he looked at her. It was bad enough that he had no control over the desire which consumed him at her lightest touch!

They had continued to stroll as they were talking and he now realised that their eastwards direction had taken them as far as Royal Crescent.

'It is very elegant,' said Ianthe, admiring the sweeping curve of tall houses fronted by a garden. 'And I like the sea view, but I'm not sure I wouldn't prefer plain stone to those dark tiles.'

Luke explained that the houses had been fronted with black mathematical tiles to help the stonework resist the salt-laden air. 'Would you care to see inside?' he asked, pointing out the house he had rented from the Earl of Dover. 'Or would you prefer to eat a nuncheon?' he continued with a glance at his gold verge watch.

'I rather think we should be in the way,' Ianthe murmured, watching as a couple of servants dashed out carrying rolled-up rugs. 'And this sea air has given me an appetite.'

'Then we shall return to the Castle Inn,' Luke said decisively. 'The food there is excellent.'

Ianthe nodded and as they turned away from their future abode she began to ask him about the balls given at the Castle Inn. Luke answered her with every appearance of concentration, but he was preoccupied with other thoughts.

Perhaps he ought to have a private word with Lottie. She

was a dear soul, but somewhat feather-brained, and he wasn't sure he trusted her discretion. Since it seemed likely that they were going to bump into each other on a regular basis, it might be a good idea to remind her not to treat him in too familiar a fashion!

The Assembly Rooms at the Castle Inn were spacious and elegant. They had been designed, so Lord Kildare informed his wife as they entered the ballroom, by John Crunden, a disciple of the renowned Robert Adam, and they were thronged with as fashionable a company as might be seen at any London *ton* party during the Season.

Ianthe was impressed. She hadn't enjoyed her time in London, but she felt quite sure that Brighton was going to suit her much better.

'Would you care to dance?' Luke asked, indicating the set which was forming for a cotillion.

'I'd love to,' Ianthe replied happily.

It was a delightful experience to dance with her husband, she decided. He was accomplished at the art and looked remarkably handsome in his superbly cut black coat of Bath superfine and white satin knee-breeches. Aware of the envious looks from several damsels not blessed with such a superior partner, she tried not to feel smug.

Luke was also aware that they were attracting attention. Ianthe was in particularly good looks tonight. In the last few weeks she had gained weight, and while he doubted that she would ever become fashionably plump, her figure was now elegantly slender rather than thin. Her dress was also eye-catching. Utterly plain, it relied for effect upon its fabric, a Chinese shot silk woven in shades of blue and green which rippled with an iridescent sheen in the candlelight. Silver ribbons dressed her upswept hair and she wore the aquamarine and diamond necklace and earrings which had been her mother's.

'You are the loveliest woman in the room,' Luke said softly as the set ended and they left the floor.

Wild rose suffused Ianthe's cheeks as she met his eyes and saw a gleam of desire break through his control. It was odd to think that a month ago she would not have understood what his expression meant. Even more strange, was to feel the answering leap of passion run like molten lava though her veins!

She was busily employing her silver-sticked fan to cool her hot cheeks when Mrs Murrell spotted them and came hurrying over. Her companion, a tall, red-haired cavalry officer who was stationed at the nearby barracks on the Lewes road, was swiftly introduced as Captain Regan and he and Luke fell into easy conversation.

Charlotte Murrell gave a satisfied chuckle. 'I thought the two of them would hit it off,' she confided to Ianthe.

Ianthe smiled back. She was perfectly prepared to like Mrs Murrell, although she found the older woman's exuberant manner a little overwhelming.

'May I compliment you on your gown? Such a pretty colour!'

'Thank you, Mrs Murrell. You are very kind.'

'Oh, do call me Lottie! All my friends do and I hope we are going to be friends.'

There was a slight thread of anxiety beneath the blonde's jolly manner and Ianthe suddenly realised how uncomfortable it must be to feel an outsider. Mrs Murrell did not possess the advantage of good birth and her wealth could not automatically guarantee her entry into the circles she wished to frequent.

'I hope so, too, particularly as you are a friend of my husband's,' Ianthe replied.

Lottie gave a wide grin and then hastily schooled her expression. 'Oh, indeed!' She took a big gulp of breath and rattled on. 'I hear you have taken the Earl of Dover's house. Do you like it? I was told it was a marble mausoleum of a place.'

Ianthe hid a grin. Tact was obviously not Lottie's strong point! 'It is certainly severe in style, but it is well appointed and the location is very pleasant.'

'No doubt Luke had to pay a fortune to secure it. Dover was apparently planning to install his mother there for the rest of the summer. She was due to arrive this week, but now he's going to take a house for her in Worthing.'

Ianthe blinked. It was considered rather vulgar to discuss money in such frank terms, although everyone gossiped about it in private of course.

'Oh, dear! Shouldn't I have said that?' Lottie looked at her anxiously. 'Only I thought the whole world knew that Luke was as rich as Croesus.'

'I don't think he cares to have it discussed,' Ianthe said gently.

Lottie took the hint. 'Oh, I see,' she muttered thoughtfully to herself.

At this point Luke broke into their conversation to ask Mrs Murrell if she would stand up with him for the quadrille. Lottie had promised this dance to Captain Regan, but she blithely accepted and allowed Luke to lead her away.

There was a slightly indignant look upon the Captain's pleasant-featured face, but he politely asked Ianthe if she would care to join the dance.

'I think we are too late,' Ianthe replied. 'The sets appear full. But I would love a glass of lemonade if you would be kind enough to procure one for me.'

'I should be delighted to do so, ma'am,' the Captain replied gallantly.

He escorted Ianthe over to where several gilt chairs had been set out for those not dancing and, with a polite bow, left her to seek out refreshments for them both.

From her position Ianthe had an excellent view of the dancers. She noticed how Luke was laughing at something Lottie had said. They seemed very friendly.

Stop it, she told herself crossly. If you are going to be jealous of every female who flirts with Luke, you are going to be a very miserable woman!

She deliberately removed her gaze from the dancers and surveyed the crowded room. Thanks to the quiet life she had led at Northwood she didn't think she knew anyone here, although she recognised one or two well-known leaders of the *ton*.

After a moment she realised that she herself had been under scrutiny as a middle-aged matron, resplendent in purple satin and feather-bedecked turban, came across to greet her.

'Miss Garland, is it not?' she said in a high, well-bred voice. 'Forgive me for accosting you so brazenly, but I am Mrs Coventry. I believe we met three or four years ago in London when you made your come-out. My son, Hugh, was one of your escorts.'

Ianthe thought for a moment and a mental picture of a shy quiet youth popped into her mind. Once she had placed him, she remembered his mother too and returned the older woman's greeting with a friendly smile.

Mrs Coventry seated herself next to Ianthe. 'I saw you dancing with Lord Kildare,' she announced. 'Do you know him?'

Ianthe nodded. She had just remembered that Hugh had five unmarried sisters!

'I am not acquainted with him myself,' Mrs Coventry went on without giving Ianthe time to speak. 'And I was wondering, if he was a friend of yours, whether you would be so good as to introduce him to me.'

'I should be delighted to do so, Mrs Coventry,' Ianthe replied demurely. 'I am sure my husband would be happy to make your acquaintance.'

'Husband?' Mrs Coventry's rather protuberant brown eyes widened in astonishment and flew to Ianthe's left hand where Luke's heavy gold band shone next to her sapphire betrothal ring.

'We were married a week ago.'

'I had no idea he was contemplating matrimony!' Mrs Coventry's plump features wore an indignant expression.

'Ours was a brief engagement,' Ianthe murmured apologetically, hiding her amusement as she wondered how many of Hugh's sisters remained unwed.

Mrs Coventry took a deep breath and seemed to recover her composure. 'Ah, well, I wish you very happy, my dear,' she said, giving Ianthe a philosophical smile.

'Thank you.' Ianthe had always known that the size of Luke's fortune and the speed of their marriage would leave her open to gossip and envy, but as Mrs Coventry continued to chatter away without any sign of malice she decided that she could acquit her present companion of bearing her any ill will for having, in vulgar parlance, snapped up the biggest matrimonial prize on the market.

'I see Lord Kildare is acquainted with Mrs Murrell,' Mrs Coventry remarked, as the quadrille came to an end.

Ianthe nodded, returning a reply somewhat at random as she watched Luke escort the lively blonde widow off the floor.

Where were they going? They had disappeared into the crowd and Ianthe couldn't help feeling faintly resentful that he had not returned to her side to offer his support.

Doing it too brown, said the honest voice of her conscience. You aren't some shy little mouse who needs to cling to his arm and he knows it. He left you well attended and he must have seen that you were not alone before he withdrew. If it wasn't that he had gone off with Charlotte Murrell, you wouldn't mind at all. You just don't like him paying her so much attention.

O, beware, my lord, of jealousy!/ It is the green-eyed monster, which doth mock/ The meat it feeds on.

The quotation from *Othello* suddenly burnt her memory. It was no use. She was jealous of the widow and telling herself that Luke had probably just taken her to obtain some refreshments didn't help!

'A very wealthy woman, so one hears, but shockingly ill bred,' Mrs Coventry pronounced with a little disdainful sniff that reclaimed Ianthe's attention.

'I don't know her well. We only met yesterday, but she seems pleasant enough,' Ianthe said carefully.

'She makes a habit of being pleasant to everyone, my dear.'

Mrs Coventry gave a little laugh and leant towards Ianthe in a confidential manner. 'However, I would be on your guard.'

Ianthe stiffened. 'Are you implying that she is...pursuing my husband?'

'Well, she was his mistress for a while last June, and it is obvious she still finds him attractive—' Mrs Coventry bit off what she was saying. 'Lud, I fear I have said too much.'

'I...I did not know.' Ianthe could feel the blood draining from her face.

'Then I am sorry to be the bearer of such news.' Embarrassed by her *faux pas*, Mrs Coventry fanned herself vigorously. 'I hope you will believe me when I say I had no intention of making mischief. I assumed you must have heard the rumours. It was the talk of London.'

Ianthe accepted this apology. 'Thank you for enlightening my ignorance.'

Mrs Coventry shot her a considering look. She had recovered a little of her colour. Indeed, there was a militant gleam in those magnificent sapphire eyes!

'It is not my place to interfere,' she said hesitantly, 'but I know you have no mother to advise you.' She gave a little cough. 'You will find married life much more comfortable if you simply ignore what I've just told you.'

Ianthe knew that wives were not supposed to concern themselves if their husbands were unfaithful. That side of a man's existence was considered completely separate from his life at home and none of a wife's business.

'I shall try to take your advice, Mrs Coventry,' she said slowly.

'I hope you can, my dear. Men are strange creatures. They view such matters in a different light and it would be a pity to spoil your honeymoon with a pointless quarrel.' Mrs Coventry gave her a sympathetic smile. 'I am sure he has broken with her and there is nothing for you to worry about.'

This *volte-face* might have made Ianthe smile in other circumstances, but as she wasn't at all convinced that Luke no longer had a fancy for the dashing widow, her sense of humour failed her.

Mrs Coventry rose to her feet. 'I am holding a little soirée next week. May I send you and your husband a card?'

Realising that the older woman genuinely regretted alarming her, Ianthe made haste to reassure her that she would be happy to accept the invitation if Lord Kildare had made no other plans.

'Then I shall look forward to seeing you.' With a nod of farewell, Mrs Coventry moved away just as Captain Regan hove into view.

Ianthe thanked him for the lemonade and allowed him to introduce several of his scarlet-coated brother officers to her.

Watching her dance and smile her way through the rest of the evening, no one would have guessed that beneath her light-hearted manner Lady Kildare was prey to any number of disturbing thoughts.

Chapter Ten

Over breakfast the next morning Ianthe mentioned to Luke that they had been invited to Mrs Coventry's soirée.

'Shall I accept?' she asked.

'If you wish. I have no objections,' he replied and took a sip of coffee.

'Did you enjoy last night?' he continued, putting down his cup. 'You were so tired on the way home we hardly spoke.'

'Too much dancing, I'm afraid.' Ianthe gave him a sunny smile.

In truth she had pretended to be more fatigued than had been the case, but she had not trusted her tongue. After a surprisingly good night's sleep, she now felt more cheerful and inclined to dismiss her fears.

'But I did enjoy my evening,' she added, answering his question.

'Good, since I dare say we shall be besieged with invitations,' Luke remarked sagely.

Lord Kildare's prophecy proved correct. Within a few days they had received dozens of cards requesting their attendance at balls, routs, picnics, breakfasts and all manner of other entertainments.

'Heavens, but I shall need to buy another pair of white evening gloves,' Ianthe said with a chuckle on the Wednesday morning as she surveyed the latest cream-laid gilt-edged card to arrive in Royal Crescent. 'We have only been here a week and the ones I brought with me are already the worse for wear.'

'The price of success,' Luke informed her drily.

Ianthe chuckled. 'You flatter me, sir. I am merely a new face and my appeal will soon fade.'

'Too modest, sweetheart,' Luke retorted with a grin. 'People like you. You are excellent company.'

Contrary to his expectations, he had enjoyed the last few days. Ianthe *was* good company. Exploring the town with her had been extremely agreeable. Dancing with her even more so.

While they had been here he had met several old friends and introduced them to her. They had all thought her charming. Their congratulations had made him realise that he was proud of her. Her beauty, poise and intelligence were assets any man would appreciate in a wife.

It would be very easy to release the floodgates which held back his deep feelings for her...

'What are your plans for today?' he asked abruptly, determined to banish such dangerous thoughts.

'Well, I mean to write to my grandmama about our doings and then I shall change my book at Donaldson's,' Ianthe replied, adding with an impish grin that it would give her an opportunity to air her new *toilette*, an outrageously expensive eau-de-nil jaconet that did wonders for her hair.

'And there is the Duchess's *fête champêtre* this evening,' she reminded him.

'I shall make sure I am home in good time,' Luke said.

Ianthe remembered that he had engaged himself to watch a horse race out on the Downs. It was to be an all-male party and he had told her that he would be away until evening.

After he had left the house Ianthe went upstairs to write her letter at the elegant little rosewood secretaire which graced her boudoir. Since she had a lot to tell her grandmother this took some considerable time, but at last it was finished and she went to change her simple morning gown for her pale green promenade dress. It had long sleeves, ornamented with ruches at the wrist, and a triple flounced hem.

It was a windy morning so Jenny advised her to wear her lemon spencer instead of taking her Norwich silk shawl.

'A good idea. Shawls can be so awkward in a strong wind,' Ianthe replied.

Deciding not to take her parasol for the same reason, she selected a pretty bonnet with a poke front to shade her complexion. Neat flat slippers in dark green leather completed her outfit.

Jenny was to accompany her and they left the house a few minutes later.

The breeze along the sea-front was invigorating and Ianthe enjoyed her walk to Donaldson's. As usual, the Circulating Library was busy and it took some time for Ianthe to change her book. She had just finished when she noticed Mrs Murrell at a nearby table flicking over the pages of one of the many periodicals which were on display.

'Good morning.' Ianthe went over to greet her. 'What an outrageous dress!' she said, pointing to the illustration that Lottie was gazing at in the latest issue of Ackermann's *Repository of Arts*.

It featured a sausage-shaped bustle tied under the top of the gown's skirts to create an outline known as the Grecian bend and Lottie's preoccupied expression lightened. 'Oh, indeed. It makes her look quite hump-backed!' she giggled.

They spent a further few minutes in conversation, but Ianthe couldn't help feeling that the widow was somewhat distrait.

'Pray excuse me,' she finally blurted. 'I…I have some shopping to do in North Street.'

She hurried off and Ianthe turned away with a slightly puzzled expression, which vanished on being hailed by Mrs Coventry. Her ladyship was accompanied by her two youngest daughters, who were both unmarried and enjoying a holiday by the sea with their mama.

A few years younger than Ianthe, they were pretty girls

with cropped dark curls and engaging manners. Ianthe found them easy to talk to and their party spent a comfortable quarter of an hour chatting before they parted with promises to meet up again at the Duchess of Bradford's al fresco entertainment that evening.

Ianthe decided it was time to return home. She emerged from Donaldson's and was about to make her way down Marine Parade when she suddenly spotted Mrs Murrell. The widow had taken one of the sea-front houses and Ianthe was just thinking that her shopping trip must have been very brief to allow her to return home so quickly when the gentleman who was escorting Lottie turned round.

Ianthe sucked in her breath. It couldn't be!

'Oh, look, there's his lordship,' Jenny piped up innocently.

The front door of the house opened and Ianthe watched Luke follow Lottie indoors.

The door slammed shut behind them.

Becoming aware of her mistress's silence, Jenny wondered whether to risk a cheery remark on the lines that Mrs Murrell had probably just invited him in for a polite glass of sherry, but one glance at Ianthe's frosty expression warned her that any well-meant reassurances would fall on stony ground!

Ianthe had not spent so long getting ready for a party since she was sixteen, but she very much wanted to look her best tonight. Jenny washed her hair for her, adding rosemary to the rinsing water to bring out its dark lustrous sheen, and then Ianthe soaked in a bath of warm, rose-scented water. When she was dry she rubbed a little orange flower lotion into her skin. It made her bare shoulders gleam.

'Shall I paint your face for you, my lady?' Jenny asked.

Ianthe rarely used cosmetics, but she nodded consent. Jenny had learnt the art when working for her previous employer and Ianthe was delighted with the results.

Her cheeks had a delicate glow and her lips were glossily pink. Jenny had darkened her eyelids too and Ianthe scarcely recognised the sophisticated young woman in the dressing-table mirror with her romantic tumble of soft ringlets.

Jenny brought over Ianthe's jewellery case. 'Will you wear your aquamarines, my lady?'

This necklace and earrings set had belonged to her mother and, as stipulated in her father's will, Maria had reluctantly handed them over on the morning of Ianthe's marriage. Ianthe was very fond of them, but she felt that her ice-blue *mousseline d'Inde* gown needed something with more colour to offset its pale, delicate lines.

She was just debating whether the garnet and pearl pendant, which had been her grandmother's wedding gift, would suit when a knock came at the door and her husband strolled in.

'Aren't you ready yet?' Luke began impatiently and then fell silent as he took in her appearance.

The sudden admiration in his eyes was balm to Ianthe's wounded pride.

'Almost, my lord. I am just deciding what jewellery to wear.' Part of her wanted to confront him and demand to know what he had been doing visiting Lottie, but Mrs Coventry's advice had rung in her head all afternoon. Was it better to let sleeping dogs lie?

In any event, now was not the time to raise the subject. The Duchess's moonlit picnic was due to begin at ten and the clock on her mantelpiece had already struck the hour.

'One moment.'

To her surprise, Luke went through into his own room. When he came back he was carrying a flat velvet jewel case.

'I have been meaning to give you these for some time,' he said gruffly, handing it to her.

Ianthe took it with a hand that shook slightly.

She stared at the sapphire necklace in awed silence. A pair of matching earrings had been arranged within the circle it formed and against the bed of white velvet the jewels glowed with a deep blue fire. At the heart of each gem a sparkling six-rayed star shone. 'They are beautiful,' she breathed.

'The phenomenon is known as asterism,' Luke informed

her gravely. 'There are inclusions of foreign mineral in the original stones. If a star sapphire is cut wrongly, the effect is lost and the stone is spoilt, but my chief stone-cutter at Ratnapura was very skilled.'

Ianthe nodded in agreement. She had never seen such lovely gems and their simple gold setting merely enhanced their beauty.

'Will you wear them tonight? They match the colour of your betrothal ring…and your eyes.'

Ianthe's heart hammered against her ribcage. Surely he must care for her a little to give her such a magnificent gift…and pay her such a lovely compliment?

Not trusting herself to speak, she nodded and handed the case to Jenny. With a big grin the maid proceeded to fasten the necklace on for her. She then handed the earrings to Ianthe, who slipped them into her ears.

She shook her head gently and watched how they sparkled in the light, an eye-catching contrast to her pale gown.

Ianthe stood up and took the gold net scarf which Jenny held out. She draped it elegantly over her arms and said, 'I am ready, sir.'

Their carriage had been driven round from the mews and, as they left the house, Ianthe was glad to note that the wind had dropped to nothing more than a light breeze.

'It's a lovely warm evening. The Duchess has been lucky with the weather,' she murmured, feeling an urgent need to break the silence.

'Aye, rain would have ruined a *fête champêtre*.'

His tone was coolly polite and Ianthe wondered what he was thinking. He was so skilled at masking his feelings!

It was only a short drive to the Duchess of Bradford's magnificent villa, which stood a little way out of town on the road to Newhaven. It took somewhat longer for them to alight and make their way into the house because of the crush of carriages all waiting to set down their passengers.

The Duchess, a well-preserved woman in her mid-thirties who wore a striped gauze evening gown and an osprey-bedecked turban, greeted them with her customary debonair vivacity. 'Bradford is in the card-room with his cronies,' she announced. 'Some of my more elderly guests are gossiping in the drawing-rooms and everyone else has gone out into the gardens. Do venture forth and enjoy yourselves, my loves!'

She held out her hand to Luke, who was an old friend, and he bowed over it gracefully. 'I'm sure we shall, Sally.'

The villa's pleasure grounds had been transformed into a fairyland lit by numerous coloured lanterns. The pale gowns of the ladies glowed in the silvery moonlight and music, from a terrace where the quartet hired by the Duchess played, floated out on the gentle breeze.

Ianthe surveyed the vista with a little tingle of excitement. She had never attended such an exotic party.

Luke smiled when she confided this to him. 'Sally prides herself on creating a dash!'

In the centre of the greensward the Duchess had caused a broad wooden platform to be laid for the purpose of dancing. A country dance was in progress as Ianthe and Luke descended the stone steps which led from the central terrace into the garden. They watched for a moment, sipping a glass of the Duchess's excellent champagne.

'Good evening. Isn't this a delightful party?' Mrs Coventry came up with her youngest daughter and they fell into conversation. Then, as the country dance ended, Luke politely invited Emily to stand up with him for the boulanger which followed.

'Such wonderful sapphires, my dear!' Mrs Coventry exclaimed when she and Ianthe were alone. 'I am quite envious!'

'They came from my husband's mine in Ceylon,' Ianthe replied proudly.

'Forgive my vulgar prying,' Mrs Coventry said, lowering her voice. 'But I have heard it rumoured that it is the main source of his wealth.'

'Quite true.' Ianthe decided that there could be no harm in satisfying her new friend's curiosity. 'Luke accepted the mine in payment for a debt. The man who sold it thought he was being clever. He'd lied about the mine being productive, but Luke had the last laugh.'

'You mean it wasn't barren after all?'

Ianthe nodded. Luke had said it was pure luck, but he had treated the mine-workers far better than the original owner. 'In return, they worked harder and made a new rich find.'

On one of their morning rides at Kildare Park Luke had explained that gemstones were found in the alluvial gravels of the lowlands. 'In the beds of rivers where crocodiles lurk or in the dark jungles where elephants appear as great grey shadows or in snake-infested swamps, the gems lie waiting to be harvested,' he'd said with a faint smile.

'I'm not surprised they worked hard for Lord Kildare. He is skilled at bringing out the best in people,' Mrs Coventry commented, watching him dance with her daughter. Emily was barely seventeen and was still shy in the presence of gentlemen, but she was chatting happily to his lordship whenever the figures of the dance brought them together.

The boulanger ended and Luke returned his partner to her mama.

The musicians struck up a waltz.

Luke quickly held out his hand to Ianthe. 'I claim a husband's privilege, ma'am, before one of your admirers descends upon us.'

Ianthe smiled. She could see two of Captain Regan's fellow officers hovering hopefully.

'Pray excuse me,' she murmured to Mrs Coventry and allowed Luke to sweep her onto the dance floor.

Held in his arms, she circled gracefully in time to Hummel's lilting music.

'You waltz beautifully,' Luke whispered in her ear.

'Thank you.' Ianthe smiled up at him.

It was heavenly dancing in his arms. They moved so well together. She felt as light as thistledown, all her cares dissolved in the pure happiness of this magic moment.

Ianthe could have waltzed all night, but at last the music ended and reality intruded once more.

'Would you like something to drink?' Luke asked as they walked off the floor.

Ianthe nodded, pleased that he had remembered that dancing always made her thirsty.

He left her talking to one of her new acquaintances and made his way over to where a refreshment buffet had been set up under one of the trees, which was festooned with several lanterns to give sufficient light for the waiters to work.

Beyond this table the character of the garden changed. A number of shady walks led off into secluded groves, which, as Mrs Coventry had noted with some disapproval earlier, were scantily lit.

'It is quite remarkable how my guests always seem to disappear in pairs to enjoy the moonlight,' said the Duchess, materialising at Luke's elbow.

'You ought to know by now, Sally, that this kind of al fresco party always turns into a romp,' Luke replied, his severe tone belied by the twinkle in his eyes.

'But that is the whole point, my love. I do so enjoy fluttering a few feathers,' the Duchess murmured with a wicked grin.

He handed her a glass of champagne and she took a sip.

'All the same, you ought to take better care of that pretty wife of yours,' she said, surveying him over the rim of her glass.

He raised his brows and she went on calmly, 'I have been hearing rumours about Mrs Murrell.'

Luke felt a chill slide down his spine. 'Really? What kind of rumours?'

Sally laughed. 'I've no mind to tell tales, Luke.' She turned to leave. 'Just don't say that I didn't warn you. No wife wants to be humiliated, least of all on her honeymoon.'

Luke watched her drift away, a frown tightening his features.

Obtaining two glasses of champagne he began to walk back

to where he had left Ianthe when out of the darkness a voice spoke his name.

He turned and beheld a shapely female form in the shadow of one of the beech trees. Her fair hair glinted in the moonlight filtering through its leaves.

He stood very still for a moment and then strode rapidly forward towards her.

Engaged in conversation, Ianthe at first did not notice Luke's absence. It was only after she had completed a country dance with Captain Regan that she realised he had been gone for a considerable time.

Looking around, she could not see him anywhere. Then she remembered the Duchess saying that some guests were inside the house. Perhaps Luke had gone indoors.

With a shrug of her white shoulders, she attempted to dismiss the faint unease which niggled at her.

'Since my errant husband has neglected to furnish me with a drink, I think I shall go in search of some champagne before they start letting off the fireworks,' she said to Miss Mary Coventry, her companion of the moment.

The young Lieutenant who had been dancing with Mary earlier and remained glued to her side gallantly offered to procure this refreshment, but Ianthe smilingly refused.

'Do stay here, both of you, or your mama won't know where to find you, Mary. I'm sure she will be back with Emily in a moment.'

'Don't be long, Lady Kildare,' Mary urged. 'They are going to begin the display any minute now.'

Mrs Coventry had taken Emily to the ladies' retiring-room so that a torn hem-flounce could be repaired. Safe in the knowledge that the crowd who had gathered in this prime spot to observe the pyrotechnics could act as chaperons to the young couple, Ianthe left them to their shy whisperings.

The champagne had been packed in ice and was deliciously cold. Ianthe drank it quickly and then handed the empty glass to the servant to be refilled.

Sipping the wine more slowly, she moved away from the buffet. Spotting a couple slipping away into the darkness beyond the trees, she dawdled to a halt. No doubt Mary's swain would like to ask her to take a walk with him in this romantic setting, she thought, with a little stab of amusement.

Well, Luke had warned her that Brighton was noted for its raffish parties!

A gleam of silk in the moonlight caught her eye. Just at the limit of her vision she could see a couple standing at the edge of the grove. Even as she watched, the woman reached up to twine her arms around the neck of her partner.

Not wishing to be a peeping Tom she began to turn away, but even as she did so a sudden flare of brilliant light from the first rocket lit up the sky. It was gone in an instant, but not before she had seen that the man was Lord Kildare.

Trembling with anger, Ianthe stalked back to the buffet and demanded another glass of champagne.

The face of the woman in his arms had not been visible, but her voluptuous figure had been clad in a pink gown and her blonde hair had glittered in that brief flash of light.

Ianthe's mouth compressed into a tight line. Charlotte Murrell was here tonight. Ianthe had not spoken to her, but she had seen her dancing with Captain Regan.

Dancing and wearing a pale pink silk dress!

'Please leave us.'

The maid, who had been instructed by the Duchess's housekeeper to attend any of the female guests who required her services, opened her mouth to protest and then closed it again.

They said redheads had a shocking temper and this one looked angry!

'Yes, ma'am,' she muttered and slid out of the ladies' cloakroom, closing the door firmly behind her.

Charlotte Murrell swallowed hard to moisten her dry mouth. 'Now that we are alone, Ianthe, would you mind telling me why you insisted on a word in private with me?'

'I don't care to be overheard,' Ianthe replied in a tight voice.

Lottie attempted a smile. 'It must be something serious.'

Ianthe threw her a contemptuous look. She had seen Lottie go inside the house a few moments ago and had followed her. 'I would regard it so, but perhaps you are in the habit of making advances to other women's husbands and take a more casual view of the matter.'

Lottie gasped. 'What are you talking about?' she demanded indignantly.

'You know very well!' Ianthe's voice cracked with rage. 'I saw you just now in the garden. You were kissing Luke! And I'll vow it's not the first time!'

Lottie blushed. 'You…you are mistaken,' she stammered.

Ianthe's blue eyes flashed fury. 'You were entertaining him this very afternoon!'

Lottie sat down abruptly on a sofa. 'How…how do you know about that?'

Ianthe glared at her. 'He told me he was spending the day out on the Downs with friends. You told me you were going shopping and yet I saw the two of you going into your house together.'

'I do not deny he visited my house, but you are quite wrong if you think anything improper took place between us.'

A harsh snort of disbelief greeted this pronouncement.

Lottie winced. 'Please, Ianthe, I can see that you are upset, but, really, you have got it all wrong.'

'Then you are not his mistress?'

'I was for a short while, but our relationship came to an end when he left London. I swear to you that the affair is over.' Lottie gazed at Ianthe earnestly. 'And I would not dream of trying to revive it. Not now.'

'And why not pray?' Ianthe demanded scornfully.

'Because today Captain Regan has asked me to marry him.'

'Oh!' The simple honesty of this answer penetrated the blind fury which had swamped Ianthe. She sat down heavily. Her knees felt wobbly and her head was beginning to ache.

It had been a bad idea to drink so much champagne, she wasn't used to it!

'I did meet Luke this afternoon, but it was quite by chance, I do assure you. His race-meeting finished early and I was hurrying home because I felt too agitated to carry on with my shopping. He could see that I was in a tituppy state and insisted on escorting me back to Marine Parade. When he asked me what was the matter I invited him in for a glass of wine and begged him for advice.'

Lottie smoothed her pink skirts. 'You see, I haven't decided whether or not to accept the Captain.'

'Do you love him?' Ianthe asked in a low voice.

'I care for him a great deal,' Lottie nodded. 'But I suspect he is penniless and I am worried his regard for me might not be genuine.' She gave a little shrug. 'A woman in my position is always at the risk from fortune-hunters.'

'So what are you going to do?' In spite of her own problems, Ianthe was intrigued by Lottie's dilemma.

'Luke suggested I make enquiries into his background. John might not want me to know his true circumstances out of pride. However, if he refuses to be honest with me…' Lottie threw up her hands in a telling gesture.

'I hope it goes well for you,' Ianthe said awkwardly.

Seeing the worst of Ianthe's fury had blown itself out, Lottie risked a slight smile. 'I never meant anything to Luke, you know,' she murmured, a faintly rueful note in her voice.

Ianthe pushed back a stray curl from her hot face. She regretted the effect the Duchess's champagne had worked on her tongue. Lottie would have been justified in returning her accusations with an answering anger. 'I'm sorry I screamed at you like a fishwife. I let my temper get the better of me.'

Impulsively, she held out her hands to Lottie. 'Can you forget my appalling display of bad manners? You have shown me friendship and I had no right to accuse you without any proof.'

Lottie went pink with pleasure. 'Nay, there's no need to apologise.' She took Ianthe's hands in her own and gave them a little squeeze. 'Besides, I would have done the same in your position! I was always jealous if I caught any woman sniffing round my Alfred.'

A slightly strangled laugh escaped Ianthe.

'I suppose somebody tattled and told you about me and Luke?' At Ianthe's nod, Lottie sighed. 'I'm sorry you had to find out that way, especially on your honeymoon.'

'I never imagined Luke was a monk.' Ianthe's wide mouth twisted in a wry smile.

''Tis foolish to get upset over a man's past amours,' Lottie agreed sagely. 'But, truly, I swear I wouldn't have tried to fix my interest with Luke again, even if Captain Regan wasn't courting me. I don't believe in frolicking with married men and, anyway, as soon as I saw him with you, I knew he wouldn't look at another woman.'

Ianthe gazed at her uncertainly.

'He loves you. Any fool can see that.'

'Can they?' Ianthe asked bitterly. 'If he wasn't kissing you, Lottie, then who was it that I saw in his arms?'

Lottie shifted uncomfortably in her seat and a look of dismay stole over her round features.

'Have you guessed her identity?' Ianthe asked quickly.

The door to the retiring room opened and another of the Duchess's guests entered. Glad to be saved a reply, Lottie jumped to her feet. 'Let's get back. I do enjoy a firework display and we are missing it.'

Ianthe nodded and rose silently to her feet.

She did not speak until they reached the terrace overlooking the gardens. The pyrotechnics had just ended and the servants were re-lighting those lanterns which had been extinguished.

'Oh, what a shame!' said Lottie brightly. 'Never mind, shall we go and find the others?'

'Lottie, please tell me! Is there something that I should know?' Ianthe whispered urgently as they began to descend the broad shallow steps.

Lottie hesitated. 'Promise me you won't create a scene?'

Ianthe bit her lip. Her emotions were churning so violently

that she felt as if she might explode. 'All right, I give you my word that I shall think before I speak!'

This promise seemed to satisfy Mrs Murrell. 'Well, I cannot pretend to know how Luke feels about her reappearance in his life, but I do think you should be on your guard.'

'What do you mean?'

They had reached the midway point of the staircase and Lottie pointed out a figure in the crowd below. 'See that woman in the pink satin gown?'

Ianthe's eyes followed the direction indicated and beheld an extremely beautiful blonde.

'The Countess of Lomond. She's the one you should watch!'

Lord Kildare raised his hand to knock upon his wife's bedroom door. Before his knuckles made contact with the wood, however, he paused and an unusual look of indecision descended upon his well-cut features.

It had already gone three by the time they left the Duchess's *fête* and Ianthe had looked tired. When they arrived home she had gone straight upstairs. Needing to think, he had poured himself a final glass of wine and gone into the study.

The Earl of Dover had appointed this room as his private sanctum in which to escape the demands of his family. It was furnished with a pair of comfortable tub-shaped armchairs and a sofa upholstered in matching green Genoese velvet, a handsome desk, a buffet cabinet in calamander wood with a black marble top and several sundry chairs and small tables. Sporting prints decorated the plain green walls.

It was a very masculine retreat and, being at the back of the house, was always quiet. The silence folded itself around Luke as he sat down in one of the armchairs.

He hadn't known that Georgiana intended to visit Brighton. If he had, he doubted he would have come within a mile of the place!

When she had spoken his name out of the darkness, he had recognised her voice instantly. At first, he'd thought he must be dreaming until he turned round and saw her standing under the trees. Her smile when he had walked towards her had been as warm and tender as on the day she had agreed to marry him.

Realising that he was drumming his fingers on the arm of the chair, Luke forced himself to stop. He took a deep gulp of wine.

Rendered speechless by shock, he had listened to her apologies and heard her express regret for rejecting him.

'I should never have married Andrew,' she had whispered. 'But I was already missing you. You had left for India and I knew it was too late for us. I thought Andrew could fill the emptiness in my life. I was wrong! He is dull beyond bearing! All he thinks of is farming and hunting. His crops and dogs mean more to him than I do!'

She had laid her hand upon his arm and looked up at him with a pleading expression. 'Say you forgive me, Luke! I never meant to hurt you. You came home from Spain so changed and I was young and foolish...'

Her low voice had faded into silence and Luke had spoken for the first time. 'Why are you telling me all this?' he had asked unsteadily.

'Can't you guess?' she breathed and, throwing her arms around his neck, kissed him.

Bittersweet memory had caught Luke in its grip. The sensuous chypre perfume she had always worn tantalised his nostrils and she felt as soft and warm in his arms as she had done six years ago...

Luke took a deep breath and set down his empty wineglass. Hellfire, what a mess!

Rising abruptly, he abandoned the study. His reflections weren't getting him anywhere. Maybe he would be able to think more productively in the morning.

He stood outside Ianthe's room, ready to knock and hesitated...

Ianthe had come up to him with Lottie after the firework display had finished. He'd thought she looked upset for some reason and was about to ask her if she wished to go home when the Duchess had appeared.

'One of my guests would like to meet you, Lady Kildare,' she had announced, beckoning Georgiana forward.

A warning flash in Sally's brown eyes reminded Luke that they were being watched with interest by half the *haut ton*.

There had been no time to alert Ianthe. Unsure if she knew who Georgiana was, Luke watched her smile and greet the Countess. At the time he had put her composure down to good breeding, but now he wondered if someone had tipped her the wink.

After the introduction had been performed she had stayed laughing and talking for several minutes until one of her admirers had whisked her away to dance. This partner had been followed by a succession of others and it was some while before Luke was able to ask her if she wanted to go home. She had refused sweetly and proceeded to dance the rest of the night away.

If she was upset, she wasn't going to admit it!

Luke's hand fell from the door. With a muttered expletive he turned on his heel and walked away.

Inside her room, Ianthe heard his footsteps receding. Taking a shaky breath, she sank back against her satin pillows.

Every night since they had arrived in Brighton, Luke had come to her room. No matter what had happened during the day the bond of attraction between them had succeeded in drawing them together. In the silent darkness they had been able to forget the mistrust and wariness which invaded their waking hours and let warm lips and bodies speak of feelings which pride and stubbornness concealed.

When they made love the outside world and all its suspicions vanished, leaving them free to enjoy a wonderful closeness, a harmony of mind and spirit as well as body. Ianthe had been hoping that this sense of belonging together would eventually spill over into their daily lives and erase the doubts which kept them polite strangers.

In time, she prayed, Luke would learn to believe that she had spoken the truth when she said that she loved him. And when he believed her, he would know it was safe to trust her with his heart.

Georgiana's arrival had been a bombshell, shattering hope and confidence alike. Luke's angry coldness towards her had thawed, but perhaps she was mistaken in thinking he was beginning to care for her. Perhaps all he felt was lust.

Stop it, Ianthe told herself sternly. You can't be certain that he prefers Georgiana. Anyway, she is married.

Not that this fact seemed to weigh with the Countess of Lomond! She had flirted with several gentlemen quite outrageously tonight and when asked about her husband she had made a cruel joke about his dull preference for bucolic pursuits.

It was obvious that she had no great affection for the Earl.

It was equally clear, to Ianthe at least, that she wanted Luke back. Leaving aside the painful matter of that secret embrace under the trees, the way she kept touching his arm and smiling up at him declared her intentions.

And Luke? Did he want her back? He was skilled at hiding his real feelings, but Ianthe couldn't help hoping that Georgiana's rejection had cut too deep for him to wish to resurrect the past.

If only she wasn't so beautiful! With her flaxen blonde hair and big green eyes she was as dainty as a fairy. At least a head shorter than Ianthe and fashionably curved, she made Ianthe feel like a skinny beanpole.

A deep sigh escaped Ianthe. Luke had occasionally praised her appearance, but she couldn't hold a candle to Georgiana and she knew it.

Any red-blooded man would desire the Countess of Lomond and, as her encounter with Lottie tonight had reminded her, Luke was no monk!

Unlike many theatres in the land, which closed during the quiet summer period, the Theatre Royal offered a number of performances for the entertainment of visitors to Brighton. Luke had asked Ianthe if she wished to see *Wild Oats* and she had agreed eagerly. She had enjoyed the few plays she had attended, but on the evening following the Duchess of Bradford's *fête champêtre* her enthusiasm was tempered by a sinking feeling that they were bound to encounter Lady Lomond there.

Half-inclined to throw the tickets away, she bolstered her courage by donning her aquamarine dress, which she knew Luke admired. To her relief, she did not spot Georgiana's fair head amongst the theatre patrons and she was able to settle down happily to watch O'Keeffe's witty comedy.

'I have ordered supper at the Ship,' Luke informed her as they emerged into the fine balmy evening. 'I thought you might enjoy their crab patties.'

The Old Ship Inn was one of the town's leading hostelries and renowned for its elegant suppers. Ianthe, delighted by Luke's thoughtfulness, was happy to agree to his plan, but no sooner had they sat down than the Countess of Lomond, escorted by a well-dressed cavalier, sailed into view.

'Luke! What a delightful surprise!' she exclaimed, stopping at their table.

He had risen politely at her approach and now bowed with a grace that concealed his irritation.

'May I introduce Sir Charles Fraser? He is an old friend of my husband's. They were shipmates together.' Georgiana turned to her escort and batted her eyelids at him. 'Isn't that so, Charles?'

'I had that honour,' Fraser answered. 'We were midshipmen together and then we both served as lieutenants aboard the *St George*, but that was many years ago.'

Ianthe surveyed him. He was a man in his late thirties, of medium height with a lean figure and light brown hair worn *à la* Titus. His eyes were an indeterminate colour and his features were somewhat heavy, but his expression was good-natured.

'We were about to order supper,' Georgiana said, an expectant note entering her voice.

Luke was trying to think of a polite way of fobbing Georgiana off when Ianthe surprised him.

'Why don't you and Sir Charles join us?' she invited, her gracious smile at odds with her churning stomach. A delightful *surprise*? She'd wager her sapphire necklace that Georgiana had deliberately planned this encounter, but she'd be damned if she let her have things all her own way!

Georgiana threw her a triumphant look. 'Thank you,' she said carelessly and promptly sat down, choosing a seat next to Luke.

Ianthe noted the little frown which creased Sir Charles's brow.

A waiter appeared and began to lay fresh places. He offered to bring a bill of fare, but Georgiana waved him away. 'We will have whatever his lordship is having,' she said impatiently.

She turned to Luke with an engaging smile. 'Wasn't it fortunate that I should bump into Sir Charles this afternoon? I know many people here, we have often visited Brighton, but in Andrew's absence it is nice to have a reliable escort I can call upon whenever necessary.'

Ianthe took a sip of hock to hide her amusement. *She talks about the poor man as if he were a pet poodle.* 'Why didn't your husband accompany you this time, Lady Lomond?' she asked innocently.

Georgiana gave her a sharp look. 'He was busy,' she snapped. 'However, he has no objection to my spending a few weeks here while he remains in Scotland with the children.'

Ianthe widened her eyes. 'You have children?'

'Two boys,' Georgiana answered curtly.

Ianthe had the distinct impression that she regretted mentioning her children. Unless she had missed her guess, Georgiana wanted Luke to think of her as the young girl who had captured his heart, not a staid matron.

'How old are they?'

'Andrew is almost four and James is two.'

'How can you bear to be apart from them?' Ianthe was genuinely curious. She did not think she would care to leave her children for such a long period, especially when they were so young.

The Countess shrugged her white shoulders. 'They have their nurse and any number of servants to look after them,' she declared airily.

Ianthe wasn't going to let her off the hook so easily. 'And your husband, don't you miss him?' she asked.

Georgiana laughed, a bright hard sound that grated on Ianthe's ears. 'Newly-wed as you are, my dear, you may find it hard to imagine, but in time you too may come to prefer your friends' company on occasion to that of your husband.'

'I suppose so.' Ianthe nodded solemnly. 'How long exactly have you been married?'

'La, what does it matter!' Georgiana fluttered her painted chicken-skin fan, plainly irritated by this question. 'Our honeymoon was over long ago!'

Ianthe smiled, as if appreciating the caustic humour of this remark, but persisted, repeating her question with a charming show of interest that left Georgiana no option but to answer.

'Five years,' she said curtly.

'Six, come November,' Sir Charles chimed in. 'I was Andrew's best man so I remember the date well.'

Ianthe saw Luke's fingers tighten on the stem of his wineglass. It was as she had suspected. The little jade hadn't cared a straw for Luke or, if she had, Lomond's offer had quickly eased her heartbreak!

Luke had never known the exact date of Georgiana's wedding. He had taken care not to know it, but now he realised that she must have taken up with Lomond the minute she had given him his *congé* on his return home at the end of September.

Or had she been flirting with Lomond during his absence?

There was a slight silence which Ianthe broke by saying brightly, 'Do let's eat or all this lovely food will get cold!'

The crab patties, the *petites croustades de mauviettes au gratin* and the turbot *à l'Anglaise* were delicious, but Ianthe's appetite vanished swiftly as Georgiana embarked on a story of the first party she had attended at Kildare Park.

'I was very nervous, but your dear mama was so kind to me!' she trilled with a charming smile. 'Do you remember, Luke, how we danced together so often that people began to whisper?'

Watching how her husband's expression softened as the flow of reminiscences continued, Ianthe struggled against the urge to grind her teeth. She was very clever, the little Countess! By constantly reminding Luke of that golden interlude when they had been young, she was strengthening her hold over him!

Turning to Sir Charles, who was equally excluded from this tête-à-tête, she asked him when he had left the Navy.

'Ten years ago, ma'am,' he replied. 'After Trafalgar things were never the same and when my father died I decided to resign my commission.'

'You mentioned the *St George*. Wasn't that the ship in which Lord Nelson sailed to do battle at Copenhagen?'

He nodded and, encouraged by the interest in Ianthe's face and her intelligent questions, went on to give her his impressions of the great man.

To Ianthe's satisfaction, Luke's attention was caught by Nelson's name. He admired the late Admiral, and with an apologetic smile for Georgiana, he joined in their conversation.

Georgiana stared across the table at Ianthe, a look of fury in her green eyes.

Ianthe smiled back sweetly and, under the cover of the table, swiftly crossed her fingers for her luck to continue.

Chapter Eleven

On the first Sunday of August Ianthe and Luke attended Divine Worship at St Nicholas's church. This old parish church contained several memorials to people who had lived in Brighton and Ianthe whiled away a long dull sermon in trying to read the one nearest to the pew in which she was sitting. When they emerged into the bright sunny morning, Luke, who had noted her wandering attention, began to tell her the story of Phoebe Hessell, who had enlisted in the Army as a man in days gone by.

'She served in the 5th Regiment of Foot and was wounded fighting at Fontenoy. She is buried in this churchyard.'

'You mean she was able to keep her identity secret from everyone?' Ianthe exclaimed, much intrigued.

'I dare say her close comrades knew,' Luke shrugged.

'What a fantastic tale! But why did she do it?'

'They say it was for love.' A slightly uncomfortable look appeared on Luke's handsome features. 'Her man enlisted and she wanted to stay with him.'

'How romantic,' Ianthe murmured.

Luke raised one eyebrow. 'My dear, if you had ever served in the army, you would know better than to make such a remark!' Something in the old story had touched him too when he had first heard it, but he wasn't going to admit it. 'The woman was a complete eccentric and must have been as tough as old boots to survive a week, let alone seventeen years of such a hard, unnatural life.'

'Perhaps, but at least she had the courage to follow her heart,' Ianthe retorted defiantly.

Luke snorted in derision and, thoroughly disgruntled, Ianthe removed her hand from his arm and marched off down the path.

'Good morning, my dear. Wasn't that a most boring sermon?' Mrs Coventry hailed Ianthe with a smile.

Hastily schooling her features, Ianthe greeted her friend. Both Emily and Mary had accompanied their mama to church and the conversation quickly turned to the party which the Prince Regent was giving in a few days' time.

'It is so exciting,' Emily exclaimed. 'I have never attended a party given by royalty before! I am quite terrified!'

Ianthe was also nervous, although she was trying to hide it. Luke had carelessly told her that Prinny was a charming host. 'There's no need to fret. Just wear your prettiest dress and smile a lot,' he'd said with his usual cynicism.

If he hadn't been in such an unapproachable mood, she would have thrown a cushion at his head!

A tiny sigh escaped her. That lovely companionship they had shared at Kildare Park seemed like a dream! Even his passion for her seemed to be cooling. Since the Duchess of Bradford's party he had not visited her bed. He had told her that he was suffering from bad insomnia, but she was afraid it was just an excuse to avoid her.

In truth, she didn't know what he was thinking these days and the constant presence of Lady Lomond didn't help. The wretched woman was everywhere!

'Haven't you managed to find a suitable mantua-maker, my dear?' asked Mrs Coventry, misinterpreting Ianthe's glum expression.

'Oh, yes, I did, thank you,' Ianthe answered rather incoherently.

Talk of the Devil! In the few moments she had been away from Luke's side Georgiana had appeared and was now cling-

ing to his arm, a sweet smile on her beautiful face as she
gazed up at him.

'Excellent. I am looking forward to seeing your new gown.'
Mrs Coventry had also noticed the Countess attaching herself
to Lord Kildare.

She frowned and, raising her voice, greeted him.

Luke responded by strolling towards them, but to Ianthe's
disgust, Georgiana came too, her hand still possessively clinging to his arm.

'Good morning, ladies,' Georgiana said, treating them to a
brilliant smile. 'Was it that dreary service which put such a
serious look upon your faces?'

'Oh, no, ma'am,' Emily piped up. 'We were discussing
what we are to wear to the Prince's reception on Wednesday.'

'A most important decision.' Luke smiled at her.

Emily blushed and ducked her head, but her smile told
everyone how much she enjoyed his gentle teasing.

Not liking him to pay attention to even so insignificant a
chit, Georgiana tapped him lightly on the arm. 'Don't torment
the child, Luke!' she said in such an intimate way that Ianthe's
hackles rose. 'I have ordered a new gown myself. From
Francine,' she added self-importantly.

'Isn't that the mantua-maker you were just talking of, Lady
Kildare?' Mary asked.

Ianthe nodded. 'Mrs Murrell recommended her.'

'She is the best in town,' Georgiana asserted, patting her
own bodice in a satisfied manner. 'She delivered this gown
to me only yesterday.'

She was wearing pink again, which Ianthe guessed to be
her favourite colour, but this time the bright lightweight silk
was overlaid with a soft aerophane of white net, which produced a shimmering effect whenever Georgiana moved. It was
a very fashionable style. Together with its shorter, heavily
flounced hemline and very puffed sleeves, the Countess
looked as if she had just stepped out of a fashion-plate.

Meeting Mrs Coventry's eye, Ianthe saw that her friend also

thought the gown more suited to a ballroom than a Sunday morning at church!

'I am sure you will find Francine's services satisfactory, but if you have any problems, just mention my name.'

Ianthe smiled politely, refusing to be ruffled by the patronage in Georgiana's tone. 'I am sure there will be no need. My dress is almost finished.'

'From that Indian stuff I gave you?' Luke, who had been wool-gathering, a look of boredom in his grey eyes, suddenly took an interest in the conversation.

Ianthe nodded. The bolt of decorated silk gauze was one of several Luke had presented to her after the wedding. It was extremely pretty with unusually fine embroidery and she had brought it with her in the hope of finding a good dressmaker. She had mentioned taking it to Francine to Luke last week, but she didn't think he would have remembered. 'I wanted something special for the occasion,' she now told him with a shy smile.

He grinned back at her, obviously pleased that she thought so highly of his present, and then Georgiana dropped her glove.

Ianthe was sure this action was a deliberate ploy to demand his attention, but as Luke stooped to retrieve it, the damage was done. Georgiana gushed her thanks, patting his arm and fluttering her long eyelashes at him.

Their brief moment of closeness was lost and Ianthe curbed a sigh, wondering whether it would ever return again.

Two days later Ianthe was gratified to receive a letter from her mother-in-law. Halfway down the sheet of notepaper she let out a loud whoop that brought Luke hurrying into the morning-room.

'Good God, what is the matter?'

'The Bishop has consented to Harry's suit!' Ianthe waved the letter at him. 'Your mama writes that they are planning on a winter wedding.'

'That is good news indeed!'

'Sophy must be so pleased.'

Luke nodded. How pretty she looked with that joyful smile lighting up her face!

Unaware of his scrutiny, Ianthe had returned her gaze to her letter. 'Your mama also says she is thinking of paying a visit to Brighton!' she exclaimed.

Luke had written to inform Amelia of their change of abode. With frequent and fast mails running between Brighton and the capital, he had felt sure that she would receive his missive before she departed for Hampshire. He hadn't wanted her to return without warning to an empty house, but it seemed his mother had other plans.

'Does Nicodemus travel with her?' he asked.

Ianthe nodded and then handed him the letter. 'Here, read it for yourself.'

'Wouldn't it be nice if he and your mama made a match of it?' Ianthe murmured, watching him swiftly scan the single sheet.

Luke's dark head jerked up. 'What on earth do you mean?'

Ianthe chuckled at his astonished expression. 'Haven't you noticed how well they get on together? And they are both lonely, I think.'

'My mother knows she will always have a home with us,' Luke said stiffly.

'I'm sure she knows she will always be welcome at the Park,' Ianthe replied, choosing her words with care. 'But I don't think she wants to rely on us too much.'

Luke snorted. 'Families belong together,' he stated firmly.

Ianthe had no quarrel with this opinion. 'I agree, Luke, and I'm sure we could all live together in harmony, but you know your mama was talking of buying a house in Alton or Winchester. She has been mistress of Kildare Park for over thirty years. It will not be easy for her to step down.'

Luke suspected Ianthe was right. The only thing stopping his mother from rushing into buying a property of her own was the necessity of finding a house that could accommodate a painting-studio.

'My mother met Nicodemus at the same time as my father,' he said slowly. 'They have been friends ever since, but I do not believe she is interested in him as a husband.'

Ianthe hid a smile. Apparently, Luke hadn't noticed how Amelia had blossomed in Nicodemus's company. Ianthe had never known that her mother-in-law could flirt so charmingly!

Still, it was notoriously hard for children to acknowledge that their parents were capable of romantic feelings!

A slightly rueful smile touched her wide mouth. She had resented Maria when her father had brought her new step-mother home and, while Luke did not have the excuse of being merely eight years old, it was probably going to be hard for him to accept that his mother was entitled to a life of her own.

'It was just an idea,' she said softly. 'Most probably, I am mistaken.'

Luke silently noted her generous retraction.

'On the other hand, if you are right, it might be a good thing for them both,' he said slowly. 'They both deserve to be happy and I certainly shan't cast a rub in their way.'

Ianthe's heart turned over with love for him. So often he tried to hide his generosity of spirit behind a mask of cynicism!

'What are your plans for today?' Luke asked casually, handing the letter back to her.

'I am expecting callers,' Ianthe replied, maintaining her calm expression by sheer will-power.

'Ah yes, today is your at-home morning. I had forgotten.' He had been about to ask her if she would like to accompany him.

Ianthe glanced at the handsome Friesland wall clock which graced the morning room. 'I ought to go and change my dress,' she murmured reluctantly.

This was the longest conversation they had shared since Georgiana had appeared in Brighton. She did not want to bring it to an end, but her guests would be here soon. 'It's the first entertainment I have offered and I want everything to go off well.'

Luke realised she was nervous and decided to remove himself. 'And I promised Charles Fraser I would meet him at Donaldson's.' He grinned suddenly. 'I believe he wants me to introduce him to Mrs Coventry and she is usually to be found there at this hour.'

Ianthe's brows rose. 'If he is interested in Mary, she is *épris* with that young officer—'

Quickly, Luke shook his dark head. 'It's young Emily who has taken his fancy.'

'He is too old for her!'

'Perhaps. But it may not come to anything anyway.'

Ianthe considered the matter. A summer flirtation and why not? Little Emily would enjoy the chance of testing her powers and her watchful mama would not allow the game to go too far.

And if the pair should find themselves truly suited, Sir Charles would make a very eligible *parti*!

'Mrs Coventry promised to call on me later. Why don't you bring Sir Charles back with you? Both Mary and Emily will be here.'

'A capital idea!' Luke grinned at his wife. 'I am beginning to think you have a talent for matchmaking, Lady Kildare!'

Ianthe laughed, immensely cheered to see him so light-hearted after his withdrawn mood of the last few days.

Bidding him farewell, she hurried upstairs to change the simple round-gown she was wearing for her more elegant blue-sprigged muslin.

She had barely seated herself in the drawing-room than her first guests arrived and the next hour was busy as she entertained a stream of callers. It was the first time she had played hostess as a married woman, but her confidence rose as the minutes ticked past. Everything was going splendidly. Her guests praised the lightness of Cook's macaroons and drop cakes, glasses of iced orgeat, lemonade and wine were drunk and the conversation never faltered.

When Luke walked in a little after noon he took in the scene with a quick glance and felt a flicker of pride. No one could have guessed how Ianthe had been fretting earlier!

He introduced Sir Charles to Emily and was in turn drawn into conversation by her mother when Abbott, the butler hired along with the house, announced the arrival of a new guest.

'Dear Lady Kildare, I hope you don't mind me dropping in on you,' Georgiana exclaimed gaily as she swept confidently into the room in a cloud of perfume and rose pink spider-gauze.

Ianthe forced herself to return the Countess's greeting with a polite smile. Since Lady Lomond was brass-faced enough to push in without an invitation, good manners dictated that Ianthe must pretend the omission had been an oversight.

'Luke!' Without bothering to exchange another word with her hostess, Georgiana immediately darted over to where Luke stood.

Finding it painful to watch them together, Ianthe quickly turned away.

When she looked back again some minutes later she was surprised to see that Luke was talking to Emily Coventry and Georgiana was nowhere to be seen. Concealing her relief, she began to move towards them, but was waylaid by another guest.

Nodding and smiling, she listened to the young man, an officer friend of Captain Regan's, with all the appearance of attention, but her concentration was focused on what Luke was saying.

He appeared to be telling Emily an Indian legend. Ianthe had no idea how they had got on to such a subject, but Emily was plainly fascinated by the story of how an Indian prince had found a beautiful woman weeping in the forest when he was out hunting deer. The lovely stranger told Ali Mardan Khan that she was a princess from over the mountains and that all her family had been killed by enemies and she was lost and alone.

'Falling in love with her at first sight, Ali Mardan asked

her to marry him and they lived in his marble palace on the
shores of a lake,' Luke continued, smiling down into Emily's
rapt little face. 'But soon their happiness was disturbed by the
fearful stomach pains which assaulted Ali Mardan. His new
bride nursed him tenderly, but he grew worse day by day.
Then one morning, when the prince was taking air in the
garden, he encountered a holy man asleep under a tree.
Princess Amali wanted to throw him out, but Ali Mardan said
holy men were a blessing and invited him to stay.'

'What happened next?' Emily demanded.

'Delighted by the prince's kindness, the holy man offered
his knowledge of medicine and examined Ali Mardan. Then
he asked if the prince was newly married. On hearing that
this was so, at dinner that night he secretly sprinkled extra
salt upon Princess Amali's plate.'

Luke smiled at Emily's confusion. 'He knew, you see, that
she was a Lamia.'

The odd-sounding word made Ianthe edge a little closer.
Unfortunately, at that moment the lieutenant chose to let out
a loud bray of laughter and she missed some of what Luke
was saying.

'The bedroom door was locked and the windows were
barred with iron grilles. Desperate with thirst, Amali stretched
and her body grew thinner until her bones melted away and
a ten-foot serpent stood there, glistening green in the moonlight. Out through the filigree ironwork she slithered down to
the lake to drink her fill before returning to the palace.'

Her eyes wide, Emily begged him to continue.

'In the shadows the holy man waited, a little silver hatchet
in his hand,' Luke obliged. 'The moment her head went
through the iron bars he struck, but she was too quick and
escaped. Next morning he went to Ali Mardan and apologised
for failing to kill the wicked creature who was feeding on his
lifeblood. Ali Mardan refused to believe that his wife could
be a three-hundred-year-old evil monster who could change
her form at will, but when the princess came into the room

her arm was bandaged. "Oh, I dropped my mirror and cut myself," she told them.'

'Did he believe her?' Emily asked.

Ianthe watched Luke shake his dark head. 'He was in love and did not wish to think ill of her, but in the end he was convinced and asked the holy man what he must do to be free. "The only cure is to kill her," answered the holy man.'

To Ianthe's irritation, the Lieutenant announced his intention of leaving and she was obliged to give him her full attention as they said farewell. By the time he had bowed and departed, she had missed how the deed was actually done.

She turned back to listen and out of the corner of her eye noticed a flick of rose pink skirts behind her, but she was too interested in hearing what her husband had to say to turn round and acknowledge Georgiana.

'The next morning Ali Mardan woke up free from pain at last and the holy man bade him goodbye with an injunction to beware of women for they are all too cunning to be trusted,' Luke said, concluding the story.

Emily giggled. 'That is a fascinating legend, my lord,' she said. 'But I am not sure you didn't make that last bit up to tease me!'

'How so, Miss Coventry?'

'Well, Amali wasn't a woman, was she?' Emily pointed out. 'She was a Lamia.'

More perceptive than the younger girl, Ianthe saw how her husband's tall figure stiffened slightly. 'Indeed she was but, as Ali Mardan found out, sometimes it is hard to tell the difference between a monster and an untrustworthy woman.'

Thinking him to be teasing her yet again Emily let out a squeal of scandalised laughter, but Ianthe shivered, turning icy cold as Luke looked up, his gaze scanning the room.

He was staring straight at her and, in spite of his debonair smile, his grey eyes were glittering with fierce conviction. He meant every word of what he'd just said!

The prospect of being entertained by Royalty made Ianthe take considerable pains over her appearance. When she came

into the drawing-room where Luke was waiting to escort her
to the Pavilion he let out a low whistle of approval.

The deep blue colour of her new gown matched the star
sapphires she wore. Tiny puff sleeves showed off her white
arms and she had chosen a simple, high-waisted style, which
flattered her tall slim figure.

'It looks very well on you!' he exclaimed, deciding that
extra trimmings would have spoilt its lovely flowing lines.

Ianthe thanked him quietly. Francine had delivered the
gown that morning and Ianthe could not fault the result. The
gown was lovely, bringing out the colour of her eyes to perfection, but she was disappointed that the mantua-maker had
somehow managed to use up all the material. She'd thought
there would be enough left over to present a length to Mrs
Coventry, who had greatly admired its unusual silver embroidery.

During the short drive to the Pavilion Luke chatted amiably
and was somewhat surprised by his wife's monosyllabic replies. Perhaps she was nervous at the prospect of meeting the
Regent?

A tiny frown touched Luke's brow. Now he came to think
on it, she had been in a quiet, withdrawn mood since yesterday. Not that they had spent much time together. They had
both had separate engagements, which had kept them apart
until this evening.

'Tonight, after this reception is over, we must talk,' he said
abruptly as the carriage came to a halt outside the fairytale
domes and towers of the Pavilion.

Ianthe nodded, hiding her unease behind an acquiescent
smile.

Was he going to tell her that their marriage was a mistake?
she wondered nervously. Her optimistic belief that she would
eventually succeed in winning his heart had been severely
shaken by his cutting remarks about an untrustworthy woman.

But perhaps there was still hope, she told herself as she
stepped across the threshold of the palace and found herself

in an octagonal vestibule lit by a large Chinese lantern. At least he still seemed to find her attractive.

They moved on into the famous Chinese Gallery, an immensely long apartment decorated in luxuriant pinks, reds, amber and blue. Its ceiling seemed largely to consist of an amazing stained-glass skylight depicting the Chinese god of thunder and Ianthe could barely contain her gasp of awe.

'A veritable kingdom of bamboo and fine porcelain, ain't it?' Luke whispered with a little chuckle.

Ianthe didn't answer. She had just spotted the Regent, his corpulence unfortunately emphasised by a dazzling waistcoat and skin-tight bright blue coat, affably receiving his guests in the centre of the Gallery.

Luke took her over to be presented and, sinking into a deep curtsy, Ianthe found her hand being taken very cordially into the Regent's own.

'So you are Lord Kildare's new bride, my dear,' he said in a genial tone. 'And a very lucky dog he is, too, if I may say so.'

There was a rather arch twinkle in the prince's blue eyes and Ianthe blushed rosily.

The Regent, who for all his faults was a gentleman and had no wish to embarrass a guest, promptly changed the subject by asking her how she liked Brighton. Her enthusiastic reply pleased him so much that he kept her talking for several minutes until it was impossible to ignore the next party of arriving guests.

'You are a hit,' Luke murmured as they moved away.

Ianthe grinned at him, feeling suddenly light-hearted. 'He approves of my liking for the exotic!'

The Regent had admired the unusual pattern of silver flowers and birds decorating her dress, a compliment which had led to a discussion of Indian art and architecture. Thanks to Luke's discourses, Ianthe was able to converse intelligently on the subject and her remarks had impressed the prince.

A footman offered them a tray of refreshments and they were swept up into exchanging greetings with the numerous friends and acquaintances who were present. Separated by the crush, Ianthe did not realise that Luke was missing until Mrs Coventry came up to her to inform her that the Regent had asked Luke to join him in the Red Drawing Room for a few minutes' private conversation before the entertainment was to begin in the Music Room.

'He probably wants to talk to Luke about India,' Ianthe said, her heart swelling with vicarious pride.

'Indeed,' agreed Mrs Coventry with a smile.

The Regent was fond of entertaining his guests with selections from Handel or the Italian operas and Ianthe guessed that he would not keep Luke long. Deciding to wait for her husband to emerge, she urged Mrs Coventry to go on ahead when people began to move off in the direction of the Music Room.

The last few guests were drifting away when a latecomer entered the Gallery.

Ianthe, who had just decided to follow the others and meet Luke in the Music Room, halted abruptly as the woman walked towards her and she recognised Lady Lomond.

'Where did you get that dress?' she demanded, staring in consternation at Georgiana's lavish outfit.

A tinkling laugh escaped the Countess's painted lips. 'Oh, dear! How very careless of Luke to give you the same gift as he gave me!'

Georgiana observed the horrified dismay which flashed over her rival's expressive face and smiled. 'I do think he should have warned us and then perhaps we could have avoided this embarrassing situation. Now everyone will jump to the inevitable conclusion and his secret will be out.'

'Are you saying he is your lover?' Ianthe forced the words out between her clenched teeth, unable to take her eyes off the silver embroidered open robe which Georgiana wore over a pale pink satin slip.

There could be no mistake. The design was too unusual. Everyone seeing it would know that Luke must have given it to her...and recognise the implication!

Georgiana shrugged her plump white shoulders in answer to Ianthe's question. 'I'm sorry you had to find out in such a humiliating fashion,' she purred insincerely. 'But, you see, he has never been able to forget me.'

A wave of despair swept over Ianthe. How little Luke must think of her if he gave his mistress a present which was identical to the one he had given her!

'I dare say he never stopped to consider the gossip that would inevitably ensue when we were both seen wearing identical gowns,' Georgiana continued. 'It is doubly unfortunate that it has happened under the Regent's roof. The tattle-mongers will have a field day!' She fluttered her pink fan at Ianthe and gave her a coy smile. 'Unless...would you like me to leave before anyone else sees me?'

This solicitous offer was the final straw! Rage replaced the mortification which had twisted Ianthe's stomach into a tight knot. 'Pray do not trouble yourself, ma'am,' she snapped and, whirling on her heel, stalked towards the exit.

'Ianthe! Wait!'

A touch on her arm brought Ianthe's flight to a halt as she reached the Octagon Hall and she turned to find Charlotte Murrell regarding her with a sympathetic expression.

'I saw Georgiana talking to you,' Lottie said simply.

The compassionate understanding in her eyes merely exacerbated the black rage which had invaded Ianthe's heart. 'Please let me go, Lottie,' she grated. 'There is no point in my staying.'

'You should talk to Luke,' Lottie urged, but obediently removed her hand from Ianthe's arm.

Ianthe shook her head violently. 'Luke has made his choice, but I have no intention of being publicly humiliated by his preference for that woman.' She gave Lottie a twisted smile. 'He never wanted to marry me so I am sure he will appreciate being given back his freedom.'

'Let me take you home. We can send a message to the Regent saying you were taken ill. I'm sure Luke will understand—'

'I don't give a fig what Luke thinks,' Ianthe interrupted wildly. 'I'm leaving Brighton and I'm not coming back.'

She summoned one of the gorgeously liveried footmen who stood like blank-faced statues by the main door with a flick of her fan and ordered him to have her carriage brought round.

'Ianthe! You can't!' Lottie gasped when the footman disappeared to carry out this command. 'Only think of the scandal!'

Ianthe shrugged defiantly. 'I don't care! I won't go on living with a man who despises me.'

Lottie decided that there was no sense in trying to reason with her when she was so distraught. 'Where will you go?' she asked quietly.

'I'm not sure yet.' In the midst of her fury, Ianthe suddenly realised the impossibility of returning to Northwood. 'Anywhere will do so long as it is far away from *him*.'

'What about money?' Lottie suddenly became practical. 'I can lend you some if you need it.'

'I still have most of this quarter's allowance and there are my jewels.' Ianthe gave her a somewhat watery smile of thanks. 'Perhaps I shall go to France. I will have enough to live on there for a while if I am careful.'

The footman returned at that moment with the information that her ladyship's carriage was waiting for her beneath the canopy of the *porte-cochère*.

Ianthe thanked him and hurried out into the warm night.

'I do wish you wouldn't rush into running away,' Lottie wailed, tagging along at her heels. 'Pray reconsider! Things will look different when you've had time to recover from the shock.'

Ianthe ignored this plea and bent to kiss her cheek. 'Goodbye, Lottie, and thank you for being such a good friend,' she said and quickly got into the carriage.

Lottie watched it drive away at a spanking pace and then turned away with a sigh to return to the party.

The peace of Marine Parade was severely disturbed in the early hours of Thursday morning by violent knocking upon the door of the house hired by the rich Mrs Murrell. After several minutes it brought Lord Kildare the result he desired as one of the upstairs windows had its sash flung up and an indignant voice demanded if he had run mad.

'Go away, Luke! You will wake the neighbours!' Lottie added in a loud hiss.

'I don't care if I wake the Devil himself. I am not budging from this step until you agree to receive me so tell those mutton-headed servants of yours to open this door and let me in.'

Deducing from his lordship's angry voice that he would continue to hammer upon her door like a lunatic if she did not submit to his wishes, Lottie sighed and told her maid to go down and inform the footman to admit him. 'Have him shown into the drawing-room and tell him I shall be down in a few minutes when I am dressed.'

Lottie had returned home as early as could be contrived from the Pavilion. She had gone to bed, but she had not been able to sleep a wink. The Regent had kindly overlooked Ianthe's breach of protocol, apparently accepting Lottie's stammered excuse that Lady Kildare had been obliged to leave in haste due to sudden illness, but Lottie had seen how the royal gaze had fastened itself thoughtfully upon the Countess of Lomond's dress.

He had not been the only one to notice the similarity and the whispering had begun even before Lottie had left. Luke's grey eyes were so stormy that she had lacked the courage to approach him directly and had cravenly ordered one of the footmen to deliver the same message to him as she had given the Regent.

Evidently, he had discovered that it had been a lie!

When she entered the elegant crimson-hung drawing-room, Luke was pacing up and down in a fashion that made her worry for the houseowner's Turkey carpet. 'Won't you sit down?' she invited nervously.

He shook his head impatiently.

Her offer of refreshment was greeted with a similar look of irritation. 'Good God, Lottie, I didn't come here to drink tea!' he exclaimed.

'I wish you hadn't come here at all,' Lottie retorted frankly. 'It won't do my reputation a particle of good.'

A rueful grin flashed briefly across his lordship's handsome features. 'I'll square things with Regan if he kicks up a dust,' he promised.

Lottie's severe expression softened. For an instant he had looked like a naughty schoolboy caught out in mischief, but the bleak misery quickly returned to his eyes, confirming her suspicion that he had discovered Ianthe's flight.

'I suppose you think I know where Ianthe has gone,' she said, seating herself upon one of the elegant giltwood chairs which graced the room.

'I came here in that hope.'

'Didn't she leave you a note?'

Luke shook his head. 'Not a word,' he growled.

It wasn't strictly true, but his pride would not allow him to reveal that he had found the dress Ianthe had worn and all the sapphires he had given her thrown across his pillow. A torn-out empty page from the back of his sketch-book lay next to them with a single line scribbled upon it.

Rich gifts wax poor when givers prove unkind.

Luke had recognised the quote from *Hamlet*. They were the words Ophelia used when trying to return his gifts to Hamlet, who no longer appeared to love her.

Numbly, his mind still refusing to accept the evidence of her decision, he had picked up his sketch-book, which lay on the floor by the bed. He had left it on his night-table and Ianthe must have grabbed it in a hurry to serve as notepaper. It had fallen open at the page he had been working on. A bitter taste of bile had filled his mouth as he stared at the sketch of Georgiana. He had finished it earlier that afternoon and the tender curve of her rosebud mouth smiled up at him.

Clutching at a faint hope that Ianthe might have looked at the rest of the sketches which filled the book, he had forced himself to quell the sick dismay choking his throat and return to her bedroom to search for any evidence which might tell him where she planned to go.

Discarded clothes lay scattered on the bed and her dressing-table lacked several toilette articles, but the room revealed no other clues. Furiously angry at being thwarted, he woke all the servants to question them and to his astonishment discovered that his wife had left her maid behind.

Jenny, however, was no help at all. After explaining that she had gone to bed early—Ianthe having told her she need not wait up for her return—she had burst into noisy tears. Out of the other servants, only Abbott, who had admitted her, had seen Ianthe, but he stammered that he had not been aware that her ladyship had left the house again.

Luke had eventually roared dismissal at the lot of them and stamped into the study to try and think. Such was the turbulent state of his mind it took him some time to remember that the footman at the Pavilion had murmured that Mrs Murrell had asked him to convey the message that Ianthe had been taken mysteriously ill.

What's more, Lottie had disappeared early from the party, which was unheard of for her. Coming to the conclusion that the widow must know something, he had sped hotfoot round to Marine Parade.

'I'm sorry for forcing myself upon you like this,' he now apologised roughly to his hostess. 'But I won't leave until you tell me everything you know.'

Lottie sighed. 'I wish I could help you, Luke, but I don't know anything of significance.'

'Didn't you speak to her before she left?'

'Yes, but only for a few moments.' Lottie gestured helplessly with her hands. 'I tried to persuade her to stay, but she wouldn't listen to me. She was much too upset!'

Luke winced.

Exasperated by this lack of logic, Lottie gazed at him crossly. 'You have only yourself to blame, you know! What on earth did you expect? Ianthe has far too much pride to swallow such an insult. If you did not wish to offend her, why did you give Georgiana an identical gift—?'

'I gave Georgiana nothing! I don't know how she came by that dress, but I assure you it wasn't a gift from me.'

The anger in his voice silenced Lottie for a moment and then she rallied. 'But you cannot deny you have been flirting with her ever since she arrived in Brighton.'

Luke ran a weary hand through his thick hair. 'Correction. *She* has been flirting with me!'

Lottie chewed over this distinction thoughtfully. 'I suppose it would have caused a lot of gossip if you had cut her dead.'

'Exactly so. With everyone's eyes upon us, I judged it better to try to act in a civilised fashion. After all, we were bound to run into each other sometime and a public estrangement would only fuel further tattle.' He shrugged. 'I thought the surest way of defusing the situation was to show the world that our former passion had dwindled to nothing more than polite friendship.'

A heavy frown creased his forehead. 'My mistake was to believe that Georgiana would accept that it was over between us.'

Lottie lifted her eyebrows. 'She wanted more?'

'At Sally Bradford's *fête champêtre* she told me she was tired of her husband and wanted my love again.' Luke gave a cynical laugh. 'She talked a lot of nonsense about leaving Lomond, which I don't think she would ever do. She enjoys his wealth and position far too much to throw it away for a whim.'

'You don't think her feelings for you are genuine?' Lottie asked cautiously.

'Of course not! She is playing silly games because she's bored and thinks an affair with me would be exciting.'

'And you? How do you feel about her?' Lottie asked curiously.

'That is my business.' A muscle at the corner of his well-cut mouth twitched betrayingly and Lottie was satisfied. If he wasn't in love with Ianthe, she was a Dutchman!

'However, this time she has gone too far. I will not tolerate her parading herself before the *ton* as my mistress,' Luke vowed grimly. 'If she does not agree to leave Brighton, I will expose her pretence and reveal her as the shameless liar she is to the world.'

Lottie's mouth fell open. The scandal would be immense! But she had no doubt that he would do it and be damned to the consequences.

'However, Georgiana can wait. Right now I am more interested in discovering my wife's whereabouts.'

A snatch of conversation rose to the surface of Lottie's memory. 'Ianthe said something about settling in France,' she murmured. 'I thought she was joking, but during her at-home morning the other day someone was talking about a local smuggler who has acquired a name for himself by offering cheap passages across the Channel with no questions asked. We were all laughing about abandoning our everyday cares and escaping to a new life.'

She gave a little apologetic shrug. 'It was just playful nonsense, of course, but Ianthe seemed quite intrigued by the idea and maybe—'

'Maybe she has decided it would be the surest way to get away from me,' Luke interrupted, his mouth twisting bitterly.

He had already come to the conclusion that she would not head for Northwood. It was too obvious a bolt-hole and since it was now legally his property she would not feel safe from him there. The Turners were still living in the house since he had given them a generous period of time to find themselves a new home, but he could not believe that she would want to ask them for help. Nor would she wish to worry her grandmother.

He had wondered if she might have fled to friends, but Lottie's suggestion made alarm bells ring in his head. In her present frame of mind, Ianthe might well have decided to embark upon such a crazy scheme.

She had always wanted to travel!

'What is the name of this smuggler?' he asked Lottie.

'I can't remember,' she answered and Luke's face fell. 'But I'm sure Sir Charles Fraser will. He was the one who told us. He seemed to know quite a lot about the fellow.'

'Thank you.' Luke came forward and bowed over her hand. 'I'll leave you in peace and seek Fraser out.'

At the door he paused and looked back at her with a warm smile. 'If you decide to accept him, Regan will be a lucky man.'

'Don't be a goose, Luke.' Lottie blushed with pleasure. 'I'm glad if I have been of help. I like Ianthe and it is my sincere hope that you will manage to find her swiftly and settle the differences between you.'

A crooked grin lit up his lordship's face. 'God willing, that's just what I intend to do!'

The only thing Ianthe had known about Shoreham until this moment was that King Charles the Second had escaped to France in 1651 from its small harbour. Her knowledge of the place, however, was expanding rapidly, she concluded with a frustrated sigh as her gaze swept the High Street once more.

A pair of drunken revellers spilled out from the lighted doorway across the road and she drew back hastily into the shadows. Even on a hired nag which had seen better days and dressed in a concealing riding-cloak, she felt horribly conspicuous.

Perhaps it was a stupid idea to seek out Joe Wilkes at this late hour. No doubt it would have been better to wait for the morning and safer still to have sought passage on one of the regular packet-boats. Unfortunately, both of these sensible plans would have involved delay.

Speed was essential. The longer she delayed, the more chance there was of Luke catching up with her. Not that he cared one iota for her, Ianthe thought, repressing a doleful sigh as she quietly urged her mount forward again. Pride, however, he had in plenty and he would not care to figure as a deserted husband.

For an instant Ianthe's conviction that Luke would follow

her wavered. Perhaps he cared for Georgiana so deeply that he was willing to let the world say what it wished!

Ianthe struggled to breathe normally as she tried to crush the pain filling her heart. She must face facts. Luke did not love her. If she had ever doubted that it was Georgiana he wanted, tonight had shown her the error of her ways.

Her hands shook on the reins as she remembered the sketch of Georgiana she had found by Luke's bed. It had been drawn with such tenderness! The instant she had seen it, her last stubborn hope that there could have been some mistake over their almost identical gowns exploded into oblivion.

No, Luke did not want her, but it would be a mistake to underestimate the effect her flight would have on him. He would hate to become a laughing-stock! Recovering his errant wife would help still wagging tongues and allow the *ton* to wink at his dalliance with Georgiana.

Once he realised that she had gone, it was likely that he would bend all his considerable energies into finding her, which was why she was willing to take the risk of bribing a smuggler to take her over to France.

She would be able to disappear without a trace if what Charles had said about Wilkes was true. He sounded just the kind of man who could be paid to keep a secret. Luke hadn't been present when the discussion about Wilkes had taken place. With luck, he would imagine she had fled to one of her friends in Hertfordshire. Even if by some chance he guessed she was heading for France, he would assume she meant to travel on one of the packet-services across the Channel. By the time he discovered she had not booked a passage on any of them, she would have covered her tracks so that he would never find her.

Unwilling to examine why this last thought should depress her so severely, Ianthe forced herself to concentrate on the task in hand. Charles had said that Wilkes had a cottage down by the harbour, near to the church of St Mary de Haura. All but one of the small dwellings there had been in darkness, but when she had knocked upon its door she had struck lucky.

'Aye, Joe Wilkes lives here right enough,' said the tawdrily dressed young woman who had answered her summons. 'But he ain't in.'

Praying that the smuggler was not away at sea, Ianthe had begged to know where he could be found.

'He's most likely still drinking.' The girl, who was pretty in a thin-faced, haggard kind of way, yawned and scratched at her dirty auburn head. 'Try the inn, the Royal Oak, in the High Street.' She gave Ianthe a sharp look. 'What do you want him for anyway?'

'A matter of business.' Ianthe had backed hastily away, fearing further questions.

The trouble was, she thought to herself as she scanned the noisy hostelry again, was that she looked completely out of place. She had taken the precaution of dressing plainly in her oldest riding-habit, but its excellent cut and material could not be disguised. What's more, as soon as she opened her mouth she revealed herself as well-born.

Which made it very difficult for her to step inside the building she was watching. There was no hope that she could blend in with the locals. Wishing that the hour wasn't so late, she was screwing up her courage to dismount and enter the premises when a scrawny child of some ten years or so came hurrying down the street.

'Hey! You, there,' she called to him as he drew abreast.

The boy came to a wary halt. 'What do ye want?' he demanded, regarding her with deep suspicion.

'Would you be willing to do me a favour?'

'Depends.'

'I'll give you a shilling for running an errand for me,' Ianthe said quickly.

A thoughtful frown touched his grimy face. 'Mam told me to fetch m'brother home from the inn before he gets himself too drunk and she'll clout me if I'm late.' Then, obviously tempted by the generosity of her offer into risking retribution, he shrugged. 'All right. I reckon I can spare a couple of minutes.'

Ianthe fished out a coin from the small purse she had stowed within the jacket of her riding-habit. 'Here.' She tossed it down to him and he caught it deftly.

He laughed cheekily when she told him what she wanted. 'That's easy, but I can't promise he'll come out and talk to ye.'

'Just ask.' Ianthe urged him on with a wave of her hand and, whistling cheerfully, he disappeared into the inn.

Waiting impatiently, Ianthe wondered how much Wilkes would charge if he agreed to take her as a passenger. She had hidden most of her money and her jewellery in a soft leather draw-string bag, which she had tied around her waist beneath her skirts. She could feel it digging into her whenever she moved too abruptly and there was a tell-tale bulge if one looked closely, but she felt it was better to be uncomfortable than risk having a pickpocket relieve her of what now constituted her entire fortune.

It was all she had in the world, apart from the contents of her purse and the small bag of clothes and personal possessions she had tied on to her saddle. Even her horse was hired! Not that she would have dreamt of owning such a sluggard!

A bitter smile flickered over her face. She was sure the owner of the livery stable had not believed her story of needing a horse in a hurry to visit a relative who had suddenly taken desperately sick. The excuse was all Ianthe could think of on the spur of the moment when she had seen his look of astonishment at her entrance to his small establishment so late at night.

He'd demanded an outrageous fee, and then insisted she paid him double if she did not wish to return the horse herself. When she had protested at the steepness of the price, he'd pointed out that he would have to send someone to collect the mount from Shoreham.

'Take it or leave it, miss,' he'd smirked. 'And I'd be obliged if you could make your mind up right away. It's nearly eleven and I want to get off to bed.'

If she'd had any other choice, Ianthe would have told him

to boil his head and walked out. She suspected the fellow knew she couldn't afford to quibble for, with a sly grin, he had pocketed her money and then saddled up this poor old beast!

All her skill had failed to quicken the cob's pace. Luckily, there was a fitful moon to light her way and she had ridden the road before on a pleasure-jaunt with the Coventry girls so it wasn't entirely strange to her. All the same, it was now well after midnight and the silent darkness of the empty street seemed suddenly very threatening as a burly-shouldered man came out of the inn and walked towards her with a rolling gait.

Chapter Twelve

'**Y**ou want to talk to me?'

'If you are Joe Wilkes, I do,' Ianthe said in a composed voice that was at variance with her shaking knees.

The moon peeked out from behind the scudding clouds showing her a mouthful of broken teeth as he grinned up at her. 'Aye, I'm Wilkes. And you'll be?'

'My name is none of your business,' Ianthe retorted hastily.

His smile faded. 'Mebbe not, but I'm damned if I'll do business with ye sitting up there looking down your nose at me.'

Realising she had inadvertently offended him, Ianthe gave him a conciliatory smile and slid down from her horse.

Standing next to him, she saw that he was taller than she had first supposed. Young, too. No more than a few years older than herself, if she was any judge, though it was hard to be sure in this light.

It was too dark to make out his features clearly, but he wore a woollen cap pushed back on his head and his clothes reeked of tobacco smoke and ancient dirt. Resisting the urge to wrinkle her nose, she said, 'I want to book immediate passage with you across to France.'

'Do you now?' His gaze raked her up and down. 'And who told ye that I might be able to help?'

'Does it matter?' Ianthe shrugged airily.

Inwardly, she was struggling to preserve her confidence. She had known that Wilkes must be something of a ruffian but, now that she had actually met him, the lunacy inherent in her plan was beginning to make itself felt even through the haze of fury and pain which clouded her thoughts.

'Not if you've got the ready.' His broken teeth flashed in the moonlight as he answered her. 'My price is high, ye see.'

'I can pay you well. All I ask is that you do not tattle about me to anyone.'

He lifted his brows at her. 'Mebbe we'd better go inside and discuss it over a drink.'

Ianthe hesitated.

'What's the matter?' Wilkes demanded. 'Too high and mighty for sharing a bottle with the likes of me, eh?'

Hearing the ugly note in his voice Ianthe decided on frankness. 'I've no objection to drinking with you, Mr Wilkes,' she said in her most soothing tone. 'However, I'd prefer not to be seen by too many people.'

He nodded, mollified. 'Fair enough, but we can't stand here jawing all night.'

'Couldn't we go on board your boat?'

He shook his head. 'High water ain't for a few hours yet and I've no mind to hang about waiting on the *Seagull* when I can sleep in my own bed.' He gave a short laugh. 'I'll warn ye now, she ain't some luxury yacht.'

Ianthe's confidence sank still lower. 'What about your cottage?'

He thought about it for a moment and then nodded. 'All right, but ye'll have to stable the nag here.'

'Very well.' Since she had intended to leave the horse in the care of the Royal Oak's landlord in any event, Ianthe had no objection to his curt stipulation.

They walked round to the back of the inn and entered a straw-littered yard. Wilkes removed her small valise from the cob's back and handed it to her. 'Wait here if ye don't want to be seen,' he muttered.

He led the horse forward and lent over the open half-door

of the ramshackle building which she guessed to be the stable-block.

'Jem! Get your lazy bones out here.'

His low growl roused a sleepy-looking groom and Ianthe pulled the hood of her riding-cloak further over her face as she watched him exchange a few words with the man.

Whatever he said seemed to do the trick. With a nod the groom led the cob inside and Wilkes returned to her.

'Come on,' he instructed, and, leading the way back to the street, began to walk in the direction of the harbour.

He didn't offer to take her bag and his lack of courtesy was a sharp reminder to Ianthe of how far she had strayed from her own world. A feeling of unwilling apprehension grew in her as she followed him. Concentrating on her anger, she stubbornly ignored it. This was her best chance to get away from her despicable husband and she wasn't going to let namby-pamby missishness prevent her from taking it!

Within a few minutes they had reached the cottage, which was now in darkness. 'Good. Maggie has gone to bed,' Wilkes muttered, producing a key from his pocket and unlocking the front door.

Once inside, he quickly lit a candle. 'Well, don't just stand there, woman. Come in and shut the door behind ye,' he ordered.

Crushing her reluctance, Ianthe obeyed.

'Sit down.' Wilkes waved her towards the large deal table which stood in the centre of the room. 'I'll get us that drink.'

Ianthe took one of the rush-backed chairs he indicated while the smuggler lit another candle. Leaving one candlestick in the middle of the table, he walked across the room with the other to forage in a tall oak cupboard. His back was turned towards her so Ianthe seized the opportunity to indulge her curiosity and look around her.

The parlour, which also seemed to serve as a kitchen to judge by the cooking utensils clustered around the hearth, was in dire need of a thorough cleaning, but it was furnished with a degree of comfort that surprised her. A handsome long-case clock stood in one corner, thick rugs were scattered over the stone-flagged floor and silk cushions graced a dainty sofa.

He liked to live well on the result of his ill-gotten gains, she supposed, with a flicker of wry amusement.

Her host returned to the table carrying a squat black bottle and two elegant wine-glasses. 'Best French brandy,' he announced, a smug note in his voice, confirming her suspicions.

Ianthe accepted the long-stemmed goblet he handed to her and sipped cautiously. She was not accustomed to drinking spirits, but the dark gold liquid was reassuringly smooth and it lit a comforting glow in her churning stomach.

Wilkes sat down. 'So you want to go to France.'

Ianthe nodded.

'I have contacts in Dieppe.' He scratched his chin thoughtfully. 'I might be able to pick up a cargo there at short notice. Would that suit your plans?'

'Anywhere will do so long as we can sail on the next tide,' Ianthe affirmed.

'Running away from your family, are ye? Or is it a husband?'

Glad that her riding-gloves concealed her hands, for although she had left her betrothal ring behind she hadn't been able to bring herself to remove her wedding-band, Ianthe remained silent.

'Aye, well.' After a moment Wilkes chuckled. 'It's none of my business, I suppose, providing you can meet my price.'

He looked her up and down and Ianthe had the uncomfortable feeling he was assessing the depth of her desperation as much as her well-clad appearance.

The sum he named took her breath away. 'Good God!' she exclaimed. 'I want a single passage, not to buy your whole boat!'

Wilkes laughed again, but there was no mirth in the sound. 'Beggars can't be choosers, my fine lady,' he said softly.

There was a taut silence for a second or two.

''Course, I could be mistaken,' Wilkes took a leisurely pull at his brandy. 'Mebbe there's no one looking for ye. Aye, mebbe ye've got all the right papers an' all.'

Ianthe bit her lip. In her frantic haste, she had overlooked her lack of documents and she had no permission of entry! She would probably be able to bribe the French officials, if necessary, but it was one more thing to worry about.

She did quick calculations in her head. Wilkes had guessed she was in the suds and didn't want to travel in the normal way. Her plight had excited his greed and he was asking for far more than she had reckoned upon. Unfortunately, she doubted she could bargain him down. There was an avaricious look in his narrow hazel eyes, but her jewellery was valuable. Once sold, she could live on the proceeds for a considerable time.

'All right,' she said calmly. 'But you get paid when we get to France and not before.'

He pursed his full lips. 'Half now and half when we land.'

Ianthe shook her head. 'No,' she said firmly and pushed back her chair as if preparing to leave.

'Not so fast!' He reached out a large meaty hand to detain her, a flicker of respect passing over his face. 'Tell you what. Give me twenty pounds now as earnest of your good faith and we'll call it a deal.'

'Done,' said Ianthe with an inward sigh of relief.

Luckily, she had enough left in her purse to pay him without having to extract any money from her secret store, but just as she reached to withdraw it from her jacket the door at the rear of the room opened.

'Joe? Ain't ye coming to bed yet?' The pretty young redhead Ianthe had met earlier stood in the doorway rubbing her eyes and yawning.

Her gaze sharpened when she noticed Ianthe. 'Who's she?'

'Go back to bed, Maggie.' Impatience filled the smuggler's voice.

The girl's hands balled on her hips. 'I wants to know what's going on,' she announced, her tone turning shrill. 'Why are ye drinking with that stuck-up doxy? She was sniffing round here earlier looking for ye.'

'It's business,' Wilkes growled, glaring at her. 'Don't interfere.'

'Aw, Joe, ye know I don't likes it when ye keep secrets.' A whining note entered the redhead's voice and she began to advance into the room.

'I said out!' Angry colour flooded the smuggler's face.

Maggie halted and threw Ianthe a filthy look. 'See ye keep your hands to yourself,' she threatened.

'Maggie! Do as you're bid or I'll leather ye.' Joe Wilkes half rose from his chair.

'All right, I'm going.' Maggie retreated from the menacing expression on his face.

She slammed the bedroom door shut behind her.

'Stupid bitch. Any one would think we was married!' Joe shrugged dismissively. 'Pay her no mind.'

Half-amused, half-offended by Maggie's assumption that she was interested in Wilkes, Ianthe murmured something inconsequential by way of reply.

What could have prompted the girl's extraordinary outburst? Ianthe wondered if Wilkes was regularly unfaithful. He held no appeal whatsoever for her, but the better light of the cottage had revealed regular features framed by unkempt blond hair. A closer acquaintance with hot water and soap might even have rendered him handsome.

No doubt some women would find him attractive, but Maggie need have no fears concerning her!

Dismissing the smuggler's mistress from her thoughts, Ianthe handed over the twenty pounds he had demanded. Wilkes unfolded the bank-notes and examined them carefully before tucking them into his waistcoat pocket with a grunt of satisfaction.

'When can we leave?' Ianthe asked, trying not to sound too eager.

'Tide'll be high at six. We can set sail then.'

'Is it all right if I go aboard now?' Ianthe asked, quickly

adding that she didn't expect him to stay. 'I know you want to sleep in your own bed, but I'd rather not wait here, if you don't mind.'

To her relief he didn't take offence at her remark.

'Ye needn't heed Maggie, but, aye, all right,' he said with a shrug of his burly shoulders. 'Ye can sleep on the *Seagull* if that's your wish.'

Ianthe rose to her feet and picked up her valise. She followed him out of the cottage. A few steps brought them to the harbour and she breathed in the clean salty air, grateful for its freshness after the fusty parlour.

'This way.' Wilkes pointed to a small sloop.

It was too dark to see much and Ianthe knew little of ships in any case. Praying that Charles Fraser had been right in declaring that the *Silver Seagull* was a trim seaworthy vessel, and extremely glad that her bag was not heavy, she climbed the gangplank after the smuggler. At the top he exchanged a few words with a dark figure. The night watchman handed him a lantern and melted away.

'Follow me and mind your step.' Wilkes led her down below. The companionway was steep but thankfully still. She could hear the water lapping at the sides of the boat, but the sloop was hardly moving at all.

'Do you think the weather will allow us a swift passage tomorrow?' she asked as he showed her into a small cabin.

'Reckon so.' He flashed her a sly grin. 'There's a bucket in that corner over there if it ain't calm enough for ye.'

Ianthe was tempted to retort that she was a good sailor, but decided wearily that it wasn't worth the effort.

'Will you leave me the lantern, please?' she asked, setting down her bag and scanning her new quarters.

The cabin was tiny and none too clean, but she felt suddenly too exhausted to care.

''Fraid of the dark, are ye?' Scorn tinged the smuggler's tone.

'No, but I don't like rats and I dare say you have several on board.'

'Aye, and some of the two-legged variety an' all.' A wide grin split his face and alarm prickled between Ianthe's shoulder-blades.

He laughed at her expression. 'There's only old Ned on board and I warned him to stay clear of ye. The rest of 'em have leave to stay ashore until I send 'em word to return, which I'll do in the morning.'

He hung the lantern up on a conveniently placed hook. 'I'll see ye in a few hours, then.'

Ianthe nodded, anxious for him to go. 'Good night, Mr Wilkes.'

By this time tomorrow, she would be starting a new life. Wilkes and this nightmare evening would be part of her past.

She would never have to see her detestable husband again!

The sky was paling, heralding the advent of dawn, as Lord Kildare rode into Shoreham. Finding Charles Fraser and extracting the information he needed had taken more time than he liked, but at least Charles had been able to give him some useful tips.

Knowing that the *Silver Seagull* would be confined to harbour until high tide had helped soothe his desperate anxiety. Ianthe must be still here, assuming his hunch was right and he wasn't fruitlessly pursuing some wild goose-chase!

Closing his mind to this dreadful possibility, Luke forced himself to concentrate. Had Ianthe already made contact with the smuggler or had she opted to spend the night at the inn before speaking to Wilkes?

Given the lateness of her arrival, it seemed more likely that she would wait for morning before trying to persuade Wilkes to accept her as a passenger. Shoreham was a small place and Charles had told him that there was only one inn of any repute. He would try there first.

The grey's hoofbeats sounded loud in the silence. It was too early for anyone to be a-stir. A grim smile touched his well-cut mouth. He'd rouse the whole damned Royal Oak Inn if he had to!

Reaching the harbour he halted, his gaze drawn to the craft bobbing about on the dark water. Charles had told him to look for a small sloop. Two boats fitted that description. Both were in darkness, apparently deserted, and Luke turned his mount's head away. If the landlord had no information concerning Ianthe, he would come back. Wilkes lived somewhere hereabouts and he would find him.

He was riding past a huddle of cottages when a sudden movement caught his eye. The next instant a figure staggered into the road and almost tumbled beneath the grey's hooves. Drawing rein with an explosive oath, Luke managed to avoid riding the careless pedestrian down.

Pausing only to reassure his startled mount, he swung himself down from the saddle, his light eyes snapping with annoyance. 'What the devil do you think you are playing at? You could have been badly hurt!'

The girl, a gaudily dressed young redhead, gazed up at him blearily and gave a loud hiccup.

'You're drunk,' Luke exclaimed in disgust, hauling her to her feet.

He released her and she muttered something that could have been a words of thanks.

Anxious to be on his way, Luke was about to remount when he noticed the tear-stains on her dirty cheeks.

'Can I assist you indoors?' he asked, his annoyance tempered by a sudden flare of pity as he surveyed her red and swollen jaw and bruised cheekbone.

Her eyes widened with fright and she shook her head. 'I wants to keep out of his way 'til his temper cools,' she whispered, swaying tipsily on her feet.

Luke nodded. Someone, probably her husband, had beaten her. He disliked such brutality, but she would probably be the first to tell him it was none of his business and, besides, he had pressing concerns of his own. 'Very well, ma'am, but for your own safety you must find somewhere other than the public highway to act as your refuge.'

Gently so as not to frighten her, he took her arm. She stank of brandy. 'Allow me.' He steered her to a safer spot in the shelter of a garden wall. 'May I suggest you rest here until you feel recovered?'

She blinked up at him. 'Lawd, ye and your breaketeeth words!' Tears welled up in her eyes and ran down her thin cheeks. 'Ye talks just like that stuck-up doxy.'

Luke released her arm. 'What did you say?' he asked, an alarm-bell ringing in his head.

'Her. Ye talks like her.' The girl looked up at him with owlish impatience. 'She came home with Joe last night. Fancy bitch!'

'A lady visited you last night?'

'Aye.' An ugly look robbed her face of its gamin charm. 'Sweet-talked my Joe, she did. Going to take her to France, he says.'

'On his boat?' Luke asked, carefully controlling his excitement.

'On the *Seagull*, aye.' The girl waved her arm wildly in the direction of the sloop Luke had noticed earlier. The sudden movement made her teeter alarmingly but, recovering her balance, she said, 'That's the *Gull*. Nice, ain't she?'

'Very,' Luke replied absently, his mind whirling.

He'd been wrong. Somehow Ianthe had already contacted Wilkes and he'd agreed to take her across the Channel.

'Do you know where the lady is now?' he asked, forcing himself to sound calm.

'She's on the *Gull*.' A savage frown replaced the girl's lopsided smile. 'Joe don't let me sail with him.'

Abruptly, she yawned. 'Wish he would.'

'I'm sure he will soon,' Luke replied soothingly.

She nodded, her eyelids drooping. 'Lawd, but I'm tired,' she muttered and, with a drunken excess of confidentiality, added that she'd had a mite too much brandy after Joe had gone to bed. 'To con…console meself, ye see.'

'Is Joe on board the *Seagull* with the lady?'

She shook her tousled head. 'Nay, he's still abed. Wouldn't talk to me when he came home.' She fingered her jaw. 'Gave me this 'cos I asked too many questions.'

'Do you think the lady is alone?'

She frowned at him blearily. 'Reckon so. Only old Ned on board at night. Why do ye want to know?'

'Just curious, that's all.' Luke gave her his most charming smile and she nodded, her suspicious look vanishing.

Another wide yawn split her face and he caught her as she staggered. The brandy was taking effect. She was almost asleep on her feet and he knew he would get no more sense out of her.

But she had told him all that he needed to know!

He glanced about him. It was getting lighter. Very soon the village would be stirring. He didn't have much time to find Ianthe before Wilkes returned to the boat.

Coming to a swift decision, he steered his companion quietly towards a nearby cottage garden, where he had spotted an old wooden bench amid a profusion of summer flowers.

The unlocked gate creaked open at Luke's touch and he paused, alert for any sign that they had been heard, but no one came out of the cottage and the grey cloudy dawn remained undisturbed.

He pushed the girl down gently on to the bench and she immediately collapsed, sagging sideways into a half-lying position. 'Rest for a while.'

Too far gone to answer him, her eyes closed and she began to snore.

He left the garden quietly, satisfied that there was little risk of her alerting anyone to his presence. Most likely, she wouldn't even remember their meeting.

What he had to say to Ianthe was going to be difficult. Probably she wouldn't even want to listen to him and the last thing he needed was an audience of irate smugglers who could see the prospect of their nice fat fee disappearing!

* * *

It was more simple than Luke had expected to slip aboard the *Seagull* unobserved. The night watchman was curled up in a sheltered corner of the deck, asleep and snoring. He didn't stir when Luke crept past him.

Below deck it was silent and Luke reflected that in his home port Wilkes must feel able to relax. On a foreign shore he would have more men guarding the ship. Here, none of the locals would dare try anything. Smugglers were not noted for their tender mercy!

It was very dark, but once his eyes adjusted he could make out that there appeared to be two cabins in the stern. He knocked softly upon the nearest door. Receiving no answer, he turned the handle cautiously.

The cabin was deserted. Light filtering in through a porthole revealed nautical charts strewn over a desk and he guessed that this was where Wilkes lived when on board.

Ianthe must be in the other cabin. He knocked quietly as before, wary of startling her. Silence answered him and he knocked again more vigorously.

Was she asleep? If he knocked any louder he might wake the watchman. Hoping he was not about to burst in on a stranger, he tried the handle. For an instant, it resisted and he thought it must be locked. Then the stiff wood gave way and he stepped inside the cabin.

In the faint grey light he could make out a figure lying on the cot-bed against the far bulkhead.

'Ianthe? Is that you?'

A muffled cry greeted his soft query and the prone figure began to thrash like a stranded fish.

Luke hurled himself across the cabin and dropped to his knees beside the nailed-down bed.

'Dear God!' His fingers worked frantically at the knot securing the gag which covered her mouth. 'Who did this to you?'

He pulled the gag free and she began to cough.

'It was Wilkes,' she gasped when she had recovered her breath.

'What happened?' Luke asked. Her hands were bound behind her back with strong rope, which was resisting his efforts. Bending forward, he slid a small Indian dagger from inside his boot-top, glad that he had followed his instincts and armed himself before setting out on this journey.

'He was leaving...I had my back to him...I didn't see...then he grabbed me.' Ianthe shuddered, her voice dry and hoarse.

Black rage filled Luke at her disjointed words. 'Did he harm you?'

She shook her head. 'He was rough when he tied me up, but that's all. He said he was too tired for frolicking.' Her mouth wobbled as she tried to smile. 'I suppose I should be grateful for small mercies.'

The rope parted. Luke longed to enfold her in his arms and comfort her, but he forced himself to direct his attention to untying the bonds which imprisoned her ankles.

'I thought I was being clever hiding my valuables, but he must have seen the bag around my waist,' Ianthe said, rubbing her freed wrists to restore the circulation. 'And decided he wasn't content with just my passage money.'

'Do you still have the bag?' Luke asked quietly, finishing his task.

'Yes, he said that it was safe enough here with me.' She gave a slightly hysterical laugh. 'He thinks no one knows I'm here, apart from a few of his cronies who would never betray him.'

A shiver feathered down Luke's spine and as their eyes met he knew Ianthe had come to the same chilling conclusion.

Wilkes was planning to kill her. It was the only way he could guarantee her silence after the theft. It would be easy enough to drop her over the side once the sloop was out at sea. A weighted body would sink and disappear and he would deny that he had ever seen her should there be any questions.

'I knew my plan was dangerous, but I ignored my instincts and trusted him.' Ianthe sat up, wincing as the blood flowed back into her cramped limbs.

'God, what a fool I've been!' Her head slumped forward on to her chest and her shoulders began to shake. Luke reached out a hand to touch her, but dropped it unseen as she added bitterly, 'No doubt you think I am well served for running away from you.'

'I suggest we leave recriminations until we are safely away from here,' he said stiffly, hiding his anguish.

Ianthe gulped back her tears. He was right. She could have the vapours later!

She scrambled from the bed and followed him from the cabin, abandoning her bag, which contained only a few simple gowns and toiletries, without a second thought.

They had reached the companionway when they heard voices.

'Go and fetch that barrel of ale Dawson owes us. He said he'd have it ready.'

'Shall I round up the others on my way?'

'Rob's doing it. Now hurry up, you lazy old rascal, I want to set sail the minute everyone is aboard.'

'Aye, Captain.'

'And don't let me catch you asleep on duty again!' The more assertive voice was coming nearer.

Laying a finger to his lips, Luke motioned Ianthe to move away before he positioned himself to one side of the steep companionway, knowing that the dark shadows would conceal him from anyone above.

They heard footsteps and Luke withdrew his pistol from his waistband. A large figure blocked out the light and he tensed.

The man began to descend. He had barely reached the bottom of the ladder when Luke sprang out of his hiding place.

'What the—?' Wilkes let out an exclamation of astonishment. He attempted to turn and fight but was too slow and the heavy butt of Luke's pistol cracked against his skull before he had time to say another word.

He dropped to the deck like a stone.

'Is...is he dead?' Ianthe gasped in horror. The lightning

speed of Luke's reactions had startled her even though she had guessed what he planned to do.

Luke bent down and felt for the pulse in the unconscious smuggler's neck. 'He'll live,' he replied curtly, straightening up again.

Ianthe stared uncertainly at her captor. His ruddy complexion was pale and he was breathing stertorously.

'Are you sure?'

'Do you want to wait and find out?' Luke demanded with impatient sarcasm and she flinched.

'I'll see if it's clear.' Luke wished he had not been so harsh, but there was no time to apologise.

He climbed the companionway with lithe speed and after a second beckoned her to join him. 'Come on. He'll wake up soon and we've got to get well away from here before the rest of his gang arrives.'

Only too well could Ianthe imagine the unpleasant consequences if Wilkes managed to get his hands on them and she ran down the deck after Luke as if her feet had acquired wings.

Luke had left his horse tied up by the harbour wall. He sprang up into the saddle and extended a hand to Ianthe to pull her up behind him.

It was fully light now and a few folk were stirring. They attracted several curious glances as they trotted sedately out of the village. Ianthe was sure someone would try to stop them and she breathed an enormous sigh of relief as they passed the last cottage.

'That's the first hurdle over.' Luke urged the grey into a brisk gallop. 'Now, hang on tight!'

Lord Kildare pulled up his tired horse by a coppice of ash, which straggled the side of the Brighton road.

'We'll rest here for a while,' he announced.

'Do you think we've got far enough away for them not to follow us?' Ianthe asked nervously, unclasping her arms from his waist.

Luke nodded. 'I imagine that Wilkes attacked you on the spur of the moment. You were too much of a temptation to resist, but to come after us now might entail risk and, since he has the reputation of being shrewd, I think we are safe enough.'

Ianthe slid down to the ground and wiped her brow with the sleeve of her jacket. It was growing warm now that the sun had come out from behind the clouds. Her knees were still shaking and she went to sit on a fallen tree trunk. Someone had been working in the coppice, but it was deserted at this early hour and only birdsong disturbed the silence.

She watched Luke walk the grey to cool him down. He was speaking softly to the animal, giving him an occasional re-assuring pat. Resentment boiled up in her and she glared at him.

Becoming aware of her angry scrutiny, Luke tethered the horse loosely and strode over to join her.

'I had thought it best to postpone any discussion until we were back in Brighton and you'd had time to rest,' he explained carefully. 'But perhaps you think I am mistaken.'

'You've been wrong about many things, particularly about me!' Ianthe's eyes flashed sapphire fire.

He lifted his brows at her bald statement. 'Should I have left you to your fate?' he enquired mildly.

Hot colour flooded Ianthe's face. She had not even thanked him for rescuing her. 'I am aware I owe you a debt,' she muttered. 'But gratitude comes hard when one knows one is unwanted and despised!'

He winced. 'Is that what you truly think?'

Ianthe bounced to her feet. 'You treat that horse better than you treat me!'

'Don't be ridiculous!' Luke snapped, goaded into losing his precarious self-control. 'I know you have had a severe fright, but—'

'Oh, pray don't mention it. I can do without your sympathy, my lord.'

Infuriated by the sarcasm in her tone, Luke was about to

launch an angry retort when he saw the tears glistening in her lovely eyes. 'I'm sorry if you thought me unfeeling,' he said, struggling to regain his composure. 'I wanted to offer you comfort, but logic dictated that I concentrate on our escape rather than your distress.'

'Sometimes other emotions demand precedence over logic,' Ianthe murmured unsteadily. 'If I had been behaving logically I would never have run away in such a crazy fashion. I knew I was taking stupid risks, but it didn't matter.'

'Why did you feel you had to run away?'

Ianthe took a deep breath and met his penetrating gaze defiantly. 'Because I cannot bear to live with you when I know that you want Georgiana instead of me.'

To her utter astonishment he laughed. 'You couldn't be more wrong! I wouldn't swap you for her. In fact, I don't want Georgiana at all!'

'But...but...!' Ianthe stared at him in shock. 'I don't believe you! How can I after the way you have behaved?'

Luke sat down on the tree trunk. 'Give me a chance to explain.' He took her hand and tugged it gently, silently begging her to join him. 'Please?'

Ianthe nodded and sank down beside him, her throat tight with unshed tears.

'Georgiana threw me over as soon she realised that the Kildare estate was virtually bankrupt on my father's death,' he said softly. 'My scar was just another reason to be rid of me, but when you have been rejected in such a public and hurtful way, the one thing you long for above all else is to hear that it was a mistake. A part of me always grieved for my loss and I could never completely forget her, no matter how I tried.'

Ianthe bit her lip. She wanted to scream at him to stop, but he had been willing to risk his life for her today and she owed it to him to listen, no matter how painful she found his explanation.

'When she turned up that night at Sally Bradford's party I wasn't expecting to see her. My surprise turned to delight when she began to apologise for rejecting me so brutally.' He took a deep breath, determined to be honest. 'I was flattered when she told me that she preferred me to her husband and wanted to become my mistress.'

'So you accepted her offer.' A bitterness she couldn't suppress filled Ianthe's voice and she pulled her hand free of his. Oh, she could hardly blame him, she supposed, but how this confirmation of his infidelity hurt!

He shook his dark head. 'I was very tempted, but something—call it conscience, if you will—stopped me. Neither Georgiana or I were free and even in those first moments of transport I knew I did not want to inflict pain on you.'

There was a tiny silence while Ianthe tried to digest what his restraint could possibly mean. 'Are you saying that you have fallen out of love with her?' she asked carefully.

'I was in love with a dream, a girl who existed only in my own head.' Luke's tone was rueful. 'I never knew the real Georgiana before. Now, without the rosy glow of infatuation to blind me, I can see what she is truly like.'

His mouth twisted. 'And I don't like what I see! She is shallow and vain and has no idea of loyalty. That her husband might be hurt by her infidelity doesn't seem to bother her in the least. All she cares about is her own pleasure and she is willing to use lies and manipulation to get what she wants.'

Ianthe stared at him, a tiny tendril of hope unfurling in her heart.

'Then you didn't stop coming to my bed because you wanted her instead of me?' she asked hesitantly.

He shook his head violently.

'And you didn't give her an identical gift?'

'If it were not for the need to curb gossip, I wouldn't give her so much as the time of day,' Luke answered firmly. 'She is still a beautiful woman, but her behaviour disgusts me.'

He shrugged his broad shoulders, his expression rueful. 'Once I found her prattle charming. Now I realise that she is selfish to the bone and sadly lacking in the intelligence I prize in a woman.'

Ianthe remembered him telling her that he could not abide to marry a simpering ninny.

This time she did not pull away when he took her hand. 'I regret that I did not have the sense to make my feelings clear to you,' he said quietly. 'I suppose I was ashamed.'

'*Ashamed?*' Ianthe ejaculated.

'After all the terrible things I said to you on our wedding night I knew I did not deserve to be forgiven.' Luke's light gaze fixed upon her face with a painful intensity. 'I accused you of being manipulative and deceitful. Georgiana's behaviour last night showed me how wrong I was. *You* would never have played such a trick!'

Living with Ianthe had opened his eyes to the truth. She was as kind and honourable as she had first seemed to him at Kildare Park. Instead of accepting her word that she had not wanted to compromise him into marriage or deliberately deceive him on their wedding night, he had stubbornly clung to his anger and cynicism.

His pig-headed determination to compare her to Georgiana had almost cost him his marriage!

'I know now that I behaved very badly and I ask your pardon for doubting you.'

Hope flowered in Ianthe. Ruthlessly, she held it in check. She had always known that he was a man of honour. Just because he had apologised, it did not mean that he loved her!

Her silence dismayed Luke. With an unaccustomed nervousness, he wondered if she understood what he was trying to tell her.

'How did you know where to look for me?' Ianthe asked hastily. She longed to throw her arms around him, but the fear that she might be allowing optimism to mislead her was too strong!

Luke told her of Lottie's hunch, which had resulted in him seeking ing out Charles Fraser. 'He was anxious to help, partly because he likes you and also to crush the possibility of scandal tainting the Lomond name.'

'He is a good friend of the Earl's.'

'Aye.' A note of anger infused Luke's deep voice. 'When he took her back to her lodgings last night after the reception ended, Georgiana admitted to him quite brazenly that she had bribed Francine, your mantua-maker, to provide her with the left-over silk gauze from your gown.'

Somehow this piece of information did not surprise Ianthe!

'Charles is furious with her. He's been aware for some time that her behaviour was teetering on the edge of scandal and he told me that he intends to escort her home to Scotland today before there is any more vulgar speculation. Whether or not she wishes to do so, I think Georgiana will go with him since he has her husband's ear. If she won't listen to him, I shall convince her to leave.' Luke's expression was grim.

Ianthe could not pretend that she wouldn't be pleased to see the back of the Countess of Lomond. But her flare of satisfaction quickly died when she realised that the rumour-mongers had already been busy.

'I'm afraid so,' Luke replied when she asked if her abrupt departure and Georgiana's dress had been noticed. 'Shall you mind the gossip very much?'

Ianthe shook her head. 'Not now that I know it was Georgiana, and not you, who planned to humiliate me.'

In spite of the burgeoning sunshine she gave a little shiver. Thanks to her own angry impulsiveness, Georgiana's scheme to drive her away from Luke had almost succeeded! 'I suppose she thought she would have a better chance with you if I left Brighton.'

'I imagine so.' Unaccustomed colour tinged Luke's tanned face. 'However, I beg you to believe that, apart from those first few minutes when my guard was down, I had given her no encouragement to think that I would welcome her into my bed. On the contrary, I told her several times that I was not interested in her offer, but she refused to believe me.'

The leaden lump of misery which had lain in Ianthe's stomach ever since Georgiana had approached her at the Pavilion dissolved. 'I *do* believe you, Luke.'

He broke into a jubilant smile, but when he would have put his arms around her, Ianthe hastily drew back. 'Please don't!'

She was trembling. 'There has always been desire between us, but there is more to marriage than four bare legs in a bed. Kisses cannot solve every problem.'

'Maybe not, but it's fun trying,' Luke replied, essaying a light smile.

An answering gleam of amusement lit her gaze for a second before her expression grew sombre again. 'I think that I should return to Northwood for a while. Alone.'

Luke's heart sank. 'Are you still angry with me?'

Ianthe quickly shook her head. 'I understand how strong first love can be. If Philip had walked into the Duchess's party, I am sure I would have still found him attractive, although this time I think...I *hope*...I would have been able to resist his blandishments!'

Luke's stomach turned over. He had never let her explain what had happened with Lieutenant Fenton, but he thought he could guess.

Facing battle, the boy had taken advantage of her generous nature. It had been reckless and unfair. He might have left her with child. He had certainly left her brokenhearted.

'I really did love him, you know,' Ianthe whispered, her gaze fixed on the grass at her feet. 'I know that is no excuse for my behaviour, but even now I can't regret giving in to his persuasion, not when I think of what happened to him afterwards.'

Luke wondered if he would have had the strength at that age to behave any better than Fenton. He hoped so, but the temptation might easily have overcome all notions of honour!

'If you are willing to forgive my lack of understanding, then perhaps we can lay the ghosts of our past and forget them.'

Ianthe's head jerked up. He was smiling at her with an awkward tenderness that told her as plainly as words that he was no longer angry that she had not been the virgin bride he'd had every right to expect.

'When I was in India I thought I hated Kildare Park. Coming home made me realise I still love the place. I'm ready and willing to settle down to the life of a country gentleman, but it will be Dead Sea fruit unless you are there at my side.' Luke raised her hand to his lips and kissed it. 'I did not dare allow myself to believe you when you told me that you loved me. If my folly has not destroyed your feelings for me and you are willing to give me another chance, I shall try to become the husband you deserve.'

She stared at him, her eyes enormous in her pale face. 'Do you…can you…?' she floundered, hardly daring to hope that she had understood him aright.

'Sweetheart, I love you to distraction!' he said shakily. 'I fell under your spell on the first day we went riding together. It was such a strong attraction that I couldn't resist detaining you that night in the painting-studio though I knew it was foolish. Then I pretended my marriage was merely for convenience, which puzzled Harry and Nicodemus, who knew me well enough to realise that I was deluding myself!'

A faint smile touched his mouth. 'I told myself that I wanted to get away from you, but I couldn't even resist the need to bring you to Brighton with me! I remained too stubborn to admit the truth until Georgiana came back into my life and I realised that the real reason I didn't want her was because I was in love with you!'

'Oh, Luke, are you sure?' Ianthe gazed at him mistily.

'Irrevocably,' he said with a firmness that brooked no denial and drew her into his arms. 'You will just have to get used to being adored by me, I'm afraid.'

'I think I can manage that,' Ianthe sighed happily, her mouth curving into a smile of delight that proved too much for Luke's self-control.

His dark head bent to hers and their lips met in a long slow kiss that left them both breathless and shaking with passion.

'Let's go home,' Luke said, his deep voice husky with desire. 'I want to make love to you!'

'What an excellent suggestion, my lord!' Ianthe's eyes sparkled with willing anticipation as she allowed him to pull her to her feet.

His arm around her waist, they walked over to where his horse stood patiently waiting.

'There is one thing that still puzzles me,' Ianthe announced as he untied the grey. 'I accept that you no longer love Georgiana, but why did you make such a tender drawing of her?'

'I thought you might wonder about that,' Luke replied and took out a folded wad of drawings from the deep pocket of his dark green riding-coat. 'I didn't draw Georgiana from life, but from memory. That is how she looked to me when we first met.'

He shrugged in a faintly embarrassed manner. 'I had decided to ask your forgiveness when we came home from the Regent's party. I was going to admit that I wanted us to start afresh and I suppose it was my way of saying goodbye to the past.' He handed the wad of paper to Ianthe. 'This is what I hoped the future would hold for me.'

Ianthe unfolded the drawings and gave a little gasp. Every one was a sketch of her! Some revealed aspects of Kildare Park in the background, the others had Brighton scenes framing her figure.

'You have flattered me shamelessly, sir!' Ianthe exclaimed with a catch in her voice. She had never realised he was sketching her, but there was unmistakable love and tenderness shining out of every single drawing.

'I drew you exactly as you look to me, as beautiful as you are kind and accomplished,' Luke answered with a sincerity that made her heart sing with joy.

Ianthe folded up the drawings carefully and Luke tucked them back into his pocket. 'Will you let me draw you again?' he asked.

'I shall look forward to it.' Ianthe suddenly grinned at him. 'Your mother says I am a good sitter.'

Her comment reminded Luke that Amelia and Nicodemus were due to arrive in Brighton tomorrow. 'If, in spite of Georgiana's departure, the rumours about last night continue to persist, I am sure they will both do all in their power to help us scotch them. My mama can be formidable when her wrath is roused!'

'She said you had inherited her temper,' Ianthe teased, a warm feeling of security chasing away the last lingering fragment of her concern at the thought of returning to face the gossips. She was part of Luke's family now. Her lonely days of having to fend for herself were over.

Luke nodded. 'In a rage I often say things I do not mean,' he replied ruefully. 'It is a fault I deeply regret.' He paused. 'When I think of all the vile accusations I have flung at your head—'

'Don't.' Ianthe quickly reached up to lay a finger against his lips. 'It doesn't matter any more. We have both made mistakes. Let's consign them to the past along with our ghosts and promise ourselves to do better.'

One day she would tell him of how Turner had threatened her and how she had feared for her grandmother's health. She had no desire to keep any secrets from him, but the whys and wherefores behind her journey to Kildare Park were no longer important. In the end she had resisted Augustus's infamous proposal and won Luke's love fair and square.

Luke turned her hand over and pressed a kiss into her palm. 'An Indian mystic once told me I would marry a woman who was as wise as she was beautiful. I discounted his prophecy at the time, but I see now that he was right.'

A wild rose blush coloured Ianthe's cheeks. 'You pay a pretty compliment, sir, but I seem to remember you comparing me to a Lamia not so very long ago!'

He stared at her, a frown creasing his brow. 'What do you...Good God, you didn't think I meant that story about a treacherous woman for *you*, did you?'

'You were staring straight at me!' Ianthe protested indignantly.

'Sweetheart, I was looking at Georgiana. She was standing right behind you.'

Ianthe's lips formed a little circle of astonishment. 'So she was, but I never thought...' She began to giggle. 'Oh, Luke, what a pair of deluded idiots we have been!'

He grinned back at her. 'They say that the course of true love never runs smooth.'

'Then we must prove the proverb wrong from here on in.'

'Indeed, we shall, my lady,' Luke answered and catching her in his arms, kissed her with a warmth that left her in no doubt that he meant to do his best to make their marriage a success.

'Come on, sweetheart. Up with you.' Releasing her, Luke lifted Ianthe into the saddle and vaulted up after her.

Still smiling, Ianthe snuggled contently against him and he bent to press a kiss against the smooth skin of her nape. Then, wrapping his arms around her slim waist, he urged the grey into a trot and they rode off into the morning, which, like their future, was now glowing with golden promise.

* * * * *

Modern Romance™
...seduction and
passion guaranteed

Tender Romance™
...love affairs that
last a lifetime

Sensual Romance™
...sassy, sexy and
seductive

Blaze
...sultry days and
steamy nights

Medical Romance™
...medical drama on
the pulse

Historical Romance™
...rich, vivid and
passionate

29 new titles every month.

*With all kinds of Romance for
every kind of mood...*

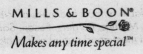

MILLS & BOON®

Makes any time special™

MAT4

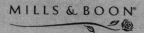

Treat yourself this Mother's Day to the ultimate indulgence

3 brand new romance novels and a box of chocolates

= only £7.99

Available from 18th January

Available at most branches of WH Smith, Tesco, Martins, Borders, Eason, Sainsbury's and most good paperback bookshops.

0202/91/MB32

2 FREE
books and a surprise gift!

We would like to take this opportunity to thank you for reading this Mills & Boon® book by offering you the chance to take TWO more specially selected titles from the Historical Romance™ series absolutely FREE! We're also making this offer to introduce you to the benefits of the Reader Service™—

- ★ FREE home delivery
- ★ FREE gifts and competitions
- ★ FREE monthly Newsletter
- ★ Exclusive Reader Service discount
- ★ Books available before they're in the shops

Accepting these FREE books and gift places you under no obligation to buy, you may cancel at any time, even after receiving your free shipment. Simply complete your details below and return the entire page to the address below. *You don't even need a stamp!*

YES! Please send me 2 free Historical Romance books and a surprise gift. I understand that unless you hear from me, I will receive 4 superb new titles every month for just £2.99 each, postage and packing free. I am under no obligation to purchase any books and may cancel my subscription at any time. The free books and gift will be mine to keep in any case.

H2ZEA

Ms/Mrs/Miss/Mr ....Initials................................
BLOCK CAPITALS PLEASE

Surname ....

Address ....

....

....Postcode.................................

Send this whole page to:
UK: FREEPOST CN81, Croydon, CR9 3WZ
EIRE: PO Box 4546, Kilcock, County Kildare (stamp required)